THE WORLD OF OLDER MEN

JEAN-LOUIS CURTIS

The World of Older Men

Translated from the French by
ROBERT BALDICK

LONDON
MICHAEL JOSEPH

Published in France by
Editions René Juillard
30 *Rue de l'Université*
Paris

© 1966 *by René Juillard*

First published in Great Britain by
MICHAEL JOSEPH LTD
26 *Bloomsbury Street*
London, W.C.1
1969

© *English translation* 1969 *by Jean-Louis Curtis*

7181 0086 7

Set and printed in Great Britain by
Tonbridge Printers Ltd, Peach Hall Works, Tonbridge, Kent
in Janson ten on twelve point, and bound by
James Burn at Esher, Surrey

'Well,' said Bruno, 'I don't know about you, but I feel perfectly game for the second half of the century.'

'Oh, you athletic types are always game for anything,' said André Comarieu. 'I was speaking for myself.'

'You are as young as you feel,' said Claire Comarieu.

Her husband turned towards her, a smile on his lips, and it was obvious what he was going to ask her, but he was beaten to it by Bruno:

'You are right, Claire. As long as you have plans for the future, as long as you enjoy what you are doing, you are still young. The main thing is to love life and the people around you . . .'

'Has the second half of the century started?' asked Juliette Marcillac, who was one or two remarks behind. 'Or is the first just coming to an end?'

'I think,' said André, 'that we are still in the first.'

'Well, I only hope the second will be quieter. With two world wars and God knows how many revolutions, we've had a busy fifty years.'

'When I saw the photo of President Lebrun in the paper the other day, I told myself: a whole epoch is vanishing with him.'

'Why, yes, we spent our youth under the reign of Lebrun.'

'The poor man's death didn't cause much of a stir, did it? And he always wept bucketfuls whenever things went badly.'

He had never been really popular, in spite of being regarded as typifying the average Frenchman. Was the present President any more popular? His Toulouse accent and his familiar ways were a help to him. London had just given a warm welcome to this chief of State who cared so little about protocol. Bruno expressed the opinion that he was not a very good advertisement for the French male, and they discussed the importance of a fine presence for people in positions of power. Nobody could say that George VI was the most handsome of men, and what was more he stuttered, yet his people seemed extremely attached to him. On the other hand the romantic good looks of Leopold II had not been enough to save his throne. The Belgians were about to vote on the question of their sovereign's return. The four of them weighed up his chances. Wasn't a king, in this day and age, even in a constitutional monarchy, an anachronistic relic? There was no doubt about it, the world was moving towards universal socialism.

Either this prospect seemed rather gloomy to the Marcillacs and their guests, or the rarefied altitudes of abstract ideas had temporarily robbed them of the power of speech, for silence fell over the room. Just as it was threatening to grow deeper the maid made a timely entrance to announce that dinner was served.

'We won't wait for my little sister-in-law,' said Juliette, standing up. 'She's always late. She may not even come home till two in the morning.'

'I don't advise her to,' said Bruno.

'She takes no notice of your advice,' Juliette said gently. 'In any case she's over twenty-one.'

'You mean that as her elder brother you haven't any authority over her any more?' asked Claire.

'Good heavens, no! What can you expect? Beatrice arrived fourteen years after me. I took no notice of her until she was a big girl, and then it was too late: her bad habits had already taken root. She has been terribly spoilt.'

'By you most of all, and you can't deny it. You never bothered to help with bringing her up.'

'Her parents were there, weren't they? But they let her do whatever she liked. Whereas with me, when I did the slightest thing . . .'

'Times had already changed,' said André. 'After the war everybody was much more indulgent with their children.'

6

'That's true. It's fantastic how much our attitudes have changed within a few years.'

'Wars always speed up progress.'

'If you can talk about progress in this context. I'm not sure that it's such a good thing to give children free rein. But it's the fashion.'

'When I think,' said Juliette, 'that I wasn't allowed to go out at night until I was eighteen, and even then I had to be home before midnight. It was ridiculous,' she added with a show of retrospective rebellion. 'Especially when you consider that here in Sault a girl didn't get raped on every street-corner!'

This moderately daring remark drew a polite smile from Claire and André, although the former had lowered her eyes. Bruno for his part was delighted and gave a broad smile.

'My dear pet,' he said, 'if I'd met you at midnight in that shrubbery near the station, I might well have done you wrong.'

'I'd have put up a good fight, big as you were,' she replied. 'And please don't call me your pet!'

However, she didn't seem at all annoyed. The reference to an amorous encounter between her husband and herself had established a current between them from which both were obviously deriving pleasure. André's gaze, suddenly sharper and harder, noted this brief moment of conjugal complicity.

'I trust you wouldn't have put up any sort of fight,' Bruno went on in the same bantering tone. 'You'd have been only too happy to . . .'

'Stop bragging,' said André. 'At eighteen you wouldn't have dared. Even at midnight in the station shrubbery.'

'That's true,' Bruno admitted. 'We were terribly shy in those days. We would have thought we were committing a crime if we'd done anything with a girl. That was the way we were brought up. You remember those sermons?'

Here we go with the reminiscences. He's going to do the

7

famous swallow sermon. Doesn't he realise he's already done that turn for us umpteen times? Our life is made up of routines... I felt a slight twinge of jealousy when they exchanged that glance. Because the brute is still very good-looking. And so is she. And it's obvious that they're still very much in love with each other.

Bruno was doing a parody of pulpit oratory.

'Imagine, children, a swallow which came once every hundred years and brushed its wing against a bronze globe as big as the earth. How many centuries would it take to wear the globe away and reduce it to dust? Well, children, that terrifying length of time is nothing compared with the eternity during which you will have to suffer unspeakable pain if you die in a state of mortal sin.'

'They really overdid it,' said Juliette. 'Terrifying poor little kids with stories like that. Nowadays they don't talk to them about hell any more. The Church has evolved in that respect too.'

'Naturally,' said Bruno. 'I wouldn't like to have my kids scared with that kind of sermon. What sin deserves an eternity of torture?'

'Not one!' said Claire nodding her head; and she gave a sarcastic smile. 'Not one!'

There was a moment's silence. With a brief glance André checked to see whether his hosts had noticed the tiny pebble fall into the still water, or whether they could see the ripples spreading out in widening circles. No: they looked the same as ever; they mustn't have noticed anything.

'It's the same with politics,' Bruno went on. 'The young people nowadays don't give a damn about politics, whereas we used to get all worked up about them. Do you remember the arguments we had in February '34?'

'We'd left school by then; we were already students.'

'You're right. I got into scraps on the Boul' Mich more than once.'

'If I'd been in Paris you'd probably have found me fighting

on the other side. Because you were for the Leagues, weren't you?'

'I certainly was! I wonder who still remembers the Patriotic Leagues apart from us? All that seems so long ago.'

I've just put my foot in it. I've reminded everybody that he was on the extreme right before the war, and something of an admirer of the Marshal at the beginning of the Occupation. It's true that he made up for all that in '44. Besides, Bruno isn't the sort to bear me a grudge for a boner like that. I didn't mean any harm by it. Anyway, they didn't turn a hair, either of them. Claire sensed the danger though: she batted her eyelids.

'Ages ago, and yet have things changed all that much? In politics, I mean. The Fourth Republic is even more of a mess than the Third. And look at the strikes: yesterday the metro and the buses; today the gas and electricity. Just as it used to be under the Popular Front.'

The two women exchanged opinions about the domestic inconveniences caused by the gas and electricity strikes. They were very slight, because in the south-west the unions hadn't been unanimous.

'They weren't unanimous anywhere,' said Bruno. 'The Working Force didn't come out.'

'I wouldn't like to be running the country just now. What a job!'

'The most important thing would be to halt the rise in prices, but to do that you'd have to ...'

Bruno did not have time to enlarge on his economic theories: a girl had just come into the room.

'You take things easy, don't you?' Bruno went on. 'You're only an hour and twenty minutes late, that's all.'

'I'm terribly sorry,' said the girl whose serene expression belied her words. 'No, please don't get up, André. Good evening, Claire. I hope,' she said to her sister-in-law, 'you aren't too cross with me?'

9

She sat down on her brother's left, without the slightest sign of embarrassment or regret at her lack of politeness.

'We stayed too long at Letitia's,' she said. 'I wanted to come home, but Michel went on blethering away.'

'Did he bring you home on his motorbike?' asked Juliette. 'I don't like you going on that motorbike of his. He drives like a lunatic and I always get so worried.'

'What was it like at Letitia's?'

'The same as usual. People from the coast. One or two quite interesting characters.'

And she went on talking about the party in little chopped-up phrases which she brought out in a bored, weary tone of voice, as if she had really had enough of the world and its paltry feasts.

'But if you find it such a bore,' said Bruno, 'why do you go to the woman's house? She must be a hundred, mustn't she?' he asked André.

'Oh, no. Madame Dolfus must be ... wait a minute.'

He did a rapid calculation.

'I think she must be just over sixty.'

'That's funny! When I was a kid I always regarded her as an old woman.'

'She keeps herself in form,' said the girl. 'I'd like to be like her when I get to her age.'

André gazed intently at her. It was hard to imagine a sixty-year-old Beatrice. How pretty she is! Or rather, how pretty she would be if she didn't spoil everything with that bored look she puts on, with her excessive self-assurance and her bad manners. She didn't even bother to apologise when she arrived. We don't matter to these young people. I'd like to beat her and kiss her at the same time, she looks so fresh and shapely. Claire must loathe her, judging by the way she's looking at her: the eyes a bit too bright, the smile a bit too forced. She must loathe her for everything that girl represents, everything Claire has never had and wouldn't want: freedom to live as one likes, the cult of self, contempt for others.

There I'm on Claire's side all the way. We'll try to make sure our children don't turn into little monsters like that ravishing creature.

'Bonneteau was there,' Beatrice added casually.

The name meant nothing to either Bruno or his wife, but André was better informed.

'Bonneteau the writer?' he asked. 'What is he like?'

'A sort of English elegance. He must have been a great lover in his day. He certainly talks about love very well.'

'He writes about it very well too. But I thought you members of the younger generation had nothing to learn on that subject?'

André seemed to be getting somewhat heated.

'Nobody has ever finished learning,' said Beatrice.

'And what that old gentleman told you didn't seem too out-of-date?'

'He's more modern than you think.'

The conversation turned to the books they had read recently. Juliette admitted that she hadn't been able to stop reading the very end of *Falling Bodies*, although the crude realism of that book had frequently shocked her. Beatrice said that she was reading 'the whole of Sade' all over again. Claire, when it was her turn to reply, hesitated for a moment before declaring that she was deep in *Fragments of a New Teaching*.

'My wife,' said André, 'is an adept of the secret tradition of esotericism.'

He promptly regretted opening his mouth, for on the one hand Claire protested: 'That isn't true!' while on the other hand his hosts probably didn't know what he was talking about, so that they would think he was being pedantic. In all likelihood this was the first time Bruno had ever heard of esotericism; but when anything was mentioned that he knew nothing about, for example in literature and the arts, he was in the habit of taking refuge in silence. This was not a silence of anger or humiliation, but on the contrary a very com-

fortable silence, accompanied by a polite, appreciative smile
suggesting at once the modesty of the non-specialist declining
to express any opinion and the interest of a well-bred man,
who, even if he takes no part in the conversation, can take
pleasure in intellectual exchanges. Sheltering behind this smile
whose almost Buddhist discretion was the equivalent of a
noli me tangere, Bruno could give himself up completely to
the joys of the table, which until then he had been unable to
savour fully, because he had been making an effort to talk
in order to entertain his guests. Now the food at the
Marcillacs' was excellent. Scarcely a day went by without
Bruno congratulating himself on having married a woman
who, apart from her charm, her good nature, and her utter
devotion to her husband and children, was also a *cordon bleu*
cook. Sometimes the pleasure Bruno took in his food (and
there were supreme culinary delights that returned with the
seasons, like ragout of wood-pigeon in October) was somewhat spoilt by the fear of developing a paunch; but this
danger was being kept at bay for the time being by playing
football. One day Bruno would stop playing – few men go
on with the game after forty – and give up what he respectfully called 'training'; and then his muscles would collect a
little superfluous fat; that was inevitable, and he would have
to resign himself to it. In the meantime this *foie gras* was
absolutely delicious.

'That's something like occultism, isn't it?' asked Juliette.

'More or less,' replied Claire. 'Yes, occultism.'

'And you really believe in all that nonsense?' said Beatrice.

'I didn't say I believed in it,' retorted Claire, unable to
prevent a noticeable stiffening in her attitude. 'I said I was
reading a book that dealt with esoteric doctrines.'

'But you've always been interested in that sort of thing,
darling,' said André; while Bruno scowled and said to his
sister:

'Featherbrain, what do you know about it? You didn't even
bother to sit for your second *bac*.'

Having thus punished juvenile insolence with an act of immanent justice, Bruno returned majestically to the enjoyment of his *foie gras*. He made a mental resolution to give the girl a stern talking-to when the guests had gone. Not satisfied with arriving late, she took the liberty of being disrespectful to a lady like Claire Comarieu, who was older than she was and worth a hundred of her. Bruno couldn't bear seeing anybody being humiliated or even annoyed. On that point he was extremely sensitive. His wife had often pointed this out to him, adding that it was a virtue you found in strong men but never in weaklings, whose weakness, on the contrary, often made them mean and cruel. In her opinion, keen sportsmen had tender hearts. Bruno readily agreed with her, just as he agreed with everything Juliette said.

'Remember that it was you who once got me to read a book by Madame Blavatsky.'

I wonder why those two still call each other *vous*. After ten years of marriage. Try as I might, I can't get used to it. He must think it's the snobbish thing to do. All I know is that if I had to say *vous* to Juliette ... No, it's unthinkable. And do they say *vous* to each other in bed too? (Here Bruno imagined the dialogue and was seized by a fit of merriment. He had to put his napkin to his lips to hide a smile.) In any case it's difficult to imagine Claire making love ... She's always so dignified, so stiff, almost forbidding. She'd put me right off my stroke. Poor André. It's true that he probably isn't cut out for it either. I'd rather be in my shoes and have Juliette. It's always gayer here. And we at least call each other *tu*. I'm really very happy – touch wood. If I really believed in God, I'd thank him for everything he's given me. I ought to try saying my prayers again – not mechanically, but thinking about what I'm saying. After all, you never know. It's like going to Church: I go because a man in my position, here in Sault, can't do anything else; but I ought to try to follow the Mass, instead of daydreaming about all sorts of things and ogling the women and so on. All the same,

I'm going to say on the off chance: 'Thank you, God, for giving me what you have given me.' If he exists, that may please him, and in any case it's better than touching wood ... I wonder how that superstition of touching wood started? It can't prevent things from happening. Anyway, nothing is threatening me, as far as I know. Nothing and nobody.

'There's somebody who used to be very keen about occultism in the old days, and that's our old schoolmate Jean Lagarde.'

'Really? ... Have another helping, André.'

'No, thank you. This *foie gras* is delicious, but ...'

'Jean Lagarde,' Beatrice said languidly. 'Isn't he that character Michel used to argue with sometimes last year?'

'Why do you refer to him as "that character"? Believe it or not, Lagarde is a highly intelligent man. If he hasn't done very well for himself in life, that isn't his fault. Circumstances have been against him.'

'But I never said he was stupid. He can't be if Michel condescended to argue with him. He just looks rather seedy, that's all.'

'Seedy? Nonsense! You don't know anything about it! ... Am I going to be the only one to have a second helping ...'

'Go on, don't make such a song and dance about it,' said Juliette. 'Help yourself: you're obviously dying to ... I don't think Jean Lagarde looks particularly seedy, but I must admit he sends shivers down my spine. Though I've no idea why. On the rare occasions Bruno and I have happened to meet him and exchange a few words with him, I was on pins and needles.'

'He's a tormented character, I think,' said André. 'He had a religious crisis; then he broke completely with religion and started expressing extreme left-wing opinions. After that he became a theosophist or something like that. I should add that at a certain period he used to do quite a bit of elbow-lifting. He must have cut it down since. Otherwise he would probably have lost his job at the bank.'

'I'll tell you the trouble with Lagarde,' said Bruno: 'he's never been properly appreciated. He's got tremendous energy but he's never known how to use it. So far he hasn't been able to find his element, the sphere where he belongs.'

Not bad. I would never have thought Bruno capable of such a precise judgment. Or rather, I would never have thought he could take the trouble to pass a precise judgment on somebody who doesn't matter to him. This isn't the first time Bruno has surprised me by a sort of quiet sagacity, a real flair. He's much sharper than his little pest of a sister.

The little pest, not in the least abashed by her brother's recent reprimand, was expounding her personal point of view on the subject of religion: all religions were relics of primitive, pre-logical thought.

'You really must read Frazer,' she advised Claire in a faintly condescending tone of voice. 'Nowadays people throw themselves into the most farfetched beliefs simply because they've been frightened ever since the Bomb. It's the great fear of the year one thousand all over again.'

She for her part didn't seem seriously disturbed by millenarianist fears; and she was enjoying the profiterolles she had just been served with the tranquillity of a well-tempered soul. The planet could blow up: this particular stoic was prepared to take disaster in her stride.

The reference to the Bomb hadn't made anybody round the table jump. Bruno recalled that two months earlier Einstein had issued an 'anguished appeal' to the world's leaders, asserting that the destruction of all life on earth had now entered the realm of technical possibility.

This time the little spoons remained suspended above the helpings of profiterolles, either because the company wanted to pay attention to Bruno out of politeness, or because mention of universal annihilation by so irrefutable an authority as Einstein was undeniably impressive. According to André, who had read the article in *Le Monde*, there was already talk of a hydrogen bomb whose destructive power would be equivalent to a thousand times that of the bomb which had pulverised Hiroshima, but a physicist at the University of Chicago had declared that it was impossible to manufacture it yet.

Provisionally reassured, everyone moved into the drawing-room for coffee.

A rather short young woman with a swarthy complexion was beating eggs in a bowl. Next she poured into a frying-pan the liquid she had put to warm on a gas-ring. While performing these actions she seemed to be thinking about something that had nothing to do with her work. She turned towards a man who was sitting at a table laid for two, and said:

'I'd do that if I were you. Even if you haven't seen anything of him for a long time, he's still your uncle and you're his only relative. I'd go and offer to buy his farm, leaving him a life interest in it. If you wait until you inherit it, what with all the tax you'll have to pay, you'll have only just enough to pay the death duties.'

'What sort of price is he likely to ask for the farm?'

'It wouldn't be very high,' she assured him, 'in view of the relatively modest acreage.' He mustn't hesitate. If necessary they would borrow money.

'Borrow money!' he said, looking almost frightened.

'Yes, borrow money. That isn't a crime you know. And you'll be able to get a loan, seeing that you own a house.'

'Oh, *my* house! Who would want to raise a mortgage on this tumbledown shack?'

'I wish you wouldn't always belittle what you've got! It's a house, after all. There's the site, which is in town. On the outskirts, I admit, but in town. That's a security, and you can borrow money on it.'

'I had never thought of that.'

'Well, you've got to think of it. You've got to go ahead, improve your position, make plans.'

She tipped the frying-pan to spread the omelette properly before rolling it up and sliding it on to an earthenware plate decorated with a red cockerel. She sat down and cut a loaf of bread into slices.

'I haven't gone to much expense,' she said unsmilingly. 'A ham omelette and a salad, some cheese and a tart.'

'It's a feast.'

'It will be better than the grub they serve in your restaurant, but you can only have one glass of wine.'

'All right, all right. Whatever you say.'

He for his part smiled as he looked at her; the smile lit up his plain features, which life hadn't treated kindly.

'It's for your own good, you know,' she said.

She started eating. There was a brusque determination about all her gestures, and her dark eyes darted fire. They were sitting in a narrow room in which considerable ingenuity had been used to fit in a divan bed, a table, a small armchair, two upright chairs, some bookshelves and a cupboard. The washstand served as a sink. Everything was meticulously clean. Flowers in an earthenware vase, copies of not too famous pictures, a few knick-knacks, and the very arrangement of the books made this cell a snug and almost stylish refuge.

'It's pretty here. You've made a nice job of this room.'

'Your place could look just as good if you took a little trouble over it.'

'Since my mother died I've just left everything lying around. What do you expect from a bachelor? . . . I thought it was good enough for me.'

'A hovel is no good for anybody.'

She had put no harshness into her words. She was simply saying what she had seen and calling it by its name, without any tact but without any malice either: it was like that, and that was all.

17

'A hovel,' he repeated. 'So I've lived for over eight years in a hovel without noticing.'

'That's what poverty is: not noticing that you're living in it.'

'You don't mince your words, do you?' he said, and again he gave a gentle, appealing smile.

'It's simpler to say what you think.'

'But sometimes you risk hurting people that way.'

'Did I hurt you?'

'No, but only because it was you. I know that you don't mean to be hurtful. In that respect you're like a child.'

'Oh, you're making a mistake there! Children are very cruel; they love hurting people.'

'You think so?'

'I know them. When you've worked as a schoolteacher for a few years, you've got no illusions about children being kind.'

'Are you tough with them?'

'Not tough. I don't allow them to get away with anything and I'm absolutely fair. They know that and they respect me.'

'Are they afraid of you?'

'In respect there's always a tiny element of fear. What do you think of my omelette?'

He raised his eyes towards heaven in an ecstatic grimace.

'Then finish it off. I'm not going to give you any wine until you start on the ham, and you'll have to make it last until the cheese.'

'A real cure for alcoholics!'

'I'm going to look after you, you'll see! In less than a year you'll be a different man.'

'I've been trying to be a different man for twenty years.'

'Yes, but you'd have liked to change your skin or your face, be six inches taller, turn into someone else. That's a futile dream; it's ridiculous. I've dreamt of being someone else too, but only until I was twenty. At the age of twenty I

realised that that dream destroyed me, and that I had to...'
(here she fumbled a little for her words)...'I had to accept
myself as I was, trying to improve myself where that was
possible. Through education, for instance. At the age of
twenty I decided I was going to be somebody.'

She looked almost happy.

'I haven't got very far, of course; at least, not yet...But
when you know how far I've come!'

With a hesitant gesture he stretched out his right hand
across the table and laid it on the young woman's left hand.
She looked a little surprised, but tolerant.

'I know how far you've come,' he said. 'And I admire you.'

She shook her head.

'There's no cause for admiration. All you need is a little
common-sense and a bit of will-power. But it's true that I
was nothing at twenty. Less than nothing. When you do the
washing-up for other people, you are less than nothing.'

There was no bitterness in her voice or her tone: she was
simply stating one of the laws of the world; she wasn't affected
by it, even if she had once been subject to it. So much the
worse for those who resigned themselves to being 'less than
nothing'.

The open window revealed a patch of night sky and some
foliage.

'I was lucky enough to find this room overlooking the park.
There's always a little air and light. It smells of buds opening...If it's fine on Sunday, how about going to see your
uncle? Twelve miles on a bike is nothing.'

'If you like, but he's going to wonder who we are and
what we want with him. God knows how he'll receive us!
Probably with a pitchfork.'

'Don't you worry: I'm the one who'll talk to him. I know
how to talk to peasants.'

'He hardly knows me.'

'Well, this will be a good opportunity to renew acquaintance with him.'

'But what are you going to tell him?'

'The truth. That we want to buy his farm and his land, first of all because it's in our interest to do so; but that it's in his interest too to sell it to us and to get an income out of it instead of leaving everything to the State, without bene-fiting anyone. Peasants understand that sort of reasoning.'

'He's a savage. He's bound to be stubborn and stupid.'

'Leave him to me. I've already dealt with some real boors and I know how to handle them. How much will you bet that before we've been talking for an hour he'll offer us a drink? And that by the time we leave in the evening, every-thing will be settled?'

She held out her hand in a laughing challenge.

'I'm not betting. With you I'm almost certain to lose.'

She put on a serious, frowning expression again.

'I tell you, we must buy some land. Especially in that region, close to the gas deposits. It's a gilt-edged investment.'

'But will I be able to pay his life interest?'

'There'll be two of us to pay it. I've already worked it all out. With my salary added to yours, we'll manage. And next year, if I succeed in getting my diploma, I'll earn more at the technical college.'

They must fix the date of their marriage (the words 'we must' kept coming to her lips) and carry out the most urgent repairs to the house. She would do the easier jobs, such as painting and papering. Bit by bit, through their combined efforts, they would turn the house into a place that was 'quite pleasant to live in'.

'I get the impression that you can work miracles.'

'I enjoy planning, organising, doing things. I can't stay still for a moment. I've always got to be getting on with some-thing. Have you finished your ham? I'll give you some wine. But be careful: don't empty your glass at one go. How much did you use to drink before you met me?'

'I've already told you.'

'I've forgotten. Are you ashamed of it? What can it do to

you now, when it all belongs to the past? Well, when things were going badly, how much did you use to drink?'

'A couple of bottles... Sometimes a bit more.'

She allowed a brief silence to pass.

'You wouldn't have lasted long at that rate. A drunk is a horrible sight. My father used to drink quite a lot. I saw him drunk two or three times. Very drunk. I'll never forget. It was horrible.'

She returned to their plans for the future. The wedding would be a very simple affair, with as little expense as possible. They would invite nobody but the witnesses. There would be no honeymoon, of course: after the age of thirty it wasn't the thing any more, and besides, it was just a bourgeois custom. They would take it later on, when their situation had improved, when they themselves had become bourgeois. She didn't feel much curiosity about foreign countries, but she would quite like to go back to England, to the town where she had spent a year *au pair*. The family she had been with hadn't exploited her, as often happened with *au pair* girls. They had been very kind to her and had taught her a great deal.

'What, for example, apart from English?'

'Well, ordinary things in everyday life. For example, how to eat my food – what they call table manners. Yours aren't very good: I must teach you how to eat properly. What are you blushing for? Have I annoyed you? There's no need to get annoyed about that, seeing that you've never learnt. I was the same when I arrived in England: I ate like a peasant girl, with my arms spread out and my elbows on the table. The people I was with taught me to sit up straight, with my elbows tucked in, and to use my knife and fork like they did. I became civilised in their house. They introduced me to boys and girls of my own age. Over there, the fact that I'm not very pretty didn't matter as much as it does here, because they aren't much to look at themselves. I learned how to dance and all that. I grew quieter and not so awkward. Before, I was a little savage ... So you see, my stay in England was very useful for me.'

'Is it hard to learn English?'

'Very. It gave me a lot of trouble at first, and I've never succeeded in losing my French accent. Or perhaps I should say my Béarn accent!'

He was examining the books on a shelf above the table. He pulled one out at random and opened it.

'English poems with French translations. Were these in your course?'

'Just a few of them.'

He leafed through the book, reading a line here and there; and all of a sudden he stopped and read something carefully, in complete silence. His features had frozen. When he had finished he said:

'This poem is absolutely extraordinary! Do you know it? It's called *A Poison Tree*.'

'No. That one wasn't in my course. What is so extraordinary about it?'

'Listen,' he said. 'I'll read it to you.'

And he read, clumsily, but in a toneless, slightly feverish voice which was more impressive than the diction of any professional reader. He was short of breath and stumbled over certain words, either out of shyness at hearing himself reciting poetry aloud, or out of emotion; and probably it was out of emotion. Struck by this new appearance he had taken on, this face of his that she had never seen before, this sudden passion for which the poem was probably just a support or a pretext, she fastened a sharp, penetrating gaze on him while he read. Wide-eyed with interest, she looked like a little owl.

I was angry with my friend
I told my wrath, my wrath did end.
I was angry with my foe:
I told it not, my wrath did grow.

And I watered it in fears
Night and morning with my tears,
And I sunned it with smiles
And with soft deceitful wiles.

And it grew both day and night,
Till it bore an apple bright,
And my foe beheld it shine,
And he knew that it was mine, –

And into my garden stole
When the night had veiled the pole;
In the morning, glad, I see
My foe outstretched beneath the tree.

He paused to get his breath back.

'It's superb, isn't it?' he said.

'I don't know. Maybe. What's superb about it?'

'Why, it's a terrifying thing! That curious image of a hatred, a spite which you grow, like a plant, in pain, which you water with your tears, and which ends up by producing a fruit, a poisonous fruit ... You understand, don't you? It's the poem of vengeance.'

And looking at her without seeing her, because he could see beyond her something that was no longer her, he slowly repeated the last two lines:

In the morning, glad, I see
My foe outstretched beneath the tree.

'Have you any enemies?' she asked calmly.

'No. At least, not as far as I know ... I mean to say that I don't hope for anybody's death, like the person who says "I" in the poem. But that doesn't matter: vengeance doesn't have to have one person as its object ... You see,' he went on, getting more excited, 'that's all symbolic: the fruit, the enemy who drops dead...But suppose...Suppose, for instance, that you've suffered from the indifference and contempt of other people, or of a few people, or of one person. And then, one day, the situation is reversed, and you can despise the others in your turn, because they are underneath you, as the result, say, of a change of fortune. Then, all of a sudden, they see you, they are forced to see you, these people who until now had never seen you, they are forced to recognise your existence, perhaps even your superiority. At bottom, what that poem is saying is that resentment, even hatred or humiliation, can also be a source of life and energy...'

The fervour he had put into this speech must have surprised him himself, for he gave a disarming smile and concluded in a lighter tone:

'That poet must have been quite a character!'

She had watched him and listened to him without moving, her chin resting on one hand.

'I think I understand,' she said at last.

That was her only comment, but it was obvious that she had indeed understood.

'I'll tidy up tonight,' she said, getting up. 'How about going for a walk?'

With their coffee and liqueurs they abandoned the world to its doubtful future and talked about a less dramatic present, that of the theatre, the cinema, fashion and local gossip. Beatrice had a lot to say about the theatre. She had just come back from Paris, where she had seen 'everything that was worth seeing'. Bruno and Juliette were planning to go and see *Le Don d'Adèle* when it came on tour to Biarritz or Pau.

'Yes,' said Beatrice, 'that's just the sort of play for you: theatre for pleasure.'

'Well, that's better than theatre that gives you pain,' retorted Bruno with a good-natured laugh.

24

In the cinema, Beatrice went on, there was nothing good apart from *Kind Hearts and Coronets,* and of course – but everybody had already seen it – there was also . . .

'*The Third Man,*' the others chorused.

'That Harry Lime theme!' groaned Juliette.

The children whistled it all day long. It really got on your nerves. Pierre, their eldest child, wanted a zither for his birthday. Think of it: a zither! They had laughed till they cried at the idea of their chubby, lisping little Pierre playing a zither. André said that the Harry Lime theme was a clever piece of work, 'with reminiscences of Kurt Weill'. In any case, it had made the composer a rich man. Nowadays, said Bruno, it was only in the world of entertainment, the cinema and popular music, that you could hope to make a fortune, because business, well, business wasn't doing very well. 'You know that the sale of pit-props is finished,' he told André; 'it doesn't bring in anything any more. I'm going to have to sell all those acres of forest in the Landes, because why hang on to useless capital?' And the two men, although they probably had no desire to broach the subject, started talking investments, dividends, social levies, tax rates and price increases, because that was the sort of thing men talked about after dinner, it being understood that it would be discourteous to bore women with such austere discussions. The three women meekly obeyed this unspoken rule by forming a little group of their own. Even Beatrice condescended to chat with her sister-in-law and her guest on such frivolous subjects as the length of dresses this season. They were beginning to get away from the New Look, and about time too; they had had enough fussiness, it was time to get back to simplicity, to sober lines. The new hairstyles were very practical too; with your hair short you felt freer, and you could comb it in no time at all. At this point Bruno, who had already exhausted the harrowing subject of the nation's finances, pricked up his ears. Delighted at this diversion, he expounded his masculine point of view to the ladies: he was not in favour, not at all in favour, of this vogue for short hair. Were they going back to the style of the emancipated young women of the twenties? Hair hanging down to the waist, or even to the feet: that was what Bruno would have liked. Yes, heavy chignons and 1900 hairpins...Seeing a woman's hair coming undone and spreading over her bare shoulders...'For thine hair is a warm river,' murmured André, but nobody seemed to recognise the quotation.

A certain languor began to weigh upon the evening. Several times Claire Comarieu made as if to get up and assumed the expression of a person about to say: 'I think it's time we went home,' but she failed to find a favourable opportunity: every time somebody started the conversation going again. Now they were talking about the 'scandal of the leaks' in which some generals had been compromised. It wasn't surprising that the war in Indo-China was at a standstill: our Intelligence Service was deplorable. Other countries must be laughing at us...Anyhow, it wasn't the first scandal of the Fourth Republic, and it wouldn't be the last. And what could the ordinary citizen do? Absolutely nothing. A sigh of despair. 'I think,' Claire said firmly, 'that it's getting late,' and she stood up, smiling. 'André, perhaps it's time?...'

Bruno and Juliette accompanied their guests to the door. There was a breath of spring in the air. While they were exchanging the usual courtesies a couple passed by on the other side of the street, going up the hill. In the dark they failed to recognise them straight away. It was André who identified them first, from the rather stocky silhouette of the man; and as the couple were now about a dozen paces away, they thought they could safely talk about them in an undertone, without realising that this sudden whispering might strike the attention of the two passers-by. 'Who is she? Do you know her? It's the first time I've seen him out at this time of night with a woman. Well, well! Does that mean he's going to get married at last? Poor fellow, so much the better for him ... They're going up to the Navailles Tower, the local lovers' walk. What are you laughing at? ... We aren't laughing!'

'They're talking about us,' said the young woman. 'Do you know them?'

'I know the two men. I went to school with them.'

'What can they be saying?'

'Oh, they must have been wondering whether we were lovers, or something like that.'

'They didn't say good evening to you.'

'They probably didn't recognise me straight away. Besides, we don't see much of each other any more.'

'Why not?'

'I don't know. It just happens that way. We don't belong to the same class. They are middle-class and always have been. At school you can get along together at a pinch. But afterwards the different classes form up again ... Anyhow, I don't give a damn, you know. We've got nothing more to say to each other, them and me.'

'If they are middle-class, you ought to renew acquaintance with them. If you've got interesting contacts, you keep them.'

'But I don't think they *would* be interesting. When I ran into them by accident, I never knew what to say to them.'

'If you had to stop seeing people simply because you've nothing to say to them, you'd end up seeing hardly anybody.'

'But what interest would there be in seeing those people?'

'More interest than in seeing nobody. You just talk. You say anything that comes into your head, provided you talk. You're mixing with people, you're in company. That's good for you.'

'You think so?' he asked, and as his tone of voice wasn't genuinely doubtful, the young woman replied straight away:

'Yes, and you think so too. Besides, I wasn't just thinking of us, I was thinking of our children. If they can mix with middle-class children when they're little, then things will be easier for them later on.'

He couldn't help smiling and squeezing her arm.

'Are you thinking of our children already?'

'We're getting married to have children, aren't we? In any case, speaking for myself, I want two or three.'

There was not the slightest hint of sentimentality in this statement. It was just as if she had said: 'I want a refrigerator and a washing-machine.' She made no response to the pressure of the man's hand on her arm. Yet he was not offended by this apparent coldness, this down-to-earth attitude, this instinctive rejection on her part of vain words and gestures. He felt safe with this girl who seemed prepared to take their common destiny into her firm hands. They would marry in front of the mayor and in front of a priest, since that was how the world wanted it; but there was already an unspoken pact between them.

'What a dinner you gave us, pet!' said Bruno, coming back into the drawing-room. 'It was delicious!' And he went on to heap extravagant praise on the meal they had eaten.

'Really? You really thought so?' said Juliette, her eyes shining. 'I thought the guinea-fowl . . . No? It was all right?'

'Everything was perfect,' repeated Bruno. 'You're marvellous, you know! There's nobody to touch you.' And he kissed her passionately.

'Have you finished?' said Beatrice. 'Anyone would think you were still engaged. It's almost sickening.'

She was smoking, deep in an armchair.

'Sickening?' Bruno exclaimed indignantly. 'If there's anybody sickening in this room, it's you. I'm beginning to get fed up with your airs and graces! Who do you think you are?'

'Bruno, please . . .'

'But it's true, you know, she'll get me to lose my temper in the end! If you don't like it here, my girl, you know what you can do: go back to your mother and father. Yes, back to the country! No, really! You keep us waiting for dinner, you don't even apologise, you're rude to our guests...'

'They're idiots.'

Bruno turned to his wife.

'You hear that? Our guests are idiots. So are we, I suppose. After all, we go to the theatre for pleasure. She told us so to our faces. That's how she...'

'Beatrice, dear, you ought not to talk like that. Just because you're younger than we are, that's no reason for...Oh, I can understand that you find it a little boring here, because you're used to...'

'So Mademoiselle finds it a little boring here, does she? Well, she can get the hell out of here, dammit! She can go back to Paris, and bloody quick!'

'Bruno, please don't shout like that. You're going to wake the children.'

Beatrice didn't seem at all alarmed by this outburst. She took a last drag on her cigarette, stubbed it out in an ashtray, and stood up.

'I'm going to bed. Good night.'

Bruno had to drink a glass of armagnac to calm his nerves after this little scene. Juliette pointed out to him that his sister was still very young, and assured him that she would change, that she would lose her pretentious manner and her affectation of rudeness; she wasn't a bad kid. 'You're too soft with her,' he replied. They went upstairs and went on tiptoe to look at their three children asleep in their respective rooms. Pierre, the eldest, the one who wanted a zither for his birthday, was sleeping all curled up, pink and chubby with a little sweat on his upper lip; they exchanged tender smiles over this big ball of childish flesh. Nicolas, the younger of the two boys, was stretched out on his back with his arms lying alongside his body; pale and delicate, with faint purple shadows under his eyes, he had a solemn, rather mysterious look about him, like a recumbent figure on a tomb. Line, the youngest, was just a baby face framed in tulle. She hadn't cried yet that evening; she was a good little girl ... This inspection of his family calmed Bruno down completely. In their bedroom he stood in front of the open window and breathed in the scents rising from the garden. He even did a few breathing exercises: you had to think about keeping fit. The rich food and the armagnac warmed his blood agreeably. When he turned round, Juliette was already more than half undressed, her lovely shoulders shining in the halo of light from the standard lamp. A greedy gleam lit up Bruno's eyes.

'The evening was beginning to drag,' said André as they walked up the Rue de Navailles – their house was only about thirty yards from the Marcillacs'. 'They're a delightful couple, but after three hours of their company ... Luckily I can always count on you to give the signal to leave.'

'You seemed to wake up all right when the little sister arrived.'

André gave a rather forced laugh.

'Now what do you mean by that? It's just like you to have an idea like that. She's a pretty little thing, and pleasant to look at, like a pretty object, but she's just too stupid for words. No, really, you can rest assured that you've nothing to worry about.'

'Oh, I wasn't at all worried. I found it amusing to see you putting on a show for her at the beginning: that's all.'

'I put on a show for her?'

'Yes. When you were talking about Madame Dolfus and that writer. It was obvious that you had an audience all of a sudden. You trotted out one or two of those "brilliant remarks" you only serve up on important occasions ... Oh, it was very amusing.'

There was no spite in her voice, but rather a somewhat tense irony.

'I can't remember what I said. When you're at a dinner-party, you do the best you can; you say whatever comes into your head, on the spur of the moment.'

'But I'm not criticising you. You play your part very well, and it's only natural that the presence of a pretty girl should stimulate you a little. I was only joking.'

At this hour of the night the street was empty, lit here and there by dim electric lamps fixed to the corners of houses. Claire and André had walked along this stretch of street between the Marcillacs' house and their own dozens of times, in every season of the year, at about the same time of night, and they knew every inch of it by heart. During the German Occupation, in the early days of their marriage, the street wasn't lit and every source of light was covered; they used to go home just before the curfew, which was fixed at either ten or eleven, according to the whim of the Kommandantur; the windows were draped with blue material, and a thin ray of bluish light filtered through the closed shutters. At that time the street was bathed in a grey, lunar silence which was not at all depressing, for behind all those blue-striped shutters you could sense the warmth of firesides where families huddled together around radio sets from which an angry voice was piping above the crackling of the jamming transmitters. Besides, in this little town fed by an inexhaustible countryside, this town whose everyday routine was not seriously disturbed by the war, and whose walls were not stained with blood, except during the last days before the German defeat, life under the Occupation had not been entirely devoid of charm. This was because of the constantly renewed feeling of an ever-changing situation, because of the excited rather than anxious wait for news, and also because of the local incidents which filled the day like the scenes in a *commedia dell'arte* – the butcher's wife, as patriotic as any of Daudet's characters, had given a piece of her mind to the captain of the Kommandantur which had left him speechless; young Lacoste had got himself arrested crossing the demarcation line; the Gaullist Darriolas had fallen out with the

31

Pétainist Coustous – a comedy which could be distressing at bottom but which wasn't seen in that light at the time. After the liberation of the town, the electric lamps, which were still very provincial and nineteenth-century in appearance, had been lit up again at the corners of the houses, whose wide-open shutters afforded glimpses on warm evenings of a kitchen with a family eating in it, or, through muslin curtains, the cushioned comfort of a middle-class drawing-room. The silence of the night had lost something of the crystalline purity it had had in wartime, shattered as it was now by the occasional blare of a radio and soon, when prosperity returned, by the roar of a car; but about midnight, when Claire and André used to return home after dinner at the Marcillacs', it was still an almost silent street in a sleeping town.

Claire went up to the first floor, 'to see if the girls are asleep'. André sat down, lit a cigarette, and started lazily looking through one of those glossy monthlies devoted to interior decoration, the furnishing of country houses, and the pleasures of antique-hunting for thrifty millionaires: the French were beginning to take an interest in such things, all the French and not just a small section of aesthetes and idlers – that was what was new about it. André had taken out a subscription to this magazine because that sort of thing was done among what he still called 'our sort of people'. He looked around him. The house differed from the Marcillacs' only in odd details, a more confident, enlightened taste. The arrangement of the different rooms was identical. The same garden at the back stretched as far as the ruins of the town's old fortifications. The furnishing of their house had been an interest in common for Claire and André during the early years of their marriage. They had gone round all the antique shops, choosing materials, ornaments and pictures together, although André always left the final decision to Claire, in conformity with an ancient tradition that the decoration of the home was the wife's responsibility, and also out of basic indifference: provided he was comfortable, it was all one to him. He was not cut out to be an antique-collector. All the same, he loved this house, of which Claire's parents had given them the use but not the deeds, but which, one day, would nonetheless be theirs, and which they already regarded as such. Like the Marcillacs' house, it was an imposing edifice with huge rooms and thick walls, which had been built about two centuries before, at a time when a bourgeois putting up a house did not skimp on space, when the materials used were millstone and tile, and when men built, not only for themselves, but for endless generations to come. Over the street door, which was approached by a flight of four semi-circular steps, a carved inscription gave the date of the building, 1772, and the name of the architect: *Jacob Toula fecit.* The prestige and attraction of this patrician house, and the prospect of living in it, of becoming a resident of the Rue de Navailles, which was the old aristocratic street of the town and which, although now a little proletarianised, still numbered four or five noble dwellings, had played no small part in the decision André had taken one day to marry the 'very lady-like' Claire Bartissol. The same considerations had coloured the feeling he had for her during their engagement: not love, admittedly (or at least, not what at that age he imagined love should be), but an affectionate, somewhat condescending, rather tender regard, which he also tried to think of as rather poetic, as if he were engaged to a Francis Jammes heroine who was also bringing him a dowry of an eighteenth-century house and a guarantee of social advancement.

Claire came downstairs again – their bedroom was on the ground floor, overlooking the garden. She reported that the little girls hadn't woken up. She picked up a notebook that was lying on a table and in an undertone, as if talking to herself, she listed the things she had to do the next day. She was methodical to the point of fussiness; she took care to make a note of all her appointments, although she had an excellent memory, was as punctual as the stars, and could have managed without a watch. The 'very lady-like' girl had become a 'very lady-like' woman, but with nothing left of the poetic quality André had thought he could discern, or had wanted to see in her; in ten years of marriage he had learnt that condescension was not a suitable attitude to adopt towards Claire.

'Aren't you coming to bed?' she asked.

'I've got a slight headache. I wouldn't be able to go to sleep straight away. I'm going to stay in the library for half an hour.'

'You aren't going to work at this time of night, are you?'

'I may do a little writing.'

'Oh, you and your scribbling,' she said with a little smile. 'I thought that ages ago you ... Well, good night. I shall probably go straight to sleep. Don't wake me up when you come to bed.'

In the library André opened the bottom drawer of a writing-table with a little key he took out of one of his pockets, and pulled out an exercise book with a black cover. He switched on a lamp standing on the corner of the table, but before sitting down he glanced at his reflexion in a mirror. That was a reflex action he had had constantly during his childhood and youth and which he was gradually losing. For a few years he had noticed that he was taking less interest in his face. He had often wondered whether other men had the same reflex action, but he had never dared to ask any of those he knew, not even friends like Bruno. However, he noticed that young men going into a public place, such as a café or a cinema foyer, never failed to steal a furtive glance at their reflection. Some even stood openly in front of the mirror to comb their hair or straighten their tie. He concluded from this that coquetry, or more simply the urge to check on your physical appearance, on the effect you are producing, was just as common in men as in women, though more discreet in the former, and this reassured him about himself, although to tell the truth he had never worried about this symptom of narcissism. Tonight he thought he looked especially young, really quite handsome. He had scarcely changed at all in the last ten years: the lower part of the face had grown a little heavier, a little thicker, that was all. Claire, on the other hand, hadn't weathered the passing years so well.

He sat down and opened the exercise book at the page where his writing stopped. He re-read the last paragraph he had written, which ended with a quotation dated 16ᵉ January of that year:

The real drama of old age (at least for certain people, and most of all for poets) is that it does not exist. So long as the body has not suffered the first of those terrible blows of the axe which strike the old human tree at the intersection of the spirit and the flesh and make it shudder in every limb, nothing changes except that face whose destruction surprises us every morning in the mirror, as if we had been expecting some miracle: the miracle which will indeed take place when, on Judgment Day, the angel's trumpet will rouse from the dust of ages millions upon millions of incorruptible young bodies.

There followed this note: 'It is the last lines of this quotation, after the colon, that are the most beautiful, worthy of Chateaubriand; unfortunately they mean nothing to me.'

They had reached the top of the hill, where the Rue de Navailles became a country road. On the left a steep bank led up to a flat strip of ground on which there stood a tower, all that remained of a vanished castle. A narrow platform, overlooking gardens and roofs, dominated the whole town, which lay enclosed within a semi-circle of gentle hills. Leaning on the railing, they amused themselves identifying first monuments, then houses, and spotting the one in which they were going to live, although it was no easy task to make out a bit of roof lost among other roofs similarly shrouded in darkness. Because it was dark and they were wrapped in silence, they talked in an undertone, almost a whisper.

'I don't think I could live anywhere but here,' said Jean Lagarde. 'I've often thought of going away and settling down in some other town, but I couldn't do it: anywhere else, even fifty miles from Sault, would represent exile to me. I don't know why. It's funny, really. It isn't that I've been happy here, but just . . . When I was young I went to Paris for a while and I was even lonelier than here, which is saying something.'

'Don't talk about it any more, because it's all over: you aren't alone any more now.'

'All the same, you can't help remembering certain . . .'

'I too,' she broke in with a hint of impatience, 'have been lonely and unhappy. I told you about it once, I told you what my life had been like, so that you should know about it once for all; but I'll never talk about it again. I've written *finis* to all that: it's all over, done with, dead.'

'All right, all right,' he said light-heartedly. 'I'll do the same. It's forbidden to be sad, forbidden to recall unpleasant memories.'

'Strictly forbidden.'

'But you know, it can be very pleasant recalling unpleasant memories when you are happy, just to be able to say to yourself: that hell is over, and to feel your happiness with more . . . to be more conscious of your happiness.'

'Maybe, but what I don't like is the way in which you recall painful memories, the tone of voice in which you talk about certain things. Anybody would think you took a sort of pleasure in hurting yourself. It's a kind of self-indulgence,' she added rather stiffly: this word, or at least the use of it, was probably a recent acquisition, a small enrichment of her language which didn't date back to her schooldays but to a more recent period, so that she wasn't sufficiently familiar with it to use it without thinking.

'Perhaps,' he said after a pause, 'it's also the fact that sadness can act as a stimulus . . .'

' "I've been unhappy, so I'm going to make the world pay

36

for having hurt me, I'm going to make it pay dear." Is that what you mean?'

'There's no need to explain anything to you: you understand everything in advance. It's terrible.'

'That isn't hard to understand: you've been talking about nothing else all evening. I don't know whether you are right, whether you can make the world pay for anything... Still, let's suppose you can. In that case, why have you waited until you're nearly forty? You should have begun at twenty, instead of vegetating as you've done... It's shameful, having talent and education and not trying harder to succeed. By now you ought to be a director of your bank. You shouldn't still be sitting behind bars, like a little monkey, counting banknotes.'

Her scolding tone of voice was tempered by an affectionate gruffness.

'I've never been interested in the bank,' he said. 'It isn't my line.'

'Then you ought to have tried something else. Besides, why weren't you interested? If I had had your training, I'd have found it very interesting, handling other people's money and making my own little pile at the same time.'

'I can well believe it,' he said with a laugh, 'from the way you used to count the notes when you came to the bank, and the way you put them away in your handbag... I used to watch you when you were checking your modest little account...'

'Look here, are you making fun of me? Do you know how much pinching and scraping that modest little account represented? Can you imagine what it meant to me to have a bank account? The first time I held my first cheque book, with my account number and my name printed on it, I almost felt I was a different person.' And in a very natural, almost childlike tone of voice, as if referring to something that went without saying, she added: 'I had even more self-respect than before.'

This last remark must have touched him, for he took her by the shoulder and drew her towards him.

'In any case,' he said gently, 'it was when I saw you checking your account that I started saying to myself: that little woman who isn't exactly pretty' – he tightened his embrace – 'but who has such lovely eyes, I wonder if . . .'

'I wonder if I might condescend to marry her?' she asked suspiciously.

'No, on the contrary: I wonder if she might accept.'

'And we know what happened after that,' she said briskly. 'Nobody can say that our love-story is one of the greatest of all time, but it's good enough for us.'

'The evening of the Sault fête, when we went for a walk and . . .'

'Yes, yes, I remember.'

'You didn't feel the slightest hesitation? You were determined to accept me if I asked you to marry me?'

'I was that! You were the first, and I wasn't going to let the opportunity slip!'

He loosened his embrace and let his arm fall to his side.

'It's incredible,' he murmured, 'the things you can say. 'Anybody would think you didn't realise . . .'

She let out a burst of fresh, girlish laughter.

'Why, you idiot, I was joking! Listen, you were the first, that's perfectly true. But I'm no fool. I wouldn't have thrown myself at just anybody.'

'At last, the sweetest of all admissions.'

He drew her towards him again. She didn't resist, but only, he felt, out of a good-natured desire to please him, or perhaps out of a wish to conform with what she thought was expected of her, or what she considered to be the right attitude in the circumstances, since they were by themselves, after midnight, in a spot which was a traditional meeting-place for courting couples. She was troubled, not by emotion but by uncertainty, not knowing what she should do next, whether it was right to put her arms round the man's neck and offer him her lips, or whether she should leave the initiative to him. She was clearly not used to this kind of situation, and it was also obvious that her feelings were not exactly passionate; but he knew that already, and if anything, he was touched by his companion's awkwardness, her anxious, resigned submissiveness. Until now he had only known very ordinary and sometimes very stupid women, for whom he was just one nameless man among many, or else, when he went to nearby towns where that sort of game, unknown in Sault, was available for the local garrison or visiting tourists, prostitutes whom he paid to go to bed with and whose very venality had ended up by stimulating him like a drug. So this clumsy kiss was something new for him. He had the feeling that he was in command, that he was the master; and for the time being, that made up for a great deal that was sad in his life.

Back home after dinner at the M——s'. An evening like all the previous evenings there. B—— and his wife bursting with health, flourishing, and still obviously very much in love with each other. J—— is a dark-haired Rubens. She is in danger of growing fat. Already she has the beginnings of a double chin; but she has such pretty dimples, such a spontaneous, jolly laugh. It is impossible to imagine that one day she will be a fat lump like her mother. Yet it is inevitable: she will be a fat lump of a woman. B——is filling out too. With his enormous appetite, that isn't surprising. He is still magnificent, in a rather vulgar way: the classical athlete, of the massive variety (the pugilist) rather than the graceful type (the discus thrower). The little sister was there tonight. Ravishing and stupid. Very badly brought up by parents who had her late in life, when they were almost old enough to be her grandparents. She was aggressive towards C——. As soon as the girl arrived, I realised that C—— was on the defensive and that there would probably be some sharp exchanges. There were one or two, which were very slight but didn't go unnoticed. Poor B—— was very embarrassed. Back home, an acid remark by C—— suggesting that I had 'put on a show' for that stupid girl. Which, of course, may be true. Beauty and youth have always stimulated me, and I haven't lost the desire to please. After all, why should I lose it? Every time I am, or try to be, courteous and charming, C—— treats it as an insult to her. Any liking I arouse offends her. To please her, nobody should like me, and I should like nobody, outside the family circle.

What I have just written may be unfair. The fact is that C—— still hasn't forgiven me for that wretched peccadillo seven years ago. If it can even be described as a peccadillo, which is doubtful. In any case it was a sin of thought rather than of deed, but for a puritan like C—— the intention is as heinous as the act.

I haven't written anything in this book since 16 January. A long break for what is or pretends to be a diary. When I told C—— tonight that I wasn't going straight to bed, and that I might do a little writing, she didn't fail to say sarcastically: 'Oh, you and your scribbling . . .'

'My scribbling . . .' I should never have told her about it. She knows that I am keeping this diary, in more or less regular fashion. Not once has she shown the slightest curiosity about it, or asked me to read her a few pages. Does she regard this habit of mine as a weakness? I wouldn't dare to ask her what she thinks of it, because she would be quite capable of telling me bluntly: 'A provincial lawyer, stung by the literary tarantula; still, it's a hobby that doesn't cost us anything. I'd rather see you keeping a diary than collecting Chinese porcelain.' Would she be capable of answering me like that, or am I blackening her character to reduce my own responsibility with regard to her, or out of masochism?

How can I ever make head or tail of C——'s feelings towards me – that mixture of hurt affection, devotion, disappointment, bitterness and hope – and with all that, a rigid sense of duty? Is it possible to be as wrong about somebody as I was about her, at the time we got engaged? But I don't want to return to that subject yet again.

The last lines I wrote in this book, on 16 January, are a quotation about old age and the resurrection of the flesh – a quotation in which it is easy to recognise the author's tone and rhythm. It is followed by a note in which I declare that the resurrection of the flesh doesn't concern me. Well, two nights ago I had a peculiar dream. I was shut up in a cavity which fitted me tightly and from which, against my wishes, for I was very comfortable in it, I was due to be expelled. The operation turned out to be extremely difficult. I felt as if I were suffocating and I had spasms of agonising pain. I wasn't in the required position (though how did I know that?) and I kept trying to turn in all directions, to move about, to roll up into a ball, to curl up... The feeling of suffocation and anguish woke me up with a start, bathed in sweat. At first I told myself: 'I have had a dream that I was going to die,' and it was only on reflection that I realised the nature of my dream: that it was not a dream of death, but of birth, a prenatal memory, the recollection of what I had experienced just before coming into the world. Since then I have read in a psycho-analytical work that it is possible to have memories of the period before birth. But if the child about to be born has the feeling that it is going to die, why shouldn't a man who is dying be on the point of being born into another form of life, of which we have no idea whatever, any more than the foetus provided with food and oxygen by means of the umbilical cord can have the slightest physiological presentiment of what breathing with the lungs and eating with the mouth will be? The removal of the child from its mother must represent, for the child, a sort of death – until the respiratory system starts working. I am noting this down because the dream made a profound impression on me, but without really attributing any importance to it. For the moment, as I feel I am still a long way from my own death, I am resigned to being mortal. Besides, the idea of eternity has always terrified me. One of my games, when I was a child, was to shut my eyes and repeat: 'Always, always,' until I had an intuition of what that could be – an intuition as brief as a flash of lightning, which used to make me feel dizzy and slightly sick.

B——'s sister said that she had seen the writer Bonneteau at Letitia's. She repeated a few remarks he had made, which suggest that he is extremely pleased with himself and his work. How comfortable it must be, that self-satisfaction, that feeling that you are somebody important and that what you are doing is important too. What wouldn't I give to... It was Bonneteau's remarks that made me open this note book again. How many men and women, all over France, at this very moment, are writing either a diary, or a play, or (in most cases, probably) a novel? The thought of that silent, fervent, slightly crazy crowd is enough to make you shudder ... To shudder and to blush a little at being one of them. Three times I have begun writing a novel. Not once have I got further than the thirtieth page. It was so bad, so very bad! The worst sort of novel: autobiographical, without any attempt at transposition. A white, spongy, insipid, colourless, uniform lymph. Oh, I could have gone on with it, and written my hundred and twenty little pages. From the grammatical point of view it was correct, and a few passages could even be regarded as 'quite successful'. Yes, but so what? Disgust forced me to give up.

If I had the sort of imagination which allows you to project yourself, to multiply yourself, to give life to creatures who are not you, or who are just variations on you, I would have written that novel already, I would have had the courage to keep going to the very end. Not that I really feel any compulsion to do so. The fact of the matter is that I am just an amateur. C—— is right: a provincial lawyer who devotes some of his leisure time to writing, because he is bored.

'Because he is bored' ... It wasn't C—— who said that. It is I who have just written it, without thinking, and it has taken me aback: until today I had never admitted that I was bored. But how have these last ten years gone by? Learning a job, my marriage, the birth of my daughters, and settling into this house, have occupied a goodly part of the time. I can't say that during, say, the first six years I had that feeling of emptiness, of uselessness, of endless duration, which is boredom. Besides (and I am writing this down because I believe that to a large extent I have passed this stage) I was carried along for a long time by a sort of ambition which perhaps ought to make me blush (again!) – an ambition which would probably raise a smile anywhere but here, because it was limited to the comparatively petty setting of Sault. (Not that I attach any pejorative sense, or the slightest hint of condescension, to the word 'provincial', which in any case strikes me as completely out-of-date: the provinces, as a sociological and cultural reality, no longer exist; everything has been standardised, and people of my class are exactly the same in Paris and in Sault.) In short, I wanted to be, so to speak, the headman of the village, and by and large I have succeeded. What I mean is that I have reached the summit of the little social pyramid of the town; there are richer men than I but none more distinguished; with the M——s and a few others, we form the upper crust of the town, and that isn't a matter of indifference to me: I would find it even harder to adjust myself to existence if I had been forced to remain on a slightly lower social level, the level of people who are not my equals in either intelligence or culture, etc. Let us say that reaching the highest point in my comparatively restricted environment was a sort of basic minimum, starting from which I might try to do something and become somebody ... All right. So that has taken me a few years. Now it has been done, the goal has been reached, the pleasure I obtained from drawing nearer to it has vanished; and apart from my everyday work and a family life on which it would be better not to dwell, I don't know what to do ... But is it absolutely essential for me to do something? Is it really necessary? And what can I turn my hand to? ... Why can't I let myself live ever so gently, just as people let themselves die? ... That is what nearly everybody does ... What do I love in this world? I haven't any overpowering passions, nor a very sensual nature. I don't drink, I don't gamble. I am mildly interested in politics, and rather more so in literature and the arts, but not to the extent that you could talk about a vocation. The liveliest thing in me is probably a feeling of curiosity about other people, in which I have sometimes flattered myself I could distinguish the germ of a literary talent; but that can't be enough, for concierges too are curious about other people. All in all, if you can calculate that sort of thing, I am not unhappy; but I am not happy either. If I were, I imagine I would know.

André put his pen down, read quickly through what he had just written, then closed the notebook and put it away in the drawer, which he was careful to double-lock. Every time he took out this diary and added a few pages, he felt the satisfaction both of duty done and of a sort of moral progress, as well as a slight uneasiness, into which there entered the feeling, completely opposed to the idea of progress, of standing still, of marking time in a rather absurd fashion, and also a very vague feeling of guilt, doubtless connected with the somewhat clandestine, solitary, nocturnal character of this conversation with himself; but usually it was satisfaction that won the day.

He looked at his watch: two o'clock in the morning! He ought not to stay up so late. All the same, it was pleasant writing late at night, in a house where everything was asleep. The air coming in from the garden, through the wide-open window, was beginning to freshen a little. It carried with it the scent of the orchard in blossom; and how peaceful this silence was! Silence? No, not completely. Somewhere in the town, or on the outskirts, a vehicle was making a loud humming noise – one of those little motorcycles from Italy, green machines which had just begun to appear in the streets of Sault, ridden by adolescents and young men. It moved away, but the angry wasp-like buzz, diminishing in intensity with every second, lingered on none the less, like a hidden threat.

'I've come to see you,' said Jean Lagarde, 'to ask you for a piece of advice. It isn't anything very important, at least for you, who must be accustomed to much bigger transactions, but for me . . . But let me explain.'

An uncle of his had died, leaving him a farm and a few acres of land, about fifteen miles from Sault. The farm wasn't in very good condition: no repairs had been done to it since the Great War at least. Should he sell it as it was? Or would it be better to restore it, modernise it, and then try to sell it at a higher price? What price could it fetch in its present condition?

'I don't know quite what to tell you,' said André, 'first of all because that sort of question is more a matter for a notary than for me. And secondly, to make a reasonably accurate valuation, I would have to see the property, where it is situated, how far from the main road, and so on. That isn't my speciality. If you want expert advice, you must go to one of my notary colleagues, or even better an estate agent in Pau.'

'Yes, I know that this sort of business is usually handled by

44

a notary, but if I came to see you first, it's also because we've known each other a long time, and then too ... my wife and I think it's important to have your own lawyer, just as you have your own doctor. It isn't that we're planning to launch out into business, at least not yet ... The fact is that now I'm a family man, I'm going all middle-class.'

He's smiling, looking as if he's making fun of himself. But I know the trick: pretending to despise the very thing you are proud of. Like people who complain of having had an unhappy childhood because their English governess was too strict ... What exactly does he want with me? He must have already made up his mind about that farm. Asking my advice is nothing but an excuse. He's looking for or waiting for something else. But what? Picking up with me again perhaps ... No thank you!

'Having a lawyer,' Jean went on, 'is part of being middle-class, I believe?'

'In any case it's a beginning,' André said coldly.

'It is, isn't it? I'm glad to hear you say so. When somebody says: "I've seen my lawyer," it sounds impressive, it inspires confidence straight away. I've begun to feel a yearning for respectability recently.'

He says that jokingly, so it must be true ...

His gaze was riveted on André, unblinking, unmoving. The imperturbable fixity of his eyes seemed to indicate the existence of vast hidden plans even more than if they had shifted about. Whatever he had to hide, his gaze didn't let him down; it was his mouth, too mobile and occasionally twitching at the left corner, that wasn't under control.

'I don't think you know my wife?' he asked, as if there might be some doubt about it.

'I scarcely knew you were married,' said André, growing colder every minute.

'A husband always sounds rather a fool when he praises his wife, but ... she really is a remarkable woman. Every day

45

I congratulate myself on having been lucky enough to meet her. You know, I was beginning to turn into a fussy old bachelor; I was getting really bogged down. And then I met her and everything changed.'

Is he going to offer to introduce me to her? What's he got in mind?

'You have some children, haven't you?' he said, making sure that the politeness of the question revealed, instead of disguising it, the lack of interest he felt in the answer. He was very good at that sort of dosage.

'A little boy. He's three years old now.'

'Congratulations.'

He gazed hard at this ex-bachelor who had ceased to be 'bogged down'. There had always been something rather awkward about Jean Lagarde. None of his features could be described as ugly in itself; it was the whole face which, through an accumulation of minor defects (the low brow, the long nose, the greasy skin with the dilated pores), attained ugliness. The thickset body, with the long torso ill matched with short legs, did nothing to improve his appearance. He had the sort of build that breaks a tailor's heart. André noticed that the dark grey suit was well cut, but it was no use: Jean Lagarde would never look smartly dressed. They had been boys together at the local Catholic school. At that time Lagarde had already been regarded as a difficult, prickly sort. A good pupil, he tried to compensate with academic success for the real or imaginary inferiority which he obviously felt very keenly. He had gone off to Paris, and his teachers had expected great things of him. Then, one fine day, he had reappeared in Sault, a broken creature who seemed to have given up all hope. People sometimes met him in the street; he would keep close to the wall, pretending not to see them. They accepted this pretence all the more readily in that they hadn't the slightest desire to renew acquaintance with the fellow. Various rumours had reached André's ears; he had heard one of the curates say something about a 'conversion', or a revival of religious fervour. That hadn't lasted, for shortly afterwards Lagarde had joined the Party and become the brains of the local Communist cell. That had been another temporary experience: soon people heard that he had been expelled from the Party, possibly for petty-bourgeois intellectual deviationism. Where would they go looking for petty-bourgeois deviationism next! After that, he was lost from sight for years. Then a cleaning woman who was a neighbour of his and worked for the Comarieus gave them news of him: he had got a job in the bank; he lived all alone in a tumbledown little house; he drank rather a lot; and now and then he had 'a loose woman' in the place. Could that old cliché of the seedy bachelor, living in squalor between a whore and a bottle of rotgut, really correspond to a reality in one's own town? Of course it could: all clichés are true, and life is terribly conventional. Claire had suggested one day that they might try to help him: she meant by giving him moral support. Wasn't the Old Boys' Association, of which André was a member, going to do something for him? Yes, of course, André would have a word with the secretary. 'But what about you? You were in the same form: why don't you go and see him one of these days? Or invite him round here?' André made an anguished protest: 'Oh, no, not likely! I don't mind mentioning him to the secretary of the Association, but as for going to see him, and above all inviting him here, no, you can count me out! I'm not a boy scout or a St Bernard.' Claire hadn't pressed the point. Feeling a little embarrassed, perhaps, André had added: 'Besides, you know, with his touchy pride, he wouldn't take kindly to any approach we made. He's a professional outcast, and he'd smell out our charitable intentions a mile off.' To which Claire had replied with her exasperating gentleness: 'But it isn't a question of having charitable *intentions;* it's a matter of *being* charitable, of showing a little of the friendship you used to feel towards him.' André had not thought fit to continue this little argument, and he forgot to mention Jean to the secretary of the Old Boys' Association.

Well, apparently that wouldn't be necessary any more, seeing that Jean Lagarde was no longer 'bogged down', and seemed to have made a go of things.

'It's a pity to get out of touch, when we live in the same town ...'

You didn't see anything of your old friends, life went by, and one fine day you noticed you were forty, over forty in fact. It was incredible, wasn't it ... yes, forty-two ... Yes, it was hard to convince yourself that ... So, well, Jean had thought that it was a pity to get out of touch and that ...

'I am a very busy man,' André said quickly. 'My wife and I hardly ever go out, and we don't see anybody.'

Jean lowered his eyes abruptly. With the tip of his forefinger he started stroking the braid on his armchair in a mechanical movement. He was still smiling.

'Except for the Marcillacs,' he said.

'Yes, it's true we sometimes see the Marcillacs. After all, they are neighbours of ours.'

'How is Bruno these days?'

'Fine.'

'I seem to remember hearing that he wasn't doing terribly well?'

'Really?' snapped André. 'As far as I know, they are doing as well as ever.'

'And you are in a position to know,' said Jean, raising his eyes again, 'since you are the family lawyer.'

André made no reply, but looked his visitor up and down in such a way that anybody else would have got up straight away and walked out. But Jean's only reaction was to broaden his smile and increase the sharp brilliance of his gaze.

'They say he's selling his farms one after the other. But since you say that isn't true, so much the better. Bruno is such a nice fellow, I would be terribly sorry if ... Give him my regards, won't you.'

'I certainly will,' said André in the tone people adopt to mark the end of a conversation; and he put both hands on his desk, as if he had realised that Jean was going to stand up and he was preparing to do the same.

'Well, what sort of reception did he give you?'

'He was just a little colder than an iceberg, but that was what I expected.'

'You didn't go about it the right way. You ought to have flattered him, told him what a success he was, insinuated that you admired him. You didn't flatter him, of course, did you?'

'No, but that wouldn't have made any difference.'

'It would have made all the difference in the world. But I can imagine how you spoke to him: just as if you were making fun of him. I've told you a hundred times, you have to learn to be humble when it's useful.'

'You're too inclined to think that people allow themselves to be won over. They're sharper and tougher than you think.'

She asked him for an account of the conversation, and he gave it to her, omitting only one detail: the reference to the Marcillacs.

'All right, let's say no more about it,' she decided when he had finished. 'From the point of view of possible contacts, we've failed this time. Ten years from now, and possibly sooner, it will be his turn to approach you. Let's say no more about it.'

She returned to what really interested her, their chief interest at the time: the property that had just come into their hands.

'I've had an idea,' she said. 'Why don't we convert the whole farm from top to bottom, modernise it, and let rooms to people working for the gas company?'

'Have you any idea how much capital we would need to . . .'

49

'We borrow it! The State itself grants loans for improving property in the country.'

'Besides, you're forgetting that the company is building a town just for its workers.'

'It hasn't been built yet, and it won't be ready to live in for five or six years. Work it out for yourself: four rooms, just four rooms, at thirty thousand francs a month for five years. That comes to nearly five million after tax.'

'Perhaps you're right.'

'Of course I'm right. But five million is scarcely worth the trouble. What's five million nowadays? We ought to be able to make ten times as much.

'I married an adventuress ... That's the title of a film.'

'I'm in a hurry. I want to move fast. We've started late in life, the two of us. We've got to make up for lost time.'

And they went on discussing their plans for the future.

'I had a visit from Jean Lagarde. You remember you took an interest in him a few years ago and wanted to help him. Well, you'll be pleased to hear that his situation has greatly improved.'

Claire replied that she was delighted, that he deserved this improvement in his circumstances, and that she was happy for his sake. She was probably telling the truth. She was only conventional in company, either because she was anxious to conform to the ways of society, or because a certain shyness prevented her from expressing her ideas frankly, like Juliette Marcillac for example; but at home, with her husband and her daughters, and at times when she wasn't on the defensive, there could be no doubting the spontaneity of her reactions, which revealed a character in which praiseworthy feelings far outweighed the rest. André had to admit to himself that from the moral point of view his wife was better than he was; he didn't resent this superiority, since it didn't involve qualities such as intelligence, which he rated more highly;

besides, he would have found it hard to bear having a petty-minded wife, envious of other people and given to back-biting. He didn't mind people not being openly charitable (that required too much effort and implied a belief in values he didn't accept), provided they were not actively evil or destructive either. A moderately benevolent neutrality was what seemed to him best suited to a person of breeding, equally remote from the ignoble and the sublime.

If he compared Claire to other women they knew, he couldn't help congratulating himself, because the comparison was in his favour. Juliette was a gay, charming woman, very sociable, easy to get on with; but without being stupid, she uttered a lot of platitudes, and that would have irritated André in time. In other women, inadequacies of character, position or class were glaringly obvious. The idle ones annoyed him with their frivolity and selfishness. The needy ones, burdened with children and housework, and obsessed by the need to keep up appearances, repelled him. Claire was certainly the most distinguished by far of all the women he knew; she was the epitome of 'good taste'; and that, he readily admitted to himself, flattered his vanity. She dressed well, without slavishly following the latest fashion, so that the sensible, rather severe clothes she preferred (a twin-set and skirt, or a simple dress in one colour) had a timeless elegance, like the clothes of those English women of the landed gentry who are so sure of their social eminence and splendid complexions that they scorn the advice of the dressmakers and put comfort before all else – believing, in any case, that old country tweeds and flat-heeled shoes with crêpe soles, excellent for walking through field and forest, only emphasise, through the contrast presented by their coarse material, the aristocratic refinement of those who wear them. However, this last motive played no part in Claire's choice of clothes, which was dictated rather by a sense of economy, a desire for self-effacement, and a tasteful concern to match her dress with her looks.

Just as her clothes possessed a timeless elegance, so Claire's face had an ageless charm. About the age of thirty her figure and her features had attained an equilibrium which seemed destined to remain undisturbed. You could tell that she would look much the same twenty years later, and that only her ash-blonde hair, by turning grey, would mark the passing of the years. André often told himself that he would never suffer the painful shock of seeing his wife turn into a plump matron, but perhaps felt a secret resentment at the realisation that she was 'wearing' better than he was, that he had not only caught her up but passed her on the inexorable chart on which, for those who know us, the declining curve of our decrepitude is marked. The thought occasionally occurred to him that it was her spiritual rectitude that kept Claire in good physical condition and that strict morality might well be the best recipe for eternal youth. He had even made a note on this point in his diary, promising himself to come back to it and study the question more closely, with a view to trying something on those lines; but for want of knowing precisely where to concentrate his efforts at improvement and what method to adopt – a humble tabulation of his faults and weaknesses, daily exercises in meditation as in yoga, or prayers to the unknown God? – he put off from day to day the implementation of a programme of spiritual gymnastics designed to preserve his waistline as long as possible. Slimming products, walking, and a careful diet struck him as easier methods.

This evening André was a little on edge, for he and his wife were due to dine with Madame Dolfus in Biarritz; and he suspected, though without being sure, that Claire was going to cry off at the last moment, as she had already done on a previous occasion.

The Comarieus' relations with Madame Dolfus were intermittent and hung by the merest thread. André had been at school with Madame Dolfus's son, but the young man had gone off to the States at the age of twenty-five and André had never seen him again. All the same, having met André when he was an adolescent, Madame Dolfus had been kind enough to remember him, and to invite him to dinner now and then, during the period she spent every summer in her villa on the coast. These were evenings to which he attached a certain value, not simply because of their rarity, but also on account of their exoticism: they made a change from his usual routine, there was something of a 'high society' atmosphere at Madame Dolfus's villa, and the people you met there were colourful and often amusing. There was nearly always one celebrity among the guests. Depending on the hazards of the seasonal migrations, it might be a youngish millionaire already famous for his sensational divorces, one of those men the illustrated magazines were beginning to call 'playboys', a well-known painter, a noted author, or an actress. Sometimes a season proved disappointing, and the international summer migrations, for reasons more mysterious than those governing the annual flight of the swallows, neglected Biarritz in favour of Deauville, Monte Carlo or Tangier. Then, on evenings when there was a lack of visiting celebrities, Madame Dolfus would fall back on the local *Who's Who*, inviting, say, a Russian princess who since the October Revolution had been living at Guétary in elegant poverty.

André had a feeling that Claire was a little out of place in this environment: her middle-class characteristics became more noticeable and jarred with the setting. Although she made an immense effort to behave naturally, she was ill-at-ease, and her embarrassment communicated itself to him. Madame Dolfus liked her guests to be gay. Claire wasn't. But was *he*? When he felt relaxed, when conditions were favourable, and when the atmosphere was exactly right, he managed to play his part reasonably well.

'You haven't forgotten,' he said to Claire, 'that we're dining at Madame Dolfus's? If we leave at seven we'll have plenty of time.'

He guessed straight away, from her face, that she had

decided not to come, and tried to adopt an expression that would not reveal the relief he felt, but on the contrary suggest disappointment and even distress. All the same, he mustn't overdo it. For a fraction of a second he arranged his features, his eyes and his tone of voice to 'betray' the annoyance of a guest afraid of offending his hostess, rather than the sorrow of a husband left to go to a dinner-party by himself: that would seem a likelier reaction on his part, and Claire would probably believe it. The important thing was that she shouldn't think he was happy to go without her.

'No, listen, I'm definitely not going. I haven't the slightest desire to. You'll find an excuse all right.'

'It's a pity, though, because you cried off last time too. Madame Dolfus is going to think we're terribly casual.'

'Is that so important?' she asked, her head cocked to one side and a smile playing about her mouth.

'Is what important? Madame Dolfus's opinion or your crying off?'

'Both...Oh, come now, you know perfectly well that Madame Dolfus only invites me out of politeness and isn't at all keen to have me at her table.'

'What on earth are you talking about?'

'You know as well as I do.'

'If you don't come, I'm not going either,' said André, quite skilfully and without overmuch fear of her taking him at his word.

'Nonsense! I don't want to make you miss an evening at Madame Dolfus's. You enjoy her dinner-parties. I don't. No, no, go and get ready.'

'Bonneteau is going to be there tonight, and it should be interesting. Wouldn't you like to meet him?'

'I quite like his books, but...No, I wouldn't know what to say to him; besides, I imagine he's just like anybody else. No, I'm going to stay here; I've got something to read.'

'Claire wasn't able to come with me,' he told Madame Dolfus a little later. 'She's very tired and sends her apologies.'

54

'Claire refuses to come here; she's too grand for my little parties. Tell her I'm very cross with her.'

André muttered a vague denial but Madame Dolfus didn't listen to it, for she was getting ready to introduce a new arrival to the guests already gathered on the terrace. The latter had grouped themselves into a semi-circle around an elderly man whom André recognised immediately as the writer Bonneteau. He still looked like the photographs of him that appeared in the papers, although they dated back to the thirties, the period when he had reached the height of his fame. As with a few other writers and artists, the Liberation had dealt his career a serious but far from mortal blow, from which he was gradually recovering, thanks above all to the enthusiasm of five or six young authors who, reacting against the critical edicts which came into force immediately after the Armistice, advocated the return to an uncommitted literature and chose as their masters writers who had begun their careers during the previous post-war period. The old man to whom Madame Dolfus introduced André made only the beginning of a movement which, if he had finished it, would have brought him to his feet, and with a sigh he agreed to give way to the newcomer's insistence that he mustn't think of moving. In spite of the lack of hair and the fine network of wrinkles, he was a handsome man and it was perfectly possible to believe that he could still obtain the favours of beautiful young women, as Madame Dolfus hinted. His age was most apparent in his slow, slightly asthmatic elocution which speeded up now and then into a nervous stammer. He spoke with a slight hiss, either as the result of an unsuccessful dental operation, or from an English affectation of talking through the teeth; but old age had made this affectation more Auvergnat than English. Was it a sign of class, or was it the physiological form the habitual practice of sarcasm had taken in this particular man? André also noticed the nervous habit, which he shared with Madame Dolfus, of ending certain sentences, even when they were in

55

the affirmative, with a blunt, interrogating 'what?' as if he were demanding unreserved agreement from his audience, rebuking an interrupter, or asking for the repetition of a question which he hadn't heard and which nobody had asked. Finally his laughter, announced a few seconds in advance by a mischievous gleam in his icy green eyes, which was emphasised by a sudden narrowing of the lids, came in a series of staccato gasps, like a machine that was beginning to misfire now and then. All this went together to create an act, a special turn, which had the natural quality of an exercise perfected over a period of years, in which the artist is in complete control of his effects and can allow himself to perform the most astonishing variations.

'Are you a native of this region, Monsieur?' he asked André; and without waiting for an answer which was a matter of complete indifference to him, he went on in the same breath to inform the other guests: 'I like local-born people. There are fewer and fewer of them, wherever you go. Last year I went to Greece, to stay with my friend Michel who has bought a house on Hydra and lives there very quietly with his delightful young wife – he chose to go into exile because literary life in Paris is fatal to the writer, it sterilises him ... As soon as I landed, I said to him: 'Michel, show me some Greek men and Greek women, especially the latter.' Three days later, except for an octogenarian waiter, a ship's captain and an old woman who sold lemons near the harbour, I hadn't seen any Greeks, any real ones I mean. Most of them had gone off to the United States, and those that were left had been crossed with Maltese, Syrians, and heaven knows what else. There were Americans on the island, Germans, even Belgians, but no Greeks. And it's like that everywhere: ethnic integrity is a thing of the past. Even here, don't you think ... What did this young man say?' he asked Madame Dolfus, nodding towards André. 'Is he a native of the region? You are a full-blooded Béarnais, Monsieur?'

At a nod from the young man, and while Madame Dolfus

was shouting: 'I told you he was a friend of my son's, they were at school together,' though without any hope of being heard, for his slight physical deafness was complicated by an intellectual deafness which prevented him from hearing what other people said, he put on an almost ecstatic expression and a sepulchral voice to declare, with oracular slowness and pomposity: 'Ad-mi-ra-ble! At last a provincial, a genuine local, an authentic native! Whatever you do, don't change!' he told André, who was slightly embarrassed at being the centre of attention. 'Stay what you are: a Béarnais. Marry a local girl...' – 'He's already married!' Madame Dolfus shouted in vain – '. . . to preserve your precious racial purity.'

'What a man! I tell you he's married!' Madame Dolfus shouted louder than ever.

He cupped his hand round his ear. 'Married?' he repeated, as if in amazement. 'To a Béarn girl, I hope? Bravo! And what do you do in life, young man? I like knowing what people do,' he added, speaking to the other guests as if André weren't there. 'It's always interesting, isn't it, to learn about trades, professions, the social background.'

A little more of this, and anyone might have thought that he was a professor of anthropology and André a specimen of an archaic tribe, an Amazonian Indian for example who had been brought along that evening to tickle the curiosity of these enlightened Europeans, much as a well-behaved savage had been shown to the court at Versailles in the eighteenth century.

'I'm a lawyer,' said André, 'and not so young as all that.'

An expression of utter rapture appeared on the face of Monsieur Bonneteau, who had caught only the first half of the reply.

'A lawyer!' he murmured, dwelling delightedly on every syllable, rather as he would have exclaimed: 'Mozart!' on hearing the first bars of *Eine Kleine Nachtmusik*. He raised one hand into the air. 'A wonderful profession! A lawyer or a notary – that is what I would have liked to be if fate hadn't made me a coal-merchant – what?'

His gaze swept round his audience who looked slightly surprised at the revelation of his occupation.

'My father,' he went on, 'sold coal, like my grandfather and my great-grandfather. I have followed in their footsteps. I have sold coal all my life.' André recalled that for several generations the Bonneteaus had indeed been at the head of one of the biggest firms in the French coal industry, and enormously rich.

'After all, literature isn't a profession,' continued the old proletarian (who had doubtless just taken a shower to cleanse himself of soot and slag). 'No self-respecting man can earn his living from books: a self-respecting man sells coal or wheat, he keeps a grocer's shop, he makes chairs, but he doesn't earn his living writing books. Literature has to be an extra; it is an art cultivated in leisure moments, a useless, unnecessary activity ... Professional writers (and all writers are professionals nowadays) are wretched creatures – what? I knew poor René Maran; nobody knows who he was, but he had his little hour of fame and thought he could live off his books. Well, he was a failure; literature ruined him and his wife; that ebony couple broke my heart whenever I met them ... René Maran was a Negro,' he added for the benefit of those who might have been puzzled by the ebony quality of the couple in question. 'I always tell my friend Michel: "Michel, take a job when you return from your Greek exile, sell something, cloth, nuts, anything, but don't try to live off your books. A lawyer, a notary – those are real professions,' he repeated, looking at André as if he saw him in the splendid dual light of his occupation and his race. 'Those men know the human heart much better than we novelists. What does a professional writer know of the human heart? Nothing. But provincial lawyers – ah, *they* know all the plotting that goes on inside families, and *they* have access to the best kept secrets. *They* could write the most remarkable novels!'

He had scarcely uttered these last words before admiration gave place to alarm. 'Young man, you don't write, I hope?' When André shook his head he looked vastly relieved. 'Don't ever write,' he advised him. 'You see, you might easily say to yourself: "I am a provincial lawyer, I know the secrets of the human heart, I am going to write a novel." He raised his hand to turn André away from such a terrible danger. 'Don't do it! You are much too young. Wait. Wait till you are thirty-five or forty.'

'I *am* forty,' said André, to no purpose.

'Then perhaps, when you are thirty-five, you can write, if of course you have the desire to do so, the vocation... You can assure me that you don't write?' he continued anxiously. 'No novels? Not the smallest essay? Not even a private diary?' André shook his head and reddened slightly. 'I congratulate you,' said Monsieur Bonneteau earnestly, as if he were going to award him a medal. 'A full-blooded young provincial who doesn't write...He possesses all the virtues! Don't you agree,' he went on, speaking to his entire audience, 'that people write too much nowadays, not only too much but too soon and too fast. Those young authors even publish their private diaries – it's incredible! Or else they resolve to publish them when they have become, so they fondly believe, famous writers. A flood of private diaries is going to descend upon us in twenty, thirty years. They will all be identical, they will all describe exactly the same things, the same dinners in town at the same houses; they will all repeat the same anecdotes, the same witticisms... It will be Louis-Gabriel Pringué a hundred times over... Absolutely heartbreaking! I always discourage young men from writing, especially those who have already begun. I always tell my friend Roger, who is a clever young fellow and a wonderful stylist, I always tell him: "Roger, you are a wonderful stylist, you have great gifts, and one day you will be the greatest writer of your generation, but you have the misfortune to be too young. Wait, garner your wheat, don't hurry. You have published two admirable books. Now promise me that you will remain silent for ten years." '

'Is it Roger Nimier you are talking about?' asked one of the two women present. 'I met him last year, at Louise de Vilmorin's I think. What an astonishing young man! And how amusing!'

'People write too much,' continued Monsieur Bonneteau, who had magnanimously tolerated this brief interruption, but wasn't going to overdo things by allowing the conversation to break up and wander at will... 'Too many books, too many words, words, words! Too many films... By the way,' he said anxiously, turning his head in every direction to see if he could spot her anywhere, 'where is that beautiful girl who wants to go into films, that dark-haired girl, I forget her name...'

'Beatrice,' said Madame Dolfus.

'I thought you had invited her,' Monsieur Bonneteau said sternly. 'What is she called? Let me see, she has a Dantesque name... Beatrice!' he exclaimed, having found the name thanks to an ingenious mnemonic technique while everyone had maliciously left him to hunt for it by himself. He looked overjoyed... 'Beatrice,' he repeated. 'She has a complexion like a peach, and you feel like singing her that song that asks a girl where she's going, so lightly clad, without her shawl... Can anybody here sing it for me?'

There was a moment's hesitation among the guests, who looked at each other with amused smiles; then one of the two young women plucked up her courage and started singing the song in a thin, piping voice. Monsieur Bonneteau listened to her with his head on one side, a rapturous expression on his face.

'Ad-mi-ra-ble!' he said, cutting short the singer's disinterested effort. 'Don't you agree that it's in the songs of the people that poetry has taken refuge today, that poetry which deserted literature long ago – what? Young girl, where are you going, so lightly clad, without your shawl?... It has rhythm and freshness, it's grace itself ... So much better than Claudel. Where is Beatrice?' he asked Madame Dolfus again, knitting his bushy, angry brows.

'She's with Michel Argelouve,' she shouted. 'They'll be here soon. They are always late.'

'You promised me she would come, but I don't see her. People make promises to me, they say: "Beatrice will be there," I come along, I don't see her. That young fellow she always goes around with, I forget his name, it doesn't matter, that young fellow who is mad about the cinema – are they lovers?'

'I hope so for their sake,' said Madame Dolfus genially.

'I don't know whether they are lovers: I suppose so, young people have complete freedom nowadays, it means the end of love – what? No, don't deny it; love can only flower under constraint, whether that constraint is religious or moral or social. Look at the book of that young woman who has just been awarded the Prix des Critiques – what's her name?'

'Françoise Sagan.'

'She has written a story I imagine you have all read. I knew Éluard slightly, he looked like a fish, and his poetry is shapeless ... You think I'm getting senile and beginning to ramble, but set your minds at rest, I always find my way through my meanderings.'

He laughed, choked slightly, and got his breath back.

'Well, in that young woman's novel there are a girl and a boy who go to bed together, just like that, like a couple of young animals, without uttering a single word of love. That's because they don't know the language of love any more, and they can't invent it again; they are too free, too easy-going, too empty ... That young novelist ... Ah, I've just remembered her name: Françoise Sagan!'

He seemed delighted at this feat of memory.

Now that he had ceased to be the object of a half-sarcastic, half-benevolent interest (for the author of *Laure* was obviously sincere when he asserted his rather reactionary love

61

for unspoilt provinces, his esteem for lawyers and notaries, his contempt for writers who were nothing else, and his shocked amazement at the constantly growing number of his colleagues), André was enjoying the sight presented to his eyes. He resolved to find an opportunity to tell Bonneteau how much pleasure he had obtained from reading his recent works, how much he admired the limpid quality of his style, a conciseness which was not dryness but had mysterious undertones. While listening to the speaker, he was mentally rehearsing the compliment he was going to pay, the homage to which he thought a writer of longstanding and well-earned fame was entitled to receive from a stranger who had had the honour to be introduced to him. When he had imagined, not Bonneteau's face, since he knew that from his photographs, but his manner, his way of talking, his general demeanour, André had pictured a character who combined the upper-middle-class Protestant, the spiritual director for society women, and the romantic hero of the twenties – the man with the Hispano. Certain aspects of Bonneteau were not out of keeping with this ideal picture, but André had not foreseen that the author of *Laure* would be what he obviously was: even more than a wealthy bourgeois, or than the coal-merchant he claimed to be before all else, or than a Don Juan, or than any of the other aspects that went to his making: Monsieur Bonneteau, to the core of his being and the tips of his fingers, was a man of letters. There was no harm in that; it was just rather odd to hear this author *par excellence* heaping contempt on those people who were weak enough to want to be professional writers. What also surprised André was that the author of solemn, sad, and sometimes even deliberately dull books should turn out to be this sneering carnivore who savaged other people's works and reputations, this inexhaustible chatterbox who was delighted to have an audience, and whose eyes sparkled with cruel gaiety.

He took in with a single glance the scene before him: in

the foreground the little group of men and women in evening dress, arranged, like the figures in a picture, in a pyramid-shaped pattern in which the point was the speaker towards whom their attentive faces were all turned. Behind this group, the terrace bathed in a uniform, milky light, which might have been attributed to the moon but which came in fact from concealed floodlights. Beyond the terrace, the horizon of the sea and a roll of foam under the bluish sky. The smell of seaweed and salt reminded André of the Sunday outings of his childhood, when the names of Biarritz, Saint-Jean-de-Luz and Hendaye suggested ideas of wealth and luxury and a privileged class (for in those days children who weren't rich didn't spend their holidays at the seaside). That superior species, the people who went to the coast in the summer, lived in palaces also known as casinos, huge cakes the colour of whipped cream, among the tamarisks, a stone's throw from the waves. As soon as you could make out the smell of seaweed and salt, you knew that you were getting near your magical destination, already foreshadowed by an intoxicating name, 'Chiberta,' and that round the next bend in the road you would receive full in the face the green and blue splash of an ocean stretching away to the sky and fringed with sand the colour of the desert; but as you walked about in your 'Sunday best' among the princes of this world dressed in linen or flannel, you felt regret at not being one of them, a nostalgia for the fabulous pleasures which were probably their lot; and the sunny day which had begun in the joy of setting out and the wonder of the names of Biarritz and Hendaye gradually lost its magic ... André knew now that the privileged were not really privileged, that their pleasures were insipid, and he no longer had any desire to set foot in the casino ... But the smell of the ocean remained the smell of luxury; and luxury tonight was this terrace, the bare arms and shoulders of the women, the jewels, the white-jacketed waiters in the background, the expectation of a dinner which was sure to be excellent, and the amusing talk of a famous old writer. The setting was the same, but the contents and the meaning had changed: the disappointed illusions of childhood had given place to the reasonable pleasures of maturity. And André reflected that it was good to grow older.

Accompanied by a young man, the Michel Argelouve Monsieur Bonneteau had mentioned, Beatrice made her entrance. André hated the young fellow almost at sight: he was too sure of himself, and looked both weak and pretentious. He thought Beatrice rather less attractive than when he had first met her: she had lost the miraculous bloom of adolescence and become a young woman. It didn't suit her to wear trousers, even if they were evening trousers in bronze silk, and to wear her hair in such an untidy style, or rather no style at all, just tumbling carelessly over her forehead. You had to be eighteen to carry off such a wild style, and time goes by for everyone... *If you imagine, little girl...* Michel was talking about films. What! Had somebody really succeeded in interrupting Monsieur Bonneteau? Why yes, youth stopped at nothing. Michel was not in the least intimidated or overawed; he was talking to him as an equal, and he had had no scruples about raising the subject of the cinema, with which the great man was unfamiliar. A glass of whisky in his left hand, a cigarette in his right, relaxed, well-fed, shining with health and self-assurance, he was saying that the only films that counted nowadays were those that bared the sores of society, and denounced poverty and the exploitation of man by man. When Michel came to make films himself, what subjects would he deal with? Hunger in the underdeveloped countries, strikes, the vicious way in which the capitalist states hunted down Communists... Here Monsieur Bonneteau's face expressed the deepest distress.

'President Coty is hunting down Communists?' he asked, gazing at Michel with eyes sharpened by loathing.

'Haven't you ever heard of Senator McCarthy?' the young man retorted coldly.

'McCarthy,' said Monsieur Bonneteau, 'is in America.

McCarthyism is a phenomenon peculiar to America.' And as Michel was opening his mouth to reply, he raised his hand and said in a tone of voice that sent a chill through his audience:

'Let me finish, please.'

Cowed at last, Michel remained silent.

'I don't believe that either here in France, or in Italy, or in England, the Communists are being hunted down. And don't start thinking that I deplore the fact: I am not anti-Communist. I am not anti-Communist, first of all because I believe that Communism is going to be our future; in less than twenty years France will be a little popular republic, a little satellite state like Bulgaria or Albania, and not much better off than those two countries. You have to accept the ineluctable march of History. Secondly, I was the first Socialist writer of my generation – the first to commit himself, and indeed the only one, when Mauriac was satisfied with being a little Bordeaux dandy who had "come up" to Paris – Mauriac who since then . . . The great idol of my youth was Jaurès. People have forgotten all that, or decided to forget it, and it doesn't really matter. As I grow older, political agitation strikes me as futile and ridiculous. You say that you want to put politics into your films. Do as you wish, but I shan't go to see your films, for I shall know in advance that they won't contribute anything essential. What each of us regards as essential is something limited, temporary. For a writer it is a perfect sentence, in other words the rarest thing in the world, something that may never have existed . . . Apart from that, nobody knows what is essential.'

'For us, the essential thing is to go and have dinner,' shouted Madame Dolfus, who had been waiting for several minutes for a break in this speech.

As the group of guests was moving towards the house, Monsieur Bonneteau took André by the arm.

'A lawyer!' he sighed. 'Just what I would have liked to be! My dear sir,' he went on graciously, 'you don't know how lucky you are. Above all, remember my advice: don't write! Not yet!'

10 September. Back from the country. Relieved to return to my old routine. Holidays are a waste of time. If I were not obliged to close my office for three weeks every summer, I wouldn't take any. Or if I did, it would be on my own, and that's out of the question. C—— isn't bored at Saint-Blaise: she loves the country and enjoys getting up at dawn and going for long walks through the fields. But all I can do is read and listen to the radio when there's a good music programme; and I just die of boredom. The girls are bored too, especially Suzy, who has tastes older than her twelve years: she would already like to go dancing, and she misses the cinema twice a week and the company of her boy friends. She worries us, C—— and me; but what C—— is chiefly afraid of is Suzy becoming too frivolous, even shameless. What worries me is that as she gets bigger we may not be able to pass off her silliness any more as a weakness of character, and that we may have to recognise it for what perhaps it is: stupidity. The poor little thing sometimes irritates me beyond words: her yelping laugh, her inability to concentrate, and above all her accent, which is flatter than usual even in this area, and which we have tried in vain to correct and tone down. In Suzy flatness of accent is linked with laziness of mind. C—— and I and Catherine have the standard middle-class accent of the south-west: it has a few southern inflexions, admittedly, but it isn't either ugly or ridiculous. When you hear Catherine talking, even without seeing her, you can tell straight away that she is a well-bred, 'refined' little girl. As soon as Suzy opens her mouth, it's a catastrophe, she sounds as common as dirt. The very timbre of her voice is common; worse still, it is stupid. If, as she grew older, she were to remain as she is now, it would be the most terrible disappointment of my life, and even a sort of disaster. It is hard to resign yourself to stupidity in your own children. But I haven't given up hope entirely. Some minds wake up after the age of twelve, or, on the contrary, go to sleep for ever, after holding out tremendous promise.

C—— told me that she would like to live in the country all the time, and make Saint-Blaise her home. She would have a garden, an orchard, a henhouse. She would get along perfectly well without the town and its pleasures. 'You can stay in Sault with Mariette. We are lucky enough to have a model servant, and after all, that's all you need: a housekeeper.' She said this with a smile, without any trace of bitterness, at least as far as I could see. She was very relaxed – she is always more relaxed after a few days at Saint-Blaise. I treated it as a joke and said yes, the arrangement she suggested was perfectly possible, but how could we justify it to the outside world? 'Well, we could say my health forced me to live in the country. You could come and spend your week-ends with me, and I would go to Sault now and then, when you needed me for a dinner-party.' I replied that she was deliberately trying to upset me. Once again I kept my voice down and spoke almost light-heartedly. Still, these things have been said and can't be taken back. I used to think that a husband and wife couldn't live together unless they got on very well, and unless love immediately smoothed away all difficulties and broke the force of any collisions. Well, I was wrong: they can. All that is necessary is that they should be a well-bred couple and both have an equal dislike of scenes. Tonight, before dinner, I went round to the M——s' to say hello and ask after little Nicolas, who has had his adenoids removed. On the way there, going down the hill, and on the way back, coming up the street again, I had an impression of something unusual. To be more precise, I felt a vague uneasiness. I asked myself: 'Well, what has changed? This is the same old Rue de Navailles I have always known. In three weeks' absence it can't have become unfamiliar to me.' And I stood in the middle of the street, with my arms dangling and my nose in the air, looking at the houses to make sure that everything was in its place; but I couldn't see anything unusual about the houses. Then, all of a sudden, having to walk round a car that wasn't mine to get to our steps (I still don't know who is the owner of that Dauphine, and I intend to ask him to park his car somewhere else and not in front of *my* house), I saw at a glance what it was that had changed: the left-hand side of the street, in other words our side, was nothing but a long car-park from top to bottom. I counted a good fifteen cars lined up one in front of the other. They must have been there already a month ago, if not all fifteen, at least nine or ten; but as they have arrived gradually, one after another, over the last two or three years, the increase in their number has never struck us. But I have just spent three weeks in a village where there are no cars yet (except for a van belonging to a rich peasant), and I came home remembering the Rue de Navailles as I have always known it, throughout the forty years of my life: a pretty provincial street, quiet and graceful, dotted here and there with the silhouettes of a few passers-by, as in an old print. And all of a sudden I saw those machines lined up in front of the houses, and taking up a good third of the roadway – those big stupid machines, with their steel shells shining in the September sun... It was quite a shock. It annoyed me and worried me. If the number of cars increases even more, what is going to become of my street, my town?

This growth in the number of cars is one of the many signs that we are moving towards a society on American lines. Part of me applauds this progress towards a world in which wealth and comfort will be distributed more fairly; but the inevitable consequence will be the destruction of certain things by which I set some store, to which I attach a sentimental or aesthetic value. A rather shamefaced reactionary inside me would like to preserve the resemblance of the Rue de Navailles to a nineteenth-century print, and the 'prestige' of the little society in which he has carved his niche. Already, beyond any shadow of a doubt, three quarters of that prestige has disappeared. What are we in Sault: the Marcillacs, the Vignemales, the Argeloses and ourselves? We don't count. We aren't the people who control local politics: none of us plays the smallest part in the running of the town. We are a relic of the past to which before long nobody will pay any attention any more (though I may be wrong on that point). And to think that my poor mother worked so hard to enable me to belong to this little society, and that by marrying C——— I made her happy, if not myself, and that her happiness still endures: my mother still lives under an illusion... I shan't do anything to open her eyes, but if she only knew... If she only knew that as a class we no longer arouse anybody's envy.

Except perhaps somebody like Jean Lagarde, because he is still living in the past; but as far as he is concerned, things are much more complicated, I think. Social envy is probably combined with more obscure feelings. What a life he has had! When I think that in all probability nobody has ever loved him, except his mother... And his wife now, I hope; though that has yet to be confirmed.

68

I have 'taken refuge' in the library, not because I felt like opening this note-book again, for I write in it less and less – I think that Bonneteau's advice, 'Whatever you do, don't write,' has borne fruit – but to avoid the moment when, after dinner, C—— draws the curtains in the drawing-room. It would take too long to tell how I have come to dread that moment, to live through it, however brief it may be, with a feeling of irritation or malaise – a malaise which, on certain evenings, comes close to anguish. I think it must have started fairly soon after we were married, during the second or third year perhaps. The fact remains that tonight I fled. That action of drawing the curtains is perfectly reasonable and legitimate in itself: it is performed in every home in the world. At nightfall somebody draws the curtains of the room where the family are sitting, to shield them against the outside world and the night, and to wrap the cosy intimacy of the house round the family circle. In this house it is Mariette's job to draw the curtains in the other rooms, our bedrooms, etc; but in the drawing-room C—— insists on performing the rite herself. Every evening, at a fixed hour, she walks towards our two big windows with a determined step. She always begins with the one on the right. She raises her arm, grasps the cord, pulls it, and – lo and behold! – the curtains close. Anyone would think she were operating a guillotine ... Next comes the turn of the left-hand window. Now the curtains are closed and the outside world has been abolished; the night, all nights, the cool, scented nights of spring, the summer nights with their stormy skies, the autumn nights with the maddening south wind blowing, and the crystalline winter nights, frosted with stars – all these nights are shut out together with the world; and we are reduced to our own company, in this drawing-room which is vast but none the less restricted ... And that will happen every day, until the end ... Once the rite has been performed, C—— turns towards us, towards me if the girls have gone to bed, with a face smooth with compunction (or am I deliberately deceiving myself?). Naturally I tell myself that if I were very happy, this moment when the curtains are drawn would be a moment of bliss ... There must be a poem about it – Verlaine perhaps? But on the contrary, I dread it. I dread it more and more. As if a claustrophobic complex had secretly developed inside me ... On certain evenings, sitting in my armchair, I feel my heart beating faster as the fateful moment approaches; at other times my stomach gets in knots, or else I experience the feeling you get before fainting, when you break into a cold sweat. It isn't normal. Perhaps I ought to see a neurologist about it. Or a psychiatrist. But what would the psychiatrist tell me? Probably that my claustrophobia is an infantile fixation. Which wouldn't explain very much. Poor C——, of course, doesn't suspect a thing. Sometimes I've been on the point of asking her to leave the curtains open for an hour or two – to let the outside world and the night come into our home. But what would she have thought of me? She would have told me that, our drawing-room being on the ground floor and its windows overlooking the street, passers-by could see us, and that that was embarrassing; and she would have been right... The fact remains that tonight I couldn't stand it. I have left her with the girls; and here I am, incurring Bonneteau's well-merited disapproval, writing, poor wretch that I am, my diary...

There was the sound of footsteps on the gravel. The front door creaked. Somebody was trying to walk on tiptoe along the corridor.

It's him.

Juliette stretched out her hand towards the bedside lamp. The pink light made her blink. A glance at the clock. Twenty-five past three.

I must have fallen asleep.

She hadn't been able to fight off sleep. After midnight it was impossible for her to stay awake. Bruno! At last he had come home. She got up and put on her dressing-gown.

I must take care not to wake the children. What is he up to? He's going into the kitchen. He's knocked a chair over ... Heavens, is he drunk?

She tied the belt of her dressing-gown and quietly opened the door. On tiptoe – the floor always creaked in the same places, she must make up her mind to have the planks re-placed – she walked along the landing, without turning on the light, and went downstairs. In the hall she saw the kitchen door half-open, forming a narrow oblong of yellow light. She felt a wave of anger against Bruno welling up inside her. She mustn't show him an angry face, especially if he was a little tipsy. She must behave as if she thought it perfectly natural for him to come home so late. She stopped and took two or three deep breaths, to slow down the beating of her heart and recover her composure – a tip she had picked up in a magazine. She imagined what she must look like at that moment, and made an effort to relax her tense muscles and raise the corners of her mouth which bad temper had turned down.

He could have had an accident, he drives so fast. I'm always afraid when I know he's on the road late at night. I ought to be relieved that he's here, that he's come home safe and sound.

Almost certain now that she looked all right, she pushed open the kitchen door, getting ready to say to him in a whisper, so as not to wake the children, and if possible with a welcoming smile: 'Ah, here you are at last. I was beginning to get worried.' He was standing at the sink with his back to her. At the sound of the door opening, he turned round, holding a glass. Juliette put her hand to her mouth, choking back a cry.

'Bruno! What have you done to yourself?'

He put a finger to his lips and glanced up at the ceiling. Round his right eye there was a huge bluish patch, streaked with brown under the lower lid. The swollen nose and cheek-bone and the puffy eyelid gave him the inhuman appearance of a boxer after a hard fight.

'What's happened to you? Have you been in a fight?'

'Hush!' he said in a hoarse voice. 'I'll explain. It's nothing. Nothing to worry about.'

He was obviously a little high. Not really drunk. High. And he had driven twenty-five miles in the dark. Juliette pictured the car against a tree, Bruno's body shattered, his

71

head on the steering wheel, one hand hanging out of the window.

'Yes, I'd like you to explain,' she said, unable to prevent her voice from shaking, out of retrospective fear, or anger that he should give her such a fright.

He emptied the glass and put it on the draining-board. His gestures had the cautious slowness of somebody not too certain of keeping his balance.

'You were going to be home by midnight. You promised me . . .'

'Don't scold me, pet. It's true I've been in a fight. But it was a matter of honour. You'll be proud of your husband when you hear about it.'

'I shouldn't count on that,' she sighed.

All the same, she hadn't been able to suppress a smile.

'Come on, let's go into the drawing-room.'

'The drawing-room, at three in the morning? Can't you explain it all here? . . . Heavens, how awful you look! Let me put some ice on that eye.'

'No, no, it's nothing, it'll get better by itself.'

She insisted. If she didn't put some ice on it, it would be much worse tomorrow, people would wonder what could have happened to him, they would start talking. She forced him to sit down, opened the refrigerator, and took out a few ice cubes. She shattered them, put the pieces in a piece of cloth, and folded it.

'Well, fire away. Who were you fighting? And don't tell too many lies.'

'Lies – me? Really, pet, I'm offended.'

'Don't call me pet! Come on, fire away.'

'I fought tonight,' he said pompously, 'for Dien-Bien-Phu.'

'For who?'

'What do you mean, for who? Dien-Bien-Phu isn't a person. Juliette,' he went on in a voice of shocked reproach, 'you aren't going to tell me you don't know what Dien-Bien-Phu is.'

'It's a battle, isn't it?'

Bruno put both hands to his head in horror.

'Sweet Jesus,' he murmured. 'The fantastic indifference of women. The ignorance of women about contemporary history.'

'You mean it isn't a battle?'

'Yes, alas, it is indeed a battle. A battle we lost, believe it or not. And not so long ago. It was last spring. This very year.'

'All right, all right. So you fought somebody for . . .'

'What do you mean, all right, all right?' he asked indignantly. 'It isn't all right at all. It's the worst disaster France has suffered since Dunkirk.'

'Bruno,' she groaned, 'it's three in the morning and you've come home with a black eye. Don't start preaching at me. Lift your head, so I can put this ice-bag on your eye.'

'Ouch! It's cold!'

'Don't be such a softy.'

'It's cold, dammit! You're torturing me into the bargain.'

'Let's go back to Dien-Bien-Phu.'

'Yes, Dien-Bien-Phu. If I understand you correctly, it's all one to you that we've been given the most humiliating thrashing of the century and that we've lost an empire?'

'Bruno! I ask you why you've come home drunk at three in the morning, and the only answer you can give me is that we've lost an empire! Listen, just now I don't give a damn for the empire we've lost. Tell me what you've been up to – that's all I want to know.'

'Did you hear that?' he said, calling an invisible audience to witness. 'On one side the disaster of Dien-Bien-Phu. On the other a black eye. And all that my wife cares about is . . .'

'Please, Bruno. I'll lose my temper if you don't watch out.'

'All right, all right. I don't want my pet to lose her temper, do I, over such a little thing.'

A pause. He took a deep breath, as if he were going to run a hundred yards.

73

'We were provoked by some Communists we had a bit of a scrap we put them out of action I got a punch in the eye and that's all,' he babbled at top speed. He gave a sigh of relief, pleased to have got to the end of his story without any trouble. 'You see, darling, it's all very simple. There's nothing to get worked up about.'

Juliette opened her eyes wide.

'Monsieur Dutilleul?' she said incredulously. 'Monsieur Dutilleul was in a fight?'

After a pause of two or three seconds, Bruno burst out laughing.

'Quiet! You're going to wake the children!' she said.

He reduced the volume of his laughter, but was unable to limit its violence. His whole body was shaking with hilarity.

'Monsieur Dutilleul!' he managed to say at last, between two gusts of laughter. 'Can you see him in a scrap? With his stiff collar ... Oh, no, that's too funny for words. Where does she get these ideas? Oh, no, I'm going to die laughing! Monsieur Dutilleul! Why, you could knock him across the street with your little finger. No, really, it's too much for me ...'

He took a handkerchief out of his pocket and dabbed his good eye, which this fit of laughing had misted up.

'Well, if it wasn't Monsieur Dutilleul ...,' began Juliette.

'Monsieur Dutilleul! She's going to kill me, I swear she is.'

'... who was it with?' she finished.

'With some paratroopers,' he said, and started laughing again, but *pianissimo* this time: a muffled, barely audible laughter.

'You were in a fight with some paratroopers?'

'Not with them,' he said. 'What I mean is: not against them. I was fighting on their side, against some other characters, some Communists who had provoked us.'

'But what the bloody hell were you doing with those paratroopers?'

'Juliette, really, the language. "What the bloody hell..."
That isn't like you.'

'What were you doing then?'

'Me?' he asked, looking as though he didn't understand.

'Yes, you!' she shouted in exasperation. 'What were you
doing with them?'

'Why, nothing, pet. We met at the Bar des Pyrénées. I
bought them a drink. They were veterans of the Indo-
Chinese war; they had been at Dien-Bien-Phu.'

'Well? What happened then?'

'Well, there were these two characters selling *L'Humanité*
outside the bar. Can you beat that? I mean to say, can you
beat it? Sheer provocation. Under our very noses.'

'Who says it was provocation? They have a right to sell
their paper.'

'Juliette, you may know nothing about contemporary
history... All the same. Listen. We've lost Indo-China because of the Communists. And those two characters, standing
there with *L'Humanité* in their hands... we saw red.'

'You'd already got a few drinks under your belt, I imagine.

'Juliette, I swear by all that's holy...'

'Don't swear! Please don't swear.'

'...that I was absolutely sober. You don't think a couple
of drinks could... No, really.'

'Was it the men selling *L'Humanité* that knocked you
about like that? '

'No. It wasn't them. The scrap got out of control. Some
passers-by joined in. In the end there were a dozen of us
fighting on the pavement, outside the Bar des Pyrénées. It
was a real free-for-all! I wish you'd been there to see it.'

'A dozen of you! Oh, Bruno, you shouldn't...You
shouldn't do things like that any more. Not at your age.'

'What do you mean, not at my age? The nerve of the
woman! A man in the prime of life. In first-rate condition
too. When somebody insults my country, I suppose you want
me to take it lying down?'

'Oh, get along with you!'

'I'd be a poor little shit if I did,' he said, in a tone of wounded dignity.

'Bruno! That's not a very nice way of talking either.'

'No, but it's very French,' he said, and he started laughing helplessly again. 'Monsieur Dutilleul!' he repeated.

'And how did it finish, this scrap of yours?'

'Where do you think it finished? At the police station, of course. The cops came along with their Black Maria. They grabbed us all, the paratroopers, the other fellows, the two characters selling *L'Humanité* ... Eleven or twelve of us in all. What a catch!'

'What time was it?'

'About eight o'clock.'

'But what about Monsieur Dutilleul? You didn't have dinner with him?'

'My sweet pet,' said Bruno with gentle patience, 'how could I possibly have dinner with Monsieur Dutilleul when I was at the police station?'

'You didn't have dinner ... You let him know, at least?'

'Yes, yes ... Not straight away, of course. When they let us go, about midnight, I phoned him from a café.'

'About midnight?' she groaned in despair. 'You don't turn up for dinner and you wake him up at midnight to apologise ...'

'Yes, it's true I did wake him up,' said Bruno, not thinking of denying the facts. 'Poor old chap. I even frightened him. His voice was trembling when he answered the phone ... He probably wears a nightcap, don't you think?' he asked, and he started laughing again at the idea.

'How could you do a thing like that? He was probably going to buy Le Bosc. You went to Pau with the express purpose of having dinner with him and trying to pull off the deal. I can't see him buying Le Bosc now. Not after that insult.'

'Of course he's going to buy Le Bosc from us. Don't you worry: he's too keen on it to back out.'

'You say they let you go at midnight? And you arrive here at half-past three. What have you been doing in between?'

'Darling, we hadn't had any dinner. We were starving.'

'So you went and had dinner? You and those para-troopers?'

'Yes. The poor devils deserved a good meal after such a rotten evening.'

'Where did you go?'

'The Izard. You know perfectly well it's the only restaurant open after midnight.'

'The Izard? The dearest place in Pau. And I suppose it was you who paid the bill?'

'You couldn't expect me to let soldiers pay, could you? Veterans of Dien-Bien-Phu?'

'How many were they?'

'Two,' said Bruno after clearing his throat.

'You're lying. I know you're lying.'

'Listen, don't keep on scolding me like that. You're terrible. It's demoralising. You're worse than a gendarme. There were five of them. Five and no more, I swear.'

'Five! And how much did you pay?'

'About twenty thousand.'

She made no comment. She had started weeping silently. Bruno put both arms round his wife's waist.

'What's the matter, pet?' he said uncertainly. 'Are you cry-ing because I've spent twenty thousand francs for nothing?'

'It isn't because of the twenty thousand,' she said, still hold-ing the ice-bag against Bruno's right eye. 'It's because you keep behaving like a little boy.'

'I can assure you that any man in my place would have behaved the same way. Any man with a little spunk in him, I mean.'

'Oh, you and your spunk!' murmured Juliette, as if she had her doubts about the value of that attribute. 'I'd rather you had a little less spunk and a little more sense.'

She wiped away her tears with her free hand.

'Come now, don't tell me you'd like me with less spunk in me,' Bruno said roguishly, and he gave his wife's behind one or two affectionate slaps. He was in high spirits again. 'You bawl me out, you walk all over me, and I thought about you tonight. Yes, I thought about you. That has been known to happen, you know.'

He took his wallet out of the breast pocket of his jacket, opened it, and pulled out two little slips of paper.

'Theatre tickets for Sunday night. You wanted to see that play, didn't you? Well, you see, I remembered. And this time you can't say that I'm giving you a present because I've got a guilty conscience, because I bought them before eight o'clock. Besides, the box-office isn't open after that. Well, are you pleased? On Sunday night, off we go, the two of us. A nice little dinner in some restaurant, like a couple of sweet-hearts, and then the theatre.'

She was touched, but didn't want to appear to give way too quickly, to agree too soon to let bygones be bygones.

'Theatre tickets are dear too. You spend money without thinking, but from now on we ought to be more careful. The children cost us a lot, the cost of living goes up every day, and we aren't doing so well any more.'

He stood up and put his arms round her.

'Just once isn't making a habit of it. Tell me that you're pleased. Go on, tell me.'

'Yes, I am ... I'm pleased most of all because you thought about me. I only wish you'd be a bit more sens ...'

He didn't let her finish, planting kisses on her mouth, her eyelids, her cheeks, and clasping her tight, but rather as if he wanted protection and support, as if she were a tree firmly rooted in the ground, to which he was frantically clinging with all his strength, in the middle of a storm. She leaned

78

backwards and gazed affectionately at his battered boxer's face.

'Heavens, how ugly you are!' she said, and started chuckling to herself. Then she pressed her head against his shoulder. He stroked the back of her neck, looking very peaceful in spite of his black eye; but she pulled away from him again, suspicion in her eyes.

'Where did you go after dinner?'

'After dinner? I got the car and drove home.'

'You're telling the truth, are you? You didn't go with those soldiers...'

She left the question unfinished, pursed her lips, and put into her eyes what she refused to express in words.

'Go where?' he asked, with an ingenuous air.

'Where you've been at least once, you and your pals at the regimental dinner.'

Bruno immediately became a picture of injured innocence.

'Juliette, how can you think a thing like that? We left the Izard at twenty to three. I got here half an hour later. You can phone the Izard if you like. You can carry out an investigation. No, really, you're going too far. Accusing me of...'

'All right, all right, let's assume I'm being unfair this time. That'll make up for all the times I was right to accuse you, and you had the nerve to deny everything.'

'In any case,' said Bruno, with a gleam of amusement in his good eye, 'how could we possibly have gone to a place like that? You know perfectly well that they were closed down years ago.'

'You beast.'

'I'm joking, silly! How about going to bed now?'

'You say you got back here in half an hour? In the dark? You must have driven like a lunatic.'

'Sixty miles an hour on an average. That's not too fast. And I was singing at the top of my voice.'

'There was plenty to sing about. Oh, yes. You could be

really pleased with yourself. A business appointment missed. Twenty thousand francs down the drain. A black eye. Oh, yes, you'd done a good night's work. No wonder you were singing. But if you keep on like that, we'll soon be in queer street. And one of these days you'll be found with your brains bashed out against a tree.'

'I drive superbly. Have I ever had the slightest accident?'

'You drive superbly. You play football superbly. You are superb at everything . . .'

'Well, I think I can say . . .'

'. . . except business. When it comes to business, you are hopeless.'

'Now don't be unkind, pet. This is a fine way to greet me . . .'

'A good many women would have greeted you with a rolling-pin, coming home at this time of night in your condition.'

'Not you, Juliette. Come now, we are a respectable middle-class couple; we know how to behave.'

'Oh, yes, you know how to behave all right!'

Her mood kept fluctuating between indulgence and anger, between satisfaction that he had come home safe and sound, and the annoyance she felt at his childish behaviour. Missing an important appointment. Fighting in the street on a ridiculous pretext. Getting arrested by the police. Spending the evening with boys of twenty. And coming home in high spirits, singing at the top of his voice. You couldn't help smiling, perhaps, but at the same time you couldn't help crying, and trembling for the present and the future. But there he was, big and strong, without an ounce of malice in him, hugging her tight, as affectionate as ever, as he had always been since the first day they met: how could she fail to forgive him once again? And she felt angry with herself for giving in like that, for always ending up by 'overlooking it'.

Just as they reached the first-floor landing, a small voice called out: 'Mummy!' behind a door with a thin line of light shining under it. 'We've woken Pierrot,' murmured Juliette. She went right up to the door and said in a clearly articulated whisper: 'Go back to sleep, darling.'

'Is Daddy there?' asked the small voice.

'Yes. Go back to sleep. You mustn't wake Nicolas and Line.'

'I want to say good night to Daddy.'

'Don't go in,' she said to Bruno. 'You'll frighten him.'

'Frighten Pierrot? Get along with you!'

And he opened the door. The little boy was sitting up in bed, his hair all tousled, his face tinted crimson by the light shining through the pink lampshade. At the sight of his father he reacted in the same way as Juliette had done, putting his hand to his mouth and catching his breath. Bruno sat down on the edge of the bed. Wide-eyed, the child looked at the unrecognisable face, the huge eyelid, and the blue bruise streaked with brown, on which the ice had left a few drops of water.

'Have you been boxing, Daddy?' he murmured, a little scared but trying to be brave.

'I was attacked by some bandits,' said Bruno in a theatrical whisper.

'Go on, stop kidding me. He's having me on, isn't he?' he asked his mother. 'Bandits in Pau! You're having me on.'

'Well, teddy boys, then. There were six of them, with bicycle chains. It was quite a scrap, old fellow!'

'Really? Christ! Teddy boys? Bloody hell!'

'Quiet now!' Juliette pleaded in a low voice. 'You're going to wake your brother and sister. And please don't use bad language.'

But she knew that this prohibition was completely useless. Like most little boys of his age, Pierrot had a repertory of uncouth exclamations which he used all the time without understanding them, and without thinking. 'Bloody hell' was one of these exclamations, which was used indiscriminately to express surprise, unreserved admiration, indignation, and several other shades of emotion. In the presence of adults, and especially ladies, he watched his language and behaved like a well-brought-up child. But among his little friends, in exclusively male company, vulgarity reigned supreme. It was aggravated by a Pyrenean accent which likewise resisted all attempts at reform. In Pierrot's mouth the foulest expression acquired such an exotic quality that it lost its original meaning.

'I wish you'd been there,' Bruno was saying. 'I knocked four of them out straight away. But there were two of them left. I got a punch in the eye. It's nothing. You should have seen the state *they* were in!'

'Oh, bloody hell! Show me how you did it!'

And kneeling on the bed, he put up his guard, tucking his head in between his shoulders and watching warily, with his little fists clenched and one elbow raised to the level of his chin, as his father had taught him.

Delighted to be able to go on playing, and to have a son who was such a keen fighter, Bruno put up his guard too, pretending to dodge the child's punches and letting a few of them hit their target. He skilfully landed two or three very gentle punches on Pierrot's ribs. These tickled the boy, who doubled up with merriment, but stifled his laughter, partly because he mustn't wake his brother and little sister, but mainly because it was much more exciting to laugh like that, like at school when you were trying to avoid the teacher's attention; it helped to increase the feeling of closeness to your parents, of breaking the rules, of snatching a privileged moment from everyday routine.

'Come on, haven't you finished yet?' grumbled Juliette, at once happy and impatient. 'What a pair you are!'

Bruno and the little boy, suddenly as solemn as judges, looked at each other with raised eyebrows, without moving a muscle. This was obviously part of a game, a little comic ritual which was all their own.

'I say, isn't it wonderful how she puts up with us!' whispered Bruno with a contrite expression on his face; and just as suddenly they fell into each other's arms, roaring with laughter.

Pierrot finally agreed to go back to bed and swore he would sleep well, but not before obtaining a few extra details.

'Daddy, will it still show tomorrow?'

'A bit, yes.'

'You're going to tell people you were in a fight with some teddy boys, aren't you? I'm going to tell them at school. I say, will it be in the paper?'

'There'll probably be a big article about it on the front page.'

'With photos! Bloody hell! And will they talk about it on the telly?'

'Not on the telly, perhaps. It all happened so quickly, they didn't have time to come and film it.'

Pierrot snuggled down in his bed again, and playfully pulled the sheet over his head.

'He's as strong as an ox,' Bruno told his wife when they were in their own room. 'He's going to make a first-rate athlete. You know, you won't find many men who can give you such good-looking kids.'

'That's right, look for excuses. Boast away.'

'Well, isn't it true? Aren't you pleased to have kids like that?'

He had started undressing.

'It seems to me that I can claim some part of the credit.'

'Pooh,' said Bruno, his lip curling disdainfully. 'A very small part. You were just the receptacle. They get everything from their father. Why, don't you agree that your kids are the best-looking kids in the town?'

'Oh, yes! But that's no reason for ...'

'Well, then, what are you complaining about? You ought to thank your lucky stars every day. Imagine if you were married to some ordinary little squirt. Why, even to a fellow like Comarieu. He's not a bad-looking chap, I'm not saying that. You could even say he's quite distinguished. All the same ...'

And, stripped to the waist, he posed in front of her, throwing out his chest.

'All the same, compare him with that!'

'I wonder,' said Beatrice, 'whether you can see it at night. It doesn't say in the paper.'

'See what?' asked André.

'The sputnik.'

'Why should anybody want to? You've already seen planes in the sky at night, haven't you? A red dot moving among the stars. It must be just the same.'

'No, because planes are something we're used to, whereas this is the first time in the history of the world that anybody has seen an artificial satellite.'

'But the impression of something new isn't any greater than if it were just a plane with a bigger engine. It's a quantitative difference.'

'Five miles a second doesn't mean anything to you?'

'They've already broken the sound barrier. Ten years from now, the satellites will go three times faster than now. What then?'

'Well, I think it's wonderful,' she said stubbornly; and she opened the paper, which carried a banner headline on the front page announcing that the previous Friday the Russians had launched an artificial satellite, that the experiment had been a complete success, and that the news had created a sensation all over the world.

'It's funny,' she said, 'how the Russians always pick October for their big shows: the Revolution and the beginning of the space age.'

'They picked October this time precisely because it was the fortieth anniversary of the Revolution.'

'I'm glad they've brought it off. The Americans are furious

about the sputnik and they're idiots. And Khrushchev,' she added, in the sing-song voice of a little girl, 'is a sweetie, and I just love the Russians, they're darlings. I hope they get to the moon first.'

'A lot of good that will do us. And how can you call the Russians "darlings" exactly a year after Budapest?'

'What's that got to do with it?'

'What do you mean, what's that got to do with it? Exactly a year ago, in case you've forgotten, your darling Russians crushed the Hungarian revolt in Budapest with tanks.'

'Well, and what are we doing in Algeria?'

'You're right; but I've never said that we were "darlings".'

'You don't like the Russians,' she said after a pause, 'because you're a reactionary petty-bourgeois. You're scared for your bank account and your house in the Rue de Navailles.'

He gave a laugh that was both indulgent and annoyed.

'No, really, you're ridiculous...It's impossible to discuss anything with you. After all, what are you calling me a reactionary for? Because I'm not dazzled by the sputnik. That's just absurd.'

'On the contrary, it's very logical. You hate the world which is just beginning. You are too old – you belong to the thirties.'

She accompanied these words with a little grimace of feigned contempt, or rather which was meant to suggest feigned contempt, but the spite in the sidelong glance she gave him belied the double pretence and revealed a sudden burst of resentment. He loathed this technique of a vicious attack under a cover of friendly teasing.

'You don't belong to the new wave either. For that bunch you're just as old-fashioned as I am.'

He nodded towards a group of young people at the next table.

'In their eyes both of us belong to the same species: we are both of us squares.'

He stressed the word as people do with new expressions

fashion has brought into common usage. She darted a glance at the group of boys and girls, bronzed by the sunshine of the recent summer, who sat on the terrace open to the October sky, like splendid fruit with all its bloom intact. They didn't pay the slightest attention to the people sitting at the other tables, for these were all gentlemen in the prime of life and ladies approaching it. To say that they paid them no attention is an understatement: they didn't even see them. They were completely absorbed in their exclusive interest in one another, as members of a closed community jealous of its prerogatives. The rest of the world didn't exist for them, or existed only in so far as it catered to their basic needs, their games and their pleasures, or paid them homage. Sitting round the table, as if they were taking communion in their own youth in the form of chewing-gum and Coca-Cola, they chattered and smiled; and when their glances chanced to move outside the sacramental circle, they passed unseeingly through the vague shapes of the adults sitting at the other tables, since for them those shapes had neither faces nor substance.

'They haven't got much time,' said Beatrice. 'They're right to make the most of it.'

One of the girls could be heard using the words 'baby moon'. These adolescents were not interested in the space exploit performed by the Russians. As a scientific and political event which could have repercussions on the lives of individuals, it left them cold. For them the 'baby moon' was just a news item, like the latest championship fight or the latest 'discovery' in the world of the popular song: something they talked about, but with which they felt no involvement, since it wasn't the work of people of their age.

'You hear that?' said André. 'They don't find this world that is just beginning particularly interesting. They don't give a damn for it, because they are young. It's you who dates, with your enthusiasms. You're very much the post-war girl, terribly nineteen-forty-five.'

He really loathed her at that moment, and he felt angry with himself for loathing her and for stirring up this stupid and even unfair quarrel, when it would have been so much more honest to say: 'Beatrice, it's time we parted. We mustn't see each other again – alone at least. Our liaison is all wrong, not because it's a liaison but because it isn't one; we have never loved each other, not a single day, not a single hour; we have simply pretended – you out of laziness and a want of something to occupy your time, and I out of a combination of boredom and vanity which I don't feel at all proud of. Let's call it off. We are dragging it out just because we don't know how to put an end to an affair when there's no reason to put an end to it, and I admit that there's no reason. But it can't go on either; it's too stupid, too futile; neither of us is getting enough pleasure out of it, or at least the pleasure we are getting isn't worth the bother of all the precautions we have to take, and, in my case, the worry about being found out, and even a little remorse. Why don't we part, as the saying goes, "as good friends"?' Yes, it would be both braver and more honest to say that. He called the waiter.

'Are you going?' asked Beatrice.

'It's nearly six o'clock. I have to be home at seven.'

'The model husband.'

'Oh, for heaven's sake!'

After an awkward pause she asked:

'When do I see you again?'

Beyond the iron balustrade on which a few passers-by were leaning as they admired the landscape, he looked at the curved bluish mass of the mountains, which were turning pink in the late afternoon sun.

'Do you really want to?' he asked, without looking at her.

'All right, I see. So this is the parting of the ways, is it? I was expecting it.'

'That's rather a solemn way of describing something . . . Something that has never really bound us together,' he finished rather lamely.

87

'In other words, you're dropping me . . .'

'Oh, you'll bounce up again . . . No, seriously, don't you think it's the best thing to do?'

'As soon as I saw you this evening, I thought it was the last time. And when you started attacking the Russians, I was sure of it.'

He could not repress a little burst of merriment.

'You see, another example of masculine dishonesty. The man wants to break things off, but doesn't dare admit it. So what does he do? He vents his spite on the Russians.'

'I know what I mean,' she said unsmilingly.

He called the waiter again. These waiters never came when you were in a hurry to get away; it was almost as if they pretended not to hear on purpose.

'Listen,' he said, 'you don't want to go on with it any more than I do – admit it. I'm not your type. You're quite right, you need somebody younger.'

'Oh, don't start looking for excuses. In a minute you'll be telling me you feel guilty about your wife.'

'Well, believe it or not, there *is* a bit of that mixed up in it. I don't feel very proud of myself.'

'Every cliché in the book! You're the limit!'

He reflected that she wasn't upset about the break, but just annoyed; and that showed how little their liaison had been worth, it was an indication of its quality. At the same time he told himself: 'I'm trying to excuse my rotten behaviour.'

The waiter finally condescended to come to their table; and a minute later they were walking along the boulevard towards the place where they had parked their cars. Both of them were wearing sunglasses, she out of habit, he to avoid being too easily identified by one of his fellow townsmen who might have come to Pau that afternoon. He was walking fast, and she was having difficulty in keeping up with him. He suggested that she should get into his car for a few moments, because 'we can't part like this'.

'Why not?' she said, standing with one hand absentmindedly stroking the bonnet of the car.

He had a feeling that he had seen this before, lived through it before. What? Could there have been a similar scene in his past? He couldn't remember one ... And then, all of a sudden, he realised what it was: it wasn't in his past, it was in a film. Beatrice was playing a film sequence in which a man and a woman were parting after being lovers. But as she wasn't old-fashioned, but on the contrary, right up to the minute, she was playing this scene in a modern style. No tears, no convulsions. Instead, a hand absentmindedly stroking the bonnet of a car. What a brilliant idea! She was bending her head slightly to one side, an autumnal nymph by Botticelli retouched by Mademoiselle Chanel, and saying: 'Well ... So this is it ...' with an awkwardness as convincing as if a director of the New Wave in the French cinema had re-hearsed her. Yes, this was all very much in keeping with a psychology of suggestions and gropings and twilight feelings that was beginning to permeate the fashionable new films ... Dear Beatrice, always in the forefront of the *avant-garde*.

It was time to get it over with.

'Come on, get in,' he said, opening the car door.

When they were sitting side by side, he half-turned to-wards her, and she still and erect, showing him a clear-cut profile barely threatened by the beginnings of a double chin, he made an effort to find the right tone, telling her that he had been happy with her, but that it was more sensible to end an affair that was leading nowhere. As he went on talking, the ready-made phrases ended up by creating as it were an embryo of the feeling they were supposed to be expressing. After five minutes he really felt a little affection for her. He also thought vaguely that since this episode was coming to an end and would soon be filed away among the things of the past, he might as well make it a pleasant memory: after all, they had had a few good moments together, there was no denying that, and she was still a beautiful woman, although there were lines at the outer corners of her eyes and the corners of her lips, and her face was a little puffy from over-indulgence in spirits; but this evening, haloed by the autumn light, she looked very striking. He stumbled slightly over the words when the time came to pronounce the terrible little phrase 'I hope we'll remain good friends'; and out of the corner of his eyes he watched her profile of a young Byzantine empress, of a slightly over-ripe Theodora, to see whether the sinister cliché had raised a smile. But no: the profile remained as solemn as ever. He chose to think that she was still playing a part; but just in case she really had been hurt, he put his arm round the young woman's shoulders and drew her towards him to kiss her.

When she had got out of the car (he had been careful to recommend her to wait at least half an hour before leaving, so that they weren't seen arriving in Sault within a few minutes of each other) and had gone to lean on the balustrade of the boulevard, he experienced a slight feeling of fear for a few moments; everything that came to an end had this effect on him, as if what was coming to an end were a warning, a prefiguration of the final ending. However, as soon as he had left the town and was speeding along the fine smooth road between the two rows of plane trees at seventy-five miles an hour, it was a feeling of liberation that seized hold of him, sweeping away everything else. It was all over! He was free! What a relief!

It didn't last long, barely five weeks. But long enough to show me how unsuited I am to committing adultery. Too much worry, too much trouble. I hate having my habits disturbed. Inside my marriage, which isn't very happy but isn't unhappy either, I've arranged a comfortable life for myself which combines the advantages of celibacy with those of the married state. And suddenly I had to upset that harmonious timetable, arrange escapades lasting a couple of hours, invent extremely shaky stories of business appointments for the benefit of Claire and my secretary and my head clerk, drive to Pau or somewhere else in fear and trembling of being found out, go on feeling scared going into the hotel, and back home – even though with Claire there was no need to fear either a scene or a scandal – lie clumsily and know that I was lying clumsily, and all that worry, all that expenditure of time, energy and money, for what? For a pleasure which lost its novelty almost straight away. And which above all else was a matter of vanity. I hadn't thought it possible to obtain the favours of that girl I admired so much when she was eighteen or nineteen. And then I obtained them, but ten years too late. The illusion scarcely worked any more. Oh, yes, I felt slightly reassured about myself, because I could still attract a young woman. All right, I needed that re-assurance. But then what? Even that cost too much ... What a joy it is to be free, to be driving by myself along a splendid road, through this autumnal countryside. The air is fresh and scented. Let me take a deep breath. Never again. No more of these escapades ...

He slowed down, to pay attention to the fresh surge of fear affecting him. Never again. Something was closing. A door was silently swinging to, yet another door. They would end up by all swinging to, leaving only one way open, to a well-known destination.

He didn't dwell on this idea. After all, it was a familiar idea, and he had already been living with it for a long time.

Tonight, after dinner, I'll listen to some records, the two Monteverdis and the Vittoria, which I don't know by heart yet. I'm going to begin enjoying my little everyday pleasures again – music, books, food – without any ulterior motive and without remorse. I feel hungry; I shall enjoy my dinner tonight. I wonder what it will be? In any case, I know it will be excellent. I'm going to be good to Claire, to Catherine, to Suzy. Very good. A model husband and father ... How bored I was by Beatrice! When we spent that afternoon in Biarritz, the day Claire went off to see her uncle, we trailed about the streets and cafés like a couple of lost souls. I was practically sick with boredom, and for two pins I would have swooned away. Fainting with boredom – that would have shown what I was really like ... Beatrice bores me because she's never natural, everything is second-hand with her – opinions, judgments, gestures, tone of voice – everything comes from some modern mythology, some junk-shop full of films, literary fashions, current clichés, and articles in women's magazines and newspapers for enlightened middle-class readers ... An insufferable bore! You can't live or even spend more than a couple of hours with an automaton like that, even if the automaton swears by Sade, eroticism and abstract painting. How genuine and authentic Claire is in comparison! I don't care much for the word 'authentic', which is one of Beatrice's favourite words, but still ... Claire never tries to impress people or shock them; she never repeats what she has read in the paper. What she says has been thought and felt; it is her. I'm going to be good to Claire. Considerate, attentive. I haven't given her a present for a long time. What could I buy her, I wonder? But I would have to find an excuse. If I just gave her a present like that, out of the blue, it would look suspicious.

He went into his house looking fairly relaxed. He did something he hadn't done for years: he kissed Claire. She seemed a little taken aback and looked at him strangely. (Could she suspect something? No, it's because I kissed her). He gaily asked what they were going to have for dinner, and spoke jovially to Catherine and Suzy when they came downstairs from their rooms, where they had been doing their homework: their father's arrival always marked the end of their work. After putting on a pair of leather slippers and changing his jacket for a smart smoking-jacket, André collected the papers – *Le Monde, Le Figaro, L'Express* – and went into the drawing-room to rest and read for an hour before dinner. He hesitated as to whether to treat himself to an apéritif, then decided good-humouredly that it would be better to remain sober. Encouraged by his unusually affable greeting, the two girls came into the drawing-room, from which they were normally excluded during this hour of newspaper-reading. He made conversation with them. A good day at school? What had they been doing?

'Is your Latin getting any better, Suzy? ... Twenty-seventh in composition? Why, that's splendid. Last time, if I remember rightly, you were thirty-sixth ... I beg your pardon, yes, thirty-fifth. Don't hop about, Suzy, you're too big for that. A girl of fifteen doesn't hop around a drawing-room. And what about you, Catherine? Anything new? ... A letter from your American pen-friend? You must be happy, then. Go on, now, don't blush. Is he a nice boy, this Alan? ... You want me to read his letter? Darling, I don't know if I have the right to ... All right, you can give it to me to read after dinner ... But Suzy, I don't know what they are showing: I didn't go to the cinema ... Wait a minute, I think there's *Nights of Cabiria* at the Palais des Pyrénées. That can't be the sort of film for you, you know ... You know more about the cinema than you do about Latin, don't you? Fellini, de Sica, all those Italians are pals of yours, aren't they, but not old Julius Caesar? ... There now, I was only joking!'

Dinner was a relaxed meal. Suzy talked about the baby moon (she snapped up the latest words like a carp gobbling up midges) and asked whether you could see it; then, without waiting for an answer, she ran to the window and peered up at the sky. Her mother pointed out to her that people didn't leave the table in the middle of a meal, even to look for a satellite. Suzy, however, didn't come back and sit down straight away.

'There it is!' she exclaimed, pointing upwards. The other three ran to the window, but although they scrutinised the sky they could see nothing but the stars.

'I must have been wrong,' Suzy concluded calmly; and as everyone was in a good mood they didn't scold her or call her a little idiot, as they would have been sure to do at any other time. After this false alarm Suzy turned her attention to international politics. She asked whether the Russians were now 'on top' and whether they were going to 'win'.

'Win what?' asked her father.

'Whah, just win,' she repeated.

'Darling, you win something against somebody. For the time being, there isn't any war between the Americans and the Russians. Suzy, love, I've told you a hundred times that you should say "why" and not "whah". Couldn't you make a little effort?'

'It's the local accent: everybody thinks it's charming, and I don't want to lose it.'

'Charming is going a bit far. Try to improve your own anyway. Look at Catherine – she talks properly.'

'Oh, her! She just puts it on.'

'Another thing, Suzy. I'm not getting at you or scolding you, but it isn't very nice to refer to somebody who is sitting next to you as "him" or "her", because it's really common. All right? All right, and not . . . not . . . ?'

'O.K.,' Suzy answered meekly.

'Good. You won't forget, will you? You've got to understand that talking correctly is a great help in life. People who murder the language don't get anywhere . . . You understand? And not . . . not . . . ?'

'You get me,' Suzy said with a smile.

After dinner, when they were in the drawing-room, she asked for permission to turn on the radio, and permission was granted. She nearly fainted away when a woman's voice filled the room which was alternately guttural and shrill, darting up and down the scale with the agility of a monkey leaping from branch to branch, now a cooing coloratura, now a deep contralto.

'Yma Sumac!' Suzy exclaimed ecstatically. 'She's gorgeous!'

And she explained that this singer with the exceptional range was an Indian princess, an Iztec – whah, yes, an Iztec! ('An Aztec, I suppose,' said her father) – who, only six months before, had still been officiating as a priestess of the sun. 'I read it in the rag,' she added, as a guarantee of the accuracy of her statement.

'In the *paper*,' said André. 'But I seem to remember reading that it was a publicity stunt, that the woman is really a North American whose name is plain Amy Camus. If you read each name backwards, you get...'

But Suzy refused to believe this story, which had probably been started by a jealous rival. No, she admired the priestess of the sun. She was the greatest singer in the world.

'The greatest, Suzy? You're sure of that?'

'It was in the rag!'

When the girls had gone up to their rooms, André settled down in his armchair for an evening's reading. During dinner Claire had seemed perfectly natural. Perhaps she had glanced at him once or twice more searchingly than usual, but André attributed that to a rather puzzled surprise at the jovial good humour he was lavishing on his family this evening. Nothing in her attitude or her remarks suggested that she had any suspicions as to the way he had spent his time between four o'clock and seven.

He was reading the paper. Suddenly he stopped short, holding the paper in front of him. His eyes followed Claire who had stood up and was walking towards the right-hand window. With a clear-cut, precise, military gesture she pulled the cord that worked the curtains. Snap. Then it was the turn of the left-hand window. The same gesture. Snap. The outside world was wiped out. Instead of the street and the sky, there were two rectangles of red velvet. The drawing-room became an enclosed space, a walled chamber softly lit by the standard lamp and the wall brackets. Having shut out the outside world, Claire came back and sat down in her armchair, wearing the satisfied, rather smug expression of someone who has just performed a sacred rite. André had not taken his eyes off her during this operation. He gave a sigh and went on turning the pages of the paper, looking for an article to read, but apparently without success, for soon he started searching his pockets. He took out a small flat plastic box and opened it; it contained some yellow tablets. He put one in his mouth. Claire looked up from her book, noticed the gesture, and returned or pretended to return to her reading.

'You need a tranquilliser?' she asked.

'It will help me to sleep better.'

She kept her eyes fixed on her book.

'Did you do what you wanted to do in Pau?' she asked casually.

'I saw Minvielle about the inheritance. I don't think it will cause any trouble.'

The two of them went on reading, or tried to go on reading, during a silence which became almost tangible. Claire suddenly shut her book and picked up a paper. There was a sound of rustling as she turned the pages.

'Can you see this satellite, in fact, or can't you?' she asked. 'Not that I'm really interested in it.'

'The papers don't say. I think that radio stations can pick up the signals it's sending out.'

'Is it really important, all that? I mean, what good does it do?'

'Oh, yes, it's important all right: it's the beginning of the conquest of space.'

'And what difference will the conquest of space make? To our lives, I mean.'

'I don't know. It may change lots of things. One discovery leads to another. I don't know – the study of cosmic rays might help us to find one of the causes of cancer, for example.'

'All right. One curse defeated. There will be others, possibly worse. And we shall continue to be mortal.'

'Yes, we shall! You ask too much.'

'In other words, nothing will be changed.'

'You're very contemptuous about modern science. Does it mean absolutely nothing to you to be in at the birth of a new era? We had the Stone Age and so on all the way up to the age of the Industrial Revolution, and now we're in the Nuclear or Space Age. We are privileged to be living in this era.'

'No, I'm not impressed by all that. If they changed men themselves – all right – men and women, that is – I mean Man with a capital M, I *would* be impressed, or at any rate interested; but these satellites . . .'

'But it's a pretty thing, a baby moon.'

'It seems to me that the sky is sufficiently cluttered up with planes.'

'Well, *I* regard this Soviet achievement as tremendously exciting, because they won't stop there. Ten years from now they'll go to the moon, and then to Mars, and in another hundred years, they'll be exploring the galaxies.'

'In another hundred years you and I will be dead, and we may know more about the galaxies than our great-grandchildren. Or else we shall know nothing at all, and in that case what does it matter?'

'The world is made for the living.'

'I sometimes wonder . . .'

'You're very pessimistic this evening. I'm more alive than you are to the wonders of our age. This is the outside world coming into our home – and a good thing too. Everyday life is so everyday.'

'Really?'

'I didn't say that; it's Jules Laforgue . . . Well, now the world is going to change with every day that passes. We are going to go from one surprise to another. After all, you must admit that this satellite is more interesting than our dinners in Sault . . .'

'I thought you liked dining out. With the Marcillacs, the Vignemales or the Andurains. I thought that was what you wanted.'

André folded his paper and put it down. He smiled, breathing rather faster.

'What I wanted? I don't understand.'

'I thought,' said Claire in a cutting voice, 'that was what you wanted: to live in a house in the Rue de Navailles – this house – and mix with the leaders of local society...'

She had not raised her eyes from the newspaper spread out on her knees, and was pretending, no doubt unthinkingly, to be reading it.

'In other words, you think that's why I married you?'

'That may have been one of the reasons.'

'Claire.'

She looked up. He made an effort to meet that gaze of hers which was shattering his serenity.

'What's the matter?' he asked, trying unsuccessfully to keep his voice steady.

'Nothing. Or rather, yes, there *is* something, and you know perfectly well what it is.'

This was it. He was going to have to face up to all the bother of recriminations and complaints.

'I admire the way,' Claire went on, 'that you can kiss your daughters and play with them, when you have only just left your mistress. You might at least have taken a bath.'

'What do you...,' he began, but Claire's gaze paralysed him and he was incapable of finishing his question.

'I hope you aren't going to deny it.'

He stood up and started pacing up and down the room. In these cases a show of anger helped you to carry it off.

'All right,' he said. 'You know about it. I won't ask you who you've had spying on me or which private inquiry agency you...'

'Come, now,' she broke in, raising her voice slightly. 'I'm not the sort of person to have anybody spied on. And as it happened, I didn't need to. You took hardly any precautions, you and that person. You were seen leaving for Pau and coming back, each of you in your own car, at a few minutes' interval...People aren't so stupid, and they end up by finding an explanation for these repeated coincidences.'

'Oh, so somebody took it upon themselves to put you in the picture?'

She hesitated for a moment.

'Juliette came and told me,' she said. 'I knew already. But she confirmed what I thought... You had been seen, you and that person, coming out of a hotel.'

'Juliette came and told you?... What business was it of hers?... She'd do better to keep an eye on her own husband, instead of denouncing other people's.'

'It *is* her business. That person is her sister-in-law and Juliette is a friend of ours. I would have done the same if I had been in her place. She was acting for the best. It upset her dreadfully to have to tell me.'

'Does Bruno know about it too?'

'No, set your mind at rest, he doesn't suspect a thing.'

She was talking without looking at him, sitting erect with her hands in her lap. He wasn't looking at her either, standing a little way off, a prey to an embarrassment which was causing little nervous twitches in his cheeks and temples. He managed to speak, with a dull, hoarse voice. His guilty voice.

'Seeing that you know about it, I might as well tell you what has happened: it's all over. It's finished. This very evening, in fact; I broke it off. I might add that it never really counted for me. I only... gave way out of vanity.'

'Gave way?' she said harshly.

'Try to understand. It's a question of male vanity. At a certain age you want to reassure yourself...'

'Oh, don't go on! You're contemptible.'

He fell silent, stunned by her words.

'The first time,' she went on, 'barely three years after we were married, was it also vanity that made you "give way"? Not that it matters. That doesn't make it any less sordid. On the contrary.'

She stood up and seemed to be uncertain what to do next.

'If it weren't for the children,' she said at last, 'I would ask for a divorce. But that would be awful for them.'

99

Without a glance in his direction, she left the room. André heard her walk quickly upstairs and open the door of her room. He came back to his armchair and sat down. His face was completely changed. He sighed. Leaning his elbows on his knees, he put his head in his hands. At his feet, on the carpet, lay the paper he had dropped when he had stood up. There were banner headlines on the front page. World-wide sensation. Washington uneasy. The whole of mankind must congratulate the Soviet scientists (*New York Times*). A new era is beginning . . .

For some time Juliette had been 'badgering' her husband ('Don't badger me,' Bruno used to tell her) to have a serious talk with their younger son, Nicolas, who was fourteen years old. By a serious talk she meant a conversation in the course of which the father would explain the facts of life to the son and describe the dangers facing a rash or ignorant young man – in other words, give him a few healthy ideas about sex. She had read in a magazine a long, copiously documented article written especially for parents by a psychiatrist who was an expert on child education; and this article had made a great impression on her. She considered that Pierre, their eldest, who was a strapping young fellow, as high-spirited as his father, probably didn't need to be warned about, say, the prostitutes he might meet on his Sunday outings with the football team, when they went to play in the different towns in the region. He probably knew all the risks and wouldn't hesitate to go to a doctor if he got into trouble. But it was different with Nicolas. In the first place Nicolas was still very young for his age; he was also much more delicate and sensitive than Pierre. She thought Bruno ought to talk to him and tell him what every father had a duty to . . .

'Oh, leave me alone!' Bruno broke in. 'What's all this nonsense about sex education? You've just read about it in one of your magazines and taken it for gospel. Did *you* need any sex education? And did *I* get any?'

'That's just the point. When I was fifteen I didn't know a thing. I could easily have got into trouble. If my mother had warned me . . .'

'What do you mean, warned you? You didn't get into trouble, did you? So what are you complaining about? Your instinct told you not to do anything silly. That's quite enough. When a child has a decent character it doesn't need its parents to give it a course in hygiene or anything like that. Stop nagging me about it. Can you see me talking to the kid about things like that? What the hell would I say to him? I wouldn't even know what to say. I'd feel terribly embarrassed.'

'You – embarrassed.'

'Why, yes, of course I'd be embarrassed. A father does feel embarrassed talking to his children about certain things. You women, of course, have no sense of modesty. You're a lot of animals.'

'In other words, on the excuse that it might embarrass you, you're refusing to shoulder your responsibilities as a father?'

'What do you mean, my responsibilities? Don't I feed my children and bring them up and send them to school? Don't I give them everything they need? What more do you want me to do?'

'In our day parents left their children to find out the facts of life by themselves, without any help, at the risk of . . . Anyway, it was pretty hard on them. Nowadays we are more enlightened, and it's our duty to . . .'

'Oh, don't give me that stuff about how enlightened we are today! If somebody has to give them a talk about that sort of thing, what about the school chaplain? All you've got to do is go and ask the chaplain to have a word with them.'

'A priest! But a priest isn't qualified to talk to them about those things!'

'And why not? They're bloody enlightened, as you put it, the priests we've got today. And they bloody well show it.'

'Don't say bloody all the time! And please don't shout at me.'

'You're right: you'll end up by making me lose my temper! I simply refuse to have that talk with Nicolas. You hear that? I won't do it! If you're worried about him, you've only got to go and see the doctor. My responsibilities, indeed! You're a fine one! . . . Well, I'm going to the office. See you tonight. And don't badger me any more with that nonsense. 'Bye, pet. Give me a kiss all the same.'

And off he went to his office. Every time he was threatened with some unpleasant task, he took refuge in his work and pleaded that he was too busy. Juliette had her doubts about the volume of his work, but she knew very little about business and was content to remain in a state of cautious or resigned ignorance as to her husband's affairs. Bruno always created an impression of frenzied activity. He drove all over the countryside, visiting each of his farms in turn, for he owned about thirty in the adjoining departments of the Basses-Pyrénées, the Landes and the Gers, a fortune in land patiently amassed by several generations of Marcillacs, first farmers, then big landowners, and finally wealthy bourgeois who no longer did any work but collected rents from their tenants. Shortly after the Great War Monsieur Marcillac had added a pit-prop business to his farming activities, but this concern had gone downhill during the depression and Bruno was finally forced to sell it at a heavy loss. Under the new laws, farms brought in hardly anything, and on the contrary were often a burden. It therefore became necessary to sell them off, one after another, without making much profit, and it was from these sales that Bruno now derived the bulk of his income – eating his capital, as they put it in Sault. He only made a real profit when one of the farms happened to fall vacant. Then he would sell it, not to a farmer, but to a city-dweller in search of a country house. That only happened very rarely, when an old couple died whose children had preferred to look for work in the town. Normally he had to sell his farms in occupation, an arrangement which made it hard to find buyers.

In these circumstances there was no longer much justification for the office, an unpretentious room which he rented in the middle of the town. However, Bruno kept it on, partly out of habit, partly out of concern for public opinion ('You've got to save face') and also for convenience' sake: this office in which he had installed a divan and a little bar was his refuge, his den, his bachelor pad. 'Here I'm my own boss,' he used to say. 'Family life is all very well, but now and then a man needs a little rest.' His friends also came to see him there, attracted by the promise of a 'thundering good brandy'. He had never dared to take a woman there: 'Too many people can keep an eye on me here. Two minutes later you'd see Juliette descending on the place, armed with a club. Besides, I've no desire to deceive my wife.'

Bruno enjoyed touring his farms. Not that he had a sense of property, of ownership of the soil. He never said to himself with a square's pride or a miser's avarice: 'These fields of corn and wheat, these vineyards, these woods, these orchards belong to me.' What he appreciated about his bucolic outings was the fresh air, the good smell of the earth, talking dialect with the peasants, sitting down at their table as a beloved, and he thought respected, landlord, tasting the new wine and the preserved goose, the winter pork, the autumn pigeon. The more ruthlessly he was being fleeced, the more warmly he was welcomed. Far from respecting him, his farmers rather despised him, for they exploited him to the utmost; but he was certainly popular with them, as with his fellow townsmen of Sault, because, bourgeois and 'gent' though he was, he had the simple, friendly manners of a decent fellow, and in language and accent he talked like everybody else. 'He's a good sort,' people said; 'he doesn't put on airs.' Sitting at table with his peasants, he would give free rein to his penchant for bawdy talk and his passion for good food. He knew every member of these countless tribes, whom he regarded more or less as an extension of his own family, and cherished a pastoral dream in which he was both a revered patriarch and a handsome incarnation of the god Pan. Baptisms, weddings, first communions and village fêtes were all excuses for him to 'go for a drive'. From one springtime to the next he watched the growth and flowering of a few robust country girls. He chatted with them, teased them, and stole an occasional kiss – tempering the coarseness of his remarks with an entirely fatherly bonhomie. The parents regarded all this with amused indulgence: seeing that they were bleeding him white, they could afford to overlook these innocent little jokes.

He would have been greatly surprised, and even shocked, if anyone had said that he led a lazy life, that he was an anachronistic idler. He regarded himself as a powerhouse of energy. Sometimes, when he realised he had been tricked, he flew into a terrible rage. He heaped insults on the cunning, dishonest farmer, threatened to take him to court, told him he ought to be ashamed of his treachery and ingratitude, and gradually calmed down, though not without a few more explosions of anger. To seal a reconciliation about which the culprit had never had a moment's doubt, he ended up having a drink with him, his wife, his children and his farm-hand; and the pastoral dream continued in the cowshed, where they went to feel the promising sides of the heifers, and in the fields, where they enthused over the size of the ears of corn. In the evening, in the cool, scented air of the countryside, Bruno would drive back towards Sault, his anger gone, pleased with his day: he had acted like Solomon, combining the severity of a judge with the gentleness of a father.

In his office, in between arid perusals of his account books, he would read *Le Sud-Ouest* and *L'Équipe*. Politics and sport interested him to an equal degree. Every day he would meet a few friends at the café for an apéritif. André didn't belong to this well-to-do but somewhat uncultured group. The conversation turned on the recent exploits of various rugby teams, or on the stormier battles of the Fourth Republic. Bruno believed in keeping Algeria as part of France. He came close to quarrelling with André, whose culpable radicalism was forcing France and the other imperialist nations to give up their colonies, and to give them up in a humiliating fashion. Such blasphemous opinions as André professed made Bruno's blood boil. He told Juliette that if André hadn't been a friend of theirs, he would have felt like pushing his face in on more than one occasion. Juliette had no definite opinions about Algeria or about any other political problems, and she didn't attach much importance to her husband's, although she voted the same way as he did. In private she thought that Bruno ought to take a little less interest in politics and sport, and a little more in managing his property and bringing up his children; but that, she decided, was a weakness common to most men, a constant factor in the eternal male. And it was true that she loved her Bruno as he was, a thoroughly decent sort, gay and clumsy, and that it warmed her heart to see him laughing and playing with his sons as if he were still their age.

He played with his sons, but not in the same way, depending on whether his partner was Pierre or Nicolas. No doubt he loved them both with the same unconditional, boundless love, just as he loved the little girl, Line: they were his children, in other words the cream of the human race, and he would have given his life for them. But with Pierre he behaved naturally; with Nicolas he didn't. Juliette had felt this very early on, when Nicolas was only five or six. Then it had gradually become an obvious fact, revealed in a thousand little ways, a thousand details of family life. She had never talked about it to Bruno, first because she would not have known how to describe something intangible and indefinable, which was not so much a series of precise facts and actions as a certain way of behaving, a mood, a climate, or, as she put it, an 'atmosphere' ('When he's with Nicolas, the atmosphere is different'); and secondly because, if she had ventured a few words on the subject, she felt sure that Bruno would have exploded straight away. 'What do you mean,' he would have said, 'I'm not the same with Nicolas as with Pierre? Why do you say that? Where did you get that idea? Women! Always complicating everything! What a brood!' He would have denied it all; but the thing would have secretly burned deeper into him, would have curled up like a grub in a corner of his brain; he would have been worried by it, as if by a mysterious disease which defied diagnosis but was nonetheless real, and his relationship with Nicolas would have suffered from this secret anxiety. Juliette had therefore refrained from making the slightest remark to him. Besides, it wasn't as serious as all that; they could carry on quite well like this. Day after day, without appearing to do so, she watched and spied on the trio of the father and his two sons. She didn't even need to look at them; it was enough for her to hear them to register, like a barometer, the almost imperceptible changes of moral pressure as he moved from one to the other. With Pierre, Bruno was perfectly natural and at ease, and the boy was just as relaxed. A lion was playing with its cub. Sometimes there was a tremendous din, like the sound of a pillow-fight in a dormitory, the father bawling happily, the child mad with joy, giving free rein to an innocent verbal vulgarity: it was no use having them educated by priests, or reproving them and calling for a little decency, there was no stopping the torrent of bad language, and the fact had to be recognised that the two of them were incorrigible. Not that Juliette really wanted to correct them; their rascally conspiracy was one of the elements of her happiness. When they were indulging their inexhaustible passion for 'messing about' with the car (they were for ever taking the unfortunate machine to pieces and putting it together again) and she heard Pierre shout: 'Daddy! It's the ejector that's fucking things up!' she was secretly amused and couldn't help smiling. And then there were the games of football in the orchard, in summer, before dinner, with Bruno coaching his son with the authority of a former virtuoso and the boy receiving this teaching as a sacred trust. They would have gone on for hours if Juliette's repeated summons and their own appetite had not ended up by overcoming their love of the game – 'Come along, or she's going to bawl us out!' – and they came in across the lawn, conversing in the ritual language (*dribble, shoot*, and so on) that she had learnt in the old days, when she used to go to watch Bruno play. 'Pierre is no problem,' she told her women friends; 'he gives me no trouble at all'. No, Pierre was no problem: at the very most, because he was so credulous, so trusting and, for all his physical strength, so helpless, she was afraid that he might fall in love, as a young man, with some scheming, unscrupulous girl; but apart from this worry, which was a tribute in itself to Pierre's character, she knew that he would never give her any unpleasant surprises.

It would have been untrue to say that Nicolas was a difficult child. Indeed, Juliette would have liked him to be rowdier, more undisciplined. He looked rather like one of Botticelli's angel musicians: he had the same delicate features, the same sad, dreamy eyes, and in his long, loose-limbed body, the same languid indolence. This apparent languor contrasted with a highly-strung temperament which sometimes made him stammer and turn pale. If anybody spoke to him at all harshly, he started shaking from head to foot and looked completely abashed. You had to speak to him gently and cautiously giving him repeated marks of affection; only then would he open up again and recover the spontaneity and gaiety of his age. He made up for his feeble temperament with exceptional intelligence, scholastic success, and a charm which easily won all hearts. Juliette often wondered how she had come to have this rather exotic son, so different from the line of Gascon bourgeois from which she was descended, and from the dull-witted peasant stock of the Marcillacs. She would have liked to know the ancestries of both families, to try to make out among the ramifications of their crowded branches the stray bough from which Nicolas had inherited his delicacy; but the line of descent on both sides was soon lost, on account of illegitimate births and gaps in the records.

Bruno was proud of his younger son, for whom his school-masters were full of praise. His affection for him was tinged with a hint of deference. Like Juliette, he detected in Nicolas something essentially different; but he did not dwell on it, did not try to single out this difference and analyse it. For him everything could be summed up in a few vague words: 'Nicolas is the intellectual of the family. He's a clever kid. He knows everything. I don't know where he's picked it all up. And quiet too. Never shouts, never raises his voice.' Un-like his brother, Nicolas only very rarely used bad language, not out of prudishness or a desire to be different, but out of incapacity: certain words did not come to him easily, sounding strange on his lips, and you could tell that he was making an effort, trying to suit his conversation to the others, to cry with the pack. When Bruno talked to him, he in-stinctively watched his language. Occasionally, when he was looking at his son, Juliette noticed a little gleam of perplexity in his gaze, and in his voice, which was a fraction gentler and warmer than was necessary, vague overtones which suggested doubt and uncertainty. She sometimes had a feeling that Bruno was overawed by his younger son.

The article she had read about sex education contained a paragraph on sensitive, imaginative adolescents. Certain symp-toms were described which had seemed to her to apply to Nicolas. The author stated that puberty could be a difficult and dangerous period for certain delicate natures. Parents had a duty to inform their children frankly about procrea-tion, to warn them of the risks involved in promiscuity, and finally to teach them the rudiments of hygiene. She con-sidered the advice reasonable but was frightened of putting it into practice. On several points in the programme she herself had only the vaguest knowledge or none at all. But after all, it was a father's job to tell his sons the facts of life. She returned to the attack and finally, for the sake of peace and quiet, Bruno gave in.

'All right, all right, I'll talk to him when I have a free moment. But I don't know what the hell I'm going to say to him, except that he ought to steer clear of tarts and that doctors are there to cure every sort of disease. And even that is going to be bloody difficult to say. For one thing, he isn't old enough yet. But since you're so keen on it...I can see that I'll have to go through with it. You won't give me a moment's peace until it's done. You women, once you've got an idea in your heads!'

So one Sunday afternoon, urged on by Juliette and radiating goodwill, he went into his son's room. Nicolas was lying on his bed, reading a book. When his father came in he shut the book and propped himself up on one elbow. His face assumed a slightly alarmed expression. Bruno sat down on the edge of the bed.

'Well, old man, what are you doing?' he said in a fairly good attempt at a natural tone of voice. 'Reading?'

He glanced at the cover of the book.

'*Jocelyn*, by Lamartine. You know, I've never read that,' he said, as if that gap in his reading were really surprising. 'Now I come to think of it, what have I read by Lamartine? Is *Le Lac* by him? Then I've read that. I can even remember the first line: *Ainsi toujours poussés vers de nouveaux rivages* ....Is that right? Well, your father isn't as ignorant as he looks after all. That's right, go on: laugh at me. Well, is it any good, this *Jocelyn?* What's it about?'

Nicolas's cheeks flushed.

'It's the story of a priest,' he said.

'The story of a priest? That can't be much fun. Still, I'm glad to see you reading the classics. That's very good. You're a serious young fellow.'

Bruno looked at the innocent little face raised towards him and was suddenly swept away by a surge of emotion. He took the boy in his arms and hugged him tight as if he had to protect him against some mysterious danger. It was a long time since he had hugged him like that: after children were ten it just wasn't done. Nicolas, in an instinctive gesture, put his arms round his father's neck. At that moment, if a heavenly messenger had come and offered to protect Nicolas for ever against all harm if his father laid down his life, Bruno would have agreed at once, in a tumult of happiness.

He slackened his grip and the two of them exchanged a rather embarrassed look of surprise, but smiling as if they had taken an enormous step towards each other and had been vaguely aware that that step had to be taken. Bruno was wondering how to broach the subject. However, he was a little less nervous now than he had been before coming into the room. He told himself that with a boy as intelligent and attentive as Nicolas, it shouldn't be too difficult.

'You spend nearly all your Sundays reading,' he said. 'You're going to become a great scholar. I'm proud of you, you know. You do us credit. Yes, I mean that. When somebody praises you to me, I wouldn't change places with anybody in the world. All the same, I sometimes wonder if you don't work too hard.'

Nicolas's smile grew broader and he shook his head.

'Today, for instance, it's a fine day, and you could go for a walk, wander round the town. Or else go to the cinema. With a girl friend, perhaps. You have got a girl friend, haven't you?'

He felt quite pleased with himself at having found this transition, which he considered diabolically clever. Nicolas didn't bat an eyelid.

'Yes,' he said simply. 'Catherine Comarieu.'

'Ah, Catherine. But she's a childhood friend of yours. I wasn't really thinking of that kind of . . . Still, yes: Catherine . . . Well, why don't you go to the cinema with her?'

'We were there last night, Daddy. We go nearly every Saturday.'

'Yes, of course, that's right. She's a nice girl, Catherine ...
You're quite fond of her, eh? But do you think you'll marry
her one day?'

The idea made Nicolas smile.

'I don't know,' he said. 'We don't talk about that. We're
too young.'

'Yes, of course. All the same, at your age you start thinking
about those things. Not about marriage, but about those
things ... Because you're almost a young man now.'

He drew a deep breath. It was here that the conversation
was going to become delicate. How should he begin?

'You know everything you ought to, I suppose? ... I
mean, you know how children come into the world?'

Nicolas flushed scarlet, but didn't lower his eyes. He
nodded.

'Good,' said Bruno. 'I thought you'd know about that, and
that's perfectly natural. There's no need to blush about it –
it's quite normal. Well, in that case I don't need to explain
something you know already. All the same, I'd like to
give you a little advice ... Because there's more to all that
than what happens in marriage, between husband and
wife ...'

He paused. He felt as if he were floundering and wondered
what to say next. He stood up, trying to look relaxed, and
started wandering round the room, pretending to look at the
titles of the books on the shelves, picking up an ornament
here and there and turning it round between his fingers.
What sort of hornets' nest had he blundered into? Yet perhaps Juliette was right, and he ought to put little Nicolas on
his guard against the sordid dangers that lie in wait for an
ignorant boy. He knew perfectly well what his own
adolescence had been like: a period of frenzied sadness, an
oscillation between frustration and debauchery, each about as
ugly and demoralising as the other. So little real pleasure. He
was a plucky, good-looking, attractive boy and all the girls
made eyes at him. By rights he should have led the life of a

young pasha, but it hadn't been like that at all. In the Sault-en-Labourd of the thirties it wasn't so easy ... There was no hope of 'making out' with the girls who made eyes at him. Sometimes you could 'make out' with a housemaid you picked up at a dance-hall, but that was all. And then there were the local brothels ... with the terrifying possibility of catching a 'disgusting' disease. He had caught one himself, and that at a time when treatment was lengthy and expensive. You went to the clinic in secret, frightened and ashamed. Oh, no, in that respect his adolescence had been anything but happy, in spite of the advantages he enjoyed of money and physical charm. He had to do his best to spare his sons all that anguish. How did they manage nowadays? You heard people say, and you read in the papers, that young people nowadays had much greater sexual freedom. But what exactly did that mean? Did it mean that Pierre, for instance ... ? No, he would know about it, just by looking at him. There was an expression, a look that was unmistakable. Pierre was still a child. You heard and read that girls, even from decent homes, made no bones about sleeping with their boy friends. What truth was there in all these sociological investigations? Did the little Camarieu girls, for instance ... ? No, definitely not, Bruno was sure of that. He thought straight away of his little Line. She was only eight now, but one day she would be sixteen, and he gave a horrified shudder at the thought that perhaps she wouldn't remain a virgin until she married, if that was how morals were shaping in France. He hoped that she wouldn't follow the example of the other girls. It was bad enough to think that one day a man would ... It was different for boys: they had to get their freedom earlier.

'Listen,' he said at last, 'you're still rather young, but in a year or two you'll start thinking a lot about girls. You'll probably feel like a roll in the hay with one of your girl friends ...'

The slang phrase had come out awkwardly. Bruno had used it in a coarse tone of voice because he thought that that was how boys talked to each other; but now he realised that it sounded wrong and he felt ashamed. Not daring to look at his son, he went on wandering unhappily round the room, and continued:

'... but you'll have to control yourself. You see, your girl friends are decent, respectable girls from good families. We see a lot of their parents, so imagine what a disaster it would be if you made one of them pregnant... All right, you're going to say, but a fellow can't always be expected to hold back. No, of course not. There are girls who'll give you what you want, but there again you've got to be careful. When you get a girl in the family way it's your duty to marry her if you don't want to be an absolute swine. And can you see yourself marrying, say, a barmaid? ... Not that I've anything against barmaids, but it's better to marry somebody of your own class... All right. Now there are ways of having fun without any unfortunate consequences... kids or anything else... I'll discuss all that with you another time. Or else you can ask Darricau, the chemist. He's a good chap, he knows life, and we're old pals. You can talk to him in complete confidence... Another thing...'

Bruno was now puffing like a steam-engine. God, but this was hard! With Pierre it would have been easy. Pierre would have listened to him with respectful attention, as he listened to his advice on matters of football. He would have been proud to be talked to like this, feeling that he was being treated like a grown-up. Yes, it would have been a real 'man to man' talk, with no embarrassment on either side. But little Nicolas, sitting behind him, silent as the grave ... Bruno took a handkerchief out of his pocket and dabbed his temples and the back of his neck. He thought of the old expression about the bull in the china shop and pictured valuable porcelain being smashed under heavy hooves. Still, he had gone too far now, and he had to go through with it.

'Another thing,' he went on. 'When you go to towns like Bordeaux, and especially Paris, women may try to pick you

113

up in the evening, in the street. That's forbidden, it's against the law, but they do it all the same. They are prostitutes, women who go to bed with you for money. Well, if you went with them, that wouldn't be a terrible crime, but you'd have to be careful with them as well, because most of them have got diseases, serious contagious diseases. So if you found you'd got a queer sort of pimple, or if you were worried about something, you ought to go and see a doctor straight away. Don't hesitate, whatever you do. If it's caught soon enough, that sort of thing isn't serious.'

At last he had come to the end of this terrifying job. He had covered everything, hadn't he? He hadn't forgotten anything? No. Mission completed. What a relief! He turned round to face his son. His knees drawn up to his chin, his head hidden in the crook of one arm, his shoulders shaking, Nicolas was silently weeping.

Bruno's heart missed a beat. He came back and sat on the edge of the bed.

'Nicolas! ... You mustn't cry. What's the matter? Did I say something that upset you?'

The boy's shoulders were promptly shaken by still more violent spasms, and his sobs became audible, although he made a great effort to stifle them. Bruno did not dare to touch the child, but gazed in consternation at the stricken little figure. He got to his feet and went downstairs. Juliette was waiting for him in the drawing-room.

'You and your sex education!' he grumbled angrily, though in an undertone. 'You big ninny! I knew you were wrong! Well, he's crying now, poor kid. You can go up and comfort him.'

'Crying? What did you say to make him cry?'

'What do you mean, what did I say to him? What a question! I said what I had to say to him. No more and no less.'

Juliette went up to the first floor, looking worried. Nicolas was still crying. She coaxed him, but without managing to get a single word out of him; and this fit of weeping was to remain a mystery to her and Bruno.

'How can anybody read in a house where there's music playing all day, if you can call that stuff music!'

After lunch André used to rest for an hour before going to the office. He liked to settle down in an armchair in the library, for a read and a short nap. That particular day he was disturbed by a jazz tune coming from upstairs. He got up and went into the hall.

'Suzy, will you please turn off your transistor or lower the volume. I don't want to hear any more of that din. Understand?'

There was no reply; but after a few seconds, as if Suzy had hesitated as to what to do, the volume was turned down. Frowning, André went back into the library. Suzy was really becoming impossible! She thought she could get away with anything. Since she had bought that damned radio, the house had been throbbing with jazz and popular songs, almost without interruption, from morning till night. She even took her transistor with her when she went out. She took it with her to school! She did her homework to the accompaniment of the transistor, braving all the remarks her father and mother had made to her on the subject: 'You can't do two things at once, work and listen to music, it's bad for the brain.' Admittedly poor Suzy's brain was better left out of it. The fact remained that with the transistor on one hand, the record-player on the other, and the traffic outside, they were now living in a constant din. Why didn't the authorities try to curb all this noise? But they probably considered it more urgent to continue the war in Algeria – the hateful, stupid war which was useless too, since France was bound to lose it. On certain days the contempt André felt for the Fourth Republic attained an almost painful virulence. His blood boiled. He would have liked to speak his mind to the Government, and to the editors of certain papers. But his inner fury was futile, and also probably extremely harmful, spreading poison throughout his system. Nothing was worse for the nerves than suppressed anger. That was why he took these pills from America which were supposed to soothe the nervous system, reduce aggressive impulses, and restore peace and harmony. He settled down again in his armchair and opened the paper. His eyes fell on a headline: 'The Teenagers Judge Us.' He crumpled the paper up. The teenagers judge us! What next? Soon they would expect their elders to account to them for everything they did. He knew the author of the article; she was a journalist who specialised in 'problems of the day' – the young, the young writers, the young directors.

He got to his feet and went over to the bookshelves to look for a book. Now what should he read again? Why not Jean-Jacques Rousseau? Not his *Émile*, at any rate! Where were the *Confessions*? He really must make up his mind to tidy up this library, it was such a mess. Well, well – Proust. You could go on reading him indefinitely. The chapter on the little clan, to keep his anger going against cheats and idiots. No, he mustn't keep his anger going. Especially not after lunch ... Admittedly with Proust, you didn't get angry; you laughed or you were entranced. *To belong to the 'little set', the 'little group', the 'little clan' of the Verdurins, one condition was enough, but that condition had to be fulfilled: it was necessary to adhere to a creed of which one of the articles* ... Yes, that was what he needed. For the third time he went back to his armchair and settled down to read.

Not for long. He had got to the passage in which the author tells how Madame Verdurin is so accustomed to taking figures of speech literally that one day she splits her sides laughing and Doctor Cottard has to stitch her up. André was familiar with this page, like many others, but every time he read it, tears of merriment came into his eyes. Feeling positively light-hearted now, he got ready to enjoy what followed: the verses about Cottard's stupidity and Odette's sulky beauty, rather as an opera-goer looks forward to an aria he knows by heart, when a sudden noise made him jump. Practically behind his back, though in fact it was out in the street, something had just roared into action, a noisy machine which was making the whole world shake. He rushed to the window to see what it was. It was a pneumatic drill, one of those shuddering tools on which North African slaves bore down with all their weight, to break up the concrete of a pavement or the asphalt of a roadway. They were demolishing the house across the way, to put up a ten-storey apartment building in its place. André had forgotten this work, which had begun a week before and was due to last at least a year. Twelve months of that infernal din! And what would the apartment building be like? Hideous probably. The house they were demolishing was admittedly in a ramshackle condition, but its very decrepitude had a certain charm. They could have confined themselves to restoring it ... A ten-storey apartment-block in that historic street where there was not a single building more than three stories high! What the devil was the local planning committee doing? Surely the town council ought not to have allowed that sort of desecration? André gave a sigh, pressing his forehead against the windowpane. They would never have any peace or silence again. The world was turning into a nightmare. There was only one thing to do, and that was to go up to his bedroom which overlooked the garden.

He went upstairs, took off his shoes, and stretched out on his bed. He opened his book again but was unable to start reading straight away, for the thought had occurred to him that he was behaving like an unspeakable bourgeois, making such a fuss because of a little noise near his house. What if, instead of living in this historic building in the Rue de Navailles, he were one of the workers putting up the apartment building across the street? What if, instead of being merely disturbed by the noise of the pneumatic drill, he were the North African slave working the drill? Was he left-wing or wasn't he? Yes, in feelings and opinions he was left-wing, and he voted left in every election. Well, in that case he ought to put up calmly with the minor inconveniences involved in the industrial development of the world. He ought to compare his life as a privileged person with the lives of the exploited masses. Feeling a little calmer, he went back to his book, but before he had read more than a few lines, he pricked up his ears. Yes, it was that damned transistor again. He realised what had happened. At first Suzy had been listening to the transistor in her own room which was exactly above the library. After her father had spoken to her, she had simply moved into her sister's room. White with rage, André shot out on to the landing and threw open the door of Catherine's room. Surprised by this dramatic entrance, the two girls gaped at each other. Neither of them had the presence of mind to switch off the radio. André took three strides, slapped Suzy hard with the back of his hand, snatched the transistor out of her hands, went over to the window and hurled it against the garden wall. In the same second as the noise of the object shattering came a sound half-way between the miaowing of a cat and the wailing of a baby, amplified four or five times: this was Suzy crying.

André went out, slamming the door behind him. He returned to his room and dropped on his bed again, exhausted, his heart pounding wildly.

It was now out of the question for him to go on resting or reading. He put on his slippers and went down to the library again. Upstairs Suzy was howling like a damned soul.

God, I shouldn't have slapped her like that. I behaved like a brute. That slap was hard enough to fell an ox. I only hope I haven't damaged something in her head, burst her eardrum or something like that. I don't seem able to control myself any more; I ought to go and see a doctor.

He heard Claire going upstairs and Suzy's wails getting louder. 'Daddy hit me. He's broken my transistor.' Claire started talking, but he could not make out what she was saying, just a soothing murmur. Suzy's sobs gradually died down. Claire came downstairs again. A scene was obviously imminent.

She came into the library, looking very calm.

'You shouldn't have slapped her,' she said.

'No, of course I shouldn't have slapped her! But dammit all, it's impossible to have a moment's peace in this house any more, what with the din out there in the street and music in here all day long. Another six months of this and I'll have a nervous breakdown.'

'Patience has never been your strong point.'

'I'd have to have the patience of Job to put up with this!'

'All the same, a scene like that . . . . Catherine was terrified.'

'She had no need to be.'

'Try and patch things up. You ought to talk nicely to Suzy. She's in despair. She thinks you hate her.'

'She told you that?'

'Yes.'

He put his hand to his forehead.

'But what have I done, for heaven's sake, for my children to think I hate them? Why, I spoil them like nothing on earth. All right, tell her to come down and I'll try to patch things up.'

Suzy did not come down straight away. She was probably refusing out of dignity, or else to exploit the situation. Finally she appeared, a gawky figure with a puffy, tear-stained face. She stood stiffly in front of her father, hanging her head. He took her hand and pulled her on to his lap.

'I'm sorry, Suzy.' (The girl's mouth twisted and a sob came out.) 'No, no, don't start crying again! Calm down. I shouldn't have slapped you, that was a terrible thing to do. I'm sorry I did it. I'm very tired, I need a rest; so that all that music going on all day . . . You understand, don't you?' (She nodded.) 'I love my little Suzy, and I'm terribly sorry I've upset her. Give Daddy a kiss to show him you forgive him.' (She threw her arms round her father's neck and gave him a wet kiss on his cheek. She certainly wasn't vindictive.) 'You aren't angry with me any more?' (She shook her head.) 'Naturally I'm going to make good the damage. When you break something, you've got to make good the damage, if you've been properly brought up.' (The good-natured tone told Suzy he was joking, and she promptly responded with a convulsive little laugh. She found it easy to pass from tears to laughter.) 'How much did it cost, that marvel of modern technology? ... Six thousand francs? You're ruining me.'

The next day Suzy had a new transistor, even more up-to-date than the previous one. In the sphere of gadgetry progress was made every day.

' "*The Pyrenean*. Estate Agents." What do you think of that?'

'It's a bit peculiar – one name in the singular, and underneath, two words in the plural. "Estate Agency" would be more logical. Besides, "*The Pyrenean*" sounds like an insurance company. Why don't we put: "Lagarde and Costedoat, Estate Agents"? My name and yours. You're entitled to put your name, seeing that you've got a licence.'

She repeated the formula under her breath to see how it sounded.

'Look,' he said. 'Imagine I'm a woman: which name would inspire most confidence in me – "*The Pyrenean*" or "Lagarde and Costedoat"?'

'The second,' she decided. 'You always prefer to think you're dealing with people rather than a firm.'

'It would be even better if we could put: "Registered capital, so much." But seeing that we haven't a sou ...'

'We *have* got a sou – lots of sous, in fact. Maybe we haven't got our first ten million. But in a year or two we shall have.'

She wrote in capitals on a sheet of paper: LAGARDE AND COSTEDOAT, ESTATE AGENTS.' He was sitting on the window-sill above a huge square shaded by plane trees. The room he was facing was bare and empty except for the desk and two chairs; it smelt of shavings and new paint. The carpet still had to be laid and the lighting installed.

'A brass plate,' she said. 'That will look good. It'll be the first time I'll see my name engraved in metal.'

'One day it'll be carved in stone, but you won't be there to see it.'

'You're being cheerful, I must say!'

'Underneath they'll carve the words: "The first business-woman in Sault." '

A business-woman. She already looked the part, with her short hair, gently waved in the latest style, her well-cut suit, and her beautifully cared-for face and hands. It was strange how trim her little figure had become.

'All you're missing is a pair of horned-rimmed spectacles.'

'To make me look even uglier?'

'You don't look ugly. You look much better than you did eight years ago. You looked like a little weasel then.'

'Thanks.'

'It's a pretty little thing, a weasel is. What I mean is that you looked like a country girl, as if you'd come straight from the fields. Now you don't any more. You look like a real lady.'

He glanced at his own reflection in the window.

'I look a lot better too. I carry myself better. You've nagged at me so often – "Hold yourself upright!" and "Raise your head!" – that you've managed to straighten me out.'

With a swift glance she gauged the results of her training.

'Not bad,' she said. 'I'm quite pleased with my handiwork.'

And she returned to the subject which really interested her: their work, the office. There was no point in dwelling on past achievements.

'I'm going to put the filing-cabinet in that corner, the two armchairs here. And I'd like a big map of the region, to pin up behind the desk. The sort of map they have at an army headquarters.'

'With little flags you'll stick in wherever there's something for sale?'

'Naturally. You're so bright.'

'You already see yourself gradually conquering the whole department.'

'Why not? We're the only estate agents in the town, so far. The first. Oh, don't worry, in two or three years, if we make a go of it, we'll have lots of competition. But we'll also have two or three years' start. We shan't be afraid of anybody any more.'

'Are the little flags for your personal satisfaction? Like a general marking up his victories?'

'Not a bit of it. I don't need to *see* things like that. Everything's carefully classified in here.' (She tapped her forehead.) 'The little flags are for the customers. "You're looking for something fifteen miles from Sault? I can offer you this..." And I point to a flag on the map. It's quick and precise, and there's no need for explanations. I'll have photos as well, of course. All the estate agents have photos. But they haven't thought of a map yet.'

'Anybody would think you'd been to a course in business management.'

'I don't need any courses. Common sense is enough for me.'

The hardest thing for them, she went on, would be to get the town to accept them. They were lower-class people and the town knew their humble origins. This promotion to the business world was bound to annoy people, and arouse sarcasm and distrust. If only he could at least have managed to get on with people. But he didn't know how to mix with others. She didn't blame him for it: he was made that way. Besides, the trouble was not beyond repair. All that was needed was a little patience and skill. The hardest thing would be to succeed with the first few deals. After that, success would breed success, and everyone kow-towed to prosperity. Even this hard town, with its Huguenot tradition, would kow-tow to it. If they managed to acquire an appearance of prosperity, they would be sought after first by the *nouveaux riches*, the *parvenus*. They were the people they had to cultivate first of all because they formed a ready-made clientele for country houses. For the second house, the 'little place in the country', was becoming all the rage, even here. The older middle-class families had had a country house for years. Those who were going to buy one now were the tradesmen, the shopkeepers. A car was no longer a status symbol. A country house was.

'Where did you learn all that?'

He asked the question with feigned interest. In fact he was only half listening to Lucie. They had already discussed all these things many times. 'She's repeating herself,' he thought. 'But then, we probably all repeat ourselves... Life is a routine.' Lucie was really obsessed by her business. It seemed as if nothing else mattered to her.

'You'd know it all too if you paid attention to what's happening. I scent what's in the air, that's all. Why do you think I read so many papers and magazines? It isn't to keep up with politics, or the arts, or princesses' love affairs. I don't give a damn about all that. It's to find out what's fashionable, what's the latest thing, what gets people excited. Because that's where the money is.'

While she was talking he half turned his back on her to look out of the window. Beneath him was the main square of the town, gilded by the October sunshine. This square was one of the town's chief attractions, on account of its size, its imposing lay-out, and the plane-trees which edged it with greenery; but now it had been turned into a car-park. It was the first time he had had the opportunity to look down on the square and take it all in at a single glance; he was struck by the transformation. Those rows of steel rectangles, gleaming in the sunshine, were ugly and depressing, but they also proclaimed the prosperity of the town, the increase in incomes, economic expansion, the circulation of money. Lucie was right: many of the citizens of Sault now spent freely,

123

without counting the cost; savings were a thing of the past. If a house in the country was the latest fashion, then it was a house in the country for them.

A car had just drawn up outside the post-office. The driver was wearing a white sports shirt and white shorts. He looked about forty. A teenaged boy sitting beside him opened the door and got out to post a letter. He looked like the driver; he too was wearing a sports shirt, shorts and tennis shoes. Both of them looked fit and suntanned; they exhaled prosperity and well-being. As he got back into the car, the boy picked up a racket lying on the seat and laid it across his knees. A passer-by had stopped to talk to the driver. It was impossible to make out what they were saying, but as he walked away, the man called out: 'Goodbye, old chap. Goodbye, Pierrot.' The car moved away. Jean followed it with his eyes.

'Are you listening to me?' Lucie said behind him.

He turned round.

'What's the matter?' she asked. 'What did you see?'

'Nothing. You were saying?'

'I was saying that people will go there one day because there'll be no room anywhere else.'

'They'll go where?'

'You weren't listening to me! To the Landes. The Atlantic coast of the Landes. Because the Riviera will be overcrowded. The first arrivals will tell their friends: "It was wonderful, we were all alone on five miles of sand." Then everyone else will come along because nowadays people are a lot of sheep. And the Atlantis Club is going to start something there too, I can feel it in my bones. Well, we've got to beat them to it.'

'You know what you remind me of? One of La Fontaine's fables.'

'The Milkmaid and the Pail of Milk – I know, you've already told me. But two years ago, did you imagine we'd have this office one day?'

He admitted that he had not, but pointed out that the office was not open for business yet.

'And you make me laugh, with your precious Atlantic coast. There aren't any roads, there's no water, it's just a marshy waste that you can't even get to. Nobody can live there except the shepherds, and they have a hard time of it! They don't so much live there as die there.'

'Roads can be built. Marshes can be drained.'

'And are *you* going to do all that?'

'Oh, you're so stupid! No, you aren't stupid, but you don't use your brains for certain things. Suppose an enterprising council decides to redevelop a small town or a village.'

'Are you crazy? That would cost a few hundred million.'

'Well, what of it? I don't know why the idea of a few hundred million still impresses you. Really, there are times when you talk like a peasant. After all, what's a hundred million nowadays?'

'All right, all right, Mrs Rockefeller.'

He contradicted her partly out of spite, because it humiliated him to see her so sure of herself, so superior to him in her understanding of business and finance. He also contradicted her on principle, for her self-assurance frightened him. Although he knew she was cautious, cunning and extremely thrifty, he was afraid that her spirit of enterprise might run away with her. On the other hand the perpetual effervescence of that fertile brain of hers had a stimulating effect on him. She infected you after a while with her methodical, unbounded ambition. What an amazing creature she was, this little weasel who juggled with millions of francs as if they were really hers! When you thought what sort of a childhood she had had... There obviously must be some truth in the theory that poverty and hardship toughened a strong personality instead of breaking it.

That evening, at home, she returned to the subject of the Landes coast.

'Next Sunday let's go for a drive out there. We'll take our lunch with us. A day in the open air will do Michel good.'

'Don't start looking for excuses. Just say you want to go prospecting. You know, you don't talk about anything but money nowadays.'

'I like money,' she said simply.

'But why?' he asked. Did she like money for the pleasures it could provide, or out of a need for security, or because, after being poor for so many years, she had endowed it with an absolute value? She shook her head.

'You've asked me that before. I don't know. I've never thought about it. I like money, that's all.'

'It's worth thinking about. It's interesting to know your own character. Look – would you rather handle gold or bank-notes?'

'Gold, certainly. Gold is something real and solid. Paper can be devalued. Gold can't.'

'But would you get a sort of physical pleasure from counting pieces of gold, letting them run through your fingers, plunging your hands into a casket full of them?'

'Just try me! I can see myself doing it!'

'Your eyes are already shining at the idea. Let's have a few more questions. I'm giving you a test.'

'Fire away.'

She liked playing games. Despite her obsession with business, she was always ready for a game, just like a child.

'Between a taxi and a bus, which would you choose?'

'The taxi if it saves time and it's important to save time to bring off a deal.'

'How would you invest your capital?'

'That's easy: a quarter in government bonds, a quarter in mortgage loans, a quarter in shares, and a quarter in foreign exchange stock. You've got to divide your risks.'

'What are the things you find it easiest to economise on?'

'You know the answer to that one: luxury goods.'

'But you buy your clothes from the most expensive dress-maker in Bordeaux.'

'To save money. "I'm not rich enough to wear cheap clothes." That's a proverb I learnt in England. Besides, you've got to dress well if you're in business. If you look shabby you feel inferior, you talk badly, and you don't impress the customer. Oh, I know *you* don't care how you look. If I weren't here you'd be dressed like a tramp.'

'Nobody ever taught me to look smart. And nobody . . .'

He left the sentence unfinished.

'Go on, go on: and nobody . . . ?'

'Until you came along, nobody cared whether I looked smart or not. Right. If you make a fortune one day, what will you do?'

'I'll try to double it.'

'Good. But will you buy any pictures, jewellery, antique furniture?'

'Of course I will. All those things are good investments. I read in *Match* the other day that a hotel-keeper in the suburbs of Paris had a coll . . .'

'You're incorrigible! Would you buy something that doesn't represent an investment, something without any value?'

'How could I? Everything you buy has some value, how-ever small it may be.'

'All right. Would you go round the world, travelling first-class and staying only at the best hotels?'

'Yes. But not by myself – I'd get bored. With Michel and you. Chiefly for Michel's sake, for his education. To give him self-confidence and get him used to mixing with people.'

'You're a wonderful mother.'

'I know. And a model wife. You've already told me so.'

'And how do you imagine him later on? What ambitions have you got for him?'

'Oh, that depends. His teacher says he's doing very well. We'll see. We've got plenty of time to think about that.'

'The years go by faster than you think. One fine day he'll be twenty, and we'll be taken by surprise.'

'Well, what do *you* want him to be? How do *you* imagine him?'

'I want him to be . . . I want him to be everything I haven't been,' he went on in a slightly husky voice. 'If he doesn't change too much as he grows up, he'll probably be very good-looking. I want him to be . . . a prince. I want him to be successful. I want people to like him and envy him. That's natural, isn't it?' he said looking at her defiantly.

'Yes, that's natural. I'd like him to be all that too.'

Jean stood up. He lightly touched a few objects on a table: three pieces of stone in a bowl, a lump of quartz, and a long tortoise-shell paper-knife. This was a common habit with him. Whenever he was thinking of something at all serious or unusual, he felt a need to touch the things around him. She watched him from the depths of her armchair.

'There are some people,' he said thoughtfully, 'who have . . . a kind of grace. Just like that. They're born with it. Because of their looks, perhaps. Let's say they're good-looking. Well, they're given everything else as well. It's very odd. And to cap it all, they're usually decent sorts. They're "nice people". And why shouldn't they be? So if there were a heaven they'd go straight there, when they died, after having already had a heaven on earth. I think that's a bit unfair, don't you? Having everything, and then being beautiful souls into the bargain.'

'Fair or unfair, it's always been like that. But I don't see the connection with . . .'

'With Michel? Why, it's obvious,' he said casually. 'I want him to be one of the princes of this world.'

'Now you mustn't expect too much of the boy!'

'I want him to be able to walk through the town, all in white, with a racket under his arm, without feeling embarrassed or ill-at-ease. As if the world were his oyster.

And I want people to admire him as he goes past. A young aristocrat.'

'I don't know whether people will admire him,' she said. 'But as for walking through the town with a racket under his arm, that's easy. We'll buy him a racket and pay for him to have tennis lessons.'

Jean gazed at her for a long time, with a little sarcastic gleam in the depths of his eyes.

'How simple everything is for you,' he murmured, and he gave her a gentle smile.

André's secretary told him that Monsieur Thill was asking to see him. The woman had an infuriating habit. It was only very rarely that she looked you straight in the eyes; her gaze usually lingered on another part of your person, so insistently that you felt like asking her: 'Is my tie crooked?' or 'Have I got some egg yolk at the corner of my mouth?' And in fact, if you examined yourself at the place she had been inspecting, you were sure to notice a tiny detail – a stain on your shirt, a button hanging by a thread, a hair protruding from a nostril, or rings under the eyes – which betrayed either personal neglect or physical deterioration. Mademoiselle Adèle had an unerring eye for such details. 'What's the matter, Adèle? Do you think my shirt cuffs look too frayed?' – 'Oh, Monsieur!' – 'Tell me what's shocked you. Come on, now, speak up!' – 'I couldn't possibly permit myself to . . .' – 'I'm giving you permission. Well, do you think these cuffs are too frayed?' Adèle would look the picture of disapproval. At last she would say: 'It isn't my province, Monsieur.' The implication being: 'You've got a wife who ought to attend to things like that.'

André had frequently had words with her about that inquisitorial gaze of hers. Without achieving anything, of course. And this had gone on for twenty years. Apart from this touch of sadism, Mademoiselle Adèle was a model secretary. Knowing that she was indispensable, she had taken it upon herself to torment her employer with a cruel gaze which, day by day, gauged the ravages of time or the worsening of a domestic situation made obvious to everyone by his shabby appearance. During these inspections she assumed such a supercilious air that sometimes André could not help laughing. His attitude towards her was a mixture of amusement and irritation. For a few weeks now, he had had no need to ask her what she was examining: he knew the answer. Every morning, as she came into the office, Mademoiselle Adèle darted a more or less furtive glance at André's forehead and temples. The meaning of this glance was obvious: 'You're losing your hair pretty fast.' To take his revenge, André had begun staring at her upper lip, which was darkened by a moustache. This sly duel of their gazes occupied several minutes of their time every day. André was extremely distressed by the progress his baldness was making. Soon his scalp, laid bare except for a few wisps of hair, would look like the revolting pink skin of a pig. The loss of his hair gave him a feeling of embarrassment akin to shame, as if going bald were a deliberate, criminal act. He would have to submit helplessly to other dilapidations too: the falling-in of his cheeks and the formation of puffy folds of flesh on either side of his nose and mouth, giving him a surly expression. Why did you have to go through all this? Why did Nature amuse herself making you ugly before killing you?

His client, Monsieur Thill, gave him a long, involved account of his troubles. Like most people, he did not know how to express himself clearly and briefly. What is more, he failed to state the precise purpose of his visit; but André guessed what it was about, almost from the start of the conversation. Monsieur Thill complained that his father had sold his house for a life interest, thus depriving his two children (Monsieur Thill had a sister) of a large part of their inheritance. This could have been said in a few words. Instead, Monsieur Thill turned it into a family saga full of digressions about rivalries between brothers-in-law, quarrels over money, and the old man's private life – a widower, he was under the thumb of his housekeeper. It so happened that it was to a cousin of this woman that he had sold his house. The deal might never have gone through without the intervention of a certain Madame Lagarde, who called herself an estate agent, and who, in collusion with the housekeeper, had succeeded in tricking the old man. Monsieur Thill exploded in indignation against this 'scheming woman', who, of course, had received a commission. She and her husband were 'a couple of pirates', upstarts who had made enough money, probably by fraud, to open an agency. If there were any justice in this world, they ought to be 'slung into jail'. They had taken advantage of a feeble-minded old man ... Flushed with anger, Monsieur Thill ran his finger between his neck and his celluloid collar. André told him that Madame Lagarde's profession was perfectly legitimate and that he ought to be careful not to call her and her husband crooks: if he didn't watch his tongue, he risked being sued for slander. Monsieur Thill then asked in a roundabout way whether, in spite of everything, they couldn't do something, appeal against the sale.

'There's no law against your father selling what belongs to him. He can dispose of his property as he wishes. You can't make a will disinheriting your children, but you can do what you like during your lifetime. If you want to ruin yourself, for example, the law can't prevent you, except in certain cases.'

Monsieur Thill pounced on this qualification.

'Exactly!' he exclaimed. 'There are certain cases in which the law can prevent somebody from ruining himself. When that somebody is no longer of sound mind.'

'Has your father shown obvious signs of mental derangement?' André asked wearily.

He had been waiting for this from the start. This was not the first time a client had come and asked him whether they could have a close relation committed to an asylum.

'That's no easy matter, you know. Your father would have to be examined by a psychiatrist. You'd have to prove that somebody had taken advantage of his mental debility to extort a signature from him. All this would involve you in very long, expensive proceedings. Very complicated proceedings too. And unless your father is showing very obvious signs of senile dementia, you would probably lose. I don't advise you to get involved in anything like that.'

He thought about Monsieur Bonneteau's remark about his knowing family secrets of this sort: dreary and sordid, and completely devoid of any diabolical glamour. How on earth did novelists manage to find their material in all this mediocrity? Yet Balzac would have built a huge novel on Monsieur Thill's story. I've never regarded these things as specially interesting. That must mean I haven't much imagination. My job has never been anything to me but a means of earning a living. It doesn't bore me, but it doesn't interest me either. During the first few years he had tried to convince himself that a lawyer's work was 'very amusing' and that the Legal Code was a mine of picturesque detail. This deliberate illusion had not stood the test of routine. No, his work wasn't very amusing. It was as dusty as the files with the green labels in which only Mademoiselle Adèle knew where to find what they were looking for. And it was as unprepossessing as the jargon used by lawyers. Since it was no longer possible to keep up the pose of the lawyer who loves his profession, he had adopted another one: the cultured, enlightened, provincial bourgeois, the sybarite who would not leave his eighteenth-century house for anything on earth, because 'here a man can read and relax, and besides, I like having a garden and spacious rooms'. That was all true, in fact, but the social upheaval which had taken place since the war had shattered the provinces and damaged the concept of the bourgeois, at least in the eyes of the bourgeoisie itself. What did the word 'provincial' mean in the early sixties, when everybody travelled, wore the same fashions, read the same books (the

132

two or three world best-sellers), saw the same shows, and watched the same television news? Whether they lived in Paris, Kansas City, Poitiers or Sault, men were now just citizens of the twentieth century. It was useless, therefore, to pose as a provincial bourgeois, since the species no longer existed. But as he grew older, André became aware that he felt less and less desire to pose as anything at all. Posing as this or that was probably a youthful habit, a trick to prevent you from suffering too much from your deficiencies, and to enable you to put up with yourself. In later life a man didn't feel so uncomfortable in his own wretched skin.

But why was he thinking about all this? What was the association of ideas? It was Monsieur Thill, André's inability to find material for a novel in such sordid matters, and his abortive attempts to make anything of his profession except what it was. God, what a ferment of ideas! He ought to start keeping his diary again.

He thought about the Lagarde couple, at whom the kindly Monsieur Thill had hurled his anathema. Jean Lagarde's wife had opened an estate agency three or four years before. She had come to see André to ask his advice on a few points of law. A strange woman, not pretty, but not devoid of charm. A crafty creature, endowed with almost animal cunning, yet with an innocent, rather likeable side to her character. Why had she married poor Lagarde? She deserved better. You could never tell what brought certain people together. The fact remained that in a very short time the agency had become so prosperous that the woman had taken on two employees and her husband had left his bank to work with her. They now lived in an expensive flat in a modern apartment building on the outskirts of the town. Nobody was surprised any more at this sort of success story: it was just one of many examples of the economic and social upheaval that was going on. At the same time other people were going down in the world who only yesterday, in other words before the war, had been cocks of the walk. Bruno Marcillac was an example. He could have kept his place, for he had quite a considerable fortune. In his case the disruptive element was laziness, or rather a sort of easy-going nonchalance, the absence of any spirit of enterprise, an inability to adapt himself to his times, and lastly – in fairness to Bruno – a disinterested attitude towards money. He ought to have invested in prosperous businesses. He preferred the easier course of nibbling away his capital like a cake, year after year. Nobody, nowadays, could afford to live on his capital like that, and the Marcillacs' finances were in a poor way. I must phone him; I haven't seen anything of him for a long time. The last time they had met, they had had something of a quarrel about Algeria. Bruno, who was a supporter of French Algeria, had accused de Gaulle of having betrayed the Army, and had praised the heroism of the paratroopers. André had been rash enough to mention the allegations of torture; they had exchanged a few sharp words and had parted coldly. What a stupid business! Right, I'll phone him, using the Lagardes as a pretext. Bruno might be well advised to ask their advice, since he was trying to sell the estate he owned in the Landes, Le Bosc. But he would probably jib at the idea. 'Sell Le Bosc to Lagarde! Not likely!' That would be his first reaction. The humiliation of financial setbacks was felt more keenly between people who had known each other a long time. But the wisest thing was to master these feelings of misplaced pride.

Mademoiselle Adèle came in with the mail.

'Are you inspecting my scalp, Adèle?' he said jovially. 'Yes, I'm afraid I'm losing my hair. You women are luckier than we are,' and he fixed his gaze insistently and precisely on his secretary's upper lip, 'You don't lose the noblest ornament of your sex.'

Cheered up by these reprisals, he left his office at midday in good spirits. On his way home, however, he felt a twinge of remorse. Poor Adèle. Devotion personified. Twenty years in his service. And she couldn't have a very gay life. I shouldn't have been so unkind to her. All right – tomorrow I'll be very nice to her, and on New Year's Day I'll give her a big present. Feeling easier in his mind, he went into his record shop to pick up his latest order. Yes, the records had arrived. He would listen to them that evening, especially the *Structures for two pianos*, for he was curious about this new music, which was so difficult to appreciate but so intriguing. He had a fascinating evening in front of him. Modern life was not all horror and boredom after all . . .

Bruno too, that evening, felt that life was not unpleasant. It was the annual fête in his district. As a prominent local figure, he was a member of the organising committee and was therefore expected to put in an appearance at the various functions in the programme. Nothing, in fact, could have pleased him more, for a variety of reasons, which he would have strenuously denied if they had been put to him, but which his friends and relations knew very well. First, he enjoyed his own popularity. He had been very popular early in life, on account of his athletic prowess and his personal charm. He gloried in public approval, like a tribune acclaimed by the people in the forum. Secondly he loved a fête, simply because it was a gay, innocent saturnalia in which everybody seemed happy under the fairy-lights, in a smell of acetylene, nougat, white wine and sweat. For him this smell was linked with his youth, and the memory of nights when he had danced without stopping until the orchestra packed up, and after that to the music of a record-player; then, with a group of friends and those girls who were willing to stay up all night, he used to go and eat bacon omelette at a café in the cattle market; he would return home at dawn, still hot and excited and scattering pink and blue confetti on the floor when he undressed. Finally – the last but not the least of his reasons – the dance provided Bruno with an opportunity to hold a few pretty girls in his arms. He would not have sacrificed this particular pleasure for anything in the world. Juliette was well aware of this. As it was a harmless pleasure she turned a blind eye to it. The marked attention her husband paid to certain girls – and he always chose to dance with those who were known for their vulgarity and loose morals – had become the talk of the town. She knew this too, and it hurt her a little, but she pretended to laugh at it.

Every year, what Juliette called 'the scenario' was enacted according to an unchanging pattern. During the days immediately preceding the fête, Bruno made a great show of irritation and weariness: 'What a nuisance they are with their committee. It's taking too much of my time. Just imagine – three meetings this week. This is the last year you'll find me organising their precious fête. They won't get me on their committee again.' At dinner on the first evening of the fête he played the part of the tired man who doesn't want to go out but has to answer the call of duty: 'They wouldn't understand if I didn't put in an appearance at the dance. But on the stroke of eleven I'm coming home to bed.' – 'Don't be a hypocrite – we've heard all that before. At midnight you'll still be dancing dreamy tangos.' – 'They don't play tangos any more. It's all rock and roll now.' – 'Well, what difference does that make? You've asked your sons to teach you how to dance it.' – 'What a life! I'm always being bawled out in this house.' And he winked across the table at Pierre and Nicolas. Juliette refused to go with him: 'I'd be out of place there, and I know you prefer to go by yourself, so don't bother to pretend.' – 'You hear that, boys? Your mother's so unfair.' And he went off with them, just as excited as they were, and probably more so.

The 'best people' never showed up at the fête, except for those who, like Bruno, helped to organise it out of community spirit. In any case, those adults who came to the fête attended simply as spectators, sitting at the bars or on the grassy mound overlooking the square where the dancing took place. The fête was intended for the young people and it was they who

136

had drawn up the programme. Whether they came from bourgeois or working-class homes, or from the surrounding countryside, there was hardly anything to distinguish them, at least in appearance: they all had the same well-fed, well-built bodies, and the same clothes; anyone might have thought they also had the same heads, for they all conformed to a certain international type (a short nose, thick lips, hair falling obliquely across the forehead) popularised by advertisements, illustrated magazines and the cinema, and almost identical for both sexes.

Some of the boys over twenty, elders already on the verge of decrepitude, wore beards in homage to Fidel Castro, and also to display their political affiliations. However, they mixed peacefully enough with half a dozen cleanshaven paratroopers in uniform, on leave from Algeria: the fête was also a truce. The paratroopers, their red ribbons hanging down over the backs of necks bronzed by the desert sun, moved about among the crowd with the strong, supple slowness of wild beasts, chary of gestures in the midst of all the southern exuberance, their eyes expressionless and their jaws set. They had not come to the fête for a little innocent amusement, but to pick up girls: they were soldiers, and entitled to a soldier's pleasures.

After greeting a few friends, Bruno started looking around for a girl he could invite to dance. In the crowd he noticed his son Pierre with Suzy Comarieu: those two were inseparable – were they going to marry? At home he had been told that Suzy was in love with Pierre, and when the boy was teased about it, he just laughed. Suzy was a very pretty girl; she was said to be rather slow-witted, but Bruno hadn't seen any evidence of that. He would have been delighted to have Suzy as a daughter-in-law, because she seemed to be 'a nice girl' and she was the daughter of old friends of his: a good home, a good education, money and beauty – what more could anybody want?

He also spotted Nicolas and little Catherine, not among

the dancers but in the front row of spectators. Two more inseparables. It certainly looked as if the Marcillac and Comarieu families were destined to merge together. But here the feelings involved were probably of a different type, more like those between brother and sister. Since the unforgettable incident of Nicolas's 'sex education' Bruno had never dared to make the slightest reference, in his younger son's presence, to a subject which seemed to upset him so much. Their relationship continued to be marked by a somewhat uneasy reserve. Bruno watched Nicolas grow in wisdom and grace, and everybody complimented him on having such a clever, gifted son, obviously destined for a brilliant future. After hearing eulogies of that sort, Bruno would go home bursting with pride and tell Nicolas: 'I've had some more compliments about you. I'm delighted, you know. We're both proud of you.' He tried to put all the affection he could muster into his voice, so that the boy should understand, beyond all possible doubt, that he was loved. On the other hand, afraid of falling into a sentimentality which he thought would only aggravate the sensitivity of his son's defenceless nature, he spoke with a certain gruffness and even called Nicolas 'old man'; above all he took care not to kiss him, and the boy, quivering with nervous joy, smiled at his kind, awe-inspiring father, without knowing what to say in reply.

Bruno went over to Nicolas and Catherine.

'Well, aren't you dancing, you young people? Give me a kiss, Catherine. You know, you look prettier every day. Oh, if only I were thirty years younger! What are you waiting for, son?'

And he pushed them towards the crowd of dancers. They obeyed willingly enough.

Dancing, Bruno noticed, had lost a great deal of its sexual character. As practised by these young people, it consisted only of patterns in which the two partners remained some distance from each other and did the required steps without ever touching. This new style filled Bruno with perplexed pity. The poor kids! What pleasure could they get from dancing this sort of speeded-up minuet? In my time we enjoyed holding a pretty little thing in our arms. For these boys and girls, the whole pleasure of dancing seemed to lie in following the rhythm; but perhaps there was also an element of self-satisfaction in it, a mixture of coquetry and exhibitionism, as if they were dancing, not for their partner, but for the spectators. Any love they felt was chiefly for themselves.

A loudspeaker announced that they were now going to hear a few songs from a famous 'star of the record world'. A curtain was drawn to one side and a youth dressed in leather leapt on to the platform, apparently galvanised into activity by an electric guitar slung across his stomach. A high-voltage current seemed in fact to be passing through him, for his whole body was shaken by violent muscular spasms, especially in the pelvic region, which kept being thrust forward in convulsive jerks. The torture he was undergoing drew inarticulate cries of excruciating pain from the victim – unless of course they were cries of pleasure, as the accelerated movement of his hips seemed to suggest. Suddenly the star uttered a final howl and stretched out his arms and legs in an attitude of crucifixion: this must have been the orgasm.

The crowd of young people screamed their approval. Recovering rapidly from his emotion, the star bowed, then grasped the microphone. In a whisper which pretended to be confidential, although the loudspeakers amplified it to cosmic dimensions, he informed the fascinated world that he was now going to sing his favourite song, the one which had made him popular with the boys and girls . . . he was going to sing . . . a little dramatic pause, then in a loud voice: *Serenade for You*. The boys and girls roared, and the singer kicked away the cord of the microphone, which might have got in his way. He already possessed the professional *savoir-faire* of an old trouper, an unshakeable expertise. You could tell that he could easily have broken off to smoke a cigarette and tell a funny story. This little marvel of youthful innocence, who, in default of a Rolls-Royce (for it was said that that firm was particular about its customers) drove around in a Cadillac, launched into a song full of all the bitter nostalgia of working-class Paris. In uncanny unison the boys and girls joined hands and nodded their heads in time to the music.

Untouched as yet by the grace of adolescence, some little boys between eight and twelve years old started imitating the singer's syncopated lament and roaring with laughter. Inspired by the demon of blasphemy, these infant vandals dipped into cloth bags hanging round their necks and threw handfuls of confetti over the ecstatic worshippers.

When the number was over and the singer had vanished, the bandleader announced that he was going to play the latest dance, which had just been imported from America and was all the rage at Saint-Tropez: the twist. The boys and girls roared again, but few of them ventured to try this dance which they had not yet had time to master. In both rhythm and movement it was very different from their rock'n' roll. Soon, inside the circle of spectators, the young people formed a smaller circle, in the centre of which a solitary couple were dancing. Bruno elbowed his way to the front. What he saw rooted him to the spot.

The man looked about twenty and had pronounced Spanish features; but it was the girl that had taken Bruno's breath away. He knew her by sight, or rather he remembered having seen her often in the streets of Sault: a very fetching little girl, full of promise. The years had gone by, and the promise had been kept beyond all expectations. The girl seemed only a little younger than her partner and might have belonged to the same race. She was wearing a very tight-fitting dress which revealed as much of her body as the laws of public decency allowed. Bruno could not take his eyes off this surface of matt skin – face, shoulders, arms and legs – which seemed to invite kisses and bites.

'What a smasher, eh?' said somebody near him.

He turned his head.

'Good Lord, it's you!' he said, and he held out his hand to Jean Lagarde, whom he had failed to notice standing beside him, he had been so intent on watching the girl. 'How are things with you? I say, that girl's got what it takes, eh? I've never seen anything like it. And that dance!'

Jean Lagarde seemed not in the least surprised at Bruno speaking to him as if they had seen each other only the previous day, when in fact the last time they had met had been seven or eight years before.

'I know her quite well, little Maryse,' he said. 'She's a neighbour of mine.'

'A neighbour of yours! You mean to say you can sleep at night with that volcano beside you?'

'There was a wall between us, after all.'

'Oh, so she isn't your neighbour any more?'

'No, I've moved ... Not because of her, I might add.'

'And what does she do in life?'

'I think she's a salesgirl in the supermarket.'

'In the supermarket? I'm going shopping there tomorrow. Though seeing that you know her, perhaps you can introduce me?'

'Nothing could be easier.'

'Wait for me here,' said Bruno.

He ran across to the band and motioned to the bandleader, who bent down to listen to him. Bruno slipped a banknote into his hand and came back to where Jean was waiting.

'I've asked him to play a tango,' he said. 'I don't think much of these modern dances where you stand a yard away from each other.'

When the twist came to an end there was a little clapping, though not much – for at Sault-en-Labourd, even in the golden age of youth, people were reluctant to applaud a couple of pariahs, even when they were as young and attractive as this Spaniard and this supermarket salesgirl. Maryse acknowledged the clapping with a nod and a smile.

She was about to slip away and lose herself in the crowd when Jean Lagarde took her arm, whispered a few words in her ear and brought her over to Bruno. Nicolas was watching the scene from a distance. As the band played the first bars of the tango, Nicolas saw his father bow to the girl and open his arms to invite her to dance. He turned on his heel and promptly walked away, with Catherine beside him.

A tango! The young people smiled at these cadences of another age. A few of them, however, tried to dance it, but with caricatural exaggerations. Bruno and the girl, now welded together, now separate, danced to and fro, spun around, stopped suddenly in a dramatic freezing of a pose, and then moved off again with the suppleness of creepers intertwining, breaking free and swaying in the breeze. Bruno had rediscovered the grace and fire of his youth. The feel of this young body in his arms was intoxicating. He took pleasure in attempting complicated figures, and the girl followed his lead perfectly, matching every step and every pose. After the tango the band played some more pre-war dances: paso dobles, slow foxtrots, and the waltz of a prehistoric era. Bruno remained with the same companion. He was talking to her in an undertone, and from his expression it was easy to guess the nature of his conversation.

As the couple were passing a group of young spectators, one of them nudged his neighbour and said in a sneering voice: 'Just look at old Marcillac.' Bruno came to a momentary halt which was not provided for in the succession of steps. He looked at the smiling young faces, trying to discover the insolent puppy who had just taken his name in vain.

Old Marcillac. The boy had called him *old* Marcillac, and of course little Maryse had heard.

The waltz was no sooner over than Bruno walked straight over to the culprit.

'Did you want to speak to me?'

'Me? No. Why?'

'I thought I heard you say my name?'

'Yes. What of it?'

The answer was a slap in the face. It was one slap too many. In less than a minute, as if summoned by the mysterious underwater currents which bring squalls hurrying across oceans, a score of young men, including the paratroopers Bruno admired so much, had gathered around their comrade and were shouting at the old man who had insulted him.

Bruno had been in a good many scraps in his youth, and had always acquitted himself well. The demon of the fight asked for nothing better than an opportunity to reappear. But this time everything had changed. Bruno was guilty of two irreparable wrongs: he was over forty years old, and he had committed a crime of lese-majeste by slapping a young man's face.

A few punches were exchanged, in the midst of a lot of insults. Pierre had come running up to help his father. He started valiantly hitting out right and left. It was then that Bruno caught sight of Nicolas's face, some distance away, white with panic. He sobered up at once and intervened between Pierre and his adversaries.

'Never mind,' he said. 'Let it drop. I'm going home.'

And he walked away, followed by jeers from the young men.

Pierre caught up with him and the two of them walked along in silence, side by side, cold with shame.

Bruno decided to tell Pierre to go back to the dance but he changed his mind, realising that his son would refuse, both out of loyalty to him and fear of the reception he would be given by the other young men ('Your father behaved like an idiot' and so on). Dear, loyal Pierrot...How could he thank him for being there? Bruno hunted about for something to say, but couldn't think of anything. So he told himself: Tomorrow I'll give him some money. I know he needs another twenty thousand francs to buy himself a motorbike.

He had lost face in front of his sons. He had behaved in an odious, ridiculous way.

The magic had gone out of everything – the fête, the dance, little Maryse, everything.

He had to put up with a scolding from Juliette the next day. To begin with, she reproached him with insulting her in public by dancing with a girl who was already notorious for her loose morals.

'Why, every year at the fête I dance with the first girl who comes along: I don't pick her out. As a member of the committee, they expect me to . . .'

'They don't expect you to make a fool of yourself in front of your sons!'

She went on in this vein for some time. Bruno was dumb-founded. He felt guilty and put up only a feeble defence. Juliette brought out a string of grievances which went far beyond the previous night's escapade: he was incapable of managing his affairs properly; he was throwing away his children's money; he was lazy and irresponsible; he drank too much and ate too much.

'And I know that you've started gambling too. Don't deny it – people have seen you playing roulette at Pau Casino. You go out with a bunch of drunken layabouts. You've got no dignity. Look at yourself,' she shouted, pointing to the dressing-table mirror. 'Look at what you've become.'

She was wringing her hands and looked both angry and heartbroken; he had never seen her like that before. He wondered what he could have done to deserve such an out-burst. It was true that he gambled a little. A man in his position could allow himself an occasional flutter. And he had sometimes been known to have a glass too many. Was that so very serious? When she left the bedroom he remained in a daze for a few moments. Then he opened a drawer and took out a photograph album. The photographs inside showed him at eighteen, the captain of his school football team; then at twenty-one, a soldier; then at twenty-six, dressed as a footballer again; then came the photographs of his wedding-day, and another one showing him as a young father playing with Pierre. He sat down at the dressing-table and his incredulous gaze travelled from the photographs to the face of the man in the mirror. He felt as if he were seeing himself for the first time, because he was seeing himself through the picture Juliette had just drawn of him. Or perhaps the truth was that he had never been willing to look at himself properly until today. 'God!' he muttered under his breath, in a terrified voice. He touched his cheeks and eyes; he pinched his double chin between thumb and forefinger; he drew a fingernail lightly across the wrinkles on his forehead. 'God!' he repeated miserably.

Something horrible had entered his life, which until then had been so quiet and sunny. He felt as if he had been lightly brushed by a great black wing.

'I can see I'm in the way,' André said gaily. 'When the three women of the family are gathered together in the kitchen ...'

Suzy burst out laughing and Catherine planted a kiss on her father's cheek. Even Claire was smiling. The atmosphere, as Suzy would have said, was relaxed. It was Catherine's sixteenth birthday, and they were getting ready for the party that evening. Ever since the morning the women of the house had had a conspiratorial air as they went from the kitchen to the dining-room, where the buffet was going to be installed, and then to the garden, where the guests would be able to dance if it was fine. André noticed once again, as he had done countless times before, how well Claire and the two girls got on, and how much they seemed to enjoy preparing some-thing together. They really did belong to an entirely different species. I'm the hornet. The man of the house is always the hornet, absolutely useless outside his role as begetter and breadwinner. Several times, irritated by their laughter and impatient to discover the reason for it, he had gone into the kitchen, his newspaper in his hand and his spectacles on the end of his nose, to ask: 'Well, what's so funny? What are you laughing at?' But they parried his questions, and he decided that they were probably laughing at trivial women's jokes which he wouldn't have thought funny. 'They're like three schoolgirls,' he muttered, and he went back to the library, pleased that they were in a good mood, but a little jealous at being shut out of their circle. He felt dull and stupid, like the traditional husband in those American comic strips, whose wife and daughters always led him by the nose; but in spite of everything his chief feeling was one of contentment, because he liked everybody around him to be happy: it was more pleasant for him that way, and also Catherine's happiness was a guarantee of his own. He reflected, and again it was not the first time, that one day Catherine would be taken away from them, that a stranger would come and take her by the hand and make off with her. One day he and Claire would be left alone in this house, face to face.

At dinner the girls refused to eat anything but a lettuce leaf – Catherine out of nerves and anxiety, because she was afraid that the evening might not be a success, and Suzy because of her diet, for she was determined to keep her figure slim and supple for the twist. The same concern for her appearance had led her to cover her face with a 'beauty mask', a dark paste which made her look like an opera-singer made up to play the part of Aïda. She had found instructions for this mud-pack in one of her magazines. Suzy was a great reader of women's magazines and especially the love stories they published. She was mad about articles devoted to the private lives of queens, princesses, actresses, singers and film stars. Royalty went to her head. André had tried everything to wean her away from this sort of reading-matter – 'Suzy, darling, only very naïve people read that stuff' – but he had only succeeded in annoying her. She spent hours poring over these periodicals, drunk with the taste of blue blood. She went so far as to read the marriage advertisements, without even laughing at them. Such simple-mindedness ought to have put boys off, but on the contrary, Suzy was very popular with them. Admittedly she was very pretty, but other girls who were just as pretty attracted less attention. André eventually realised that what the boys liked about his elder daughter was that she was a chattering parrot endlessly repeating what she had heard on the radio or read in her magazines. She juggled with the catch-phrases of the day like a trained seal with its rubber balls, and for some reason this appealed to them. They loved her because she was so commonplace: her conformity reassured them: 'Suzy? She's the tops,' they said, giving the thumbs-up sign. 'She's right on the ball, really with-it.'

Catherine, with her wit and elegance, rather frightened them and kept them at a distance. She only attracted boys who were as clever as she was, and they formed a tiny minority. Her best friend, Nicolas Marcillac, could scarcely be described as cast in an ordinary mould.

Dinner was rushed through in a hurry. Only André ate anything, and he didn't count: indeed, he could consider himself lucky that they had laid the table for him, instead of banishing him to his room with a cold meal on a tray. They must love him after all! With the help of their maid, the three women agreed on small changes to the preparations they had been making all afternoon, the final touches that make a masterpiece. The atmosphere became quite feverish as they went to check the fairy lights in the trees in the garden, and to make sure that the drawing-room cleared of its furniture would be suitable as a ballroom. And was the buffet impressive enough? André went into ecstasies over it. Impressive enough? It was a still-life by an old master, a banquet by Veronese or Tiepolo. What good taste they had shown in the combination of salad and shellfish, what acid wit in the juxtaposition of the salmon roe canapés with the pistachio *petits fours*! A born perfectionist, and always in the lead with the latest gadgets, Suzy suggested spraying all the rooms with an aerosol deodorant. The others dissuaded her. The house had its own pleasant smell of wax, lavender and cleanliness, and that was enough. Besides, the idea of sandwiches that smelt of Pur-Odor...

At eight o'clock the two girls went upstairs to dress, and from the first floor came the sound of running feet between the bedrooms and the bathroom, and the roar of cascading water. Left to themselves, Claire and André took refuge in the kitchen, the only room left vacant on the ground floor. Sitting with their hands on their knees, tired and smiling, they exchanged a few remarks about the girls' excitement and the strange ways of the younger generation. It was the first time they had agreed to hand over the house for the whole night to their daughters' guests. For Suzy's eighteenth birthday they had simply held a big supper-party, but every year young people demanded more and more. 'In our day we would never have dreamt of... I suppose they're going to dance until dawn? Well that's the way things are, and we'll have to grin and bear it.'

The girls came downstairs, looking delightful in their short dresses, their faces made up in the latest fashion, with huge eyes, dark lashes and pale lips. They came straight out of a New Wave film. The effect was very striking but a little sad: André would have preferred his daughters to look more natural, more like the 'young ladies' of the past.

As the time for the guests to arrive drew nearer, Catherine seemed to grow more and more nervous. She gave her mother an imploring look, and Claire turned to André.

'We're going to leave them now,' she said.

'Aren't we staying to welcome all these young people?'

'No, we aren't staying,' Claire said very firmly. 'You don't think they need our help, do you?'

'Oh, well... I only thought... Still, it doesn't matter. Well, good night, darlings. Have a good time.'

He gave them a kiss on the cheek and realised straight away that he shouldn't have done, for now they would have to touch up their make-up. (These fathers who kiss you when you've spent hours doing your face ... It's really infuriating – they ought to know better ...) Claire, for her part, had thoughtfully refrained from kissing them.

'But are we supposed to hide away,' he asked as they were going up to their bedrooms, 'as if we had some shameful disease?'

'What else do you want to do?'

'But it's only nine o'clock. I don't want to go to sleep yet.'

'Read a book. I'm going to read until midnight.'

'With all the din they're going to make?'

'Then take the car and go for a drive.'

'Yes, I think that's the best thing to do.'

'But when you get back, try to keep out of sight. Come in through the garden door.'

'Because I suppose father and mother are an indecent sight when the kids have a party?'

'It looks that way,' Claire said with a smile. 'Poor André, you look so indignant!'

'You must admit that I've good reason to look indignant. Hiding from our children and their guests, just because we happen to be their parents! I had never realised so clearly before that you and I had entered a special biological category. It's all very odd.'

He went downstairs again and hid behind a clump of bushes in the garden, an observation post from which he could see the lighted drawing-room with its French windows wide open. He was burning with curiosity to see how his daughters would greet their guests, and how those guests would behave. Lurking among the bushes in the gathering twilight, like a villain in some melodrama, he felt a twinge of sadness at the memory of some of his own birthdays, which had not been such grand affairs; but he made an effort to shake off this mood of self-pity. However, the sadness

149

remained; it obviously had another cause, which he quickly discovered. This minute incision, like a cut made by a scalpel in living flesh, was Catherine's anxiety at the idea that her father might be there to greet the guests, and the glance she had given her mother imploring her to take the situation in hand. It suddenly hurt to think about that, though it was foolish of him to let it bother him. Very foolish. He mustn't be so sensitive, so vulnerable. Catherine's uneasiness, her anxiety that her father should be somewhere else (her father, who, that very morning, had given her a beautiful gold bracelet for her birthday) didn't mean that she had stopped loving him, that she didn't care about him any more. No. It just meant that there was a time for everything, and the right to complete independ . . . But here came the first guests, providing a welcome diversion. He was being ridiculous: another few minutes and he might have started crying. What a fool he would have looked! . . .

Now he could see the first guests. Pierrot and Nicolas of course, the little neighbours, the childhood friends. They kissed both girls in turn, in accordance with a ritual which André had already observed in the street, and which seemed to be a recent innovation among the young: the boy gave a kiss on the right cheek, then on the left, then again on the right. Three kisses. Why three? He couldn't imagine. Boys and girls kissed a great deal nowadays, even when they were just friends. In his day a boy would have felt silly or effeminate greeting his friends like that, but the young people of today had no inhibitions. The affection they no longer gave their parents, or indeed any other adults, they now lavished on their fellows . . .

Pierre and Nicolas looked like fashion-plates, they were so smartly dressed. Nicolas in particular looked like a little prince. They gave Catherine their presents – books and records – and Nicolas had also brought her a bunch of flowers. Exclamations from Catherine, and more kisses. Suzy gave shrieks of joy at the sight of one record, and ran to put it on the record-player. It was a tune from a film called *Never on a Sunday*. A Greek dance they were beginning to play a lot on the radio, and which threatened to become the big hit of the next few months. André reflected that her sixteenth birthday would always be associated in Catherine's memory with that tune, which was intended to be cheerful but was really rather sad, like folk music all over the world. He tried to remember which tune had been in fashion when he had been sixteen. It must have been a song by Tino Rossi or Charles Trenet – something about a boat drifting along, a girl passenger who had disappeared, and a bargee who smelt of tar ...

Now the two girls and the two boys had started dancing the Greek dance: they stood in line, arms stretched out horizontally, and swayed on the spot to the rhythm of the music, bending their knees and shooting one foot out in front. Where had they learnt that dance? They had seen it on the screen, and that had been enough. How graceful they were – like virgins and ephebes who had stepped down from the pediment of a Greek temple.

When we were their age, we were poor awkward kids. And our girl friends were no better. They were fat and lumpish. They only got their waistlines back after the age of twenty-two. How do young people manage to be so graceful nowadays, so much at ease in their bodies? Perhaps it comes from the present-day cult of youth: those who are worshipped become gods ...

More guests were arriving now and there was more kissing. He couldn't stay where he was. What would he say if they came into the garden and found him hiding in the bushes? And what would Catherine say? He thought of going for a walk, but it was turning cool and he was afraid of catching cold. He might as well go back to his room, put plugs in his ears, and try to read. Once again a wave of sadness swept over him. Not only was he shut out for ever from the fun which was going to fill the house with noise all night, but he felt as if he had never been invited to share in it. Yet he had been the same age as these boys and girls, and only yesterday. Yesterday! The thought struck him so sharply that he stopped short, a prey to the giddiness sometimes produced by the telescoping of past and present. His life had gone by like one of those terrifying documentaries which show a plant in the successive stages of its brief existence – a seed in the ground, a frail stem, a flower opening its corollas to the sun, losing its petals, withering, falling and rotting – while your heart has beaten only twenty times.

'So you want to buy Le Bosc?' said Bruno.

'We . . . It's really my wife,' said Jean. 'I don't know much about the business. It was she who asked me to come and see you.'

'How did you know it was for sale?'

'Everybody knows everything here.'

'It wasn't Comarieu who told you, was it? Because he's the only person I mentioned it to.'

'No, it wasn't him. Besides, I hardly ever see him.'

'Anyway, it doesn't matter. It's true that I want to sell the place, because it doesn't bring in any money. All the same, I'd like to know why your wife wants to buy it.'

'That's her job. She buys and sells.'

'She expects to sell Le Bosc to someone else?' Bruno asked with a tinge of doubt in his voice. 'And make a profit on the deal?'

'Probably.'

'But she won't be able to evict the tenants.'

'She's prepared to wait.'

'Surely that sort of operation means tying up a lot of capital?'

'In the property business, that's inevitable.'

'But I thought estate agents weren't allowed to buy property, but only to act as intermediaries.'

'Oh, these things can be arranged, by using men of straw.'
Bruno clicked his tongue against his teeth.

'Isn't that risky? I don't like the idea of anything illegal.'

'It isn't illegal. You've got nothing to worry about. Lucie knows the law backwards, and she's got a very good lawyer.'

'Comarieu?'

'No, another one.'

After a pause Bruno said pensively:

'If I'd ever thought that you would come to me one day and offer to buy Le Bosc ...'

Jean smiled thinly.

'The most unexpected things happen.'

Since he had come into the room he had not taken his eyes off Bruno, subjecting him to such an intense scrutiny that Bruno ended up by feeling embarrassed and was tempted to ask: 'Why are you looking at me like that?' But he didn't dare. The fellow had always been a little odd, he thought, even at school. You never knew quite how to deal with him. Nor did you ever know how he felt about you: did he like you or loathe you? His feelings probably changed from one minute to the next. Bruno had never stopped to think about Lagarde. If anybody had asked him about the fellow, he would have replied: 'Oh, Jean Lagarde is a queer cuss,' implying that he was an unusual, unpredictable character, but not despicable or even unpleasant. Lagarde had asked to see him, and Bruno had made an appointment with him – why not, after all? – but in his office in town, and not at home in the Rue de Navailles.

He was vaguely aware that Jean Lagarde's wife had opened an estate agency, but he had not expected such a new business to have enough capital already to buy a property like Le Bosc. He was glad to be able to get rid of Le Bosc at last, but his pleasure was not unmixed. As he said that very day to his wife:

'I'm pleased of course, but I don't like having to sell to Lagarde.'

'Why not? What difference is there between him and anybody else?'

'Oh, it isn't the same. With anybody else I wouldn't feel humiliated.'

Without thinking, he had just expressed a feeling which had previously remained vague and undefined. He had no sooner uttered the word than he reddened.

'What nonsense!' Juliette said gaily. 'Why on earth should you feel humiliated? You have a lot of farms and now and then you sell one. I can't see what's humiliating about that.'

'It wouldn't be with anybody else; but Lagarde . . . You see, he knew me at a time when we wouldn't have thought of selling any of our property. In those days he looked up at us. This morning he looked me straight in the eye – he was on an equal footing with me. Indeed, I was the one who felt awkward. I'm not a proud man, or at least I don't think I am. I don't give a damn about privilege and class and all that nonsense. But, you understand, this business with Jean Lagarde makes me feel uncomfortable – the idea that *we* should be selling something to *him* . . .'

When Jean for his part informed his wife that Bruno had agreed to sell Le Bosc and that the deal was practically 'in the bag', Lucie gave vent to one of her rather childish displays of enthusiasm, laughing and dancing around the room.

'We've done it!' she said, her eyes shining with excitement. 'In a year or two we'll have our hands on forty million francs.'

'You're crazy. You'll never sell Le Bosc for more than . . .'

'Yes, I will! I haven't told you everything. I was keeping it as a surprise.'

She explained that her agent in Paris, an old friend of hers with whom she had recently renewed contact, had told her that a holiday club, Atlantis (I've already spoken to you about it, but you never listen to what I say), was planning to build some camps on the Landes coast. This plan was part of a vast investment project. Her friend had business dealings with the Atlantis Club, which was how she had heard about their plans.

'And Le Bosc is in the area where they are going to start prospecting. From the point of view of accessibility it's the best part of the coast. There are two reasonable roads leading to the sea, and the main road isn't far away.'

'You say you'll be able to sell Le Bosc for forty million francs?'

'In two or three years, yes.'

'But . . . But what if the Marcillacs hear about the deal?'

'They'll hear about it all right!' she said cheerfully. 'So what?'

Jean's expression changed.

'You're absolutely shameless,' he said sternly. 'You want to make a huge profit at their expense.'

'Why not? I'm not doing anything wrong. It's all a matter of being quick off the mark. I'm better informed than they are, that's all.'

'All the same, I don't like it. What are they going to say when they find out they could have sold Le Bosc for seven or eight times the price you've paid for it?'

'They'll be livid,' she said, laughing more than ever.

'And what will they think of us?'

'I don't care!'

'Well, I do!' he cried.

Lucie froze. He seemed to be taking the thing to heart. What was the matter with him? She looked at him in bewilderment.

'If you imagine,' he went on, 'that they'll have anything to do with us, after a dirty trick like that . . .'

'Well, we'll get along without them,' she said lightly.

'I thought,' he said, his voice trembling with anger, 'that you wanted us to come out of our shell. I thought you wanted us to mix with the right sort of people – for our sake, and to help our son. It was you who told me so, one day. You reproached me with being unsociable, with cutting myself off from my friends.'

'If that's what you're getting so excited about,' she said quietly, 'it isn't worth it. Calm down. It isn't mixing with the right people that will turn us into bourgeois – it's money. When we've made our pile, the right people will come along by themselves.'

'That's where you're wrong. Things aren't as easy as that in Sault. Money isn't everything here. There are several businessmen in the town who are rolling in money, but they don't mix with the Marcillacs or the Comarieus, and they never will. They can buy country houses and drive Bentleys, but that won't do them any good from the social point of view.'

'All right, but in any case there's no harm done. I can't remember what I said to you, but things have changed since then, for us and everybody else. As I told you just now, I can manage perfectly well without "mixing with the right people". Anyhow, what are the Marcillacs and the Comarieus today? Nothing. Hardly anybody knows who they are. They don't count any more. Nowadays the people who matter are the people in business and trade, or else...'

'But I'm not interested in people like that. I've no desire whatever to mix with them. They'd bore me stiff. Whereas the Marcillacs, the Comarieus, the Andurains are different... But you, you're obsessed with the idea of money, you can see nothing in life but money. There are other things you'll never be able to appreciate.'

She had imagined she was going to give him a pleasant surprise: his reaction infuriated her, and they had a lively quarrel, their first since they had married. Lucie revealed a talent for argument, and indeed for mockery, which he had never suspected. To begin with, she expressed sarcastic astonishment at this sudden enthusiasm for social life, in a man who had endured his isolation quite happily for years. So he had waited until he was nearly fifty before suddenly wanting to cut a figure in society drawing-rooms? And of all the drawing-rooms in the world, those of the Rue de Navailles, in Sault-en-Labourd ...

White with fury, Jean retorted that she was quite right: with a wife like her, he certainly shouldn't have entertained ambitions of that sort; one could scarcely imagine Lucie in a drawing-room, *even* those of the Rue de Navailles. She countered with a quotation from La Fontaine – 'Let us not force our talent, for we would do nothing gracefully' – and added that she would indeed take care never to set foot in one of those temples of social distinction *with him*, for fear of bursting out laughing at the sight of him fawning on the ladies ... He stormed out, slamming the door behind him, and remained in a huff for three days.

Lucie was a patient woman. During those three days she talked and behaved exactly as if nothing had happened, and as if she had not noticed that he was sulking. He finally calmed down, but persisted in his opinion that selling Le Bosc to a third party at an enormous profit would be unfair to the Marcillacs. Lucie let him talk and said nothing. She knew from experience that time was on her side, but she was disconcerted by a disinterestedness which went so far as to reject as unimportant a profit of some twenty million francs. That just wasn't normal. With scruples on the one hand and twenty million francs on the other, it seemed that her husband's moral scales would tip in favour of scruples. What passion could be strong enough to justify such a renunciation, such a sacrifice? She found it hard to believe that it was a mere longing for respectability, a sudden desire to cut a figure in society, to be 'somebody' in Sault-en-Labourd, to mix with the two or three families who were regarded as the local élite. It might be that, but not just that. For weeks she mulled over the problem. Though she was not a suspicious woman by nature – except in business matters – she could not help thinking up theories. Jean's anger, and his unwillingness to burn his bridges with the Marcillacs, were clues which had to be examined and interpreted. Could he be in love with Madame Marcillac, that beautiful woman who was still very attractive? If that was the case, it was a schoolboy's silent adoration, for as far as she knew, her husband had never had occasion to go near the woman. No, that was a ridiculous theory!

During the next few weeks, Jean met Bruno two or three times in town. They now had a reason to greet each other and make a little conversation. In the course of these brief exchanges Bruno was friendly but on the defensive, which was unusual with him. It was as if Jean Lagarde's company caused him a certain embarrassment; and every time Jean made a discreet advance – 'We ought to see more of each other . . . I'd like you to meet my wife' – he avoided the issue in a noisy, demonstrative fashion: 'Why, of course! Whenever you like! Not just now, because my wife and I are very busy, but a little later, we'd be delighted!' Then, without giving Jean time to suggest a date, he would dash away, followed by a pair of eyes which had suddenly turned hard, and which a smiling, twisted mouth did nothing to soften.

The formalities of the sale of Le Bosc brought them together again, at the notary's. It was a complicated business, and when it was all over, Lucie took her Paris agent to one side, presumably to pay her commission. Meanwhile Bruno and Jean were taking leave of each other.

'You really must come to our place one evening, you and your wife,' said Jean.

Buying an estate which belonged to Bruno must have made him bolder; but selling an estate to people like the Lagardes had had the opposite effect on Bruno. For one thing, it had sapped for the first time a self-assurance which was anything but arrogant – indeed, it was tinged with kindness and cordiality – but which was self-assurance for all that, implanted in him by the knowledge that he was a rich man; and it had also exacerbated the feeling of humiliation he had already mentioned to his wife. Consequently Jean's invitation, which he had 'seen coming' for weeks, but which Jean had previously lacked the courage to put into words, threw him into something of a panic; and this utterly unselfconscious man, who had never felt embarrassed with anyone because it had never occurred to him that anyone might judge him, suddenly lost his nerve and started stammering. Pouncing on the first excuse that came into his mind, he said that he would have loved to accept, but that his wife was unwell and had to keep to a strict diet, which for the time being prevented them from dining out. And after shaking hands with Jean, as if to cut short any attempt at insistence, he walked away quickly, feeling quite distraught.

As he got into his car he muttered to himself: 'Asking us to dinner, Juliette and me!... The very idea!... He's a regular nuisance, that fellow! I've got nothing in common with the Lagardes.' Since this was not entirely untrue, it allowed him to believe that the source of his embarrassment was simply antipathy for the other man. But if Jean had invited him to dinner ten years before, at a time when the social relationship between them had been clearly defined, in other words precisely assessable in terms of money and social position, he would have accepted readily enough, out of kindness and a fear of causing offence, considering that after all, an evening with Lagarde was not a catastrophe, but just a pill to be swallowed in the name of Christian charity. Today the relationship between them was no longer clearly defined: this Lagarde whose position on the social ladder was uncertain, but in any case closer to Bruno than before, this Lagarde who was suddenly sure of himself and treated you as an equal, was very disconcerting, in that he made you aware, by his self-confidence, how many rungs you for your part had probably descended.

After this meeting at the notary's Jean made no further reference at home to either the Marcillacs or his own hankerings for social advancement. It was as if he had left all that behind him; and when, about a year later, Lucie told him as a matter of course that she was shortly going to meet one of the directors of the club to which she intended to sell Le Bosc, he didn't turn a hair. Had he forgotten the scene which the announcement of that plan had provoked? Lucie doubted it. The assumption therefore was that his feelings towards the Marcillacs had changed, or that he had 'seen sense' – in other words, in comparison with the huge profit his wife was going to make, all other considerations had ceased to count, or now at last seemed to him as childish as Lucie had always thought them. Yes, that must be it: he had seen sense, he was growing up ...

For her part, she was too deeply absorbed in her work to give much thought to a question which seemed to have lost much of its importance, and indeed of its reality. She was discovering money like a marvel she had always dreamt of, and she handled it with a sense of fierce delight. This 'little slip of a woman', as they called her in Sault, showed a sort of genius for business. From dealing with men as tough as herself, and beating a few of them, she had gained an authority which even her husband no longer thought of challenging. She managed everything from her family life to her office, and she even found time to be a mother. Being a mother, as it happened, was the only troublesome part of Lucie's existence: her son Michel, a little boy of nine, was a difficult child, whose teachers were always complaining about him.

Although they were the very picture of prosperity, the Lagardes scarcely ever emerged from their social isolation. A few advances had been made to them by other couples of roughly the same age who also earned a great deal of money; but Jean and Lucie made no response to these advances, she out of lack of interest (her work monopolised her attention and she had no desire to go to dances or bridge parties), he out of an awareness of his shortcomings (he did not *know* how to dance or play bridge) and also out of pride, disdain and anticipated boredom.

From the early fifties a craze for enjoyment had swept the provinces, together with the fashion for whisky. It affected the young less than men and women between thirty and fifty, who were beginning to experience prosperity. The result was the formation, all over the country, of 'gangs' recruited from the liberal professions and, generally speaking, from the wealthier sections of the community. These gangs were made up of couples in which the women decided everything, American fashion. A constant round of dinners in town, visits to night clubs, drives in the country, bridge and canasta parties kept them in a state of perpetual agitation which was a middle-class version of the *dolce vita* myth – the film came at the right moment to give the thing a name. France in her turn became a stereotyped consumer society conditioned by a naïve, universal snobbishness. But Jean Lagarde had no inclination for the *dolce vita*. He helped his wife in the office, scoured the country for houses to buy, and took a rather absentminded interest in his son's education. In the space of a few months he seemed to have become moodier than ever.

'Television would be the last straw,' André said crossly. 'You can put that idea right out of your head, Suzy. As long as I'm alive there'll be no television set in this house. Don't you think there's enough noise in the world as it is?'

'Everybody's got the telly now,' said Suzy, 'except us. People think we're broke.'

'Listen to me, Suzy dear. First of all, you must take no notice of what people think and say. Worrying about other people's opinions is a great weakness. Secondly, you're wrong if you imagine that people think we're broke because we haven't got a television set. They think we're snobs, which is quite different. If anybody brings up the subject with you, all you've got to say is that your father refuses to have one because he considers that it's an amusement for half-wits. Throw that in their faces.'

'Oh, you!' cried Suzy, and she made a face which exasperated André because he thought it looked stupid. When Suzy said: 'Oh, you!' or 'Oh, him!' it meant that she was annoyed.

'It isn't an amusement for half-wits,' Catherine said angrily. 'There are some excellent progammes. The news magazines for instance. Television is an instrument of culture.'

André raised his eyes to heaven.

'Ah! The magic word! Culture! Well, if television is an instrument of culture there's nothing left for me to say, is there? Have you really fallen into that trap, Catherine? If you want culture, there are plenty of books in this house. Read the classics again, or rather, read them. There are art books. There are records. There's Larousse and even the Encyclopaedia Britannica.'

'Twentieth-century culture doesn't come just out of books,' said Catherine. 'It's audio-visual too.'

'Congratulations on the jargon! It promises well for the quality of that culture of yours.'

'Please don't start squabbling,' said Claire.

'What do you expect? They really make me tired! One of them wants television because everybody's got it, and the other because it's an instrument of culture. They talk like a couple of parrots.'

'Well, you talk like a reactionary,' said Catherine.

'None of your impudence, if you don't mind.'

'You say that television is just for half-wits. That's a typical opinion of a snob and a react . . .'

'Will you shut up?' André said in a toneless voice. 'And kindly leave the table. Go up to your room.'

The girl threw him a furious look, stood up, and walked out. They heard her run upstairs and a door slam. Claire shook her head.

'You shouldn't have done that,' she said. 'She's eighteen. You can't treat them like that nowadays.'

'Are we supposed to let them insult us?'

Suzy had stopped eating. Her face puckered up and a wailing sound came from her mouth.

'That's done it! Now the other one's starting to cry!'

Suzy stood up, sobbing, and left the room like her sister. André put down his knife and fork and pushed his plate away.

'That big gawk of a girl, crying like a baby for the slightest thing. And she's twenty years old! I give up.'

Claire said nothing. She sat with her hands folded on the edge of the table, her head bowed, her eyes fixed in an unseeing stare. Her features suddenly looked drawn, her expression indescribably weary. They sat like that in silence, face to face, without eating, without looking at each other. In the huge dining-room with the dark panelling an old clock measured out the time, drop by drop.

That afternoon was a slow torment for André. In the evening, at the dinner-table, the four members of the family said hardly a word. Dessert was no sooner over before Catherine asked her mother's permission to leave the room. Her sister followed her like a shadow.

At lunch the next day, the atmosphere was no better. The main dish was chicken. After the first mouthful André said coldly:

'Where did you buy this chicken?'

'From my usual woman. Why?'

'It tastes of fish. I imagine your usual woman is keeping up with the times. In the old days she fed her poultry on corn. Now she feeds it on fish-meal and hormones. She knows all about the latest methods. Why, she may even have television. This chicken is a product of audio-visual culture.'

He pushed his plate away.

'Is it as bad as all that?' asked Claire.

'It's absolutely foul. Ask Mariette to cook us an omelette, will you?'

'The eggs will taste of fish too,' Catherine said dryly.

'That's true. It all goes together. When the spring is poisoned ... Well, perhaps we could have some bread and cheese. Oh, I know that white bread hasn't got much food value and probably gives you cancer, but so far there's only a little plaster in the cheese.'

'That isn't funny,' said Catherine.

He threw her a glance of something like hatred but made no reply. Claire told the maid to bring the cheese and dessert. Ignoring his daughters, and speaking in the toneless voice he adopted when he was angry, André said to his wife:

'A client came to see me once to ask whether he could have his father committed to a lunatic asylum because the father had sold a house which would otherwise have formed part of his inheritance. Interesting, isn't it? An incident which shows that the classics are always up-to-date. *King Lear* ... *Old Goriot* ... I wonder whether filial ingratitude is a common theme of audio-visual culture?'

'André, please ...,' murmured Claire.

'I agree,' said Catherine. 'It's insufferable.'

'I'm not keeping you. You may leave the room.'

'If it weren't for Mother, I'd leave home.'

André spent another afternoon in hell, but a little further down, in a lower circle. He thought of committing suicide. Since the beginning of the world, millions of men must have killed themselves because their children had stopped loving them. He remembered an incident in his childhood: an old man's suicide by hanging. It had turned out that his daughter used to beat him and deprive him of food. On that occasion Madame Comarieu gave her son a lecture on 'poor parents who have ungrateful children', which André listened to somewhat resentfully, for he hated being spoken to as a possible culprit. Well, Madame Comarieu was right! A day came when fathers found themselves faced by hostile strangers:

their sons and daughters. When that day came, there was nothing left for them to do but die. Otherwise they could expect the worst; and André abandoned himself to increasingly gloomy thoughts, imagining a situation in which his two daughters, Regan and Goneril, tried to prove that he had gone out of his mind and ought to be put away. Like Monsieur Thill with his father. It would be better to get it over with straight away than to allow such horrors to be perpetrated. Death held no fears for him. He had often thought about it. Every day hundreds of people died of their own free will, calmly and deliberately, because life was hurting them too much. Among the ancients nothing was simpler or more fitting for a proud soul than to take poison or have a slave open the veins of your wrists; and the warm water in your bath took on a beautiful crimson hue, while you conversed peacefully with your friends and they tried to hold back their tears. This evening he would re-read Seneca and Suetonius...

At this point he realised that he was indulging in *delectatio morosa*, as in his childhood when he had tried to imagine his own funeral for the pleasure of picturing his little friends in tears. He felt slightly ashamed of himself and banished his daydreams of suicide; but that made him unhappier than before, for deceiving ourselves does at least lessen our misfortunes by sublimating them. With self-deception ruled out, there remained a man who was unhappy because his favourite child had spoken harshly to him twice; and soon his unhappiness became so acute that he found himself incapable of giving the slightest attention to his papers. He had to lock his office door for a few minutes to be able to cry in peace, then dry his eyes and regain his self-control. Whatever happened, he had to avoid letting sour Mademoiselle Adèle see the ugly, tear-stained face of an aged, unhappy, incurable child.

All the same, Catherine had told him she would leave home if it weren't for her mother! Could she really consider doing a thing like that? No, she was a quick-tempered girl; in a moment of anger she was capable of saying anything. Maybe at this very moment she was suffering from remorse. He promised himself that when he got back he would 'make the first move', but when he arrived home the expression on Catherine's face discouraged him.

At the dinner table the two girls talked only to their mother. They took care to avoid their father's eyes. André was overwhelmed in turn by feelings of anguish, anger, and humility. Claire tried to include him in the conversation, but he felt paralysed and answered only in monsyllables.

In the drawing-room the girls sat down on either side of their mother, on the settee furthest away from the armchair André occupied every evening. The three women started chatting in low voices. Dusk was falling quickly, for it was autumn. Claire stood up and went to draw the curtains across the windows. She had scarcely returned to her place on the settee before André jumped up, his eyes flashing, his face deathly pale. He walked over to one of the two windows and pulled hard at the cord which opened the curtains. The metallic sound they made as they moved along the rods sounded like a clap of thunder in the startled silence. Then André repeated the operation on the other window and went back to his armchair.

Claire made an effort to emerge from her stupefaction.

'What's got into you?' she said in a trembling voice, while the two girls looked at their father with frightened eyes.

'You draw those curtains every night without asking me whether I like it or not,' he said, stammering with rage. 'And you've done that for twenty years. I want those curtains left open.'

'You've waited all that time to . . .,' Catherine began.

'As for you two, go up to your rooms. Straight away. I can't stand the sight of you.'

'We'll go up to our rooms if Mother . . .'

'You heard what I said? Straight away.'

He walked towards them.

166

'Go upstairs, darlings,' whispered Claire.

The two girls left the room.

'André,' murmured Claire, 'you scare me. For the past two days you've been behaving like . . .'

She did not have time to finish. Without even looking at her, he walked out of the room, slamming the door behind him. Less than a minute later she heard the grating of the metal garage door, then the sound of a car starting up and driving away.

It was now pitch dark, and the beams of the headlights snatched out of the darkness the dizzy, double line of ghostly plane-trees.

I shall do nothing to cause an accident, to bring about the collision which would put an end in a second to this boredom and suffering. What if I went away, disappeared for good? Suppose I drove through Spain and crossed over to Africa? I can be in Morocco three days from now. I'll get a job, any job. Work on a plantation. Bury myself in the wilderness, seeing that nobody needs me any more, except as a bread-winner . . . Even then, Claire's income is big enough to allow her to spend the rest of her life in comfort, in her own house; and the girls are old enough to earn their living or find a husband.

He remembered that he was not carrying his passport on him. So there could be no final departure tonight.

I shan't kill myself and I shan't disappear. I'm trapped. I'll have to go on. To the bitter end. Even if I'm bored. Even if things disgust me and I disgust myself. Even if I'm an un-bearable burden on myself . . . Something happens, a tiny incident, your daughter answering you back, a hostile gaze resting on you – and it's like a shutter snapping. There you are, suddenly plunged into a world of darkness and horror, tied to a rack in a torture-chamber . . . There have been a lot of shutters snapping like that in the course of the last five or ten years, more and more of them . . . Or else you drag your-self along, harassed by a vague unhappiness, an unhappiness to which you can't even give a name, which has no name, which must simply be the pain of living. What am I doing in this world? Why am I here? What use am I? What God is making fun of me? Why do I get up in the morning and go to work? Why do I go on, instead of lying down on the ground and not moving and waiting for my eyes to mist over and my senses to go numb ... Did it just need a little girl to answer me back and look at me coldly? Did it just need that little domestic scene for the world to become a Medusa head, bestial, paralysing, incomprehensible?

He reached the shore and parked the car. There was obviously a storm blowing out in the gulf, whipping up the ocean into huge, roaring waves. He walked along the beach, fighting against the wind. He was wearing neither his over-coat nor his raincoat, and it was not long before he started shivering. He turned back the way he had come. The beach was deserted, but there was a winking neon sign slapping red and green lights across the sand. He pushed open the door and walked down a few steps. The bar was like a dimly lit aquarium. Two or three girls in very low-cut dresses, and half a dozen customers – those pale-faced ghosts, with yellow eyes and stinking breath, who spend their nights underground, in search of pleasure. André sat down, drank four whiskies one after another, and felt a little better. He put on an act, too, playing the part of a human wreck with no illusions left. How could you help putting on an act sometimes, in this world of sham and pretence? But through his slight drunkenness he heard Catherine's voice and saw her eyes, and they cut him to the quick: this wasn't part of the game.

He returned home about three in the morning.

A week later the reconciled family gathered together in the drawing-room to inaugurate a brand-new television set.

Suzy's favourite programmes: variety shows.

'President Kennedy has just announced to Congress that

Soviet rocket-bases have been installed in Cuba. The United Nations Security Council has been informed.'

'That's serious,' said Jean. 'It could mean war.'

They were sitting in front of their television set, he, his wife and their son Michel, each with a tray on his knees. They had got into the habit of having dinner like that, watching the telly.

'You think so?' Lucie said calmly. 'They've been on the verge of starting a war for years now. They wouldn't dare. They're too scared.'

'Yes, but all it needs is for one of those rockets to be fired ... Just imagine: Soviet rockets a few miles from the American coast!'

'Why have the Russians done that? It's terribly rash of them.'

'Russia has a mutual aid treaty with Cuba.'

They listened to the television commentator. He made no attempt to conceal the gravity of the crisis; but any effect that might have been produced by the news, whose urgency was underlined by pictures on the screen of the threatening rockets pointing westwards, was almost immediately dispelled by other news items and other pictures, of a less alarming nature: the fathers of the Church arriving for a meeting of Vatican II, and the trial of a Belgian woman who had killed her baby because it had been born without arms. Soon there would be pictures of sporting events, followed by a variety show with a parade of teenage idols; and everyone would forget the Cuban rockets and the threat of imminent war.

'I'd acquit her straight away,' said Jean. 'You can't let a monster go on living. Imagine how that child would have suffered.'

'Once you start that way, you won't know where to stop. The Nazis exterminated cripples, lunatics and incurables.'

'I don't see the connection. A cripple isn't necessarily a monster, like that child without arms.'

'Who's going to decide where to draw the line between a

cripple and a monster? You, perhaps? You either respect life or you don't. If you respect it, then it's sacred, and you've no right to kill anybody at all. It's quite simple.'

'Everything is simple for you. You have a genius for simplifying things ... Respect for life is a Christian prejudice. I say that it's better to kill a monster at birth than to let it live the life of a martyr. That's where true charity lies.'

'What do *you* think, Michel?' she asked the little boy.

But he didn't hear her, hypnotised as he was by the ceaseless torrent of pictures flowing across the screen. When the sports news was over, Jean switched off the set.

'Go up to your room now. I don't want you sitting in front of the telly every evening until midnight. You've got homework to do.'

The boy protested that it was too early yet. Lucie had to raise her voice and threaten to deprive him of television in the future. He threw an angry glance at her and left the room, but she remained unmoved.

'An hour from now I'll come and see if you've done your homework.'

She took the dinner trays to the kitchen and then came back to the living-room, Jean was reading a book. She said:

'You shouldn't say things like that in front of Michel.'

'Things like what?'

'That it would be a charitable action to kill a little monster and that respect for life was nonsense.'

'I didn't say that.'

'You said it was a prejudice. He doesn't know what the word means, but he understood all the same, from your tone of voice. Now he's going to think that you consider it perfectly normal to exterminate cripples.'

'What on earth are you talking about? He wasn't even listening.'

'He listens to everything. He remembers everything. It isn't intelligence he's short of. It's something else.'

She frowned, looking anxious and preoccupied.

170

'Well, what? What's he short of?'

'I don't know how to put it. There's no kindness in him.'

'But you said yourself, one day, that children were naturally evil, that they loved doing wrong.'

'When they're little, yes; but Michel is eleven, he's passed the age of reason . . . I've watched him with his schoolmates. He's always trying to hurt them, humiliate them. They're all afraid of him.'

'I'm glad to hear it. There was a Roman emperor who said: "I don't mind if they hate me, provided they fear me." That's an excellent precept.'

'You think so? Well, I don't. And look how Michel behaves with us. He isn't affectionate with us either.'

'Oh, he's just a kid. He'll grow out of it. Don't worry your head about him.'

A cat came up and rubbed her back against Jean's armchair. He bent down, picked her up and installed her in his lap. He started stroking her and fondling her, stood her up on her hind legs, and kissed her on the nose. The cat accepted these marks of homage with weary condescension. Her silky fur was the colour of champagne: she was a lady of good family.

'Here's somebody who can't complain she isn't loved,' said Jean. 'Except perhaps by the other she-cats of the neighbourhood who are jealous of her popularity. But a beauty like you can't help arousing jealousy, can you now? The princes and princesses of this world can never be sure whether people love them or hate them.'

Lucie listened to this chatter with more attention than it seemed to deserve. Jean met her gaze.

'To come back to Michel,' he said, 'I repeat: don't worry your head about him. If he's a bit tough with the other boys, so much the better. He'll be able to stand up for himself later on. A sensitive nature is a handicap in this modern world.'

'There's a difference between being sensitive and not loving anybody.'

'Oh, he loves us in his own way, I'm sure of that. As for loving anybody else, why should he? Just to suffer? It isn't worth it.'

'What a queer idea! You can have love without suffering.'

'No. Never. It's impossible.'

'Really? So I'm to assume that either you're unhappy or you don't love me?'

She said this with a gay, laughing air. Jean gave a bleak smile. His eyes lowered, he went on stroking the cat, which had curled up in his lap.

'It's different with us,' he said. 'It always has been, right from the start. You know that perfectly well. We've always been quite frank with each other on that point.'

'Yes, I know,' she said, and there was a hint of dryness in her voice. 'With us, it's a sort of pact . . .'

'Something like that, yes.'

'But as far as Michel is concerned, I'd rather he were more sensitive and affectionate. I'd like him to have friends.'

'Oh, no! Friendship is the worst thing there is. You wear yourself out, you give the best of yourself, and always to no purpose. No, no, I'd rather he kept all his energy for himself, to fight and win. You must never give anybody anything: it's casting pearls before swine.'

'You don't know what you're talking about,' she said lightly. 'Your ideas are completely screwy. I'm not going to argue with you any more.'

She picked up an account-book lying on a table and started checking her accounts. She never opened a book nowadays and barely skimmed the papers. They rarely went to see a play or a film, and they never entertained. 'The office is my whole life,' she used to say. The patient accumulation of a fortune was enough to keep her happy, she maintained, and she certainly gave every appearance of contentment. All that mattered was investing capital and bringing off deals. 'I'm working on a deal,' she would say, and her cunning little peasant face and gipsy eyes betrayed a childish excitement. Her pride too was childish, not in its object, which was perfectly legitimate, but in the way it was expressed. 'You know,' she would say to Jean, 'when you think of all I've done in a few years...' And with a sweeping gesture she would indicate their flat, which an interior decorator had furnished for them in a very modern style. It was a style which scared both of them a little, but as they said, 'it's the fashion nowadays, it's the latest thing. People like us don't know, we've never learnt, so we had to call in an interior decorator.' The result was these large rooms with the huge bay-windows offering the best possible view of the town, these thick wool carpets, these Tachist pictures ('Do you honestly like that stuff? Because I don't care for it much... Still, it's all the rage'), these bowls, this obelisk in veined marble – the fetish objects of success in the early sixties. 'You remember when we repainted the inside of your house? We thought we were settling down for life. And that was only twelve years ago. Just think of it – only twelve years. And here we are, in this lovely flat, one of the finest flats in town, a real film set... Well, this is all my own work!' And this well-fed, well-dressed man, with his neat appearance and manicured fingernails, who could be taken for a manufacturer or a leading civil servant, with his hair greying at the temples, his horn-rimmed spectacles, his signet-ring and his expensive after-shave lotion – he too was all her own work.

André looked up at the ceiling. From the first floor – from Suzy's bedroom, to be precise – a sound was coming which he knew all too well: it began as a thin wailing noise and gradually grew louder... What was the matter with her now? Her mother was obviously with her, comforting her, for the noise died down and finally stopped altogether. If she came down to dinner with her face all puffy from crying, it would make a wonderful impression! André gave a sigh and went back to his paper. About twenty minutes later

Claire came downstairs. Her features were drawn, and she had a vertical crease between her eyes which was a sure sign of worry.

'What's the matter with her? What's happened to her now?'

'Nothing. It's nothing,' she said, without looking at him. 'A little quarrel with her sister.'

André shrugged his shoulders.

'She really ought to be told, once for all, that she's too old to cry like that over nothing. Is she going to join us for dinner?'

'No. She asks if you'll excuse her. I'll have a tray taken up to her room.'

The Marcillacs were coming to dinner with their younger son Nicolas. Their elder son, Pierre, was doing his military service as a physical training instructor in West Africa. When his friends came in, André was struck by the change in Bruno's face and figure. Those falling cheeks, those blood-shot eyes, that pot belly...

He must stuff himself with food and drink like a fish. Juliette ought to keep an eye on him. He's aged a lot lately. I know I'm practically bald, but on the whole I'm wearing a lot better than he is. My figure is still in pretty good shape.

The presence of Nicolas, with his slim, neat figure, beside his father only heightened by contrast the impression of physical deterioration. André asked for news of the young soldier. It was excellent. It was now the rainy season in the Middle Congo, with a torrential downpour every day at a fixed time, and heat like a steam-bath, but Pierre was standing up well to these tropical conditions.

'Has he heard anything about what's going on in the Belgian Congo? After all, the two countries are only separated by the river.'

Yes, Pierre had been able to talk to some European refugees, and had heard terrible stories about street-fighting between United Nations troops and Katangese gendarmes: he had told them all about it in his last letter. They went on to discuss other parts of the world which were in the news: abscesses of contemporary violence which had recently burst. There was Saigon, with its corrupt government threatened with a popular revolt. There was Cuba too, although it seemed that the danger there had been averted, since Khrushchev had agreed to withdraw the rockets. They had been on the verge of war. Some whisky, Bruno? You like water with it, don't you, and no ice? On the verge of war. Some port for you, Juliette? What a time to live in! And what a world! Still, at least France wasn't the centre of world attention any more, now that Algeria was independent. De Gaulle had managed it at last. He had taken his time about it, but he had finally pulled it off. At Loretta's in Pau – she has some Chanel models. That's a beautiful dress. A little ice, Juliette? The Americans, who had condemned French colonialism so harshly, ought to face up to their own Negro problem. They had their Algeria too, but it was worse than ours, because it was on their own territory. But wasn't Suzy going to join them? No, she asked to be excused, she didn't feel well – nothing serious, but she thought it best to stay in her room. Mariner II is only a few days away from Mars. Mariner II? Oh, of course, the rocket. There are so many of them, you can't help getting them mixed up. Why the hell did they give the name of a rocket to the Vatican Council? And frankly, what has the Church got to do with birth control? Oh, I know it's a very important question and the future of the world depends on it. All the same, Juliette thought that cardinals discussing birth control . . . Well, I ask you. Still that's the modern world for you. Everything's upside down.

André served the drinks, a gay, attentive host. Inside him a small voice was groaning: What a bore! If only I could be on my own, with a good book . . . All this chatter. World politics. The Vatican Council. I don't give a damn for the Vatican Council. Nor do they. What's the use of an evening like this? Thirty years from now, we shall all be dead, buried and forgotten. A bit of rotten flesh in boxes six feet underground. Juliette, a biscuit? Those are very good. Yes, Vatican II is one of the most important events of the century. With Bandoeng.

However, for both couples the great event of the month, and indeed of the year, was not the Vatican Council, nor the Cuban crisis, nor the interplanetary flight of Mariner II, but the construction in the Rue de Navailles, opposite the Comarieu residence, of a concrete apartment building, six stories high. It was a real eyesore, and what was worse, the building had no sooner been sold than the ground floor had been let and fitted out as a bar, complete with fruit machines and juke-box. Neon lighting of course. The place had already become the favourite haunt of the young people of the neighbourhood. Yes, don't laugh, Catherine and Nicolas, we've seen you both glued to the juke-box, you rascals. The Rue de Navailles was completely ruined.

'Not to mention the fact,' said André, 'that we can't get to sleep any more till one in the morning, because of the juke-box. We're going to have to install double windows. In the meantime, I'm getting through a frightening amount of tranquillisers and sleeping-pills. I'm slowly poisoning myself day by day.'

Juliette said that they too were suffering from noise. One of their neighbours kept his television set on at full blast, with his windows wide open. Bruno had gone and asked him to turn down the volume. He had replied that it was his own house and he was entitled to do what he liked in it. He had only given way in the face of threats: 'If you go on bothering us with your telly,' Bruno had told him, 'I'll come and give you such a pasting you'll be in hospital for three weeks.'

That was how you had to do things nowadays; people only gave in to fear or the lure of money. They were cowards and boors. And neurotics into the bargain.

'The first time I had the feeling that I was going to have to defend myself against the modern world,' said André, 'was eight or nine years ago, after a holiday at Saint-Blaise. One evening, coming home from your house, I suddenly realised that the street had become a car-park. It was quite a shock. Since then it's got worse. A real Ionesco nightmare.'

But the worst thing of all was that chalk-coloured building across the street, with its neon sign and its noisy bar.

'And do you know,' said Juliette, 'who has got shares in that building?'

'Yes,' said Bruno. 'I nearly forgot to tell you. The building belongs to a company, and one of the shareholders – wait for it – is our good friend Jean Lagarde.'

Once again astonishment was expressed at the success of the Lagardes.

'But did I tell you about the trick they played on me?' Bruno went on.

They had bought Le Bosc from him, knowing that they were going to sell it for four or five times the price they had paid for it, to the holiday club Atlantis, which at that time had been getting ready to look over the area.

'Bruno was furious,' said Juliette. 'He wanted to go and have it out with the Lagardes. I told him: "What for? They haven't swindled us – they've simply taken advantage of our ignorance." '

'I'm surprised,' said André, 'that Lagarde should have risked offending you.'

'Why should he have had any scruples about that?'

'I thought he was disinterested. I thought money mattered less to him than, say, being on good terms with you. Because you enjoy tremendous prestige in his eyes.'

'Us? Prestige?' Juliette said in surprise.

'Yes. You don't realise it, but he's quite overawed by you. He'd be flattered to be on friendly terms with you.'

'With you too, then,' she said.

'No, not to the same extent,' said André, 'because he knew me when I was on much the same social level as he was. It may seem ridiculous, this business of social standing, and it *is* ridiculous, but for people like him I think it's more important than we imagine. And there's another thing: Lagarde liked you tremendously. He almost hero-worshipped you.'

'Get along with you!'

'I mean it. You were the only one who didn't notice.'

'Well, all I can say is that he must have changed a lot. Why, the other day I passed him in the street and he gave me a look that sent shivers down my spine. I think he's annoyed because Juliette and I have never had the courage to accept his invitations to dinner.'

'There, you see! What did I tell you?'

'We were at fault there, in any case,' said Juliette. 'After all, when you get to know them, they may be charming people.'

'Anyhow,' said Bruno, 'that's out of the question now, after the business of Le Bosc. I don't bear him a grudge – I'm not the sort of person to bear grudges – but as for having dinner with them ...'

Why doesn't she say anything? She ought not to leave me to do all the talking. André did not need to look at Claire to know that her thoughts were somewhere else, that she was finding it hard to follow the conversation and play her part as the hostess, a part she usually made a point of fulfilling conscientiously. It was a good thing the two young people were there. Although neither of them said very much, by their very presence Nicolas and Catherine made the atmosphere easier. André suddenly remembered a remark Catherine had made a few days before about Nicolas. When he had asked her teasingly whether she loved Nicolas like Suzy loved Pierre, and whether there was talk of marriage in the air, Catherine, looking a little flushed and uncomfortable, had replied: 'Oh, no! Poor Nicolas. I'm very fond of him, but that's all.' André had looked at the young man. Why had she called him 'poor' Nicolas? He was just as handsome as his father had been at his age, but in a very different, much more delicate way. He was extremely intelligent, even brilliant, so they said. There was nothing 'poor' about him. Catherine probably meant that he was quiet and gentle and good-natured ... These young people didn't know how to use words any more; they handled them all wrong.

When the guests took their leave, Catherine went out with them. She and Nicolas would walk to and fro between the two houses, chatting together, until one in the morning. This had become a regular habit of theirs. André made a few remarks about the dinner, and admitted that he had thought the evening was never going to end.

'You always think that when people come to dinner,' said Claire. 'You get bored very easily.'

'You didn't look as if you were enjoying yourself much, either.'

'No, I wasn't enjoying myself.'

She was sitting in her armchair, facing him, her hands in her lap and her expression calm and composed as usual; but there were circles under her eyes and her gaze was fixed in a stare.

'Is there something wrong?' he asked.

Without changing her position or her expression, she said:

'Suzy is going to have a baby.'

He looked at her as if she had gone mad.

'What?'

'Suzy is going to have a baby,' she repeated.

He stood up, red in the face.

'What's that you're saying? She's told you she's ... ?'

'Yes, I don't think there's any doubt about it.'

He started pacing up and down.

'Well, this is a fine state of affairs! The little fool. The idiot. She's got us into a pretty mess. All we needed was a bastard in the family. This is a wonderful piece of news.'

He planted himself in front of his wife, looking at her accusingly as if he were holding her responsible for their daughter's misconduct.

'Does she at least know who she has to thank for this little windfall?'

'Yes, of course. Pierre.'

'Pierre? Pierre Marcillac? But in that case, it must have been . . .'

'Six weeks ago, yes. When Pierre was home on leave.'

He started walking up and down again, his hands in his pockets.

'Who would have thought it? We never suspected a thing.'

'Oh, yes, we did. I suspected something of the sort.'

'What a low-down rotter that fellow is! And I thought he was a decent serious-minded boy. As for Suzy . . .'

'It isn't as serious as all that,' she broke in.

'What do you mean, it isn't serious? That's a good one!'

'They were going to get married anyway. They'll have to get married sooner, that's all.'

'You're taking it very calmly, I must say. She's our daughter. It seems to me that there's a moral issue involved.'

'I don't know,' she said, still very composed. 'There may be. But I wonder if you are really qualified to talk about moral issues.'

The blow went home. He sat down again, facing her, his elbows on his knees, his head in his hands.

'I'm sorry,' he said. 'I reacted like a heavy father. But what can you expect? I'm hurt and upset. You can't understand. It's as if I were ashamed. I shan't be able to look Suzy in the face again.'

'That's a mistaken attitude.'

'Maybe it is, but that's the way I feel. I know that women feel differently about these things. You're probably closer to nature than we are . . . But for me . . . For me, the purity of daughters is something sacred.'

'That's because you have a false sense of purity. Suzy's purity isn't compromised by . . . by what has happened. As I said before, she and Pierre consider themselves engaged. They love each other. All right. They had a moment of weakness. What of it?'

'I must say I think you're being astonishingly indulgent. I can't make you out. You're usually so strict.'

'If you'd seen Suzy just now, you'd understand.'

'She's upset, is she?'

'She's prostrate. You say that you feel ashamed. She's even more ashamed than you. And she's frightened too. Frightened of your anger.'

'Honestly?'

'I told her that there was no need to be frightened, that you loved her too much to be angry with her.'

'You did right. Poor Suzy. I don't want to make things any worse for her, of course ... But what are we going to do?'

'The best thing to do is to get Pierre home as soon as possible. The Marcillacs will arrange that all right. They've got friends who can fix it. And then we'll marry the two kids, that's all.'

'People are going to talk.'

'What does that matter? Does it bother you?'

'Not really,' he murmured, looking embarrassed. 'Have you had a chance to talk it over with Juliette?'

'No, of course not. When could I have done that? I intend to go and see her tomorrow.'

At that moment Bruno and Juliette were undressing in their room.

'I wonder,' Juliette was saying, 'what was the matter with Claire tonight. She was worried about something.'

'Really? I didn't notice anything. But didn't you think André has aged a lot? It gave me quite a shock. Though I say it as shouldn't, I'm wearing a lot better than he is.'

The weeks that followed this dinner-party were a bad period for André. First of all he had to adjust himself to the new situation created by his elder daughter's condition; for several days his relations with Suzy were marked by mutual embarrassment. Then there was the bother of this marriage

that had to be arranged as quickly as possible. The Marcillacs
had managed to obtain another period of leave, a short one
this time, for their son, and the young couple were married
very quietly one day, in a village in the Aspe valley.

The weather was cold but sunny; the bride and groom
made a good-looking couple, whose embarrassment only
added to their charm. André behaved very affectionately to
them. As for Bruno, he made no secret of his delight. The
haste his son had shown struck him, not as a sign of moral
weakness, but as a splendid proof of his virility, deserving of
respect and even of applause. The news of Suzy's pregnancy
had not upset him in the slightest. He thought that Pierrot
had conducted himself valiantly (to hell with conventional
prejudices!) and that Suzy ought to consider herself lucky to
be engaged to a boy like that. In the course of that wedding
day André felt a certain sadness at the impression conveyed
by father and son – an impression of perfect harmony, and
indeed of connivance. These two simple hearts found it easy
to beat in unison. Over and above filial love and fatherly love,
they displayed a peaceful, natural solidarity, the solidarity of
two men who spoke the same language, understood each
other and respected each other.

Among the various reasons André had for irritation at this
time, the chief one was the need to face up to public opinion,
to meet the eyes of acquaintances who pretended to know
nothing of his troubles, but who made such a point of their
discretion that it became quite overpowering. Mademoiselle
Adèle, his secretary, was particularly brilliant in demonstra-
tions of this devastating tact. She would put on a mournful
expression, look at André with moist eyes, and speak to him
in gentle, sympathetic tones, as if he had been struck down
by some unparalleled calamity.

His insomnia got worse, in spite of ever-increasing doses
of sleeping pills, and he became nervous for no ascertainable
reason, afflicted with anxieties which sometimes verged on
anguish. There was a return of old obsessions which he had

thought he had done with long before. They appeared chiefly in those dreams of incompetence, ineffectiveness and unpunctuality which psychologists and psycho-analysts have classified and explained. There was nothing about them to worry about: these dreams were common to all men; they were symptoms of an uneasy conscience, of an incurable sickness inherent in the human condition; but why had they come back now, when they had stopped haunting him for years? He also had a dream of a different sort, as strange as a surrealist picture: walking past a rocky wall, he heard a clicking sound like that of a hundred typewriters all being used at once, and a crack opened in the wall, giving him access to the source of the noise. He arrived on a vast beach, on which a huge wheel, like those you see at a fair, was fixed vertically. It was turning. The clicking sound was coming from the wheel, and it was produced by the rattling of thousands of skeletons fastened to the edge of the wheel, which knocked against one another as it went round. He tried to flee in terror, but could not find the crack through which he had reached the shore: the rocky wall had closed up behind him. A dream of death, but an ambiguous dream, since according to traditional interpretations a seashore symbolised a new life, a rebirth. Perhaps a transition was taking place in him from one biological condition to another; or perhaps, if life was a cycle, these dreams were auguries of a return to emotional states he had already known in childhood?

He felt afflicted in his physical integrity, in a bodily well-being he had previously taken for granted. His health, which had never caused him the slightest concern, deteriorated. He began having dizzy fits, sudden, devastating onsets of fatigue which forced him to sit down and stop working. He also had a prolonged attack of rheumatism. Rheumatism! The machine he had regarded as indefatigable was beginning to slow down. The wheels inside were making sinister noises.

He decided to go and see a doctor of some renown who

lived in Pau. Doctor Boranges looked like nothing so much as an outsize toad, with his wrinkled parchment skin and his bulbous eyes, which were half-covered by curved lids, so that to see anyone he was obliged to tilt his head backwards. He moved about slowly in the bluey-green penumbra of his consulting-room, whose French windows opened on to a balcony crowded with potted plants which formed a vegetable screen against the draught. His long pale hands floated about in front of him like fins; and he reminded André of an amphibious reptile of prehistoric times swimming in a swamp surrounded by tree-ferns. Doctor Boranges did not know what it was to smile. He spoke in little basic sentences, in a faint, far-away voice. After going through the routine of the medical examination in absolute silence, he asked André a few questions; among them, whether he was married and whether his conjugal relations were satisfactory. André went scarlet and answered that he had no cause for complaint on that score.

'Do you and your wife sleep in separate rooms?' the doctor asked imperturbably.

André nodded.

'How long has that been the case?'

'About eight years.'

'Am I to understand that all relations with your wife have ceased?'

'Practically speaking, yes.'

'What do you mean by "practically speaking"? It's either yes or no.'

'Then it's yes.'

'By mutual consent?'

'Naturally.'

The doctor made no comment. He examined the notes he had been making, and then pronounced his diagnosis.

'I can see nothing seriously wrong with you, from the physiological point of view. The X-rays show nothing. The digestive system is normal, the liver a little sluggish. Your blood-pressure is normal. There are no perceptible lesions. The heartbeat is slightly irregular. You will take the medicaments I am going to prescribe for you. Do not tire yourself unduly. Do not make any prolonged muscular efforts. You complain of insomnia and anxiety. You must give up taking barbiturates – you have been taking too many, in too heavy doses. Your mental health seems to be more seriously impaired than your physical condition. There are certain depressive symptoms... Are you a religious man?'

André had noticed, on the doctor's desk, a crystal rosary and a mould of Pascal's death-mask; on the wall, an old crucifix; and in a corner of the room, a statue of the Virgin in painted wood which could have belonged to the Burgundian school.

He replied that he was 'rather indifferent' with regard to religion.

'You cannot be rather indifferent,' said the doctor, in the same sad voice. 'You are either indifferent or you aren't. If you say you are "rather indifferent", that probably means you aren't. I advise you to go and see a priest. Since you live in Sault, I would suggest you consult a young priest I know there who is very open-minded and very pious – the Abbé Trébucq. He might be able to give you some useful advice.'

André returned to Sault annoyed with the doctor, annoyed with himself, and determined not to go and see the Abbé Trébucq, from whom he expected no help at all. But then he felt a certain curiosity about this young priest, who did in fact enjoy a considerable reputation in the town; he was extremely active, ran a club for young people, and was said to be 'modern'. Who could tell? Perhaps this man was endowed with special gifts, and could help André to understand and overcome his difficulties. A great mind could operate beyond the limits of a hidebound faith. Perhaps there were still a few miracle-workers left in the world. 'Lord, say but the word, and my soul shall be healed.' And one day when he was feeling particularly depressed, André, in a moment of weakness, asked his secretary to ring up the Abbé Trébucq and make an appointment for him. There was perhaps an element of self-indulgence in this decision – a vague desire to arouse someone's interest, to talk about himself, to mobilise the resources of an intelligent mind.

An aged sloven showed him into a huge, almost bare room. The priest was talking on the telephone. Without breaking off his conversation, he waved André to an armchair. The visitor had time to examine the premises and their occupant. The room had seemed bare only at first sight. Closer inspection revealed previously unnoticed riches. There was a big divan covered with a multi-coloured rug. On the floor in one corner of the room, there was a record-player and a pile of records; a little further on, a guitar. On the table was a transistor radio with two aerials; a song could just be heard coming from it. On the walls were four posters: André recognised photographs of Marilyn Monroe and Teilhard de Chardin, but failed to identify the other two. There were some books on a shelf, and he managed to make out a few titles: *Gravity and Grace*, *Lolita*, *Saint Genêt*, several volumes of the Seuil series, and two James Bonds. The Abbé Trébucq was dressed in black corduroy trousers and a thick red rolltop sweater. He was short and stocky, with a round head, gaping nostrils and sharp eyes. The pebbles of all the mountain torrents in the Pyrenees could be heard in his accent.

'Listen, Dudule, I'll do the same for you another time if you can take my place at that funeral. It's a big affair, it's sure to drag on all morning, and that's hell for me, because I've got to be in Pau at twelve. Yes, that's it... I can't be late, because I'm in the chair, and I've got to make a speech and all that. So will you do it? ... Thanks, Dudule, you're a pal. See you tomorrow. Say hello to Titine for me. How is the old girl? Good. Fine. My Josépha? Oh, she chunters along as usual. Right. Ciaou.'

Seized with an anxiety as pressing as an attack of colic,

André had been on the point of getting up and taking to his heels. The Abbé Trébucq hung up and turned to face him. Too late! The priest got up and came over to shake hands with him. On the way he turned up the volume of the radio slightly. A singer, probably a 'pop star', was complaining that his girl friend had left him in the lurch. 'You let me down, yeah, yeah,' he howled despairingly. The priest seemed to appreciate the fervour of this elegiac lament. His head bowed, his hands in his pockets, he jerked his shoulders up and down in time to the music.

'That Johnny!' he said. 'He's terrific, isn't he!'

He switched off the radio, sat down behind the table, rested his chin on his hands, and said coldly:

'Fire away, Monsieur.'

André's heart sank. What could he say to this man? He had expected to find a sort of Saint Francis of Assisi, with ascetic features full of loving meekness. Someone who would have gently drawn him out, whispering in a confessional voice: 'My child, you are worried: tell me what is troubling you.'

But not this . . .

He cleared his throat. He shuffled his feet. Feeling utterly embarrassed, he opened his cigarette case and stood up to offer it to the priest. The Abbé inspected the brand of the cigarettes and made a masculine gesture of disdain.

'I smoke nothing but shag,' he said.

Confronted with such an intransigent statement of faith, the visitor found it harder than ever to talk about his soul.

His embarrassment was temporarily alleviated by a brief interruption. Someone knocked on the door, and opened it without waiting for an invitation to come in. The slovenly housekeeper appeared, with one hand on her hip.

'The Dean has sent me to ask what to give the Bishop to-morrow,' she said bluntly.

'How do I know? Give him whatever you like.'

'Roast beef, veal, chicken, or what?'

'I don't give a damn, Josépha. Whatever you like.'

'And what do you want for the first course? You've got to tell me these things, because I don't know what you serve a bishop.'

'Listen, Josépha, do exactly the same as you would have done for us. The same menu. The Bishop isn't a privileged guest. The Bishop is a priest like any other.' (Here André realised, from a certain pomposity of voice and gesture, that the Abbé Trébucq had begun talking to the gallery). 'Fuss and ceremony and red carpets – all that belongs to the past. We have gone back to the simplicity of the primitive Church. You understand?'

'How about kidneys?' asked Josépha, who did not appear to have understood.

'Kidneys will be all right,' said the priest with a sigh.

'And to begin with, a tomato salad, mushrooms, or . . .'

'Josépha, you're a bloody nuisance! I've told you to do the same as for us. Just lay two extra places, that's all.'

'Two extra places!' Josépha repeated in surprise.

'Yes, of course – the Vicar General will be accompanying the Bishop. Now get along with you – leave us alone.'

When the housekeeper had left, the priest raised his eyes to heaven.

'She's an absolute idiot,' he said. 'Forgive the interruption. You were saying?'

For fear of sounding like a chronic invalid, André made no mention of Doctor Boranges. He said that somebody had told him that the Abbé Trébucq might be able to help him. He added that for several months he had been 'down in the dumps', and didn't know how to get out of them; that perhaps he was looking for some purpose and meaning he could give his life; and that the advice of a man conversant with the spiritual realities might be able to put him on the right track. Because he was embarrassed, and aware of the unusual nature of his visit, he said all this very quickly and very badly, using ready-made phrases, the first clichés that came to his mind. And as there is nothing more contagious than embarrassment, the confusion he felt communicated it-self to his listener. André was expecting the priest to question him about his religious observances and to urge him to carry them out with greater fervour. Good. If he did that, he would listen to him, pretend to approve, thank him politely, hand over a few banknotes for the church, and take his leave with a sigh of relief.

'What are you doing for the Vietcong?' the priest asked abruptly.

'I beg your pardon?'

'What are you doing for the Vietcong?'

'For the Vietcong?' the visitor repeated in surprise.

'Yes. Or for the American Negroes. Or for the foreign workers packed together in the shanty towns. When I speak of the Vietcong, I'm using a symbol. What are you doing for others?'

'Nobody's ever asked me for anything ...'

Of the feelings affecting the Abbé Trébucq just then, the strongest was probably embarrassment; he tried to master it by adopting a somewhat aggressive brusqueness.

'What a curious reply,' he said. 'A typical bourgeois re-action. "Nobody's ever asked me for anything ..." Neutrality, indifference. I've only been in Sault for three months, and I don't know everybody. Unless I'm mistaken, you're a lawyer, aren't you? One of the most important firms in the region. You live in the Rue de Navailles, don't you? An old-style bourgeois, in fact. You've just told me that you feel de-pressed, that your life seems to have no meaning, that you're looking for a reason for living. I reply: "What are you doing for others?" With all respect, Monsieur Comarieu, your existential vacuum is just another luxury. At this very moment, on our pretty little planet, there are millions of people who are starving to death, who are mercilessly ex-ploited. Has it ever occurred to you that for the Third World your problems simply don't count?'

189

'Of course,' said André, 'But nobody's told me to solve the problems of the Third World. We are all in the same boat, whatever you may say. I came here to consult you on a personal matter. You are a priest. I was under the impression that the life of the spirit came within your province...'

'The life of the spirit! ... The Church isn't here to coddle petty-bourgeois nostalgia, or to satisfy the pseudo-idealistic aspirations of the ruling class. In any case, we, the young people of today, refuse to play that game any more. The Church has to look after all mankind, not just the small privileged class.'

'But, Monsieur l'Abbé, there's no need for you to lose your temper...'

'You don't appear to realise,' the priest broke in, more sharply than ever, 'that the Church is undergoing a radical transformation. It is breaking its ties with the forces of power and money. It has aligned itself unreservedly with the workers. What matters to us is the struggle of the trade unions, the situation of the...'

At that moment the telephone rang. The priest picked up the receiver.

'Hello? Is that you, Sylvine? How are you? ... Not bad ... Yes, eight o'clock ... Sure ... Has Bernard been working on his paper? ... Sure ... The main thing is to present the issues clearly. Tell them to think about the questions they're going to ask ... Yes, that's right, all they've got to do is put them in writing ... The issues have to be presented clearly ... The main thing is to initiate a dialogue ... That's it ... Initiate a dialogue, break down the wall of silence ... Sure ... Sure ... Oh, that's your problem, baby, not mine ... What did you think of it? ... I thought it was cool. Good, wasn't it? ...' (At this point the priest listened for a long time to the person at the other end of the line). 'I must lend you a book that takes stock of the whole question: Georges Bataille's *Tears of Eros* ... It's a remarkable work ... Sure ... Sure ... Yes, bring them along, don't forget. I love cool jazz ... By the way, I've got Johnny's latest record ... I'll let you have it ... Sure ... It's cool, isn't it? ... Right, see you tomorrow ... And don't forget to tell Bernard to present the issues clearly. That's what matters. The main thing is to initiate a dialogue ... Sure ... Ciaou, baby. See you tomorrow.'

He hung up.

'Where was I?'

Now André had no qualms left. It was in a tone of urbane politeness that he replied, with a smile which he made pointedly bland:

'Monsieur l'Abbé, I doubt if there is any purpose in continuing this conversation. I apologise for needlessly taking up your time, and thank you very much for your courteous reception ...'

'Not at all, not at all,' said the Abbé Trébucq, without batting an eyelid at this reply (for torn between Johnny's records, the tears of Eros, Teilhardism and the need to initiate a dialogue, a man may be forgiven for failing to notice irony when he meets it). 'I allowed myself to be carried away, and I may have been a little sharp; but you see, we don't want to have anything more to do with the mystifications of the past. We have a very clear understanding of our mission and ... well, I don't quite see what advice I can give you regarding your problem. You must try to take yourself in hand and recover your equilibrium ... I don't know – perhaps a change of diet ... These so-called spiritual ailments often have a physiological origin. It's nearly always a question of glands. I think the best thing for you to do would be to go and see a doctor.'

'You haven't any proof,' said the girl.

'No proof? I saw you. My evidence would be enough.'

'They wouldn't find anything if they looked.'

'Besides, you've admitted your guilt. You confessed just now.'

'I didn't confess anything;' she gasped, looking at Jean with wide eyes.

'Yes, you did; and a police inspector would make you confess even quicker than I did.'

'I doubt it.'

'You poor kid. You wouldn't stand a chance with the police. They know how to get what they're looking for.'

'There's no proof,' she repeated.

'They'll find plenty; but if ever you're arrested, I advise you not to say there's no proof. That's tantamount to admitting there might be.'

'If you're so sure about it, why don't you go and report me straight away?'

'Why, because I don't want to do you any harm! I like my sometime neighbour. I don't want to see her in prison.'

'You couldn't tell the police anything.'

'Yes, I could. I'd tell them what I saw, that's all.'

'That wouldn't be enough to get me arrested.'

'You poor kid, you'd be arrested straight away.'

Jean spoke softly, with gentle commiseration, rather like an elder brother talking to a charming but stubborn little girl. He was sitting on a corner of the bed, because there was no chair in the tiny room. The girl was standing with her hands behind her back, as far away from him as the smallness of the room would allow. 'A hunted animal.' The phrase suited her perfectly: that was precisely the impression she created. Her eyes were sparkling, her breasts rising and falling as if she had been running in a race. Yet the fear distorting her features could not manage to detract from her somewhat wild beauty.

The bedroom was an attic room with a cracked ceiling from which flakes of plaster were peeling. There was a smell of mildew, mixed with the smell of cosmetics and cheap scent. Jean registered one or two details: some photographs of film stars pinned on the wall, the jug and basin on a little deal table. There was no running water, but he knew that already: he knew all the houses in the district well, and this one in particular; they hadn't changed in a hundred years; they were the poorest, shabbiest houses in the town. His gaze came back to the girl.

'You'd be arrested inside ten minutes,' he went on. 'If you were somebody, they'd treat you gently, they'd put kid gloves on. But you're nothing. A little shop girl at forty thousand francs a month, in other words nothing. You've already got a bad reputation. Your lover is a young lout, a sort of outlaw. You've got nobody to help you. You haven't enough money to pay for a lawyer. The court would have to appoint a lawyer to defend you, and he wouldn't bother to do it properly. I tell you, if I report you, you're done for. It's prison for you and your boy friend. If you were somebody, you'd get off with a couple of months, you'd be given a suspended sentence, you might even get an acquittal. That means that you wouldn't be convicted . . . For instance, if you came from a good bourgeois family, and if you'd done the job with a pal with the same kind of background, the court would just smile indulgently. The best barrister in Pau would make a biting speech in your defence . . . You'd be acquitted to loud applause from all the other bright young things of the region. Or rather, there wouldn't even be a trial: your families would fix things on the quiet. I know how it's all done. But you, you poor kid, you don't come from a good bourgeois family; you're a pariah. A pariah means a nobody. They wouldn't let you get off lightly. You'd get the maximum sentence. That's the truth, the gospel truth. From him that hath not, even what he hath shall be taken away . . . Though I don't suppose you've read the Gospel very often, have you? . . . Well, that's the way things are in this wretched world of ours: anybody who hasn't got money is done for. That's the law. And I know what I'm talking about.'

'That's all a lot of talk. You can't frighten me.'

'Oh, yes I can!' Jean retorted with a smile. 'I can recognise fear in people straight away. Even when they think they're hiding it. And you, you aren't hiding it at all. Your voice . . . Your eyes . . . Look at yourself, and you'll see the face of somebody who's frightened.'

'You say you saw us. You don't know what we were doing.'

'I saw you drive up to your door, between two and three in the morning, and take some suitcases and a bag out of the car. Three suitcases, I think. And a travelling-bag. Were you coming back from a journey? You'll have to be able to prove it. You'll have to say where you were. That same evening there was a burglary at that villa. A small-time amateur burglary. I made the connection straight away. So will the police – and they'll also remember the small thefts that were committed in the shop where you work . . . You see, I know everything.'

'They'll ask you what the hell you were up to outside my place at two in the morning.'

'Yes. There you're right. They're sure to ask me that. But first of all I should point out to you that I was outside *my* old home, not yours.'

'It comes to the same thing.'

'Not quite. I often come for a walk around here, to see my old district. A sort of pilgrimage. I lived thirty-eight years in this street . . . And I often come back. To make comparisons.'

'At two in the morning?'

'Ten, twenty, thirty people can testify that they've seen me roaming about, at that time of night, for a year or two. People know that I don't sleep much, and that when I can't sleep I go for a walk. My doctor actually recommended me to try it. It's hard luck for you that I was here the very night you'd just done your little burglary. But they do say there's always a witness. So you see, I'm not afraid of anything. It's you who have everything to be afraid of. Come now, don't look at me like that. If looks could kill, I'd have been in my grave long ago, eh? . . . Don't look at me like that. I've already told you I don't want to do you any harm.'

'Then what *do* you want?'

'Nothing, Maryse. Absolutely nothing.'

'All right. I know what you want.'

'Then you know me better than I know myself.'

The girl's gaze shifted towards the bed and rested on it for a moment, then returned to meet Jean Lagarde's eyes. He smiled.

'How simple-minded you are,' he murmured. 'Oh, I won't pretend I haven't thought of that. I don't say that one day ... Because you're a tasty dish. And you know it, don't you?'

She made no reply.

'Your little gipsy must show you that every day. Or every night. That you're a tasty dish, I mean. Doesn't he?'

'He isn't a gipsy,' she said.

'He looks like a gipsy. But it doesn't matter. Do you love him?'

Silence.

'Answer my question. I asked you nicely: Do you love your gipsy? Answer me.'

She shrugged her shoulders.

'What do you want?'

'I want what I want. You're very persistent, aren't you? Well then, I want ... No – as I said before, I don't want anything. I like having this little secret between us. That's all. So you see, it isn't very serious. I said to myself: "Well, well, so little Maryse has broken into a villa with her little gipsy. Isn't that nice! I'm glad I know about it, because it will be a little secret between her and me, a bond between us ..." Because, you know, I can tell you this: if you want to break into every villa in town, I'm the last person to blame you. On the contrary, I quite like the idea. You've got nothing, so you take things whenever they are there to be taken. That's only fair. Very fair, I would call it.'

He gave the impression of playing a game, of deriving a certain pleasure from this gentle banter. This was just the impression required to worry a simple-minded creature, and he obviously knew it, as those whose work involves frightening other people know it by instinct: they never raise their voices, and they keep an unchanging smile on their lips, as if they had enough strength in reserve and enough time before them to allow themselves the luxury of carefree amusement.

'Come here,' he said.

She stood motionless. He waited a few seconds.

'When I say I don't want anything,' he continued in the same quiet voice, 'I'm telling the truth. I don't want anything from you. Not yet, anyway. I think you're very beautiful, it's true, and I've told you so. But if I ask you for something, what happens? You know perfectly well. You're too clever not to know. If I ask you for something, then you've got me in your power. Not the other way around. It's more ... amusing. Now come here.'

For a few seconds of tense silence he studied the rigidity of her body until the first signs of movement appeared. She took a couple of steps towards him. In Jean Lagarde's face a gleam in the eyes and a quiver at the corner of the lips indicated the satisfaction of victory.

'Closer,' he said hoarsely.

She took another step. Stretching out one hand, he brushed it lightly against the girl's cheek.

'You see,' he said, 'we're good friends, you and I.'

Two months after their wedding Suzy went to join her husband. When her pregnancy was nearing its end, she asked her mother to come out and stay with her. After a little hesitation Claire decided to go. She was to spend two months with her daughter. André accompanied her to Orly. It was a warm, sunny June day.

'I wouldn't mind going with you,' he said. 'How splendid it would be if I could simply drop everything! Just think – tomorrow morning you'll wake up under a tropical sky.'

'If anybody had ever told me that one day I would go to Pointe-Noire,' she said. 'Of all the towns in the world!'

They marvelled at the surprises life produced. Without wanting to admit it, but unable to conceal it, Claire was delighted by this journey. Standing on the airport terrace in her white linen suit, she looked young and charming, in spite of her now completely grey hair. He looked at her surreptitiously, thinking that they could have been quite happy together, if he had been less reserved and more self-assured with her. But he hadn't wanted to take the trouble, or else hadn't known how: she had accordingly turned in upon herself, and they had become rather like two strangers, or at the most two partners, living under the same roof. He felt sorry for both of them as he thought of those twenty-two years they had wasted. Twenty-two years which were the years of their youth. Twenty-two years, or about a third of a lifetime. In the meantime he was giving her last-minute reminders: whatever happened, she mustn't forget to take quinine every day, or to wash her mouth and hands with permanganate. He told her to give Suzy a big kiss from her father, adding that he hoped everything would go well and was impatient to receive the telegram bringing news of the baby's birth.

As the hour of departure drew nearer he felt his affection for Claire growing. He would have liked to do something or say something to make her understand that she mattered a great deal to him, that he felt guilty about her; but he could think of nothing but conventional phrases – the very phrases he didn't want to use, because they would ring false – and he was surprised at the difficulty of giving sincere expression to a sincere feeling. Probably you had to be a very simple soul to do that, or something of a mystic: you had to be either a child or a saint. So for want of anything better he heaped little attentions on her, but the attentions a well-bred man can show even to a woman he doesn't love: he bought her far more newspapers and magazines than she could possibly read during an eight-hour flight, a box of chocolates, and flowers she could have no use for in the plane. The result was that the other passengers waiting in the main hall looked at them closely, wondering whether she was an actress (but she didn't look like one), or a high official, or perhaps a special envoy for an important paper (but in that case, where were the photographers?). She was somewhat surprised by so much attention, and also perhaps a little touched, guessing that it was inspired by some hidden feeling; and she looked at him in smiling perplexity. Finally, at the moment of separation, when the voice of an invisible siren, amplified by the loud-speakers, was intoning a doleful appeal – 'Will passengers for Brazzaville, Nairobi, Tananarive ...' – he was moved to kiss her so warmly that she could have no doubt of his affection. She responded to this kiss with a certain awkwardness; and in her eyes, as she looked up at him, he could read the shy gratitude of someone who had waited a long time for a gesture, a sign, and who, when at long last that gesture was made, that sign given, hesitated to interpret them as she wanted to.

This last moment with Claire had eased his conscience; and driving back towards Paris, he congratulated himself on having been 'good' to Claire, and resolved to be 'good' to her always in the future. Then he realised that he was also happy because he was alone, because he was going to have three days' holiday in Paris, and because after that there would be two months in Sault of almost total solitude, among his books and records. He wasn't planning to put this new freedom of his to any 'disreputable' use, although he didn't rule out the possibility of an affair, provided that that affair was brief and discreet – after all, I don't see how it could possibly hurt Claire, since she wouldn't know anything about it and my affection for her wouldn't be altered – on the contrary; it was going to be wonderful enough rediscovering, for a few weeks, the complete independence and freedom of movement of the bachelor. He promised himself a host of forgotten pleasures: staying up till two in the morning, if he felt like it, reading or listening to music; or else getting up at dawn and driving out to wait for the sunrise on a hillside near Sault – how long was it since he had last seen the sun come up? You had to live on your own to be able to treat yourself to these modest fancies. He would go more often to plays and concerts in Pau or Biarritz. He would ask Mariette to cook him some out-of-the-way dishes, a paella just for him, a lacquered duck (she had an exotic cookery book which contained that recipe), and a sea-food pilaf . . .

For the moment he had these three days in Paris to look forward to. Since he was treating his wife to an expensive journey to the heart of Africa, he had told himself that he might as well treat himself to a little luxury too, and he had booked a room at the Ritz. For years he had dreamed of staying at the Ritz, chiefly on account of Proust and *Remembrance of Things Past*, and the modern Arabian Nights which that name and that work conjured up. Similarly he had decided to eat in restaurants of venerable reputation, and to visit the antique shops on the Left Bank and in the Faubourg Saint-Honoré. He reflected that it was pleasant not to have to economise, to be able to spend quite freely; he admitted that he was a privileged person and that the worthy Abbé Trébucq might be right after all: above a certain income level it was unforgivable for a man not to be happy.

The Ritz turned out to be luxurious enough; but it was easy to imagine a subtler, more refined luxury. This wasn't exactly Sybaris. Proust's dining-room was occupied by a prosperous-looking, rather ordinary clientele. The Ritz failed to come up to his expectations . . . As for the world-famous restaurants, they proved to be of uneven quality. In one the service was very slow, and you had to wait for ages between one course and the next. In another the sweets were obviously prefabricated and not prepared to order. All in all, André decided that he had greater comfort and better cooking at home – Mariette was worth all the chefs in the world. Without wanting to be difficult or to appear blasé, you had to admit that the luxury which satisfied the millionaires of this world left a great deal to be desired.

Later he felt ashamed of being so hard to please, when the Third World . . . What would the worthy Abbé Trébucq have said?

He spent an evening at the Lido and found it moderately enjoyable: the girls there were very beautiful. At the theatre he saw a play, an insipid imitation of Brecht, poorly acted by a suburban company subsidised by the State. The production had been given respectful notices, and the audience were very respectful too, because they had read these respectful notices, and also because the concept of a suburban company, a comparatively new concept in the repertory of aesthetic criteria, awed them into submission. André walked out during the interval.

His solitude soon began to weigh upon him. You could be alone at home, in Sault-en-Labourd, but not at the Lido, nor at the theatre, nor in a restaurant. In a bar, yes, at a pinch – but then bars are a meeting-place for solitudes. Besides, Paris had deteriorated so badly, in so short a time! André had looked forward to having a room on the Place Vendôme, but the Place Vendôme had become a cross between a speedway and a car-park, and you couldn't open a window without being deafened by the din. Outside, you walked about in a smell of diesel oil and petrol, which was sometimes so strong that it turned your stomach. You wasted hours waiting at traffic lights. You were sworn at by drivers who seemed on the verge of apoplexy or madness. People pushed you and jostled you, and there were crowds everywhere, so that it was impossible to stroll along the boulevards, or to find a seat on the terrace of the Café de la Paix or the Deux Magots.

The strangest and most demoralising thing, however, was the perpetual impression of being invisible. People took no notice of you. If you were over twenty-five, they didn't even see you. After a while, invisibility becomes intolerable: you long to exist for other people. By the second evening, André had already had enough of Paris, with its hustle, its noise, its pestilential smells. He had had enough of being an anonymous particle swept along in a perpetually moving mass. In Sault, people at least knew who he was and still greeted him in the street. Little towns in the provinces still retained, and would retain for some time to come, this provincial quality: you hadn't completely lost your identity and existence in them.

He felt a certain relief when the last evening arrived. Once again he went to the theatre. The play he saw was an indictment of the human condition: it showed a blind paralytic waiting for death between a couple of dustbins containing his parents. It was powerful and impressive, but afterwards he felt he had to look for some amusement. Perhaps the Left Bank, with its youthful gaiety, would provide what he wanted. Failing to find any room on the famous café terraces, he took refuge in an out-of-the-way café, where he was soon fascinated by what he saw. The customers consisted of two groups, the hunters and the hunted. The strange thing was that the hunted offered themselves to the hunters, who looked positively terrified; but an appetite which could never be satisfied forced them to make advances and conclude bargains in the crimson penumbra. Here young men and women were buying and selling bodies, faces, the illusion of loving or being loved. Perhaps something less than that: the repetition of a gesture first performed or dreamt of long before, in the limbo of childhood, a gesture which had seemed to promise an infinity of joy. Perhaps something less than *that*: the symbolical representation of the annihilation of one party or the other, in an act of unspeakable finality. The faces of the hunted were young in years, but an ugliness arising from some hidden source showed on the surface, like a mysterious leprosy. In the red half-light, as the night drew on, all these bodies seemed to be undergoing a process of decomposition;

and André reflected that after seeing a play concerned with the decay of human beings, he had moved in search of amusement to another place, only to find himself in the same atmosphere.

The first few days back in Sault were delightful. He enjoyed the novelty of being alone at home (Catherine was a student at Bordeaux University), and of having all his free time to himself. The weather was fine, and he went for long walks in the surrounding countryside. Without ordering lacquered duck, which would have struck Mariette as suspiciously extravagant, he asked her to introduce a little variety into his meals, to give free rein to her culinary imagination, to spoil him; he felt like a village priest being coddled by his housekeeper. He read some of the classics he had never read before, and plunged once more into the inexhaustible Proust. The Marcillacs, thinking that he must be lonely without his wife, invited him several times to dinner. There was a much greater familiarity between them and André now, for family ties had strengthened the existing bonds of friendship. 'Poor André, you must be terribly bored,' Juliette would say to him, and he would answer that time was indeed heavy on his hands: forced to choose between the conventional reply people expect and the truth which might shock them, we always pick the conventional reply, out of consideration for their feelings, or simply for the sake of peace.

Late one afternoon he was rung up at his office and the text of a telegram which had just arrived was read out to him: a boy had been born, mother and child were doing well, love and kisses. He was relieved to know that everything had gone well. He imagined Suzy with a baby in her arms and felt a certain emotion. A few minutes later Bruno called him. He was exultant.

'Come round to our place. We'll open some champagne. And of course you'll stay to dinner.'

Before leaving the office, André announced the good news

to Mademoiselle Adèle and the three clerks. He felt rather a fool receiving their congratulations.

'So you're a grandfather now, Monsieur!' said Mademoiselle Adèle, looking sourer than ever. 'How times flies!' She repeated the word several times; she gargled with it. 'A grandfather! Well, I never!'

At Bruno's there was a celebration. He drank some champagne, but said he wouldn't stay for dinner: he was tired and meant to go to bed early. He realised that he was disappointing them and spoiling their pleasure, but he wanted to be alone, at home, in silence.

Alone, at home, in silence, to be able to think about this astonishing fact: time had eaten up his life, like Saturn devouring his offspring. Yesterday he was going to school, he was wearing short trousers; yesterday he was reading for a degree in law, with a vast future stretching out in front of him, like limitless steppes; yesterday he was sick and tired of being young, much younger than his birth certificate said. He was still a child, an adolescent on the threshold of an endless existence. And now Mademoiselle Adèle had reminded him that he was a grandfather. It was ridiculous. A grandfather. You imagined a dear old man with a snow-white beard and washed-out eyes set in a network of wrinkles, hobbling along with the help of a stick, and followed by a string of kids calling him Grandad. But no, that sort of picture belonged to the past; it was a scene from the nineteenth century. Nowadays the concept of age was no longer as strict as it used to be. You could have grandchildren without giving up any of the pleasures of active life. One American film star who was well into his sixties still played romantic leads, and everybody considered it perfectly plausible. And you had to have a twisted mind to think of Marlene Dietrich as a grandmother, though that was what she was ... All the same, between the schoolboy and the student he had been only yesterday, and the man who today could be labelled 'Grandfather', what had happened? Where had the days, the months, the years all gone? They had simply gone, that was all. Gone nowhere, but at top speed, like the pictures in a jerky old film – a film with only a few frames every second. That was what his life was: one of those early films which were sometimes shown in the first part of a programme, to amuse the public. It was screamingly funny . . .

Here are the very first motor cars to appear in Sault-en-Labourd in the twenties – Citroën B.14's, the latest thing. God, but they can put on a pretty turn of speed! Here's one speeding across the main square – it's going to knock everybody down! No, it stops right outside the Café des Voyageurs, and an acrobat jumps out, leaping from the driving-seat on to the pavement in three seconds flat. That's young Vignemale, wearing a boater. He faces the camera, laughs, walks along like Charlie Chaplin. Saucy girls in cloche hats and knee-length dresses cluster round him, jumping up and down. The dresses grow visibly longer: now they are down to the ankles, and the hats are huge – like organdie parasols. Young Vignemale is suddenly bearded, with a wife on his arm and a couple of children at his feet . . . And here comes little André, making his first communion: he rushes into the church clutching a big taper in one hand; now he comes out again, walking jerkily, with some other little boys and girls just as agitated as himself. Now he's at school, in the first form, kicking a ball about, smoking a cigarette in the corner of the yard, for he's in the sixth form now, shaving for the first time (not so fast, or he'll cut himself!), and dancing with Claire at the Pau Casino (a foxtrot probably – anybody would think the floor was on fire and they were trying to put out the flames by stamping their feet!) They dash into church, the bride wearing a white veil which looks as if it were fastened to her eyebrows. Now they come out again, and Claire is carrying a baby in her arms – what, already? No, it's Suzy's christening, and soon she's trotting into the garden to look for Easter eggs . . .

But whereas cinema techniques had improved, and the

films of the thirties and forties reproduced the normal rhythm of existence, the film of life seemed, on the contrary, to speed up as you got closer to the present.

Here's Suzy growing taller and taller, like Alice in Wonderland, in a Sault populated with troops in green uniforms; and here comes Catherine, while a mushroom of fire rises above a Japanese town, and the old world, the world of my youth, falls into the abyss of History to join the ancient worlds of Rome and Egypt; here's Claire one fine morning waking up with grey hair; and the White Man beginning to lose this ancient power over there, on the other side of the world, in a village called Dien-Bien-Phu; and Bruno, a thicker, heavier Bruno, selling his farms one after the other as if he were throwing them to the wind; and that dinner a few days ago, no, a few seconds ago, when Claire told me our daughter was expecting a baby . . . And the moment when Mademoiselle Adèle, grinning like a hyena, repeated: 'How times flies!' There. The film is over. We all had a good laugh. I've been a grandfather since eight o'clock this morning.

He wondered where and when he had felt the first blows inflicted by that time which was going to kill him soon, if the film went on speeding up at the same rate. Had there been a precise moment when he had said to himself: 'Well, well! I'm not a young man any more: I'm getting old?' No, there hadn't been one moment but a thousand, a host of tiny, fleeting touches. The first time a bus conductor in Paris had called him 'Monsieur' instead of the usual 'young man'. The first time he had noticed that his hair was receding dangerously from his forehead. The first time somebody had said to him: 'I *thought* I recognised you, but I wasn't sure; Not that you've changed all that much.' The first time some well-bred young man he didn't know had respectfully stood aside to let him go through a door. The first time, climbing some stairs four at a time he had reached the top breathless, feeling as if his heart were going to burst. The first time someone had congratulated him on his healthy appearance and on looking five years younger than his age – until then he had always been given ten years at least ... A myriad 'first times' ... A host of slight deteriorations, imperceptible defeats.

Only a few days later he met one of his army friends in the street, a man he hadn't seen since the days of his military service. This Bernard had been a jovial fellow, with the grinning face of a fawn. André recognised him almost immediately, for he had a good memory for faces, but he identified the man as he might have identified the model for a caricature, for this puffy face with the bloodshot eyes was nothing but a caricature of the original Bernard. Every feature in his face seemed to have collapsed, and the bright eyes had grown dull, but the most impressive change was the substitution, for the gay fawn-like grin, of a horribly sad leer. They shook hands, Bernard staring at André with something like dismay. 'I *thought* I recognised you,' he said, 'but I couldn't be sure. You haven't changed much, though.' – 'Nor have you.'

In July Catherine came to spend her vacation, or rather part of her vacation, at home. She was doing very well at the University. André was proud of her, and just a little in awe of her, especially since the scene in which she had displayed a rebellious spirit of independence. For several days they were together a great deal. He appreciated this chance to be with his daughter, and did his best to be 'a good pal', until he realised that she preferred a more traditional father-daughter relationship in which each party kept at a certain distance from the other. He managed to comply with this unspoken demand, and to accept the rules it imposed. He also treated tolerantly Catherine's youthful arrogance, the arrogance of a budding intellectual with a solution for every problem. These sweeping judgments, which young people were so fond of making, had irritated him for a long time; but now he knew that you had to put up with them patiently, rather as you put up with the intestinal incontinence of a baby: they were one of the symptoms of that infirmity which goes by the name of adolescence. Later on, at twenty-five or thirty, Catherine would be a sweet, gentle woman, he was sure of that. At the moment he had to compromise with her, pretending to agree with her on points on which he could see she was mistaken, and to admire a great many remarks which were commonplaces, generalisations or utter absurdities – weaknesses of her youthful years which she made up for with obvious qualities of heart and mind. She was, thank God, 'a good girl'. He told himself he was lucky to have a daughter like that, so intelligent, so serious, so admirable from every point of view.

After Bastille Day she set off for Provence to meet a 'gang' with whom she was going to travel around Italy. She had told him about this journey as something which was all arranged and for which he was not expected to give his permission since he had not been asked for it. She was under twenty-one, but she planned her holidays without taking any account of her parents; and of course, he didn't bat an eyelid. How would she react if he took it into his head to say to her: 'Catherine, my dear, I'm alone in this big house, and I'm bored: will you stay here with me until the end of your vacation?' He could imagine the look she would give him, and it almost sent a shiver down his spine. He would do better to keep quiet. Catherine was fond of her father, true; but as for sacrificing a month's vacation for him, as for giving up 'the gang' for his sake .... ! If he had been at death's door, all right. But that wasn't the case.

After Catherine had gone he went through several hours of such bitter, overwhelming sadness that he thought it was irremediable. Which indeed it was, like all sadness. But eventually it disappeared, as everything does in the monotonous ebb and flow of human life.

One Saturday afternoon in September, Bruno asked him to come with him on an outing to La Houn, a little country house where some urgent repairs had become necessary. André was rather surprised by his unexpected invitation, but saw no reason to refuse: on this sunny afternoon an outing in the country should be quite pleasant. What Bruno called his country house turned out to be a ramshackle two-storey farmhouse, consisting of a huge kitchen and a smaller bedroom on the ground floor, and a loft above. The whole house smelt fusty and neglected. There were a few touches indicating a vague attempt to smarten the place up: there was a rug in the bedroom, a pair of handsome firedogs in front of the fireplace, and even an old radio in one corner of the kitchen. Bruno took down a gun which was hanging above the fireplace, checked the safety-catch, and put a few cartridges into the pocket of his suède jacket. From the front of the house there was a view of a vast expanse of reddish hills stretching away to the bluish line of the mountains on the horizon. The air smelt of crushed grapes and dead leaves. A flock of crows settled in the next field, cawing loudly.

'Juliette keeps pestering me to sell this house. She never comes here, and I only come now and then, to shoot the odd hare. The kids are bored here. It's funny how kids are always bored in the country. We could make the place more comfortable, by converting the loft for instance, but that would cost a hell of a lot. In the old days we could have treated ourselves to that little luxury, but nowadays you have to think twice about it ... So Juliette wants me to sell.'

'You'd have no trouble finding a buyer. The view is superb.'

'I've already had offers for it. But, you know, I don't want to sell the place. During the last few months I've come here quite a lot. I sit down on this bench and think.'

'You think?' André said teasingly. 'Wonders never cease! What do you think about?'

'Everything,' Bruno said simply, not noticing André's irony. 'When you look at that view all sorts of ideas come into your head.'

'For instance?'

'For instance, that that view will still be there when I've gone.'

André understood now why Bruno had asked him out here: to be able to talk to somebody, to be able to confide in him. He no longer felt any inclination to smile.

'Since when have you been thinking about that sort of thing?'

'I don't know exactly. Ever since my fiftieth birthday perhaps. All of a sudden I said to myself: Good Lord, I'm fifty years old. I've only got about thirty years left, if I'm lucky, in other words about as long as it's been since I did my military service. Well, these last fifty years have gone in a flash. So . . .'

He made a vague gesture. André darted a surreptitious glance at the bloated profile and massive figure of the man lumbering along beside him. Bruno looked like one of his vine-growing ancestors, with the same ruddy complexion, but none of the same joviality.

'Do you ever have the feeling I have,' Bruno asked, 'the feeling that you're on the decline?'

'On the decline is saying a lot, but of course I'm aware of my age.'

'Sometimes I tell myself I'm done for.'

'Oh, there you're exaggerating.'

'No, I mean done for. Just that. Two years ago, you know, I went to the local fête with my kids . . . There was a girl there . . . A lovely piece, a real dish. I had one or two dances with her. There were some young people around us. I heard one of them say: "Look at old Marcillac." It may sound ridiculous, but that gave me a shock. Old Marcillac. Like a bucket of cold water. All of a sudden I saw myself through the eyes of those kids: an old fool trying to cut a dash and not realising what a fool he looked.'

'There again you're laying it on a bit thick. At fifty a man's in the prime of life. He's got every right to dance with a girl, especially at a public fête. No, you're exaggerating!'

'And what happened next ... You must have heard about it at the time?'

'I vaguely remember hearing something.'

'I was ashamed of myself. In front of my boys, you know ... Pierrot was very decent about it; but the more decent he was, the more ashamed I felt.'

'Honestly, there was nothing to feel ashamed about, I can assure you.'

They walked a little way in silence. Bruno had his gun slung across his back. There was nothing to be heard but the crackling of dry leaves under their shoes and the cawing of the crows in the fields.

'Do you think there's anything after death?' Bruno asked abruptly.

'What do you expect me to say? My own feeling is that there's nothing, but I can't say for sure, one way or the other.'

'If there's nothing, then it's terrible.'

'Terrible?'

'Yes. Because what's the use of living, if it's for such a short time, and then to disappear completely? When we're dead, it will be just as if we'd never lived. So you begin to wonder ...'

He left the sentence unfinished. They were walking across a field which rose in a gentle slope to the edge of a little wood. André stopped to get his breath back.

'For a man who's done for, you still walk at a pretty good lick,' he said. 'I ought to be able to keep up with you without any trouble, but for the past few weeks I've felt tired nearly all the time.'

A hare bolted from a thicket about twenty yards away. In a flash Bruno brought his gun to his shoulder. His companion was amazed by the prompt reflex action, the quick movement; but while he was nerving himself for the shot, he was surprised to see Bruno lower his gun and sling it over his shoulder again.

'You're not going to shoot?'

'Poor old chap: I might as well let him end his days in peace. He can't be too unhappy here, that hare. So . . .'

'You're getting sentimental.'

'It isn't that. I can tell you what it is: I'm so afraid of death that I've got to the point of respecting even a little animal's life. Out of superstition, I suppose. Are you afraid of death too?'

'Yes and no. It depends how I'm feeling.'

André wondered why he felt embarrassed: as if he had been asked an indiscreet personal question. But perhaps that was what his friend's question was. In any case, with Bruno there was no need to feel embarrassed: he meant no harm, and for him, talking about death wasn't unseemly or 'out of place'. In that respect nobody could be less hidebound and conventional. He talked about whatever was on his mind at the moment, without worrying in the least about the proprieties. He would have been greatly surprised if anybody had suggested to him that two well-bred gentlemen shouldn't mention certain subjects such as death – that talking about such things simply wasn't done. He would have asked why not. Dear Bruno! He was completely natural, even primitive.

'Because I'm scared stiff of death. I've been even more afraid of it lately. And I hate getting older. It's so depressing, giving up one thing after another . . . The doctor's already put me on a diet: eat less, drink less, no sauces, no salt . . . No salt: just imagine! There's no taste in anything any more. It wouldn't be so bad if it were just the pleasures of the table . . . But there's the rest . . .'

'Meaning what?'

'Come now, you know very well what I mean,' said Bruno, looking slightly embarrassed. 'It may not be the same for you; but for me, there are certain days when I think of nothing else. It's become an obsession. What wouldn't I give to enjoy the pleasures I had when I was young! Mind you, I still love Juliette, but now it's more a sort of affection I feel for her.

It's not the same any more...Without wanting to be indiscreet, I suppose that things have changed between you and your wife too, and that you...'

'Yes, of course.'

'Speaking for myself, I dream of nothing but girls of twenty! There, I've said it. In the street I've the devil of a job to stop myself turning round to look at every pretty girl who goes by. And there's no shortage of those nowadays! You can hardly take a step without getting a shock. And they're all so lovely, dammit! All of them. And the trouble is, they aren't for me. They don't even see us! Sometimes I've tried to catch the eye of one of them. Nothing doing. They've got no eyes for anyone but boys their own age. It's funny, it seems to me it didn't use to be like that. In that respect the world has changed completely.'

'In every respect, Bruno.'

André was moved, a little amused, and curiously relieved. Curiously? No, not really. He was familiar with the compensatory process by which our sufferings are reduced when we discover that others are afflicted with them too. Bruno. Solid, easy-going Bruno, who always looked as if he took life as it came, without asking any questions, without suspecting that it was all utterly senseless and could be very sad. So he too was sometimes a poor animal haunted by dreams, who scented the approach of death and reared up in protest. Why yes, they both belonged to a vast community tormented by the same secret fear: the suffering Church (André smiled to himself at the phrase) of men at the beginning of their decline. Their decline, not their old age. Perhaps, once a certain point had been reached, serenity was possible? Once you had crossed the no-man's-land between two ages...Nobody cared about that silent community, which didn't dare complain. The world was made for women and young men. Yes, America had shown the way...The older men might rule the world, but they didn't really enjoy it. Yet you heard people talk about the pleasures and achievement of maturity, and no doubt there *were* such things: wasn't founding a family the finest achievement of all?

'All the same, we've got some grounds for satisfaction, you and I. We've both of us founded families. They do say that the great adventurers of the twentieth century are the fathers of families... And we've the good fortune, which is not so common nowadays, of having nice children.'

'Yes... The children... Oh, I'm not complaining about mine – they're perfect. But when all is said and done, they've got their own lives now. Pierrot is a man now, and a father himself. He's going to live far away. It's the same with Nicolas. Besides, Nicolas...'

He gave a sigh, and left the sentence unfinished.

'Yes? Nicolas?'

'I don't know what I was going to say. He's a wonderful kid, very intelligent and all that, but... I don't know him half as well as I do the other two. I don't know why. There are things about him I don't understand.'

'Such as?'

Bruno shrugged his shoulders.

'It's nothing I can really pin down. Just a vague feeling. He's very artistic, very sensitive... Sometimes I... I'm afraid for him.'

'Afraid?'

'Yes, I'm afraid he's going to be unhappy one day.'

'Nonsense, what an idea!'

'What does your little Catherine think of him? Does she ever talk to you about him?'

'Catherine? Why yes, she adores him. They adore each other.'

'They adore each other, but there's nothing else between them, eh? Or do you think there's something else?'

'No, I don't think so. They're good friends, that's all.'

'Yes, that's what I thought too. He's very serious. For a boy of nineteen, I even think he's too serious.'

'Oh, you're too hard to please.'

They turned back, for dusk was falling and the mountains on the horizon had taken on a purple tint. The air was getting cooler. Cattle-bells could be heard in the distance; and close by, the cawing of the crows. In the little house, Bruno hung the gun up again above the fireplace. Then he lit a lamp, opened a cupboard, and took out a bottle.

'Let's have a drink,' he said. 'It's a good local brandy. I always have a glass when I come here. What shall we drink to? Our future or our past?'

'Our present. Living in the present is the best rule anyone has thought of yet.'

They sipped their brandies.

'It's excellent,' said André. 'I ought not to be drinking it, because I'm supposed to keep off spirits. But to hell with it.'

'Are you on a diet too?' Bruno asked, with scarcely veiled satisfaction. 'What's the matter with you?'

'Oh, I don't know. The heart's a bit tired, I think.'

He felt very well, stimulated by the burning taste of the brandy. He smiled to himself, thinking that the two of them looked like a couple of grandfathers in a Labiche comedy. He looked at Bruno's face, sharply etched in the gentle light from the lamp on the table. Bags, creases, wrinkles. Although it was only beginning to take shape, he could already make out the mask of the old man Bruno would be one day. That was just as it should be.

'Do you think it's possible,' asked Bruno, 'that we might go on living, after death, in a different form? What they call metempsychosis. Is there a tiny chance that it might be possible? I ask you that because I was thinking of that hare I didn't shoot this afternoon, and it occurred to me that when I died I'd rather like to start living again as an animal like that. A fox or a hare ... Anything, really, rather than rotting in a box and being nothing any more, for all eternity ... Don't you agree?'

'There's no reason why we shouldn't hope for something like that, survival in one form or another. What we call death may be birth into a new form of life which we can't imagine. I ought to add that I don't think it's very likely, but it isn't completely out of the question.'

Bruno had listened to him eagerly.

'If only you could be right,' he said sadly. 'Will you have another drop of brandy? Go on! And let's drink to our future as a couple of hares.'

'Is there anything bothering you?'

'I'm worried about Michel.'

'Oh, go on! It isn't as serious as all that. I'm not worried about it.'

'It isn't so much the fact that he's been sent home from school for three days; I know they're very strict. It's what he was sent home for.'

'Just kid stuff. Copying the next boy's work. So what? Didn't you ever copy at school?'

'No, never.'

'Well, you were an exception, that's all I can say.'

'Why, did you?'

'No, I didn't either, but that was because I didn't dare. I was afraid of getting caught. I was honest out of cowardice. All my friends copied. All kids cheat.'

'Not all of them. There are some who are honest. You start by cheating at school, and then one day . . .'

'One thing leads to another, eh? Yes, I know. All the same, don't get too alarmed. Haven't you ever cheated in your business deals? Just a little bit? Go on, own up.'

'Never!' she protested. 'Every time I've seen the chance of bringing off a deal, I've gone straight for it. I may have taken advantage of other people's stupidity, but I've never swindled anybody.'

He raised a disbelieving eyebrow.

'Hmm. Perhaps we ought not to look too closely into that. Let's say you've sailed pretty near the wind once or twice. In the property business that's easy. Not that I blame you. I'd do the same if I knew anything about business; but as I don't know the first thing ... Michel, though, will know all about it.'

'I've never cheated,' she repeated stubbornly. 'Either at school or later.'

He didn't feel it necessary to contradict her on this point.

'I'm afraid,' she went on after a short pause, 'that Michel may have evil instincts.'

'Of course not. He's going to be enterprising and aggressive. He's going to know how to fend for himself. And all the better for him. I've already told you I wasn't sorry he was a resourceful young fellow.'

'Cheating isn't being resourceful.'

'You've got to fight dirty in life. Off with the kid gloves and no holds barred.'

He said this with his usual mixture of passion and mockery, the mockery disguising any indiscreet display of passion. It was never possible to say for certain whether he was being sincere or sarcastic; everything he said was in an ambiguous, rather shady area between honesty and irony. During their engagement and in the early days of their marriage he had been more spontaneous, and indeed more vulnerable. Gradually, however, his character had hardened. She couldn't have said exactly when this hardening process had begun. As their financial situation had improved, so he had acquired greater self-assurance; but whereas he should have simultaneously gained in indulgence, mellowness and bonhomie, as happens with most men when fortune smiles on them, it seemed on the contrary that his corners had lost none of their sharpness. He had not become magnanimous in prosperity. His timidity had finally disappeared, money being the most effective medicine in that domain, but his pride remained; and with it went an ever watchful asperity, which expressed itself from time to time in caustic comments on the world in

216

general – no names were ever mentioned. She often reflected that she scarcely understood him any better than at the time of their engagement, but that didn't worry her unduly: she was in the habit of taking people as they came, however close to her they were. He was often very considerate towards her: he knew how to be thoughtful and attentive. She was almost certain that he loved her a little, that she mattered to him; and that was enough for her, or at least she made sure that it was enough for her, for she had known ever since childhood that you shouldn't expect too much of men or the world. She had enjoyed herself for twelve years, with tireless patience and ingenuity, amassing a modest fortune. This had occupied her time, like a splendid game. She was happy to have won in that game at least, in default of winning in the games of love, talent and social success. I've done something in life, she told herself. I haven't completely wasted my time in this world. Her rather peculiar husband (sometimes she thought his brain was slightly cracked, probably from birth) wasn't exactly the ideal marriage partner, but after all, who am I to demand an ideal husband, and why should I deserve one? And she concluded that the best thing was to accept her fate uncomplainingly.

Jean walked across to the window and gazed out over the town. She looked up. His face had taken on a hard, arrogant expression. His eyes were fierce and splendid, the lids slightly discoloured.

'One day,' said Jean, 'our son will be the leading figure in the town. He'll have everything I didn't have. Everything we didn't have,' he corrected himself.

'Don't ask for too much. You mustn't always talk about revenge and things like that . . .'

'Are you superstitious?'

'Yes, you know I am. I don't like talking about revenge or making over-ambitious plans. You're always punished for that sort of thing. Besides, what do you want to give Michel that we can't give him now? Education, money . . .'

'Well,' he said casually, 'for one thing we could install him in a house in the Rue de Navailles.'

'Which one?' she asked promptly. 'Is there one for sale?'

'Ah, the estate agent instinct is aroused! I don't know, but the people living in that street aren't as rich as they were before the war. If we offered a good enough price, I imagine we could buy any one of those houses.'

'And who would we sell it to?'

'We wouldn't sell it. We'd live in it. Our son would live in it.'

'Oh, I see,' she said, in a disappointed voice. 'But what for? We've got a nice home here.'

He turned round, his hands in his pockets, a smile on his lips.

'You've got no imagination,' he said. 'Living in the Rue de Navailles, being somebody who ... one of the residents, one of the nobs – that would give me a kick, you know. I like a bit of poetic justice.'

'What's that when it's at home?'

'A memory of my school-days ... You haven't been to a hairdresser's for some time, have you?' he said in a different tone of voice. 'You ought to. Don't let yourself go.'

'I haven't much time to think about my hair.'

'Find it. Don't let yourself go. That would be a pity, because you're looking more attractive than you used to.'

'What's got into you? Are you feeling ill or something?'

'So I must be feeling ill, must I, if I pay you a compliment?'

'It's just that I'm not used to hearing compliments from you.'

'Nonsense! ... When I tell you that you're looking attractive, I'm being all the more sincere in that I think I'm better-looking too. And if you laugh at me I'll wring your neck. No, joking apart, we're improving with age. Like a good wine. Honestly, don't you think we're better-looking than we used to be?'

She agreed, without much conviction.

'There's no doubt about it,' he said. 'You see, that's poetic justice too. What we didn't have when we were young, we're going to have now. I'm not saying we're going to be raving beauties, but all the same...Our features have settled into place; they've taken on a sort of nobility. Yes, nobility. No. Don't laugh. I know what I'm talking about.'

While he was talking he was walking slowly up and down the room. In accordance with a long-established habit, he kept touching the objects on the tables and shelves: the stones, the paper-knife, the obelisk in veined marble which he caressed with his fingers. Gazing thoughtfully into the distance, he went on:

'You know, I've noticed that lots of people who were really good-looking at twenty have become ugly – yes, ugly ...Sort of decrepit. As if they had stopped bothering and let themselves go...People you used to turn round and look at when they were young...Well, my pet, today they're just has-beens...That's the word for them: has-beens.'

'The literature of the second half of the century,' said Monsieur Bonneteau, 'will be journalism.'

The audience respectfully recorded this observation.

'I don't read novels any more,' said Monsieur Bonneteau. 'They just send me to sleep. On the other hand I read all the papers, even the cheap popular press. There's always something to be gleaned from a newspaper, but what can you get out of a novel, I ask you?'

His gaze swept round the semi-circle of attentive heads, but he didn't wait unduly long for an answer.

'You're going to say that I've written novels myself, or at least books that have been published with that label on them ...Perhaps I'd better explain. In the old days, the only interest of a novel, or at least of what was called a novel, wasn't psychology – what is psychology, after all? It wasn't social realism either – novelists who claim to describe the world make me laugh: how can they describe it when they don't know what it's like? In order to know the world, you have to have a job: you have to sell cloth, handle money, play the Stock Exchange; well, most novelists are poor creatures who know nothing about business, book-worms who live outside the ordinary world ... The only interest of a novel in the old days lay in the style ... Now and then, from time to time, you came across a perfect crystalline phrase.' (Here the speaker went through a suitable dumb show, his eyelids puckered in ecstasy, his lips pursed in readiness to savour an exquisite delicacy – a kiss, perhaps, or some *foie gras*). 'A perfect phrase, a gift from heaven ... And lo and behold, the miracle had taken place, literature had been born for a few moments. But nowadays nobody knows how to write any more. So literature has taken refuge in journalism, and that's just as it should be.'

He turned a scowling face towards Madame Dolfus.

'Where is that beautiful young woman who works for a fashion magazine?' he asked in an inquisitorial tone of voice. 'You told me she would be here this evening.'

'She'll be coming. She's a little late.'

'To persuade me to leave my deathbed, I'm told that a very beautiful young woman will be here this evening. I come along. I don't see her. You don't keep your promises.'

'I tell you she's late. What a man!'

'Who is he talking about?' asked Beatrice Marcillac.

'Lily Gaillard. You know, that redhead you always see at the Foulques's. I invite her here just for him, I play the pimp for his sake, and look how he treats me.'

André recalled that a few years before – ten? fifteen? – it was Beatrice the old man had been worrying about. Tonight had he so much as noticed her? In his eyes she had joined the crowd of women who no longer commanded his attention.

It's true that poor Beatrice is ageing badly. Bleached hair. Surplus flesh all over, on the cheeks, under the chin, round the waist. She's obviously sodden with drink. I wonder if she pays that young fellow she's with, who looks so common. No, I don't think she's descended to paying gigolos yet. But what do people do when nobody loves them any more for themselves? Especially nowadays when nobody's willing to accept unhappiness any more. You've got to be happy at any price. So if you aren't young or desirable any more, you've got to be prepared to pay any price ... happiness, or at least that sort of happiness, being for sale like anything else – just one consumer good among others ... Do people resign themselves when they reach old age? Those two old people for instance. Letitia is as dried-up as an old vinestock; she must be bored, but I don't think there's anything she likes now but her garden and her dinner-parties. As for Bonneteau, he's still excited by the sight of a pretty woman, but purely as an aesthete, I suppose. An old habit of an inveterate womanizer. Is he happy? If he were really happy, he wouldn't be so sarcastic in his remarks, so negative, so critical of his colleagues. Some of them, who aren't as talented as he is, have been more successful and received honours he will never be given now. That must be a source of bitterness to him. But apart from that he's full of vitality, he's interested in the outside world, he has a little circle of admirers, and he amuses himself to the best of his ability. His spitefulness is a tonic for him; it keeps him in good form, physically and mentally. The tougher you are, the better you age. That's what you've got to become: a nasty, spiteful old man, amused by the comedy of life ... You've got to prepare yourself for the part, toughen yourself up ... Yes, the last twenty or thirty years of life could be the best, provided you keep healthy. I'm getting near that time. The worst isn't over yet. The links with youth haven't all been cut yet. There are still a few left which will have to be chopped at until they break. There's still a lot of blood to be shed. But in the end, one fine day, I'll wake up an old man, and when that happens, perhaps the world will recover some of its savour.

'Besides, there are hardly any novelists left. I know of only one, and that's Simenon... Nobody is writing novels any more.'

'How do you know?' asked André, who was himself surprised by the abruptness of his question.

'I beg your pardon?' said Monsieur Bonneteau, looking as if he could hardly believe his ears.

'How do you know that there aren't any novels being written? You've just said that you never read any.'

Monsieur Bonneteau remained silent for over five seconds, which must have been a record for him.

'I read more than you think,' he said at last, in a sepulchral voice.

'The question is...,' André began. Then he seemed to change his mind, pulled a face, shrugged his shoulders and muttered: 'Oh, never mind!' After which he smiled, had a drink of whisky and took a puff of his cigarette.

What the devil got into me? he asked himself, while Monsieur Bonneteau, thrown off balance for a moment but recovering quickly, went on with his bumbling soliloquy. What I did just then was barely polite. What on earth got into me? Was it annoyance at hearing the old man contradict himself? Impatience with the nonsense he was talking, and the frivolity of these well-to-do people who think that nobody matters but themselves? They aren't alone in that. And why should I consider myself any less frivolous than them? I came here because I was bored and wanted a little distraction. This terrace overlooking the sea, the smell of salt and seaweed, these well-dressed men and women, and the prospect of a delicious dinner... An evening of luxury. A certain satisfaction for my vanity. And above all, a little distraction.

'A book isn't necessarily good just because the author is young,' Beatrice was saying. There was a sharp edge to her voice.

'Anything young enjoys a certain advantage,' said one of the guests.

'I'm beginning to get tired of the myth of youth,' she retorted.

Was that Beatrice who said that? Beatrice who, just after the war, in the days of the Rose Rouge and the Tabou, was one of the personifications of that new myth? Oh, where are the snows of yester-year? ...

'All that nonsense,' said Monsieur Bonneteau, 'began with Radiguet. Grasset, who as a publisher was something of a genius, realised something very important at that time: he realised that the fact that an author was only twenty could be exploited like stocks and shares. He had the unstinted support of the fair sex, who were just beginning to be emancipated at that time. Oh, female emancipation! That was a phenomenon which changed the world more profoundly than Marxism, with which, incidentally, it was closely connected ... You may think I'm rambling, but set your minds at rest, I always find my way through my meanderings.'

Monsieur Bonneteau gave his hissing, panting laugh.

'Radiguet's success and the success of those who followed in his wake was due to a public of emancipated women. Because it's only women who read novels. Men don't read. Grasset staked everything on this new public, which was hungry for youth and pleasure. He had realised that being young pays better than ever, and on all levels. That's an irreversible movement. Before long, as in that book by Samuel Butler whose title I've forgotten, age will be a sin, and illness too. There will be laws against falling ill. Luckily civilisation has secreted antidotes for its own poisons. Luckily we have stopped growing old. Take that gentleman, for example.' (He gestured towards André, who gave a start). 'I remember seeing him here about a quarter of a century ago ...'

'Not as long ago as that! Barely half that time.'

'... Yes, a good quarter of a century. Well, he hasn't changed much. You're close on sixty, aren't you?'

'Oh, come now! I'm still a good few ...'

'He's close on sixty,' Monsieur Bonneteau informed the other guests. 'In the old days, a man of sixty had been a doddering old fogey for years. Well I ask you, does that gentleman look like a doddering old fogey? Not a bit of it. As I said before, age has ceased to have any meaning.'

There, he's had his revenge, André told himself with a mixture of amusement and annoyance. Yet it was true that he wasn't so very far off sixty. Another eight years, which would go by in a flash: another eight years, and he would be on the downward slope for good.

As everyone got up to go in to dinner he suddenly felt ill: short of breath, with a weight on his chest and a slight feeling of giddiness. What's the matter with me now? There's always something wrong. I'll have to go and see the doctor again. The engine misfiring. Sinister creaking sounds in the machine. Perhaps I ought not to have drunk that whisky. The feeling of giddiness disappeared. Nobody around André seemed to have noticed anything. He walked towards the house. Monsieur Bonneteau was walking beside him. To André's surprise the old man took him by the arm.

'I seem to remember,' he said, 'that you are a lawyer. What an admirable profession! You know every family's secrets ... But you aren't, I hope, one of those lawyers who write novels on the sly, or keep diaries?'

André reassured the old man, with a weary smile.

'Splendid,' said Monsieur Bonneteau. 'Whatever you do, you mustn't write. Writing is the vice of our age. And unfortunately a vice that goes unpunished. Life can be very pleasant, and even exciting, without a man having to write about it. You are a happy man, I'll wager, Monsieur?'

'I'm not complaining.'

'What admirable wisdom,' said Monsieur Bonneteau. He stopped, partly to get his breath back and partly to gaze in admiration at this lawyer who possessed the dual merit of not writing and not complaining: it was almost as inspiring as the dying wolf in Vigny's poem. 'You are right, Monsieur,' he went on. 'You must never complain. You can find happiness in little humble everyday things. And you know, life is terribly long. It's endless. I'm eighty years old, and I know what I'm talking about. You'll see, Monsieur, you'll see: life goes on and on!'

'So poor Comarieu has had his coronary?' said Jean.

'Yes,' said Bruno. 'The curse of our times. The third within a few months. And all three about our age.'

'But Comarieu is going to pull out of it, isn't he?'

'Probably. All the same, it makes you think.'

'From what I've heard, he was on his way home from Biarritz?'

'Yes, he'd been to dinner at Madame Dolfus's – you remember, the mother of that boy we went to school with.'

'Yes, I remember.'

'He was driving home, shortly after midnight. He was very tired. On the road he felt ill: he'd already felt sick earlier in the evening. Luckily he had the sense to pull up; and it was just as he was going to drive off again that he felt a terrible pain in his chest. He couldn't move, couldn't call out. If he hadn't had the sense to stop the car, he'd have run into a tree.'

'It was a lorry that brought him home, wasn't it?'

'Yes. Poor André had put his arm out of the window. The lorry-driver saw it hanging out. He guessed that something was wrong. That was another stroke of luck for André.'

'You'll give him my best wishes when you see him, won't you?'

'Certainly. But why don't you go and see him too? He'd like that.'

'You think so?' Jean asked in a sarcastic tone of voice.

Bruno turned his head away. He liked gaiety and good humour. He loved a spicy story. But sarcasm sent a shiver down his spine. He didn't always understand it. Sarcasm was a snake in the grass. Jean Lagarde's presence caused him a feeling of embarrassment he had experienced not long before, though to a lesser degree. He thought to himself: The fellow's a nuisance. He's wasting my time. What does he want now? Why has he come to see me? And what's he doing coming to see me without bothering to let me know, without making an appointment? He thinks he can get away with anything, now that he's made his pile. He told himself, and pretended to believe, that the only reason for his embarrassment was annoyance at the unexpected visit of a tiresome individual, and not a more obscure feeling – a vague perception of something secret, nameless, dangerous and inflexible . . . His uneasiness was aggravated by a fairly precise awareness of having lost ground financially, and therefore socially, in comparison with this man, who had gone up in the world, or at least thought he had (and in this sort of calculation, which is nearly always completely illusory, what matters is not the facts but what one believes). This was perhaps the first time in his life that Bruno had felt 'class-conscious'. Or rather, he had probably always been conscious of his class, but the feeling had been so natural, so consistent, so closely incorporated in the fabric of his life that Bruno had never really noticed it. He would have been saddened and surprised if anyone had said to him: 'You think like a bourgeois – you are very class-conscious', for he honestly believed that he was free of any prejudices of that sort: after all, he was on familiar terms with dozens of ordinary people, he was friendly with them, popular and so on. Now the fabric of his life had deteriorated; his class-consciousness had appeared in all its fragility, and was challenged today by the mere presence in his drawing-room of this man – a man in whose eyes Bruno had once enjoyed tremendous prestige. Bruno had an uneasy feeling that in relation to Jean he no longer occupied the position he had previously enjoyed by divine right. But he didn't formulate his uneasiness clearly;

it merely expressed itself in a few vague phrases – the fellow's a nuisance, he's wasting my time, what a nerve bothering me like this, who does he think he is? – superficial half-truths which gave no indication of the profound malaise underneath. Bruno shifted in his armchair and nervously clasped his hands together, unable to keep his eyes for more than three seconds at a time on Jean Lagarde's face – an attitude which could give rise to a mistaken interpretation, by suggesting, for example, not mere embarrassment, but uncontrollable aversion, or even sheer boredom. Jean, on the other hand, sat facing him rigid and erect; his eyes never blinked, as if he were trying to hypnotise an opponent, or at least to out-stare him. Every time a gesture of Bruno's, an intonation, a wavering of his gaze, seemed to betray dislike or impatience, a harder glint in his eyes was the only perceptible indication of an inner reaction.

They asked each other for news of their respective families, and 'how things were going'. As a matter of interest, or simply in order to make conversation, Bruno said:

'Do you still see anything of that pretty neighbour of yours – Maryse I think she was called?'

'Why? Have you found out something about her?'

'No,' said Bruno, rather surprised by the question. 'Is there anything to find out?'

'No. At least as far as I know there isn't. I just thought somebody might have spoken to you about her.'

'No. I've seen her in town once or twice since that evening ... As pretty as ever.'

His gaze was a little nostalgic. He gave a sigh, as if he were tearing himself away from an idle dream.

'She used to be a neighbour of mine,' said Jean. 'Nowadays I hardly see anything of her.'

'That's true – I'd forgotten you'd moved. Somebody told me you had a magnificent flat.'

'It's not bad. It's not bad here either,' he said after a short pause. 'It's very much as I imagined it.'

'Why, haven't you been here before?' Bruno asked with obvious awkwardness.

Jean's smiled broadened.

'If I'd been here before, do you really think I could have forgotten?'

'Why not? It's a very ordinary house.'

'It was your house, so it couldn't be an ordinary house for me. In any case, it isn't ordinary at all.'

'Do you know Comarieu's place?'

Every word seemed to cost Bruno an effort.

'No.'

'It's much smarter than this house.'

'Really?'

'They've got modern pictures and lovely things. It's very artistic.'

'I'm not surprised. With André Comarieu it's what you'd expect.'

And Jean's lips stretched even further.

'If you pay him a visit you'll have a chance to see the lovely things they've got.'

'In spite of that tempting prospect I don't think I'll be going to see him ... But perhaps it's time I told you why I've come to see you.'

'Fire away.'

Jean paused for a moment.

'I was told that you and your wife were thinking of moving house.'

In a fraction of a second Bruno froze. His whole body went tense in expectation of what was to follow.

'That's news to me,' he said ponderously.

'I thought it couldn't be true, but I wanted to make sure.'

'Who told you that?'

'I can't remember. It was just one of many rumours. To tell the truth, I think I got it from my wife.'

'If anybody mentions it again, your wife can say that it isn't true.'

228

'Good. I'm glad for your sake. Because you and Juliette must be very attached to this house.'

'My wife and I? Yes, we are indeed very attached to this house.'

The slight correction he had made at the beginning of his reply had not gone unnoticed: he made sure of that with a quick glance.

Like Jean a few minutes earlier, he looked around at the room in which they were sitting. Bruno couldn't have described this room if he had been asked; he couldn't even have drawn up an inventory of the furniture from memory; at most he might have been able to remember the colour of the armchairs and the curtains. For the first time in his life, perhaps, these objects had assumed a certain significance. Just now he felt that his house was a shell, a protective carapace secreted by two or three generations of Marcillacs, inside which he had only had to curl up in his turn; it was an extension of himself. He was not vulnerable only in his physical and moral being, but also in the things that belonged to him.

There were two portraits of a man and a woman, both looking very dignified, with conventionally pink cheeks and silver hair; they dated from about 1880 and might have been painted by one of Bonnat's pupils. There were opaline vases, brass lamps, lacquer boxes; there were two small oval tables with marquetry tops; there were also some framed photographs on a table. Jean stood up to go and look closely at one of them, which showed a class of schoolboys: three rows of boys wearing uniforms and caps, with a priest in a cassock in the middle. It bore the inscription: *Sixth Form, Sault College*, and a date. Jean was in the photograph: a sullen-faced youth.

'What a sight!' he said, with a little laugh. 'Trousers too short, jacket too long, huge wrists and glowering eyes... Oh, nobody could say I was good-looking at that age!'

'We all look pretty dreadful in that photo.'

'You don't. You're the only one who looks like a human being.'

'All the same, it's easy to tell when the photo was taken. We were got up like little monkeys.'

'I don't know whether your uniform was better cut than the rest; I imagine it was ... But that makes no difference. In spite of the cap and the epaulettes, you don't look dated. You could just as easily be a boy of ... let's say the sixth century B.C.'

'The sixth century B.C.? That's a good one! But why the sixth?'

'A matter of style, I suppose.'

'Well, it's a pity I can't sell myself as an archaeological curiosity.'

'What I meant was that in this photo you are eternal.'

He straightened up. The expression on his face had softened. Bruno hurriedly averted his eyes.

'I don't feel as if I'm eternal,' he said uncertainly.

'The important thing,' murmured Jean, 'is to have been eternal for a few days.'

He came back to his armchair and sat down. Still averting his eyes, Bruno kept clasping and unclasping his hands. There was a tense, expectant silence. Then Bruno seemed to pull himself together. He frowned.

'You haven't told me yet why you've come to see me,' he said coldly. 'Is there any connection between your visit and these rumours of our alleged intention of moving house?'

'Yes,' said Jean, whose gaze, as if in response to Bruno's change of tone, had immediately hardened; 'there *is* a connection. If you had intended to sell this house, I would have suggested a buyer.'

'I've no intention of selling it; but I'd be interested to know who would have thought of buying it.'

'Me.'

This time Bruno looked his caller straight in the eye.

'You? You would have bought this house? But what for?'

'To live in it, of course.'

'To live in it...What a queer idea. Are you cramped for room in your flat?'

'Not in the least. But I've always liked the Rue de Navailles,' said Jean with the smile of a connoisseur.

'You really have got a thing about my property, haven't you? First Le Bosc, and now my house...Well, that's a dream you'll have to give up.'

Their eyes met, and both felt the silent collision of two opposed wills; or rather, since the object of their confrontation was no longer the house – an object which had probably served only as a pretext – a conflict of a different sort, a very old, very obscure rivalry on which no light would ever be shed.

'It goes without saying,' Jean observed after a brief pause, 'that I would have found you a new home.'

'Really? That's very kind of you...And where would this new home have been?'

'My wife and I own several flats which we let to people. It would have been a simple matter to let you have one.'

He waited a few moments; a savage gleam kindled in his eyes and he murmured:

'You could have lived there free.'

Bruno bowed his head and seemed to curl up in his chair. He clenched his hands on his knees. Anyone might have thought that he was gathering himself up like that in readiness to spring: and the silence which followed was heavy with menace. At last Bruno raised his head. He was smiling.

'So,' he said, 'you would have liked to buy this house...'

His smile turned into a quiet little laugh, barely tinged with mockery.

'Don't you think that you and your wife would have been a little out of place here?'

'I'm not out of place anywhere,' Jean retorted in an expressionless voice.

Bruno raised his eyebrows.

'I'm not so sure about that,' he said, and he looked with distaste at the face in front of him as it went white.

'You ought not to talk to me like that,' said Jean, almost in a whisper.

He stood up suddenly and walked out of the room. The street door was quietly opened and closed.

Left alone in the drawing-room, Bruno remained motionless for a minute or two, his eyes lowered, his head slightly bowed, as if he were physically exhausted. Then he went into the kitchen to drink a glass of water. It was only then, as he was raising the glass to his lips, that he noticed that his hand was trembling.

I haven't felt so well for ages. That was an odd thing to say to yourself when your body had just suffered such a serious blow and your activities would probably be somewhat reduced in the future. Yet I do feel well . . . And during these days of idleness, lying motionless in his bed (the doctor had been insistent that he shouldn't move at all) André tried to discover the reasons for this unexpected sense of wellbeing. The word well-being had to be taken in its widest sense, for what he was enjoying was complete moral and physical contentment. Why? Probably because his existence was now within brackets. Suspended. Outside time. Outside the current of events. I'm alive, but it's rather as if I were dead, because nothing can really affect me any more. A sick man is passive, not accountable for his actions. Free at last, since he has no need to be free. He just has to let himself be cared for and coddled. To be a precious, fragile thing that others watch over. The doctor came to examine him every three days. They made him take pills, an extravagant variety of pills, at set times, in accordance with a strict programme. The house had become a sort of cocoon inside which he was cosily installed. His wife and daughter, with the help of a nurse, looked after him, taking it in turns to keep him company and read to him; they were gentle, smiling, quiet. There was only one snag: the need for intimate attentions filled him with shame, even though the nurse performed these tasks with placid indifference and apparently without disgust; but he suffered on her behalf and felt offended in his modesty. He knew that he was being ridiculously idealistic, and that he ought to learn to accept these things with simplicity. But there are matters on which a man over fifty cannot change.

Since that dagger-thrust to the heart, one September evening on the road between Biarritz and Sault, many of his views of life had altered. For example, he had the impression that every trace of vanity in him had gone. His social values had been swept away. It no longer mattered to him that he wasn't a 'somebody', that he had never known success, that he had never written a book. The idea that he had once considered it important to reach a certain rung of the social ladder made him blush. What childish nonsense! Yet most men were obsessed with nonsense of that sort, on all levels of society, all over the world. Their career and the prospect of honours really mattered to them. Some of them struggled all their lives to obtain a single decoration; and when they finally obtained it they felt fulfilled and decided that they could die in peace.

He no longer felt any desire to cut a figure in society, and he had shed other preoccupations too – old ambitions, old spites, old fears. It was as if he had gone through the purifying waters of antiquity. On the other hand, he promised himself pleasures he had previously disdained: he who had always found the country boring decided to visit his house at Saint-Blaise as often as possible; he would go for long walks and get to know the earth, the trees, the flowers, the seasons. Why had he ignored them so foolishly? And there would also be all the books he had never found time to read, the knowledge he had never found the time to acquire.

He had made the essential discovery, the discovery of his

death. Everyone knows that he has to die, but lives as if he were immortal. We waste time, energy, effort: we pay enormous attention to useless things, which are also nearly always boring things; we fail to establish a hierarchy among things, an order of importance; but once death appears to us in all its blinding inevitability, everything falls into place. Stretched out in his bed, almost as motionless as he would be one day in his coffin, he was aware of his death, lying low inside his flesh. It was there within him; it had already risen once to deliver a mighty blow; now it would go on working quietly, patiently, until its task was done. And as time was heavy on his hands, he amused himself by imagining what was going to happen in his body, in his being, once death's work was over. The old heart had swollen and contracted for the last time; suddenly its cells panicked, bathed in a blood which no longer provided it with oxygen; they died very quickly of asphyxiation. The brain cells didn't survive much longer, just under ten minutes; but during these few moments of reprieve, the ghost of thought lingered on perhaps in this body whose arteries had ceased to palpitate, and whose blood was congealing. Then, as in a power-house where the lights went out for want of electricity, the brain cells died in their turn; the ghost of thought vanished. A body without warmth, a closed face, limbs invaded by a growing inertia. These remains were placed in a box, the lid was screwed down, the box was buried six feet underground. Soon, in the darkness of the earth, these remains would become the setting of a new life, a swarming, parasitic life. The process of decomposition could last for months, even years. The worm-eaten face would become something 'with no name in any tongue'. Little by little, a skeleton would emerge from the corruption. It would crumble away, like the box which contained it. A few unrecognizable bones, mingled with the humus; and one not far-distant day, it would be as if André Comarieu had never existed. His voice, his laugh, the colour of his eyes, his favourite jokes, his plans, his work, his weariness, his loves, his hates, his anger, his intelligence, his stupidity: it would be as if all that had never been. Never. André Comarieu. A name. An unknown name on a stone. But tombs disappeared as well, to be replaced by other tombs. Records were lost. Then there would be nothing left. Not even a name. Not even a memory. Absolutely nothing.

Once he had succeeded in absorbing this very difficult, very fugitive notion of nothingness, he immediately thought of the agitation of certain men he knew, and of his own agitation before his heart-attack; and he was almost tempted to burst out laughing. He pictured the little puppet strutting about with pretentious self-importance and frenzied pomposity, and he super-imposed the picture of the dead puppet, lying all stiff in its box. He understood now why, among certain primitive peoples, the skeleton was an object of mockery, used as a disguise in masquerades.

Just as he had learnt to withdraw from himself, so he learnt to detach himself from others. The acts which people put on for themselves and for others had never appeared to him in such a glaring light. The comedy of importance, the comedy of seriousness, the comedy of rank and precedence. He couldn't help laughing at the memory of his ridiculous encounter with the worthy Abbé Trébucq. In Catholic circles in the town people were still praising the young priest's zeal; and everybody believed, or pretended to believe, that that puppet was a lofty soul; for of all the comedies enacted in this world, the comedy of false values is the most consistent.

But in the last analysis, all that was rather amusing . . .

He thought a great deal about his childhood and youth, trying to give some substance to his insubstantial past. He saw himself approaching from the depths of time – a comical, shadowy figure lost in the huge tidal wave of other shadows; and he felt a certain gentle pity for this anonymous little creature advancing into the future without any idea of his destination.

He also tried to draw up a balance-sheet. The balance-sheet of his existence. The good deeds, unselfish actions and joys on the credit side. The failures, compromises and sorrows on the debit side. The two sides seemed evenly balanced. Possibly the credit side had a slight advantage, but only in a negative sense: through the absence of major crimes and tremendous tragedies. I haven't been a good husband. At most a good father. I haven't been a bad citizen, but nor have I done anything to earn my country's gratitude. There have been times when I have caused suffering around me, probably inadvertently; on the other hand the sum of human happiness in this world hasn't been noticeably increased by my efforts. In short, the human race wouldn't be losing much if it lost me. I'm not one of those who have brought honour or glory to mankind. Well, that too was something he had to accept humbly, without despising himself for it.

One day he was looking through a photograph album with Claire beside him. Some of the photographs, snapshots taken from the speeded-up film of his life, made him laugh, but without any bitterness. It wasn't just the old-fashioned look of the clothes that was funny. Claire shared his amusement.

'Look at this one!' he exclaimed. 'You remember? It was at Luchon.'

He suddenly realised that he had addressed Claire as *tu*. She didn't seem to have noticed.

He started thinking about their present relationship. Hadn't his illness and the mortal danger he had been in produced a change here too? Claire had nursed him with irreproachable devotion, but he might have expected that, it didn't surprise him. But she also seemed more relaxed in his company; she was more affectionate to him and more natural in her behaviour. He had noticed this change at once. It was as if she had suddenly ceased to be on her guard, on the defensive. He was sick, and immobilised in his bed; he couldn't hurt her any more. He reflected that the time of difficulties, quarrels and misunderstandings was past, and that

236

shortly before entering the unknown country known as old age, it seemed as if the two of them might come together.

That evening, when she brought their dinner in on a couple of trays, he told himself: I'm going to go on calling her *tu*. But an insurmountable shyness paralysed him: he could not find a suitable moment to implement that modest but important decision. However, when she picked up the two trays at the end of the meal to take them back to the kitchen, just as she was going out of the room he plucked up his courage, and using the *tu* form of address, said: 'That was a wonderful dinner: will you congratulate Mariette for me?' She paused for a moment. His heart pounding, he waited anxiously for her reply, afraid that she might use the conventional *vous*. Without turning her head to look at him, she said in a very natural voice: 'She'll be pleased that you enjoyed it,' and went out. She had called him *tu*! He gave a sigh and sank back on to the pillow. He felt as if all his muscles had relaxed at once. A little later Claire came upstairs again to keep him company, as she did every evening before going to her room. They went on addressing each other as *tu*, each realising how strange this new relationship was to the other. Their ease of manner was tinged with a cautious prudence, like the approach of two blind insects, lightly brushing each other with the tips of their antennae to discover their respective positions and the direction of their movements. Each was as sensitive and receptive as the other, and the difficulty for them, throughout their marriage, had not been in communicating, but in preventing communication, for their misunderstandings were the result of choice, not incapacity. Now that this will to prevent communication no longer existed, the only restraint they felt was imposed by an instinctive discretion which commanded them not to go too fast, and to combine their increased familiarity with a mutual respect which could only be strengthened by the abolition of their defences. Saying good night to him, Claire kissed him, which was something she had done every night

237

since he had fallen ill; but although not a single word had been spoken about the change in their relationship, he realised from hardly anything, in other words from nearly everything – the kiss which lingered a second longer than usual, the hand laid on his forehead for a moment as if to make sure that he wasn't feverish, the barely perceptible change in the tone of her voice – he realised that they had just drawn much closer to each other and that she was grateful to him.

The following week he was given permission to get up and go downstairs. Nearly three months had gone by since his heart attack, and until then he had only left his bed for a few minutes a day, but without leaving his room. Catherine was at home at the time. Wearing his dressing-gown, and escorted and supported by his wife and daughter, he cautiously set out on this perilous journey. In the hall there were two mirrors, arranged in such a way that when you reached the bottom steps you could see your reflection in one of them, but in half-profile, so that for a brief instant you had the impression that it was somebody else. It was only after a momentary pause that you recognised yourself. This was how André, having forgotten the existence of these mirrors and the misapprehension the play of their reflexions could cause, was surprised to find himself confronted, in his own house, with a young-looking, distinguished old man, over whom Claire and Catherine were watching. He identified this old man almost immediately.

It was late November, and during the night there had been a slight fall of snow. He asked if he might go out on to the garden terrace, and they took him outside. The garden, covered with a thin layer of snow, was sparkling in the sunshine. André greedily breathed in the frosty air, absorbed the radiant light. He had visited the shores of the underworld, the kingdom of the shades. He was coming to the surface again; for some time to come he was going to be allowed to see the sun, the snow, the sleeping earth, and the shrubs under their coating of frost, waiting patiently for spring. For some time to come there would be the intoxicating miracle of the recurring seasons, the gentle rain, the primroses in the wet grass, the smell of hay, the smoke and mists of autumn over the bare countryside. He was not going to miss a single crumb of this feast which was offered free to everyone. Already he was all attention and vigilance. He came back into the drawing-room and sank into his armchair, exhausted. A fire had been lit in the hearth, and he could feel the heat of it on his face. He sat watching the dance of the flames. He would never be bored again.

He asked Claire to bring him a notebook which was locked in a drawer in the library. He gave her the little key to that drawer. Claire brought him the notebook. She knew that it was his diary, which he had been keeping for years – the secret diary into which he had consigned things he had never mentioned to her, perhaps judgments on herself.

'Do you want your pen?' she asked as she handed him the notebook.

'Oh, no. I've no intention of writing in it. I'm going to burn it.'

'Burn it? What for?'

He shrugged his shoulders.

'I think it was a futile exercise. You can be wrong about these things. What's in this notebook is of no interest whatever.'

'Perhaps the author isn't the best judge of what he writes,' she said gently, taking care that the good-will she was showing in justifying the existence or the possible preservation of the diary should not be too obvious. 'You may have written some pages which deserve to survive.'

'I doubt it.'

'Besides, it was a distraction for you.'

She must have realised straight away the involuntary cruelty of this remark, for she hastily added:

'Like any creative activity. I imagine that literary creation offers considerable pleasure too.'

'Yes,' said André with a smile, 'but this wasn't really literary creation...Listen, don't have any regrets. When I have a brilliant thought – since nothing should be wasted, least of all brilliance – instead of writing it down in a notebook on the sly, I'll try to say it out loud, for both of us to enjoy.'

As she was standing in front of him, he took one of her hands and carried it to his lips.

'I'm sure that both of us will gain a lot that way.'

He turned a few pages of the diary, reading a sentence here and there. What he read wasn't bad after all: a great many books were published which were inferior in both substance and style. But it was the diary of somebody who was trying to relieve his boredom, trying to comfort himself for living by producing a subtley flattering portrait of himself. Like all private diaries, no doubt. No, he didn't feel any desire to keep this document. All the same, he couldn't help shivering when, after throwing the notebook into the fire, he saw the pages curl up and turn black. He made an effort to remain impassive. Claire darted a furtive glance at him and tiptoed out of the room.

'What are you doing here?'

'I just wanted to see you. To say hello as I was passing. You see, I haven't forgotten my old neighbour.'

'What have you come for?'

'Why don't you let me in first? Instead of talking to me outside your door. That would be rather more pleasant!'

She gave him a spiteful look, pushed the door open, and led the way into the room. He followed her and closed the door. Then he sat down on the bed. She remained standing, a surly expression on her face, in much the same position she had adopted during Jean's first visit.

'How are things with you?' he asked in a friendly conversational tone. 'Is everything going well?'

240

'You've got no business here. In any case, your threats are finished. You can't do anything now.'

Patiently, as if he were explaining something to a child, he showed her that she was wrong, that nothing was finished, that he could do a great deal. An interval of five weeks didn't constitute a time-limitation. He explained to her the meaning of this legal term. He might indeed be reproved for having waited so long before coming forward; but the excuses he would provide – uncertainty, and reluctance to report somebody he knew well – were perfectly plausible and would be accepted; and the machinery of the police force would promptly be set in motion.

'You would be arrested, together with your boy friend; and as neither of you is a match for the police, you'd admit everything in less than ten minutes.'

'And what if I told the inspector about you coming to see me? How would you explain that?'

'I would say that before reporting you to the police I wanted to carry out my own little private inquiry, to make sure that I wasn't making a serious mistake ... No, as I've told you already, you're no match for the police. There would be a presumption against you. That means that they'll automatically suspect you of having done the job, before hearing any of the evidence. Because you're poor, because you've no connections, because you can't express yourself. But I've already told you all that, and I'm not going to say it again. No, you really shouldn't try to fob me off; I've come here as a friend.'

'I doubt that.'

'It's true all the same. I wanted to see how you were getting on. To find out how life had been treating you since we last met.'

His gaze swept round the room.

'You don't seem to have carried out many improvements here, do you? You haven't even bought a couple of chairs or installed a heater in this icy room ... What have you and your boy friend done with the money you got from that job? I suppose he's kept it all for himself? That wouldn't surprise me. I seem to remember seeing him driving a new car the other day ... So he scooped the lot, did he? That isn't fair. You took as many risks as he did. Incidentally, how did you get rid of the stuff?'

'Through some friends of his in Toulouse.'

Not expecting an answer to his question, and certainly not this one, he was taken aback for a moment and stared at her suspiciously. Then he saw that she was telling the truth and gave a low whistle.

'You were well organised, eh?'

In the young woman's eyes there was not so much fear as a sort of defiance, perhaps even a hint of malice. It was as if she were thinking: We're smarter than you think. You aren't going to get the better of us.

However, the answer she had given him had immediately altered their relationship, and that was obvious to both of them from the profound silence which followed Jean's last retort, and also from the meeting of their eyes. She had just played a dangerous card, but one which could also assure her of impunity: if he failed to report her immediately to the police he would be making himself her accomplice; to a certain extent he would be compromised. They eyed each other like a couple of card-players who were each uncertain about the strength of the other's hand and were waiting for some reaction. Jean assumed a nonchalant expression and smiled.

'Well, that's your business. I don't know a thing. I don't know how you and your boy friend operate, and I don't want to know. I'm just sorry to see that you're still ...'

Once again he looked around at the bare room.

'... so badly off. A lovely girl like you ought to be living in luxury. Otherwise what's the use of having a pretty face and a good figure! Nature has given you some wonderful advantages and you don't use them. You live in a cheap,

uncomfortable little room that isn't even properly heated ...
You're wasting your youth, and who for? For a boy who's
just exploiting you, making money out of you. If you loved
him I could understand it. But I'm not even sure that you
love him.'

'What do you know about it?'

'If you do love him, then so much the worse for you.
When I think that there are men who'd be prepared to pay a
lot for ... who'd be very grateful to you if you'd accept
their admiration. I know some myself.'

'You, perhaps?'

'I wasn't thinking of myself. I've already told you that I'm
not asking for anything. But I know one or two gentlemen
in this town who'd be glad to look after you. If you've got
to have a lover, why not a rich lover?'

'And what's your interest in all this? Are you going to get
a commission?'

'You're an impertinent little thing! ... I've told you before
and I'll tell you again that my interest in all this is nothing.
I don't want anything for myself. All I want is to see you
better off and better dressed. I'd like you to have a real
gentleman as a lover – not a young crook who gets you mixed
up in petty burglaries. I'd like you to become a lady.'

'Get away with you! Who do you think you're kidding?
I wasn't born yesterday, you know.'

Jean smiled.

'I know, I know ... But what's worrying you about what
I'm suggesting? The fact that I'm not getting anything out of
it?'

'Go on! You're getting something out of it all right. I
don't know what, but there's something in it for Number
One.'

'You sound just like my wife. It's funny how you women
don't believe that people can be unselfish.'

'I don't believe you are, anyway.'

'All right. I can see that I'll have to make up a story to fit in with your ideas. How about this? The gentleman who's interested in you would like to buy you a little flat. He's buying it through my agency. Does that satisfy you as an explanation?'

'No.'

'Why not?'

'First, because it's ridiculous. And second, because if it was true, you wouldn't tell me.'

'Of course it isn't true! I told you I was going to make up a story . . . But why do you want to know the reasons for everything? There may not even be a reason. Perhaps the whole thing just amuses me, and that's all. I'm interested in you and I'd like to see you become a lady. Let's say it's an experiment. I want to know if it's going to come off. It's interesting, don't you think? Just like a film, only this is real life . . . Listen. Imagine you meet a real gentleman. You might meet him – I don't know – at a local fête, for instance. He asks you to dance. You dance an unforgettable tango . . . Afterwards he tells you that he loves you, that he wants to do something for you.'

'So it's him who's asked you to come and see me, is it? Good. Now I see.'

'Who are you talking about?' asked Jean, raising his eyebrows.

'That fellow – I can't remember his name. Go on, don't play the innocent. You introduced us, at his local fête.'

Jean gave the impression of searching his memory.

'Oh, him?' he said at last. 'I'd completely forgotten that evening . . . But I see that you haven't forgotten it . . . No, I wasn't thinking of that gentleman; though you're quite right, why not him? Now that you've reminded me about him, I think he'd do very well. He could give you security.'

'Come off it! You fixed all this up with him!'

'There, Maryse my dear, I assure you that you're mistaken.'

He made this denial with the smiling, rather embarrassed indolence of someone who wishes to suggest that if he is put-

244

ting up a poor defence, it is because he doesn't feel like standing by a lie which has been exposed so quickly.

'He sent you to feel out the ground, because he didn't dare to come himself.'

'I assure you that he didn't ask me ...'

'Stop trying it on. When you're lying, it shows all over your face.'

'All right. You believe what you like. It doesn't matter. But listen. If you ...' (He searched for the right words and smiled at what he was going to say). '... if you should enter into relations with that gentleman, whatever you do you mustn't mention this conversation to him or say that I've been to see you.'

'He doesn't want it to look as though it was fixed up in advance?'

'You're so quick. I don't need to explain anything to you.' said Jean with quiet admiration. 'Oh, you know us all right! You know what men are like ... No, Maryse, you mustn't tell him about our little talks, or even mention my name. That would break the spell straight away ... Yes, we men are made that way. We like to think that we have only ourselves to thank for our conquests. As you put it so well, it mustn't look as though it was fixed up in advance.'

'You've no need to give me advice, since I shan't be seeing that gentleman of yours.'

'Really? Why not?'

'Because I don't want to.'

'You're making a big mistake. You're throwing away lots of advantages. He'd treat you well, you know. And you could have anything you wanted.'

'But I've already told you I'm not interested!'

'Don't be so stubborn. Think a bit before just saying no, like a silly donkey. With that gentleman you could have anything you wanted. And there'd be no need to stint yourself. Those people are loaded, while you haven't got a sou. You can ask for anything you like. What are you risking, after all?

The more you ask for, the more he'll worship you. Life's like that. Men only love women who make them suffer... But that's enough philosophising... You've got a wonderful opportunity here, and you've got to grab it quick. Because you won't be twenty for ever, you know. You've got a chance here to get your revenge. Yes, get your revenge. You look as if you don't understand what I mean... Look, you were born poor, you work hard for a wretched pittance, you live in an icy attic – do you mean to tell me that you've never wanted to blow up the world? What have you got in your veins – blood or water? Are you resigned to being poor? Haven't you ever felt like spitting at one of those rich nobs who despise you, one of those women in the Rue de Navailles who don't even see you when you pass them in the street, because you just don't exist in their eyes? Well, now you've got a chance to show them you exist. They'll be obliged to see you, covered with furs paid for by one of their men... And you'll be the one who walks past them, with your head held high... That's what I mean by getting your revenge. Now do you understand?'

He patted the bed.

'Don't stand there like that. Come and sit here beside me.'

She obeyed, after a slight hesitation which was probably intended to emphasise her independence. She sat down at a certain distance from him, holding herself stiff and aloof.

'Now if you became the lady I'd like to see you become, with a luxury flat, and a fur coat, and all the rest of it, I would naturally show you every consideration. I would even forget a certain night when I saw little Maryse getting out of a car at two in the morning, carrying a shabby fibre suitcase... Because that Maryse would be a thing of the past, and there'd be nothing to do but forget her. You see what I mean?'

He stroked her cheek with the tips of his fingers.

'Will you be bringing us together?' she asked after a pause.

'Oh, I leave all that to you. Nothing could be easier. For

246

example, he goes to the Café de la Place every evening between seven and eight. You might bump into him there one
evening. Leave it to him to strike up a conversation with you.
After that, it's up to you. Don't worry – you'll soon see how
much power you've got . . . over him.'

Although he went on smiling, his gaze became a little
harder, a little more insistent.

'Above all, don't forget that you must never mention my
name. Never. If he happens to ask you whether you ever see
anything of me, even though we aren't neighbours any more,
you must tell him that we never have any occasion to meet.
But I doubt if he'll ask you about me. It will never occur to
him.'

'But he knows that we've met, seeing that he asked you
to . . .'

She left the sentence unfinished, as if she were now uncertain about what had seemed obvious to her at an earlier
stage in the conversation. She frowned.

'He'll have forgotten,' said Jean with the gentle patience a
grown-up shows towards a child. 'That won't surprise you,
knowing men as well as you do: he'll have forgotten.'

The famous singer was talking of her art. She said that she
was going to sing Norma, her favourite part, at the Opera.
She was followed by four long-haired youths who sang a
song and accompanied themselves on the guitar. They too
were questioned about their art. Next a leading couturier
explained that the dress materials of the future would be
metals and plastics. Fashion had to be futuristic. We were
living in the age of science fiction, so that a space-woman
style had to be devised for the future Eve. The couturier
boldly declared that he for his part was ready to equip that
Eve with aluminium dresses. Yes, aluminium – why not?
What was more, the cut of these dresses would be geometrical,
masculine. No more curves or soft lines: bosoms would be

hidden behind flat, shining armour. Hair would naturally be worn short. The future Eve would be the equal of the future Adam. A painter (television was terribly culture-conscious in the sixties) gave a definition of pop art and explained why this new aesthetic had already begun to supersede abstract art and Tachism all over the world. Meanwhile Pope Paul VI was flying to Bombay for the Eucharistic Congress. There was also news of the Mariner rocket. Viewers were granted a glimpse of the film actor who played James Bond, in the lounge of a Paris hotel. A play had just opened showing the anguish of the physicist Oppenheimer at the idea of a nuclear holocaust; and the entrancing 1912 sets for *My Fair Lady* were captivating Paris as they had already captivated New York and London.

Thanks to these news magazines, these programmes about recent events in every sphere of life, the whole world passed through every home within the space of a few minutes. The world, or rather a picture of the world. That ever-present picture had a hypnotic power. It was a drug. The general level of sensitivity all over the world must have dropped slightly since the human race had been turned into passive receivers of a film which was naturally incoherent. For absorbing a singer and a rocket, the future Eve dressed in plastic and little mutated Adams with hour-glass figures and waist-length hair, fears of nuclear war and Grandmother's fallals, Pope and Pop, all in less than an hour, was surely enough to muddle anybody's ideas. But perhaps that was what they called 'belonging to one's times' . . .

André now spent long hours in front of his television set, and the whole town did likewise. Within a few months Sault had been covered with aerials, a development which had spoilt the attractive lines of the tiled roofs – but what was that paltry aesthetic flaw compared with the fantastic advantages provided by the small screen?

The telly wasn't André's only link with the outside world. Bruno or Juliette used to drop in almost every day to see how he was. Towards the end of January Bruno told him he had just had a letter from Pierre, who had been granted a long leave and was planning to come and spend it in France with his wife and son. André said that Suzy had written to him too and hinted at the possibility of this journey.

'Well, that's wonderful news,' said Bruno. 'I hope you'll be game to celebrate your grandson's visit?'

'To be game' was one of Bruno's favourite expressions. For him it presumably had virile echoes, conjuring up the energetic combat in which man's vocation was fulfilled. Whenever Pierre was getting ready to play in a football match, Bruno, who had watched over him like a manager, would ask him: 'Do you feel game?' It was a magic formula, a lucky question.

'The doctor says I can go out in a week. The lesion has completely healed. I'll be able to live a normal life again. So of course I'll be up to welcoming Monsieur Marcillac junior.'

He expected to see Bruno's face light up, as it did every time anybody mentioned that unknown descendant of his, who bore his name and would carry on his line. Sure enough, Bruno smiled, but it was a conventional, mechanical smile; his thoughts were obviously elsewhere. André sensed that a confidence was imminent, and also guessed what it would be. Bruno lowered his voice slightly.

'May I talk to you,' he asked, 'about a personal matter?'

'Why, of course!'

'We shan't be disturbed for a few minutes?'

'Claire has gone out, and she won't be back for a good half-hour.'

Bruno seemed to be wondering how to begin.

'Do you remember an afternoon we spent at my little house in the country last year? One afternoon in September? We chatted a lot about one thing and another.'

'I remember it very well.'

'Do you remember our conversation? I told you I was ...'

He hesitated, presumably hunting for the right word.

'You told me you were depressed, in poor spirits.'

'Yes, I also told you I'd have given anything to ... to experience ...'

Another hesitation, this time apparently dictated, not by uncertainty of vocabulary, but by modesty of feeling. Again André had to finish his sentence for him:

'... to experience love again. Love with a young girl.'

'Well,' Bruno went on after a short pause, 'I've done it. But perhaps you know already? I have an idea my wife has told your wife all about it. Those two tell each other everything. Has Claire said anything to you?'

'I don't want to lie to you. Yes, we know about it. Juliette told Claire that you had a mistress.'

'I thought as much. The whole town knows about it. Tell me honestly, do you disapprove? Do you think very badly of me?'

'What right have I to pass any judgment on you? I'm not irreproachable myself.'

'But honestly, do you think it's ridiculous, at my age, to have a mistress – especially such a young one? She's barely twenty, you know ...'

A little note of pride in his voice as he made this last statement.

'Ridiculous? No. All I can say is that we're sorry for Juliette, because we're very fond of her and naturally she's unhappy.'

Bruno's face changed.

'Yes. Poor Juliette. I know she's unhappy. I can see that. I'm sorry for her too, but what can I do? Yes, I know what you're going to say: break things off with the other woman. But I can't break things off with her and I don't want to.'

'It's as serious as that, is it?'

'It's very serious. You see, she loves me.'

As this declaration aroused no comment, and André was looking at him without appearing to understand, he went on:

'The girl. She loves me. I'm certain of that. There are ways in which you can tell for sure. There are ... Well, you know as well as I do what I mean,' he finished discreetly.

This reserve on his part must have been in conflict with a desire to talk, for in the face of his friend's silence he hurriedly explained what he meant:

'There are certain words, certain cries, which can't lie. I've awakened her. You understand?'

André was torn between embarrassment, a vague feeling of hostility, and a desire to laugh. 'I've awakened her...' This was straight out of the *Kama-Sutra*. He gazed in perplexity at the paunchy middle-aged man for whom a young girl uttered cries of love.

'The fact is, I make her happy,' Bruno went on, his voice almost quavering and his gaze heavy with meaning. 'I don't need to dot my i's for you, do I?'

'You've already dotted them, old chap; and you've added quotation marks too. Listen, I don't want to say anything to offend you, but ... are you quite sure that that young woman really loves you?'

Bruno gave a sibylline smile and nodded.

'I'm absolutely certain,' he said.

'Another thing: you said just now that you had so to speak initiated her. But from what I've heard, the young woman in question has had liaisons before, or at least one, with a Spaniard if I'm not mistaken.'

'That's a lie, I can tell you that! A downright lie!'

'All right, all right. I just remember hearing ... But since you say it isn't true, I believe you. But tell me, do *you* love *her*?'

'I'm mad about her,' Bruno said simply. 'I think of nothing else. I'd do anything for her.'

'I hope not! I hope you aren't going to do anything silly.'

'What do you mean? I've a chance here, a wonderful, incredible chance to start a new life, as if I were twenty all over again. And you want me to let that chance slip through my fingers?'

'Don't tell me you intend to leave Juliette? To ask for a divorce?'

'I don't know. I don't know where I am any more. All I know is that I've got that girl under my skin, and I can't do without her. Happiness for me is her and nobody else. Yes, I know what you're going to say, but don't bother. Everything you can say to me I've said to myself already, over and over again: my wife, my children, our children who are going to arrive here a few days from now... You're going to think I'm an absolute swine and I've gone out of my mind, but I tell you nothing else matters any more. Wife, children, position, reputation – nothing! And now spit in my face if you want to.'

'I've no desire whatever to spit in your face. But I'm appalled... You can't possibly feel like that. Not about a girl of that sort.'

'What sort? What are you insinuating? What sort are you talking about?'

'Keep your hair on. I meant about a girl who, apart from her age and her beauty, has nothing really remar...'

'You don't know what she's like. Nobody knows what she's like.'

'Besides, at our age, we ought to...'

'Don't talk to me about my age! That won't work. It's the last thing you ought to mention to me just now. If anybody mentions my age to me again, I'm perfectly capable of packing my bags tonight and going off somewhere, anywhere with the girl.'

'Going off with her? But where, Bruno, where?'

'I don't care! I've got a bit of money. I'll work. I'm still pretty fit, you know. I'm still a man, dammit!'

'And you'd leave your family like that, on the spur of the moment?'

'I've already told you, there comes a time when nothing else matters.'

'All the same, you wouldn't divorce Juliette, would you? To marry that . . .'

'Why not? I've thought about it, you know.'

'Bruno! You wouldn't do that!'

'Oh, it's obvious you don't know what it's like!'

'What what's like? To be in love?'

'To be completely swept off your feet. To belong to somebody else. To think of only one thing in life.'

'But you used to have a sense of duty. You used to be somebody who . . .'

'Duty, duty! You make me laugh. What's duty? Life comes first. Living, you know. One day we're all going to be eaten by the worms. Well, when I'm in bed with that girl, when I'm holding her in my arms, I stop thinking about death. I exist! That's what duty means to me. My duty is being happy, is living.'

'Don't get all worked up. Calm down.'

'But you don't look as if you understand. It's just as if I were talking to you in a foreign language. It's queer, you know . . . Listen. I'd better explain it all to you in detail.'

And he duly 'explained it all' in detail. Without restraint. Using the precise terminology of the dormitory or the barrack-room. Through these unbridled confidences André was able to reconstruct the commonplace story he had guessed at: a man consumed by a last fire, and incapable of distinguishing pleasure from a fierce tenderness; and a sensual, cunning little animal who was turning this liaison to her advantage. On the one hand an insatiable hunger, an anxiety exacerbated by awareness of age, time, and approaching if not imminent decline; on the other, the fierceness of a young creature full of vigour and strong in the consciousness of a long future. He was not disgusted by what he heard. He felt no pity either. He was simply amazed. So the famous grand passion people wrote about in books really existed? So love that was heaven and hell combined, an erotic frenzy, a torrent of surging energy, really happened? It wasn't just a

253

literary invention? You could meet it in everyday life? I shall never have known that frenzy, that annihilation of oneself in another person which is also a rebirth, an enrichment of life. Like most of mankind, I shall die without ever having experienced 'passion'. I shall have lived in a lower key, scarcely aware that I was alive. Why? Out of fear of life? Mediocrity of character? A mistaken evaluation of the most desirable aims? Excessive caution and an unwillingness to take risks? He looked at Bruno with astonishment and dislike. He was in a hurry to have done with it, impatient for the man to go. He couldn't bear to hear any more about that unknown world ... I hate listening to confidences, he told himself.

They heard the front door opening. Bruno adjusted his features and stood up.

'You aren't driving me away, Claire,' he said, when she came into the room. 'But I've been here a long time and I was just going.'

Claire asked after his wife and family, with a natural air which was barely spoilt by a hint of coldness. As always happened when she was embarrassed, she talked too fast, not waiting for answers to her questions, and looking a little flustered.

'Well, how's everything?' she asked André. 'You aren't too tired? I've found you some mushrooms for tonight. Are you pleased? I hope it's not against doctor's orders.'

Bruno had noticed her use of the word *tu*, and André saw that he had noticed it. Bruno's face was an open book. Just now you could read on it, in letters as big as those which gave the news in electric lights: 'Well, well, so now you call each other *tu*? You must be getting along better than before.' André promptly started playing the part of the happy husband, who has long since found contentment with a loving wife and would never think of looking elsewhere for compensations of which he has no need. He thanked Claire with effusive affection. He kept giving her long, tender glances. Bruno had to go away with an ideal impression of the André-

Claire couple; he had to be suitably edified. And edified he certainly was: staring at them in open-mouthed astonishment, he couldn't get over the exemplary sight presented by the Comarieus...

'You know, he's gone right out of his mind,' said André when Bruno had left. 'He's talking about getting a divorce and going off with that girl. We're in for a real scandal.'

Claire said that she wasn't too concerned about the possibility of a scandal. She was more worried about the distress Bruno was causing Juliette, and was going to cause the children, especially Pierre.

'Have you seen Juliette? How is she?'

'Shattered, the poor thing. She doesn't know what to do. I gather that Bruno doesn't bother about keeping up appearances any more: he goes to see that girl at all hours, he receives her in his office, he walks around town with her. Naturally Nicolas and even little Line know all about it. In fact that's the only thing which seems to bother Bruno – because with Juliette he's showing an incredible lack of consideration.'

'Is he treating her badly on top of everything else?'

In André's voice there was a genuine note of virtuous indignation.

'No. On the contrary, he's being very kind to her, very gentle. The trouble is that he's told her everything.'

'He's talked to her about his liaison?'

'He's told her everything, without concealing a thing.'

'It's funny, isn't it, somebody from these parts behaving like a character in a Russian novel.'

'No. I'm afraid it isn't funny at all. He told her everything, and then he begged her forgiveness. He told her he blamed himself for what had happened, but he couldn't give up the girl and wanted to live with her.'

'That's exactly what he's just been telling me. He's mad!'

'Juliette thinks it's a sort of passing madness too, the kind of crisis most men go through in their fifties. The midday devil, in fact. And she may be right. She thinks Bruno will eventually realise his...what would you call it?'

'Aberration.'

'That's it. There are other reasons too for hoping that he'll come to his senses. He's spending fantastic sums on that person. She must be getting all the money she wants from him. It's like a haemorrhage.'

A haemorrhage. André pictured the Marcillacs' money, or what was left of it, leaking out through a crack in their house and running down the Rue de Navailles, to form a glistening pool at the feet of the girl Bruno was in love with. At that very moment he realised that he found this a pleasing picture, and he immediately set out to isolate the quiet satisfaction he felt in order to examine it and give it a name. Like most men, he had spent part of his life deceiving himself; but during the last few years he had been training himself in the hard discipline of truth. Since his heart-attack he had refused to gloss over anything, he pounced on the least admirable feelings he detected in himself, he hunted them down until they admitted what they were. The one he had just identified was particularly hideous but extremely common – so common that it had to be accepted as an evil inherent in the species. *The ruin towards which I see him rushing consoles me for the envy inspired in me by the love which he feels and of which he may also be the object.* Good. The unspeakable feeling had been analysed and labelled. Now he had to look at it unflinchingly and say to himself: *That too is part of me. That is one of the reptiles crawling in my heart. Ecce homo.*

At dinner, for the first time since his heart-attack, and with an almost feverish enthusiasm, he told Claire of his plans for the future – 'for I've got plans, I don't think my life is over'. – 'Of course it isn't! What an idea! You couldn't possibly think like that at fifty-two!' Every year the two of them would treat themselves to a holiday abroad, seeing that the girls were now taken care of, or at least could look after themselves. Yes, a holiday abroad, in some country he had always dreamt about: Israel, the Lebanon, Egypt, and even – why not? – Mexico. They could easily afford that little luxury. Of course, said Claire, that would be wonderful. To-morrow, said André, he would telephone Cook's and ask them to send prospectuses and brochures...

After dinner they settled down for an evening's television, but first Claire went to draw the curtains. The street, the apartment building opposite, the café on the ground floor of the building, the young people grouped around the juke-box in that café – all this was shut out. They were on their own. André took another of the little pills that banished anxiety: it was time, in any case, for his evening doze.

On the day their son and daughter-in-law were due to arrive at Sault, Bruno asked his wife to come into their bed-room for a moment. There he told her he had to go out and might not be back in time to welcome their children home. She asked him if he was going to meet 'that young woman'. He replied that he was. But why had he chosen the very day 'the children' were due to arrive? He hadn't chosen it. Certain circumstances made it essential for him to go and see the young woman that day, but he would have preferred some other time. He was terribly sorry. He asked Juliette to find an excuse for him.

During the six or seven weeks since unhappiness had fallen upon her, Juliette had, as she told Claire Comarieu, passed through every type of feeling: anger, jealousy, despair, even hatred. She had hated Bruno. She had experienced the most unexpected, uncharacteristic impulses, which had filled her with astonishment and fear: the desire to kill, and – a more insidious temptation, this – the desire to kill herself, to destroy this wretched body which had ceased to please a husband she still loved. She had wept for chagrin and also for shame, afraid of some scene or scandal – or even worse, that Bruno's passion might lead him to commit some irremediable act. There was a spectre Juliette could never think of without trembling. It bore a commonplace name: it was called 'News'. When she was a little girl, Juliette had often gone into her elder brother's room to read a magazine entitled *Detective*, in which the spectre 'News' was photographed on every page: in sordid hotel rooms and derelict hovels, in Auvergne or Brittany, very occasionally in bourgeois houses, but always in other people's homes, and always far away. It had never ventured into Sault. But now Juliette could sense it prowling around nearby; and sometimes, when she looked at Bruno, gloomy and silent on his return from a visit to his mistress, she told herself: 'The spectre has touched him. He looks just like a picture in *Detective*.'

There were also moments when she revolted. She had lost all her composure, shouted at Bruno, used words she would never have thought herself capable of uttering. She had shown a complete lack of dignity, but what did that matter? Now she had stopped fighting, partly because she was utterly exhausted, but also because Claire Comarieu had advised her never to raise her voice again. It wasn't a matter of a show of indifference or contemptuous detachment, but of avoiding the risk of anchoring Bruno in his madness, by putting pressure on him. The 'attack' had to be allowed to work itself out.

'An excuse?' she said. 'What sort of excuse do you expect me to find? Nicolas and Line know all about it. What good would it do to lie to them?'

He shrugged his shoulders.

'Don't tell them anything, then.'

'You really have to go and see that girl today?'

'Yes.'

'You couldn't possibly wait until tonight, after Pierre has arrived? Just not to spoil his homecoming?'

'No, I can't wait.'

He turned his head away. He looked unhappy and stubborn at the same time.

'I'm not speaking for myself. I can put up with anything as long as I'm the only one concerned. But it's the children. I beg you to think of them. What you're doing is horrible.'

'Don't make things harder for me.'

'But you must have some plans?'

'No, I haven't.'

'You haven't come to any decision?'

'I shall probably leave you.'

And he rushed out of the room.

Juliette wasn't used to suffering: the experience of suffering had come to her too late in life and taken her by surprise, filling her with panic. She wandered around the house in a daze, gasping for breath. She went round to the Comarieus and told them what had just happened. André offered to go to the young woman's flat and try to make Bruno see reason. About half an hour later he came back alone: Bruno and his mistress had already gone, but André had been able to obtain some information from a neighbour. First it was known that the young woman was planning to take a train to Paris that very evening. She had already said goodbye to some friends of hers and packed her bags. It was probably in order to prevent her leaving that Bruno had come round to her flat. He had taken her out by force and made her get into his car. The resistance put up by the young woman had caused a certain stir in that working-class street, and a small crowd had collected.

'The car went off in the direction of Spain,' said André, 'which makes me think that Bruno may have taken the girl to your house in the country. I've an idea that that's where they are right now.'

It was time to go to the station to meet Pierre and Suzy. Juliette said that she wasn't going, that she didn't feel up to it. Before the train came to a stop, Pierre appeared at one of the doors, smiling and excited. When he realised that his parents weren't there, his face changed. André hurriedly reassured him: no, nobody was ill, there was no cause for alarm. 'Wait until we're in the car, and I'll explain.' In the meantime he kissed his daughter and discovered with astonishment, wrapped in a cocoon of tulle and wool, the unknown baby who was his grandson. There were the usual happy exclamations of a homecoming: they were standing on a station platform with people all around, and appearances had to be kept up.

In the car Pierre listened calmly to what André had to tell him. He had been trained to control his feelings. In his very adult, very manly face, his eyes were all that remained of his childhood. They were incapable of disguising a sadness which went far beyond mere disappointment. André knew the adoration Pierre had for his father – a rather naïve adoration, no doubt, but not something he felt like smiling at. He told himself that Pierre must have often imagined his homecoming and the moment when he would show Bruno the little creature which bore his name and continued his line; he felt embarrassed and miserable, as if Bruno's defection were his own. As a homecoming nothing could have been more dismal and pathetic.

'I think,' he told Pierre,' that you ought to go and fetch him, if, as I imagine, he's gone to ground in that house. It's the only chance we've got. He's terribly fond of you, as you know. You're the only one who can bring him to his senses. He'll only have to see you to become himself again. He was looking forward to your return so much before all this happened to him. He talked to us about it all the time, didn't he, Claire? ... Yes, the more I think about it, the more I'm convinced that you ought to go and find him. I'm giving you a thankless job to do, Pierrot, but it really is ...'

'If you think I can do something, of course I'll go.'

'Yes, please. You can take my car. I won't come with you – it's best for you to be alone. One more thing: don't lose your temper, even if that girl is there and starts needling you.

Don't reproach your father for what has happened. Just tell him you've come to fetch him.'

'I wasn't going to reproach him for anything,' murmured the young man.

This arrival in which nothing had happened as expected, and the nerve-racking rush of events, produced a night-marish atmosphere heightened by the leaden sky over the town and the imminent threat of snow. For André there was also the perplexity he felt at the change which had taken place in his daughter and son-in-law. He had always referred to them as 'the children', but it was a man and a woman he had before him. Suzy had lost the vivacity and the coquetry of her adolescence; she was a quiet young woman, sparing with words and clearly not over-anxious about her appearance: she didn't use make-up and her hair looked as if it didn't often receive a hairdresser's attention. The metamorphosis was mysterious and complete; and as Pierre got into the car and drove down the Rue de Navailles, itself unrecognisable with its cars, noise and new buildings, André, standing on the threshold of his house, was struck by an impression, already experienced many times in recent years, of the dizzy flight of time: it seemed to him that a furious wind was carrying them all away, his family, himself, even this little child who had just entered their lives, as it was carrying away Sault and its inhabitants and the world itself, swiftly and for ever.

'Is that it, the house you want to make me live in?'

Through the car window she looked at the little farm-house with its two closed shutters, standing all alone under the winter's sky. She thrust her hands into her coat pockets.

'Don't you like it? You'll see, once it's been painted and done up. We can make something very pretty out of it. I'm sure you'll enjoy living in it.'

He opened the door and got out.

'Come along.'

'I want you to drive me back to Sault. I've got a train to catch tonight.'

'Don't keep repeating the same thing,' Bruno said patiently. 'You aren't catching any train.'

'You haven't any right to stop me. My neighbours will call the police.'

'No, because we're going to get married.'

'You aren't divorced yet; and you haven't asked me what *I* think about this idea of getting married.'

'We're going to talk about that. Come on, get out.'

As she didn't move, he took her by the arm and dragged her out of the car. He pulled her towards the house, opened the door and pushed the young woman inside. He slammed the door behind him. The darkness was almost complete; there was a sharp smell of mildew in the air.

'Leave me alone. Don't touch me.'

The sound of a struggle, of panting breaths. Then a window was opened and a shutter banged against the wall. The daylight poured into the room. Bruno, standing near the window, turned towards the young woman.

'Why are you looking at me like that?' he asked, almost jovially. 'Because I kissed you?'

'You can't keep me here by force,' she said.

He took off his coat and hung it on a hook behind the door. He pointed to a chair.

'Sit down. I'm leaving the windows open for a little while, to air the house. I'm going to light a fire.'

He opened the other window.

'You see, it looks a lot better in the light. Oh, I know there's a lot to be done. We'll have to buy some furniture and a carpet ... Look at the view you've got from here. Isn't it wonderful? Just imagine waking up every morning with that view in front of you.'

'I don't care a damn about the view. Do you imagine I'm going to stay in this house? It's downright sinister here.'

'Sinister? Not a bit of it. You'll get used to it. It's wonderful living in the country.'

'Don't bother to light a fire. You can't force me to stay here, you know.'

After a brief pause she added:

'Even if you threaten to kill me.'

'Who said anything about killing?' he asked calmly. 'I'm not threatening you. I'm offering you a house.'

'I don't want your filthy old shack.'

He opened a cupboard near the fireplace and took out a faggot which he laid across the brass firedogs. He struck a match. Crouching in front of the hearth, he blew on the little flame he had just lit on one twig sprouting from the faggot, but a cloud of smoke forced him to draw back.

'The chimney needs sweeping,' he said.

At that moment a creaking sound behind him made him turn round. The young woman had disappeared. The door was wide open. He sprang to his feet and ran outside. A lane lined with hedgerows linked the house with the main road, two hundred yards away, at the foot of the hill. He saw the young woman running down this lane as fast as her high heels would let her, the skirts of her coat flying behind her. He started running after her and managed to catch up with her. She struggled and once again he had to treat her roughly. She screamed for help. Her cries echoed ludicrously in the vast silence of the countryside, a silence disturbed only by the rusty, mournful cawing of crows. He took her back into the house, locked the door, and this time slipped the key into his jacket pocket – a heavy key such as you only see nowadays in very old houses where nothing has changed for hundreds of years. Both of them were panting after the chase and their struggle, and it took them a few minutes to get their breath back. Their clothes were all rumpled, and the young woman was staring at Bruno with eyes wide with hatred and perhaps also a little fear. He made her sit down and knelt in front of her, putting his hands on her hips. He gazed at her adoringly. His eyes were bloodshot, and he was breathing hard, his breath visible above his mouth, in the cold air. He pushed aside the skirts of her coat, although she tried to keep them together. His hands moved up and down her body. In a low voice, in little broken phrases, he reminded her of the evening they had met for the first time, four years before, at the fête in Sault.

'Yes,' she said, 'when you'd already arranged everything with your pal.'

'My pal? What pal?'

'Are you pretending you've forgotten? As if I didn't know all about it!'

'Are you talking about Lagarde?' Bruno asked in surprise.

'I'm talking about the chap you use as a go-between.'

'I don't know what you mean,' said Bruno.

She saw at a glance that he was telling the truth, that things hadn't happened as she had thought. So Jean Lagarde had lied to her. Or rather he had allowed her to believe something that wasn't true. She bit her lower lip, and frowned, like someone discovering a mystery where there had been certainty a moment earlier. She began to say: 'You didn't ask him to...' while Bruno, almost at the same moment said: 'It was he who introduced us that night, of course, if that's what you mean' – and he promptly put aside that name, that scene, which didn't interest him, which had nothing to do with them now. In the tone of voice of an adult gently scolding a headstrong child who had been on the point of doing something foolish, he said: 'You wanted to leave me. You wanted to go. You little silly. You were forgetting that we are bound together for ever, you and I.' He reminded her of a certain evening, or rather a certain night, when they had been in perfect union. He spoke in a deep-throated voice, almost a voluptuous growl, as he described certain things to her: but she shook her head furiously, either to deny the truth of what he was saying, or to assert her determination to forget them, and she retained her sullen, hostile, frightened expression. He pretended to ignore these repeated denials.

'We shall have other nights like that,' he said, 'many other nights.'

'But you aren't going to force me to live here?' she retorted.

'Why not?' he said calmly. 'I've no intention of forcing you to do anything, but why shouldn't we live here? We'll have a quiet life here, away from everything. Just you and me.'

'And what are we going to live on? Your fishing and shooting?'

'Don't worry about that. I've still got a little money to my name. So don't worry.'

He pressed his cheek against the young woman's hip and put his arms round her waist.

'What more could you wish for?'

In the voice of a housewife haggling with a shopkeeper she protested:

'What more could I wish for? You've got a nerve! Why, you're old enough to be my father. You're thirty years older than me.'

'The difference in our ages doesn't matter, seeing that we get on so well together. And seeing that I make you happy.'

'Where did you get the idea that I was happy?'

He answered in a whisper.

'I was doing my job,' she said.

'What job? You were happy – that's all there is to it.'

'You poor fool,' she said. 'If you took all that for real! ... Live here with you?' she went on. 'I'd die of boredom. Not bloody likely. You heard me? Not bloody likely. Wasting my youth on you,' she said in a rather affected tone, as if she were repeating a phrase she had heard or which someone had suggested to her. 'Wasting my youth on an old man.'

Bruno winced; but he was presumably determined to disregard anything which threatened the realisation of his dream, for he pretended to be amused by the phrase, like someone smiling at a child's vulgarity.

'You won't find many old men like me,' he said amiably. 'Not even many young men as fit as me.'

'You disgust me,' she shouted. 'You're fat and ugly. You disgust me.'

'It's no use trying to make me lose my temper, because you won't succeed.'

'Get out of my way. I want to leave here. Open that door.'

She pushed Bruno's arms away and managed to free herself and stand up. He got to his feet too, slowly and laboriously. She took a few steps to get to the other side of the table, a large table in dark oak. The faggots in the fireplace were crackling merrily and the light from the flames was dancing on the walls. Bruno went over to the cupboard, opened it, and took out a bottle.

'This is local brandy,' he said. 'It's splendid stuff. Would you like some?'

Her only answer was a shrug of the shoulders. Bruno took out the stopper and drank a long draught, straight from the bottle. He clicked his tongue and put the bottle back in the cupboard. Then he walked over to one of the windows which had been left open. First he closed the shutters. Then he switched on the lamp – a solitary electric light bulb, protected by an old-fashioned round enamelled shade. Next he went to the other window and leaned out to look at the view, which the twilight was beginning to obscure.

'What a splendid position!' he murmured. 'It's unique, you know. Some days you can see all the Pyrenees. Early in the morning it's wonderful.'

He closed the shutters with a clattering noise, and made sure they were properly bolted. Then he shut the windows. After that he turned to face the young woman, who had watched these successive operations standing motionless behind the table.

'We'll be better like this, all shut in. It makes things cosier.'

266

He went over to the fireplace and switched on a small radio. There was the sound of jazz, coming through very quietly.

'We've even got a radio here,' he said. 'I'll have a television set installed. You'll have everything you want. Just like a queen. A real queen. With a lovely view to look at all the time. If you want any improvements made, I'll have them carried out. And there's another thing I haven't told you: it's a surprise. You're a property-owner. I'm giving you this house. You didn't expect that, did you? Are you pleased?'

'I've already told you, I don't want your dirty old shack. If you imagine you're going to tie me down with that, you can think again. I'd rather have an attic room in Paris with my lover.'

Bruno froze.

'There's no question of you going to Paris,' he said.

'Yes, there is. I'm taking the train for Paris at half-past six tonight.'

'What do you want to do in Paris?'

'I've just told you: I'm going to join my lover.'

'What lover? Why do you tell lies like that?'

'I'm not telling lies. My lover's in Paris, and he's written to me telling me to come and join him. What are you looking at me like that for? You can't scare me.'

'Is that the fellow you were dancing with the night I met you?'

'Right first time.'

'And you say you want to go and join him in Paris?'

'I've been telling you so for an hour! You're a bit slow on the uptake, aren't you?'

'But why do you want to go and join him?'

'Because with him, I was happy.'

'Happy? In what way happy?'

'In every way.'

Bruno looked as if he was pondering this point.

'Listen. I don't know what you're up to. I suppose you're just trying to make me jealous. All right. But give up this idea of going to Paris, because it's idiotic. Think a bit about all I'm offering you here. I'm suggesting . . .'

'I don't want to stay here!' she shouted, stamping her foot. 'You can keep your house. If that's all you've got to offer me! A tumbledown shack that isn't worth a sou! When I think that I agreed to go with you for the money! If I'd known you were all washed up, I'd never have agreed, you hear me? Never. I got myself lumbered, more fool me. But now it's all over. So go and open that door. I want to get out of here.'

'I've sacrificed everything for you,' said Bruno after a pause.

'What do I care? I didn't ask you for anything.'

'My wife, children, position, honour, everything . . . I've sacrificed everything. And you tell me you've got a lover.'

'Yes,' she shouted furiously, 'and at least he's my own age and cool-looking. If you could see the two of us together it'd drive you mad.'

Bruno made a slight movement with his arms and looked in turn at the table and the cupboard, as if he was hesitating as to what to do next. He went over to the cupboard and took another, longer swig at the bottle of brandy. He wiped his mouth with the back of his hand and put the bottle back. The young woman watched these gestures with hatred and disgust in her face.

On the radio the music had just given place to a talk. From the pompous tone of voice it was obvious that this was no announcer reading the news but a speaker aiming at oratorical effects. As the volume was turned down very low, the thin little voice could scarcely be heard in the room: it was talking about Man's victories over the Universe. If Bruno and the young woman had lent an ear to this eloquent insect, they would have realised that it was praising the latest prowesses of science. It was a singer of human achievement, a chorphaeus in the service of technocratic progress. In twenty years, it was saying, the world had undergone one of the most important and most decisive transformations in its history – and not just the world, but the human race. In the plans of the technocrats, in the nuclear laboratories, a New Man was being born. All the values on which we based our lives would have to be revised. The man of the future would not think like us, would not feel like us, would not behave like us. His attitude towards the great problems of life, love and death, would be entirely different from ours: it would be the attitude of a demi-god . . .

But in the little house with the closed shutters, all alone under the winter sky, the orator's tiny voice aroused nobody's interest, and it was drowned by the cawing of the crows over the bare fields all around.

'You're trying to torment me,' murmured Bruno. 'I don't believe a word of what you say. In any case it doesn't matter. I love you as you are. I can't do without you. Come along, there's a bed in the next room. We're going to forget everything. It's going to be just like it was before. Come along.'

'No.'

He leaned on the table with both hands and shut his eyes. He drew a deep breath, as if his chest were feeling tight. Then he opened his eyes again and raised his head. His face looked like that of a man who has been submitted to torture.

'So you don't love me any more?' he said.

'I've never loved you.'

'Listen, I want to see you happy one more time in my arms. Just one more time. Come along.'

'No.'

He walked round the table towards her but she stepped to one side; and they began a sort of grotesque ballet, he pursuing her on one side or the other, and she dodging neatly so as to keep the obstacle of the table between them. She kept laughing at him, and they might have appeared to be playing a game, if Bruno's eyes hadn't been set in a bestial stare. Clumsy and heavy-footed, he was breathing hard, and he stumbled once or twice; while all the time the speaker on the radio went on talking about the prospects of evolution and the ultimate destiny of Man. Bruno finally managed to get hold of the young woman and dragged her towards the bedroom door, while she clawed at his cheeks. At that moment the insect on the radio quoted Father Teilhard de Chardin and explained that mystical union of minds towards which mankind was gradually moving, and which the great Jesuit called the 'noosphere'.

Bruno opened the bedroom door and tried to throw the young woman on to the bed. She arched her back and in the struggle Bruno lost his balance and fell heavily on the floor, hitting his head against the metal bedstead. The young woman bent down quickly, slipped her hand into his pocket, then rushed out of the room.

Dazed by the blow he had just suffered, Bruno did not get to his feet for a full minute. Going into the other room, he saw that the door was wide open. He dashed outside. The young woman was running down the lane; in a few moments she would reach the road – the road on which a passing car might stop and pick her up to take her back to Sault. His features convulsed by panic and rage, Bruno ran to the fireplace, took down the gun and went back to the door.

He cocked the gun and raised it to his shoulder.

The shot sounded like a clap of thunder. With a tremendous beating of wings, the crows in the nearby fields all rose into the air at once to settle in the trees. The echo rolled from hill to hill, gradually dying away, and an astonished silence fell over the countryside, which was beginning to be covered by a light coating of snow.

The young woman hadn't been hit. Bruno saw her begin running faster and guessed at the panic which had taken hold of her. He felt the same panic himself. He looked at the gun he was holding in his hand, with a wisp of smoke curling up from the barrel. He looked utterly dazed. All of a sudden he threw the gun down on the ground and put his hands to his head. Down in the valley, the young woman had reached the road. She was going on running in the direction of the town, looking back every now and then to see if a car was coming. Bruno staggered down the lane. He tried to run, but he was short of breath. When he was half-way between the house and the road, he saw a long sleek black car appear on the crest of the hill. It drew up beside the young woman who was waving frantically with both arms. Bruno started shouting: 'No! No!' and quickened his pace. The front door opened and the young woman got into the car, which drove off and disappeared. Bruno's cries grew louder. He took a few more steps, tripped over a stone and fell on his knees. His cries turned into whimpers and groans. He dragged himself on his knees for two or three yards, on the hard, frozen ground. He kept clawing at his face, or else taking his head in his hands and opening his eyes wide, as if he could see something terrifying in front of him. Then he fell headlong on the ground. His moans grew less frequent, but his body was shaken by violent shudders.

He stayed like that for several minutes, the snow covering his back with a white film. Then he laboriously raised himself on his hands and knees, stood up, and walked back towards the house. Reassured by the return of silence, the crows had begun cawing again here and there, but without leaving the high black branches where they were perched. The snow was falling harder.

Bruno picked up the gun in front of the house, went inside, and hung it over the mantelpiece. The fire was almost out. The speaker on the radio had been succeeded by dance music. Bruno switched off the set. He shut the door, drew a chair up to the table, and sat down. He leaned forward, laid his head in the crook of one arm, and sat motionless.

When Pierre arrived, about an hour later, he found his father in this position. He looked as if he might be asleep. At the sound of the door opening, Bruno sat up with a start and turned round. He looked at Pierre, standing on the threshold, without seeming too surprised to see him. Neither man moved for a few seconds. Then Pierre said cautiously:

'May I come in?'

Bruno nodded and Pierre stepped into the room. He looked around him. The bedroom door was open, revealing the bed which was still made. There seemed to be nobody else in the house.

'I've come to fetch you,' Pierre said in the same cautious tone of voice. 'We were worried about you.'

And as Bruno, sitting motionless with his head down, made no reply, he added timidly:

'Aren't you going to kiss me?'

Bruno promptly stretched out his arms. Pierre bent down and they kissed. Bruno pressed his son against him.

'I'm ashamed of myself,' he said in a broken voice.

'It's all over,' said Pierre. 'Don't think about it any more.'

'But you don't know what I've done. If you knew what nearly happened!'

'I don't want to know. Don't tell me anything. It isn't worth it.'

He drew away gently, while Bruno took out a handkerchief and dabbed his eyes. He pulled a chair up to the table and sat down.

'I can't understand what got into me,' said Bruno. 'I can't understand why I behaved like that.'

'These things happen.'

'Don't try to find excuses for me. What I did was horrible.'

'Come now!'

'I did something unspeakable.'

'Nobody's immune from that sort of ... Nobody's immune.'

'You know, there are moments of madness ...'

'Madness is saying a lot.'

'I know what I'm talking about,' said Bruno, and he gave a shudder.

'You must forget all about it.'

'You aren't angry with me?'

'Me? Why should I be?'

'You know.'

'No, of course not.'

Bruno looked doubtful and shook his head. Then he blew his nose noisily.

'It's cold in here,' Pierre said briskly. 'Don't you feel cold?'

'Yes.'

'Shall we go home straight away, or would you prefer to wait a while?'

Bruno thought for a moment.

'Let's wait,' he said.

He looked closely at Pierre.

'You're looking well,' he said. 'And brown as a berry.'

'The sun's hot out there, you know.'

'Is the climate very hard to bear?'

'Not really. You can't complain. And the worst is over now.'

'So you and Suzy are quite happy out there?'

'Yes. We've got advantages we wouldn't have here.'

'Your letters were very interesting. It was nice of you to write so often, and such long letters too.'

'That's only natural.'

Bruno replied that it wasn't as natural as all that: boys generally didn't enjoy writing letters. He recalled that when he had been in the army, for example, he had written to his parents once a month, nearly always to ask them for money. Once he had given them the latest news of his health, which was invariably good, he didn't know what else to say. He used to sweat blood writing a dozen lines. No, he was no letter-writer.

They both smiled. Then Bruno turned serious again.

'What did they say at home?' he asked.

'They were worried about you.'

'They must have criticised me?'

A faint smile touched Pierre's lips.

'No. They were just worried about you.'

'And what did Nicolas say?'

'Nicolas?'

Pierre tried to remember.

'He said you ought to take a long holiday, you and Mother. In Italy or Spain. Somewhere in the sun, anyway.'

'We ought to take a holiday?'

'Yes. And have a good rest.'

'Nicolas said that? So he isn't angry with me?'

'Angry?' Pierre said in surprise. 'Why should he be angry?'

Leaning forward with his elbows on his knees, Bruno was kneading his handkerchief between his hands.

'He's very high-minded,' he said hesitantly. 'You and I, we make allowances. Nicolas is different.'

'Yes, but he's very intelligent too. So he can understand everything.'

'That's true.'

'Besides, he's a good sort. He ought to have left for Germany a few days ago. He put off his departure because of you.'

'Because of me?'

'That's what I said.'

'Poor Nicolas. He shouldn't have done that.'

'If you think we were going to leave you like that...' Pierre said gently. 'What would we do without you at home? Can you tell me that?'

Bruno made no reply; but he had to take out his handkerchief again, which he had put in his pocket. Pierre got up quietly and went and closed the bedroom door. He squatted in front of the hearth, to scatter and put out the last few embers which were still burning. Then he looked round the room, to see if there were anything to tidy up, any traces to remove.

'Where's Nicolas going in Germany?' asked Bruno. 'I've forgotten the name of the town.'

'Heidelberg. There's a big university there.'

'Yes, of course, Heidelberg. Isn't it there that his German friend lives?'

'Yes. Nicolas is going to stay with him.'

'Oh, I see . . . I didn't know.'

There was a brief silence.

'If you're going to learn a language,' said Bruno, 'the only way is to stay in the country.'

'Yes, of course.'

'He's quite right to go over there, especially if he's going to specialise in German.'

'It's the only thing to do.'

Their eyes met. There was a question in Bruno's gaze.

'Would you like to go home?' asked Pierre.

'If you like.'

He blew his nose again, then stood up. His shoulders were slightly bowed. Pierre realised that he was taller than his father. He also noticed that Bruno's hair was completely grey. It had turned grey within a short time, during Pierre's absence.

'I haven't asked you yet about Suzy and the baby,' said Bruno. 'Do forgive me. I don't know what's the matter with me.'

'They're both very well.'

'And is he a good-looking baby?'

'I think so. Everybody says he's like you.'

'Not too like me, I hope – for his sake, poor kid.'

'As far as looks are concerned, he could do a lot worse.'

'How did he stand the journey?'

'Very well, really.'

'You flew, I suppose?'

'We arrived in Paris yesterday, and took the train this morning.'

'What did you think when you didn't see me at the station?' Bruno asked unhappily.

Pierre shook his head and clicked his tongue, to indicate that he shouldn't go back to that subject. He helped his father on with his coat. They went out. It was a cold night. The snowflakes were gleaming dully in the darkness.

'I think we'd better leave your car here,' said Pierre. 'I'll come and fetch it tomorrow.'

Bruno followed him meekly. They got into André's car.

Pierre drove slowly, for visibility was poor because of the snow, which was falling hard. Bruno asked about the 'situation' in Africa, and they talked about recent political events, rather like strangers making conversation on a train journey. After the war in Vietnam, the racial troubles in America, the Common Market and the future of Europe, they had soon run dry of international topics. During this impersonal conversation neither of them noticed that a change had taken place in their relationship. A few months before, when they had talked about these things, it had been Bruno who led the discussion; and Pierre had played the secondary part of the person who allows himself to be taught and, perhaps, convinced. Now father and son seemed to have exchanged roles. Pierre expressed himself clearly and confidently; while Bruno, huddled in the seat beside him, listened respectfully, nodding and saying: 'You think so? Well, I'll be damned! Yes, you're probably right.'

A level-crossing barrier brought them to a halt. Pierre said: 'It's the Paris express, it's 6.35'; and Bruno, putting both hands on the dashboard, slowly sat up in his seat. The brightly lit train roared past with a clatter of metal. A flickering pattern of light and shade played over the two men's faces. Pierre saw his father's head in profile, straining towards the train as it sped by, a few yards away from them. The whole thing lasted only a few seconds. The barrier was raised again. Bruno slumped back in his seat. He looked exhausted. They said nothing to each other for several minutes. The snowflakes shone in the beams of the headlights, and on either side there was complete darkness.

Pierre coughed, as if to give notice that he was going to speak.

'It hasn't snowed like this for years,' he said. 'This reminds me of the first winter I saw any snow. I was five years old.'

'I remember,' said Bruno, after clearing his throat. 'You had a little red coat on. I took some photos of you in the orchard. We must still have them somewhere at home.'

'You'd brought me a record of Christmas carols. I used to sing *O Tannenbaum* all day long.'

He started humming to himself: '*O Tannenbaum, O Tannenbaum, wie treu sind deine Blätter . . .*'

'I've always thought that was such a sad song,' he said.

'Me too. French carols are much happier.'

There was another long silence. Then Bruno began:

'If I died . . .'

Pierre interrupted him with a gentle, mocking laugh.

'Don't talk about dying! You're all set to be a centenarian.'

'An accident can happen to anybody. Look at poor André. We aren't immortal. What I want to say to you is this: when we aren't here any more, your mother and I, you'll keep an eye on Nicolas, won't you?'

'Of course,' Pierre said lightly, as if he attached very little importance to this request.

'I don't want him to be left on his own,' Bruno said in a low voice.

'There's no reason why he should be.'

'No, there's no reason why he should be . . . All the same . . .'

They were already in the town. Pierre stopped the car in front of their house. Before getting out, he turned towards his father, whose face was showing a certain anxiety.

'Everybody's at the Comarieus',' he said, 'except Mother. You can come and join us when you like.'

He added quietly:

'Don't worry. Everything will be all right.'

He put his hand on Bruno's shoulder, in a protective gesture, as he might have done with a friend.

'Are you game?' he asked.

It was the old magic question. Bruno gave a faint smile and nodded his head two or three times, closing his eyes. They got out. The roadway was covered with snow, and it was impossible even to make out the cars parked beside the kerb: they were buried under a thick blanket of snow. Clothed in white, the street had a peaceful, somewhat ghostly appearance. It looked rather as it must have looked in bygone times.